C000005519

Nickolas Butler was born in Penns[...] Claire, Wisconsin. His award-winn[...] *Lovesongs*, was an international bestseller and optioned for film by Fox Searchlight Pictures. His second novel, *Hearts of Men*, was a finalist for the 2016 Prix Médicis étranger, and his third, *Little Faith*, was awarded the Edward Stanford Travel Writing Award for Best Novel in 2020. Butler, who attended the Iowa Writers' Workshop, currently lives in Wisconsin with his wife and their two children.

'A slow-burning and mesmerising read.' *Herald*, Best Books for Summer

'A study of male friendships, greed and the desire to make meaning.' *Daily Mail*

'Enthralling.' *NB Magazine*

'The writing is careful, considered; the story allowed to gradually spool out while tension builds quietly and relentlessly. It's only after the explosion – sudden, shocking - that you realise every word prior had led inevitably to that moment . . . *Godspeed* manages to deliver a credible kind of redemption without compromising the book's vivid and deeply earned sense of environmental, elemental and emotional realism.' *The Quietus*

'*Godspeed* reads like a modern fable or a contemporary western – a bloody and violent version of the American Dream in which ambition, addiction, and frailty are locked in what is at times an almost unbearably painful struggle with loyalty, love, and hope.' **Carys Davies**

'A glorious novel, as lyrical as it is suspenseful – breathless, tense, and shimmering with the sweat of desperate men. Butler delivers mystery and tragedy against a beautiful, inhospitable backdrop, anchored in the struggles of a thrummingly vivid cast of characters.' **Steph Cha**

'Set in an American West torn between its pinewood past and marble future, *Godspeed* is the story of three childhood friends and the construction contract that will make – or break – their lives. What begins as a novel of optimism and ambition morphs into a dark warning about the end-game of American capitalism. With his characteristically rich and transporting prose, Nickolas Butler continues the urgent examination of class and culture he began in his beloved debut, *Shotgun Lovesongs*.' **John Larison**

'A page-turning, race-against-the-clock novel about fatal obsession, love, violence, addiction, and faith beautifully set in my home state of Wyoming. After you turn the last page, it'll stay with you for a long, long time.' **C.J. Box**

'Butler's award-winning talent as a storyteller (*Little Faith*) propels his characters on a heart-stopping, daring race with unexpected outcomes. Godspeed indeed.' *Library Journal*

'As in his previous three novels, Butler brings sympathy and insight to the familiar rituals and dynamics of male friendship . . . An exceptional tale, once it gets going, of what money can do to those who need it.' *Kirkus Reviews*

'This ambitious thriller from Butler highlights the conflict between wealthy transplants and blue-collar locals in the increasingly gentrified rural West.' *Publishers Weekly*

'From triumph and tragedy to pathos and redemption . . . As real as anything you are likely to read this year . . . It's hard to walk away from *Godspeed* without being grateful for the life one has, and that in itself makes it more than worth reading.' *BookReporter*

ALSO BY NICKOLAS BUTLER

LITTLE FAITH
THE HEARTS OF MEN
BENEATH THE BONFIRE
SHOTGUN LOVESONGS

GODSPEED

A NOVEL

NICKOLAS BUTLER

faber

First published in the UK in 2021
by Faber & Faber Limited
Bloomsbury House, 74–77 Great Russell Street
London WC1B 3DA

First published in the USA in 2021
by G. P. Putnam's Sons
An imprint of Penguin Random House LLC
penguinrandomhouse.com

This paperback edition published in 2022

Printed and bound by CPI Group (UK) Ltd, Croydon, CR0 4YY

Interior art: Teton Range © Jez Campbell / Shutterstock.com
Book Design by Laura K. Corless

All rights reserved
Copyright © 2021 by Nickolas Butler

The right of Nickolas Butler to be identified as author of this work
has been asserted in accordance with Section 77 of
the Copyright, Designs and Patents Act 1988

This book is sold subject to the condition that it shall not, by way of trade or otherwise, be lent, resold, hired out or otherwise circulated without the publisher's prior consent in any form of binding or cover other than that in which it is published and without a similar condition including this condition being imposed on the subsequent purchaser

This is a work of fiction. Names, characters, places and incidents either are the product of the author's imagination or are used fictitiously, and any resemblance to actual persons, living or dead, businesses, companies, events or locales is entirely coincidental.

A CIP record for this book
is available from the British Library

ISBN 978-0-571-36297-4

MIX
Paper from
responsible sources
FSC® C171272
FSC
www.fsc.org

2 4 6 8 10 9 7 5 3 1

For B. Traven. Wish you were here.

This book was inspired by true events.

GODSPEED

1

Outside Jackson, Wyoming

This was the house that would change their fortunes. They could feel it. Cole had barely steered his pickup off the highway and passed through an open cattle-gate before they began climbing the dusty canyon road north, and they could feel it—*money*—like a vibration in the crisp mountain air. It was humming out there, an expectancy, a promise, and they were driving toward it, cotton-mouthed, skin crawling. They could practically see it on the wind pushing the late-summer leaves, swaying the yellowing meadow grasses, smiling down upon the dappled river water below. The whole world here looked like money. Money just waiting to be plucked up off the ground—the leaves like greenbacks, the shimmer of the water like silver coins.

They needed this house, this break; they needed this work. Work for what sounded like as much as a year, maybe more. And not the thankless, backbreaking tedium they'd been reduced to for the past few years either. No, this was something to build a reputation on, a name, something to stake a man for decades. The kind of signature house a person could point to and proudly say, *I built that—me. I built that.* The kind of house that, thirty years from now, when they were all broken-down old men, they could travel to with their grandchildren and be welcomed, like masters of some dying art.

Bart rode in the passenger seat, blinking down at the chasm that had now fallen away just an arm's length from the gravel road. Not even a mile off the highway and already the country was wild, wild, wild. Below the road snaked a river raging white and blue, cataracts tumbling, and above them, off the low mountainsides, wispy water-falls spilled down like great lengths of silver-white hair.

A prominent dip of chew bumped out Bart's lower lip, and by and by he spit into an empty Coca-Cola can. "I lived here almost twenty years, and I ain't ever been down this road," he said, peering over at Cole, who took the gravel track with white-knuckled respect. A blown-out tire wouldn't just be a pain in the ass out here; it would put them behind schedule for their noon meeting with the homeowner. "You ever been back here, Cole?"

Cole shook his head no, fixing Bart with a meaningful look for as long as he dared before turning back to the road ahead of them. *This is big, pristine, private country,* the look communicated. *You and me, we don't just get invited back here.*

"She told me she had a driveway punched in last summer," Cole said. "Another two miles or so off this road." He pointed an index fin-ger up into the mountains. "Somewhere up in there, I'm guessing."

"You imagine the kind of bread they're spending?" Teddy put in from the backseat of the extended cab. "I mean, a two-mile driveway? Up here? That's an Army Corps–type operation."

"All that goddamn California money's, what it is," said Bart. "Hell, that state's filling up. Cheaper for them to come out here and plop a house down on a mountaintop than it is to buy a nice two-bedroom in San Diego or Los Angeles. Cheaper to build a house in the clouds. Lunacy, you ask me."

It had been an unseasonably warm spring and summer in western Wyoming, and now the mountain air was sweet with sage, the late August sky overhead deliriously blue and gauzed in cottony clouds. In the backseat Teddy studied a gazetteer, biting his lower lip and running his fingers over the map. Bart hung an arm out the passenger-side window as the truck began to pull away from the canyonside. Soon they passed through a glade of trees and he reached out for the branch of a lodge pine, managing to snap off a handful of needles. Now the cab of the truck was filled with that smell, comingling with his Copenhagen chew—pine and mint and tobacco.

All three men were dressed just a bit more presentably than usual—unstained, newish Carhartt pants, plaid short-sleeve shirts with collars, scuffed work boots buffed up near to a shine. Cole glanced at himself in the rearview, tamping down his brown crew cut with his fingers and studying his newly shaved face—the razor burn beneath his jaw, his recently whitened teeth. Bart went to work with his pocketknife, cleaning beneath his fingernails, while Teddy sighed deeply and drummed his hands against his thighs.

Buzzed down practically to his scalp, Teddy's blond hair betrayed a constellation of blotchy pink-purple birthmarks that Bart occasionally pointed to as proof positive he'd been born with a host of defects—a subpar IQ, a troublingly true moral compass, and a peculiarly deep pride in his wife of twenty years and the four young daughters they had brought into the world. Teddy was Mormon; Bart had once played drums in a death-metal band named Bloody Show. They loved each other like brothers; had ever since their childhood growing up together with Cole in the red-rock, box canyon country of eastern Utah, and then, later, as adults, moving out to Jackson Hole and this mountainous country, first as ski bums chasing near-endless winters of deep powder, tourist girls, and the intoxication of brushing shoulders with celebrities at the town's bars and cafés, and then later still, as men wanting to prove themselves in that same environment, tired of being seen as just townies, the blank-faced ski-lift operators you forgot as soon as you were swept away and up the mountain, the compliant bar-tender perfectly willing to suffer yet another drunken insult if it meant a ten-dollar tip.

Which was why, a few years back, the three men formed True Tri-angle Construction, an honest-to-god LLC with business cards, letterhead—the whole nine yards. They bought three matching Ford F-150 pickup trucks, fixing a stenciled triangle on the middle of both doors, and for the first time in their lives felt perhaps what their own fathers had felt: purposeful. Yes, they would build houses and condos for the rich vacationers and tourists, sure, but more than that, they'd be building their own company, a legacy, something to leave behind when they could no longer swing a hammer or crawl onto another 11/12 pitched roof. Hell, by then, they'd have a suite of offices, a secre-tary or three, business lunches downtown, big cowboy hats, and the lean, sun-browned visage of the kind of old men you'd see about town, that particular style and gravitas endemic to old American men of the Rocky Mountains—stern, sinewy, taciturn. *Solid as Sears*, as their fa-thers once said.

Bumping upward along that gravel road, Cole pictured himself far off and into the future: Friday night at a comfortably appointed restau-rant, the bloody remnants of a prime rib and baked potato on a plate, his elegantly aged wife across the table from him, a cup of strong black coffee, a forkful of chocolaty dessert, and then, that relaxation that passes over a contented man able to pay for his meal from a wad of pocket-cash before pushing back from a white-linen tabletop to work a toothpick at the ivories of his teeth.

"If we get this project . . ." Bart began.

"*When* we get this project," Cole said, pointing a finger into Bart's biceps. "*When*, amigo. We need to believe we were destined to build this house. That it's been, you know, *waiting* for us, up there in those mountains. Just *waiting* for our hands. These fucking hands. We need to believe that."

Teddy leaned forward from the backseat until his face was framed by the jostling shoulders of his two friends. A former high school all-conference cornerback, he was susceptible to Hallmark greeting cards, impassioned locker-room speeches, populist politics, and the every whim of his four girls, most recently ballet lessons and a pair of Shetland ponies he and his wife could not quite actually afford.

"I mean, can you imagine the size of our fee for a project like this?" Cole nearly shouted. "And if we muscle down and don't farm out a bunch of the work? Shit, man. This is *it*. This is our launching pad. This is where True Triangle Construction takes off. You can see it, can't you? Building houses for rich actors and CEOs. It all starts right here." He slapped the steering wheel for effect.

Cole had no problem imagining it. He *had* been imagining it, ever since the homeowner called him a week earlier, out of the blue. The truth was, he hadn't slept much since, each night doubting himself, doubting his own capabilities; frankly, doubting Teddy and Bart. What business did they have, really? Building some multimillion-dollar house? For the past three years they'd been just scratching by, renovating apartments, ski rentals, the occasional commercial project; a shitload of drywalling, roofing, and siding work; and then the odd new construction here and there—a handful of duplexes and a retail strip mall—*Jesus Christ*, how were they possibly prepared for this?

But he'd met the homeowner just the same, in downtown Jackson, at some place called the Persephone Bakery. The baristas were cute if waifish little things, the bakery cases full of extravagant-looking pastries, the coffee strong and expensive, and he waited for her outside on a small porch with two fancy outdoor propane heaters challenging the morning chill.

Having worked in construction ever since graduating high school, Cole knew enough to be suspicious of this homeowner—as the customer was always, always referred to: the *homeowner*—before even meeting her. For starters, why had she selected True Triangle when there were so many better-established builders in the area? For two: He'd worked on dozens of new home constructions in his time doing this, and while it was more common than not for a woman to take charge of the details of a home (selecting tile, say, or cabinet pulls, light fixtures, paint colors—that kind of thing), Cole hadn't heard this homeowner once mention a husband. Look, he didn't fancy himself a Neanderthal or what not; maybe she was a lesbian—great. But she hadn't alluded to that either. Her voice on the phone was just incredibly composed and businesslike, with none of the small talk other homeowners inevitably engaged in to butter up a contractor. They'd just agreed to meet at the bakery, and there she was, clutching a crisp paper cup of five-dollar coffee in one hand as she extended the other to him. Her grip was strong.

"Good morning, Mr. McCourt. I hope you haven't been waiting long."

His voice caught—she was one of the most attractive women he'd ever met. He could not have said whether she was forty or sixty years old, but she carried herself with a patrician assurance that only compounded his confusion as to, well, why *he* was the one she'd asked to meet her here. Her hair was long and chestnut red, streaked flinty gray in places; her eyes an arresting gold-on-green. He steadied himself as he sipped his coffee, briefly looking down at the table. In the treetops overhead, birds went on chirping, while out on the sidewalk, great wealth sashayed past in expensive duds looking extremely refreshed, unhurried, on its way to the next recreational diversion. *Focus now*, Cole thought.

"Oh, no," he said, forcing himself to meet her eyes, "not long, not long at all." For this woman, he thought, he would wait *days*.

She smiled, a bit wistfully, he thought.

"How many years have you been in business, Mr. McCourt? I must say, I looked for your website, but . . ."

"Well, around here, Miss—"

"Gretchen, please."

"Right. Gretchen. Well, around here, so much of it's just . . . word of mouth, you know? You do good work, people find you. So, in the three-plus years since we started True Triangle, we haven't really needed none of that marketing stuff."

"Still, you *may* want to consider branding yourself a bit more, lest a potential customer suppose all you aspire to is, well, framing and drywalling."

Branding? he thought. He'd worked on his uncle's ranch as a teenager, branding and castrating cattle; the sizzle and smell of burnt hair and flesh was nothing he wanted a part of again, least of all his own person.

"Or maybe that *is* all you're interested in, and I'm wasting your time."

He gathered himself anew. "Gretchen, all I can tell you is this: My partners and I have been working construction in and around these parts for about twenty years now. We don't have any fancy offices, and we don't live on big ranches or take our vacations down in Turks and Caicos or anywhere like that. We're just three hardworking guys, and if you do decide to hire us, I promise we'll do right by you, ma'am. I'll give you my word on that."

She sipped her coffee. Cole was aware that beneath the table she was crossing her legs. He studied her face, realizing that the dark bronze freckles arrayed across her nose and cheeks were something he dearly wanted to touch; he imagined himself in bed beside her, in the morning, her earlobe in his mouth, her scent exotic tea and expensive perfume, or perhaps horses and honey, or just cold mountain air.

Cole and his wife were in the midst of a decidedly conclusive separation, and close, he knew, to officially divorcing. His life had taken on a wobbly quality. Cristina seemed to be living with her new guy, their once shared apartment now sitting largely vacant. He'd begun boxing up some of his possessions in a half-assed sort of way, willfully disbelieving that their separation was actually permanent. He'd been less than forthcoming with his partners about what was going on, though in the back of his mind was the dread that the most sensible thing for him to do was to move in with Bart, a surefire sign that his life was in retrograde.

"You do give the impression of a man who is trustworthy," Gretchen said, blowing lightly on her coffee.

Trustworthy? He sure as hell was. Wasn't him stepping out of a seven-year marriage. Though, sitting here, so close to Gretchen they might have been lovers out for their morning coffee, he did allow himself a moment to ponder what that might feel like—stepping out.

"I appreciate that," he said.

"And discretion is certainly something I'd value, were I to choose your firm to construct my home."

His *firm*. He briefly imagined the scope of the project. Imagined that website she had just mentioned—the one he hadn't even thought to commission—and photographs of this house, in that style of glitzy, dream-home pornography where every image seems dipped in some kind of golden dew. And perhaps, in just a few photos, Gretchen standing beside him—the builder—on a panoramic porch, or leaning against a monolithic kitchen island, clutching mugs of chamomile. Let his future ex-wife ruminate on *that*. . . .

Cole gently exhaled. "So, uh, tell me a little about your project, Gretchen. Just so I can get a lay of the land."

She sipped her coffee. "Well, let's see. It's a remote site. Roughly a thousand acres. The house itself is not going to be some gaudy faux-ranch or mega-lodge, so, if that's your forte, Mr. McCourt, I can save you some time."

His heart did snag for a moment before it occurred to him that her notion of *gaudy* might be quite different from his own. It wasn't that he endorsed gaudiness—no; it was just that *gaudy* generally meant *expensive*, and expensive of course meant a more lucrative builder's fee.

"Imagine something akin to the Schindler House, only three-tiered, with even braver lines, and embracing a mountain. Thirty-eight hundred square feet, three-car garage, carbon neutral. Geothermal heating and cooling, solar—both passive and active. A central fireplace crafted from all locally quarried stone. Four bedrooms, three bathrooms. That should give you a basic sense of it."

He nodded along with this, though the bit about the Schindler House had gone sailing right over his head; *like the Spielberg flick?* Still, as she spoke, he began tabulating costs, and against that steadily rising number, multiplied by True Triangle's ten percent builder's fee. Okay, so this house might not be some eight-thousand-square-foot monstrosity, but it would certainly carry a price tag in the upper seven-digits, with True Triangle potentially netting around a million, if he, Teddy, and Bart worked their asses off to avoid what subcontracting they could; hell, they could farm the whole thing out and *still* pocket a bundle.

"All of that sounds great," Cole said, nodding. "And so, where's the building site?"

"Southeast of town," she said. "About forty miles, give or take."

This bit of information did give him a moment of pause. He'd worked a few jobs fifty, even seventy-five, miles away from town, and he knew that after you factored in travel time and gas and the cost of transporting materials, you could lose thousands if not tens of thousands here and there with botched deliveries, little oversights—even something as benign as Teddy's girls' dance recitals. . . . It all added up. Then, throw in a penny-pinching homeowner, and suddenly your fee wasn't nearly as substantial as you'd budgeted. But he did not have long to dwell on this line of thought.

"Mr. McCourt, do you know who I am?"

He did not, though he'd spent the past week trying his damnedest to find out. Sure, he'd googled her name—*Gretchen Connors*—but that only yielded *hundreds* of Gretchen Connorses: a WNBA player, a renowned vegan chef, and a tulip magnate, among scores of less remarkable-seeming individuals. He'd even inquired around town, but to no avail. When he asked Teddy and Bart about this dearth of information, they seemed nonplussed. Every year, more and more out-of-state money poured into their quaint little ski town, more Patagonia- and North Face–wearing strangers. Nike and New Balance had long since replaced cowboy boots, and it had been this way for a while. In fact, the only thing more galling than the loss of any real cowboy culture was the interlopers' determination to dress up on a Friday night in their best western costumes—some hedge-fund manager with a Brooklyn accent wearing *thirteen-hundred-dollar* Ferrini cowboy boots, or a California surfer-girl sporting a five-thousand-dollar fringed leather jacket. . . . Point being, it wasn't necessarily a surprise that her name didn't register.

"Well, she's *building* a house," Bart had said, "so obviously she ain't from around here. Who gives a shit, long as her checks cash?"

"No, ma'am," Cole allowed, meeting her eyes. "I don't, actually."

"That's just as well, I suppose. So, are you interested in my project, Mr. McCourt? And, more to the point, is this the kind of home your firm would have the time and expertise to build?"

"It is, yes, absolutely," he said. "And we're definitely interested."

"Fine," she said. "Then why don't we meet at the site in a week? I'll shoot you the details soon enough."

Rising from the table, she reached down for a large Louis Vuitton handbag. Even Cole recognized that particular logo and design. His soon-to-be ex, Cristina, had bought a knock-off on a long-ago trip to New York.

"I'll be speaking to a few other firms in the meantime," she said, gazing away from him down the street.

He'd been sitting on a glossy navy-blue folder with True Triangle's yellow logo on the cover. And this he pulled out now, its thick, shiny stock still warm from his thigh, and handed it to her.

"Everything's inside," he said. "All our references." Cole suddenly realized, as he stood quickly to offer his hand, that he had hardly even had a chance to pitch his company's merits. That this could easily be the last time he ever saw this woman.

"We'll be in touch," she said, and he could not help feeling that he'd just been dismissed. Clearly this was a woman accustomed to adjourning meetings. He dearly wished he knew more about her, what her job was, where she lived, where her money came from, and, somehow most importantly, whether she was married, or even a little bit attached.

"How?" he all but yelped.

"I'll contact you with the location of the site," she said. "Good day, Mr. McCourt." And with that, she walked a half block down the street before ducking into a black Range Rover and driving off.

Cole was confident he'd blown it, and it was with an acute sense of defeat that he drove to their current worksite, a nondescript beige two-story condo with severe water damage stemming from an overflowing Jacuzzi. Apparently a bunch of college kids had polished off a case of Daddy's Veuve Clicquot, partied in the hot tub, and spilled enough water to totally weaken what must have already been a rotten subfloor, because the hot tub eventually crashed *through* the floor, not only leaving a hole in the first-floor ceiling but destroying everything below. The job would be perhaps two weeks of work if they could drag it out that long, at which point True Triangle Construction would be on to the next thankless gig.

Cole's truck continued its labored climb up the mountain. In the distance, perhaps a mile or more away, a plume of dust rose into the immaculate sky like proof of some dry fire.

"What's going on up there?" Teddy asked, pointing through the windshield at the column of khaki-colored dust.

"Looks like some major action is what," Cole mumbled.

They plodded forward, scanning the mountainsides and talus slopes for bear, moose, elk, or mountain goats. Down below, in the canyon holding that rugged river, they hadn't spotted so much as a single fly-fisherman. And along the road, no trailers, no horses, no ATVs—nothing but scree, mountainside, and lodgepole pine.

Another twelve minutes of jostling and bumping down the road, and they could now see that the dust originated from a road-building crew: a dump truck, an excavator, two long flatbed trailers, two bull-dozers, and a Bobcat. Cole pulled over to the side of the road, and the three partners of True Triangle swung out of the truck, stepping down onto the gravel with the swagger of gunfighters approaching a dis-agreement not yet resolved. Cole had never been able to pinpoint it exactly, but there was a kind of judgment, a kind of *feeling out*, that inevitably accompanied two groups of workers in the building trades when they encountered each other. The visitors were sure to begin at once evaluating the others' work, while the latter affected the disposi-tion of entrenched soldiers, their body language all, *Yeah, you don't know the half of it, buddy. . . . This homeowner . . . And the fucking weather . . .*

Luckily, they were able to sidestep all the macho bullshit when Teddy recognized a member of his Mormon temple and they ex-changed heartily sincere greetings. The two groups of men eased up now, and the road-building crew climbed down from their machines for pulls off insulated water jugs and maybe a quick cigarette.

"Now, who the hell are you guys?" an older man asked, looking surprised to have company on such a lonesome road.

"Cole McCourt. True Triangle Construction," Cole said, extend-ing his hand.

They shook, and there was an awkward moment when the older man, who hadn't bothered to introduce himself, stood sizing up Cole and his partners.

"Hell of a project," Cole said to the older man, gesturing up the mountain to the road's gravel base. "How long you guys been working on this?"

"Shhhiiittt," said the man thoughtfully. "Since the spring snows quit, I guess. . . . May, for sure. Been workin' like dogs. Seven days a week. She'll pay overtime and wants it down lickety-split. Never seen nothing like it."

"You know anything about her?" Cole pressed.

The older man raised an eyebrow, pulled on his cigarette. "Well, we call her the Fox," he said. "For obvious reasons. But, buddy, all *I* know is that her pockets are deep and her checks always clear. She stays out of our way, mostly, though she's up there now. You laid eyeballs on the site yet?"

Cole shook his head.

"Yeah, well, I've worked on some choice projects," the older man went on, "but I gotta hand it to her. This is gonna be somethin' special." He spat into the dust. "What's your name again?" he asked, removing an old Denver Broncos hat to scratch at his head.

"McCourt. True Triangle Construction."

"Huh," the older man said. "Never heard of you guys. Well, we better get back to it." He tipped his cap and climbed into the cab of the dump truck. "Sure we'll be seein' you around."

Cole, Bart, and Teddy climbed back into the truck and drove on. Another third of a mile down the road, Cole brought it to a stop.

"What's the deal?" Teddy asked.

"I just need a second," Cole said, closing his eyes. "I didn't want to, you know, pull in there and not have my shit together."

"Sounds like a good time to pray," Teddy said, shifting back into his seat. "I'm gonna pray for us."

"Good," said Bart, spitting out the window. "I could always use a little extra help."

The truck sat idly for two or three minutes before Cole opened his eyes, felt his heartbeat drumming regularly again.

Bart was staring at him like he was some drooling basket case.

"Well?"

"All right, all right, all right," Cole said. "Here we go."

The landscape narrowed, closing in upon them as they ascended. The new road rose up between two nearly sheer cliff-faces that held the midday sun to glow a buttery yellow. Those ridges rose a thousand feet over the road, which was funneled into a sort of V-shaped canyon, the river still on their right, though tapering, too. Finally, the road terminated at the river, with a large turnaround area shaped like an *O*. And here was Gretchen's black Range Rover, now dusted pale brown. An asphalt-paved driveway led from the gravel turnaround across a steel bridge and up to what looked like the skeletal beginnings of a house.

Climbing out of the truck, they just stood there, stretching their backs, breathing the high-country air, and gazing up at the cliff-faces shining down upon them. Far above, three or four buzzards wheeled on a thermal, and from the crowns of the creek-side pines, a passel of black rosy finches chided them. Cole was confused; she'd said nothing about the house already being under construction.

"Over here!" a woman's voice called.

Turning, they saw Gretchen picking her way up a slope from down below them, where the river roiled.

Cole walked briskly toward her, extending his arm to guide her up the last few feet of the slope where it steepened. Dressed in expensive yoga pants and a Lycra hoodie, she might have been a model in one of the women's outdoor catalogs that Cole's estranged wife received in the mail. Her red hair was pulled back into a ponytail, a light sheen of sweat showing on her brow and in the fine, nearly invisible hairs just above her lip. She dusted off her hands and blew a tangle of long red hair away from her eyes. The men stood there, simply staring at her for a moment before remembering themselves and glancing politely away.

Now Bart stole a look at Cole, who was clearly crushing on this woman. Clear from the moment he sprang over there and guided her up, like she was a queen. It was unusual to see Cole so excited, Bart thought; he hadn't been much for talking about the separation, but Bart knew his friend had been ground down by the beginning stages of the divorce, and it had been some time since Bart had seen any lightness in his friend's step, any real sense of joy, aside from when he was reaching for a well-deserved bottle of frosty-cold beer at the end of a solid day, or on those rare occasions when they shared a joint together.

Otherwise, Cole had seemed pretty well hollowed out these past two years, a shell of the man Bart and Teddy had moved here with. . . . *Fucker looks like he's in love*, Bart thought.

"Well," she said evenly, "you found it."

"Ma'am," Bart began, "we were all saying on the drive up, we've never *seen* such a gorgeous spot." Turning his head away from her, he hooked a finger inside his mouth and as casually as possible flicked away his wad of chew.

Teddy stood staring out past the river, up to where faint wisps of cloud seemed to rise from the base of the mountain. "Is that steam?" he asked.

She smiled. "Follow me," she said, and they fell in behind her.

Just beyond the turnaround the asphalt began, leading to the wide steel bridge that spanned the river. Past the rushing water the asphalt narrowed a bit, and there was the site, already in progress. A three-car tuck-under garage had been built up almost flush against the cliff-face, and above that rose two stories of house supported by I-beam construction, the first of those floors cantilevered out and nearly over what they now saw was a steaming thermal spring. A pool of crystal-clear water appeared to be fed by a seep gushing out of the side of the mountain, eventually overflowing gently into a short creek feeding down into the river below. Deeper than six feet from the looks of it; the natural pool was about half the size of a tennis court.

"You *own* this?" Teddy burst out.

Cole closed his eyes in embarrassment.

"I do," Gretchen said. "Isn't it something?"

"I mean, I've seen some places," Bart mumbled, worrying the stubble of his jaw, "but *this* here, this here. . . ."

She lowered herself to a flat rock adjacent to the springs and looked back toward the valley and the faces of the cliff-sides now shining as if lit by some internal fire.

"Only you never mentioned nothin' about the house already bein' under construction," Cole said sternly. "Respectfully."

"The thing is, gentlemen, I've run into a snag," she said, pointing up at the house. "See, I lost my first contractor."

"Well, ma'am, at this point, I'm more than a little confused," said Cole. "Because if your contractor was local, we'd have known about this project. And if you'd lost a local contractor, we would have definitely heard about that. To say nothing of the fact that the house is already damn well *started*." It was true that Cole felt something for this woman, but at the moment he was pissed—he could not deny it—and did not even bother to camouflage the tremble in his voice.

She nodded quietly, traced a fingertip in the steamy pool.

"Mr. McCourt," she began. "I was under the impression that you wanted this job. Now, I really have no interest in dwelling on the past. Suffice it to say that my first contractor and I did not see eye to eye. He and his crew are gone. I am in need of a new contractor. I am under no obligation to further explain myself to you; it is none of your business. Now, if you and your partners aren't up to the task"—she turned her back to them and exhaled—"then please stop wasting my time."

"They must've had a reason," Bart said. "You don't just up and quit on a project like this."

Gretchen sighed.

"I have a tight schedule to keep," she continued, "and I simply will not accept anything other than the finest work. Now, I am exacting. And I must insist on a rather tight time frame. I think that . . . ultimately, my prior contractor simply couldn't maintain his end of the bargain. And so, we parted ways. I would have thought you might've seen his loss as your gain."

"Who was your prior contractor?" Bart asked.

"It really is none of your concern," Gretchen said, a sharp edge to her voice. "And, gentlemen, any further questions are really fruitless. To preserve the privacy of the site, that contractor and his crew signed nondisclosure agreements. I can assure you they were all well compensated for their work here."

The men wordlessly glanced at one another: Teddy shrugged his shoulders, Cole nodded slowly as he tapped a finger against his lips, and Bart simply stared at the house, his arms crossed tight against his chest, his fingers holding his biceps.

"Somethin' don't seem right about this," he said. "I'll play ball, but I want to say it for the record."

Now Gretchen turned to face the men as her left hand finned through the steam.

"Look, gentlemen," she said flatly, shielding her eyes now from the slant of the early-afternoon sun, "the most dangerous work has already been done; all the groundwork has literally been *set*. The pilings have been poured and by now should be properly cured. The garage and first floor are poured. The I-beams were secured into place by a specialty firm out of Denver. The well and geothermal have all been drilled. The initial electrical work is already in place. What I *need* is a contractor to take this project across the finish line. I need a contractor with an attention to detail and a desire to work hard. And I'm hoping, Mr. McCourt, that you are the man to do just that."

Cole felt Bart's and Teddy's eyes on him, and he knew why. They were equal partners, the three of them, and yet here she was talking to him as if he were the foreman. . . . But hadn't they all agreed he would be the one to meet with her that first morning? There was nothing to do but to plunge forward.

"Ma'am, I don't know what to say. . . . All this is just, uh, highly unusual. All of it, really, and I'd be lying if I didn't admit I'm having some cold pricklies."

"Cold pricklies?" she asked, frowning.

"That feeling where the little hairs on your neck pop out," Teddy offered. "You know. Bad juju."

Now Gretchen stood, rolling a pebble between her fingers. "Nonsense," she snapped. "I have built houses before, gentlemen. I know what I am doing. I had no choice in the matter, I can assure you. To finish this house on time, I needed a new contractor.

"Look, everything has been worked out and approved, all the

permits paid and signed for. This should give you time to gather your-selves and begin finding bids for the other work: what framing needs to be done; the roofing; the steel; windows, trim, cabinetry, flooring. . . . The only subcontractor I must insist on is my mason. The fireplace is already about a third done. He's been with me for more than a decade, and I wouldn't entrust that fireplace with anyone else."

"I don't know," Cole said. He meant it, too; this wasn't at all what he expected. Contractors got fired—sure, that happened. But contrac-tors rarely walked out on a project like this. And now there was some-thing in her voice, something like desperation, urgency. For a woman who seemed so reserved, so professional, she was suddenly speaking more rapidly and more loudly, too, as if pushing them.

"Why us?" Bart blurted out. "Huh? I mean, let's put our cards on the table, huh? You've got all this cash. Why choose three dudes who were repairing Sheetrock last night? What gives?"

She threw the pebble into the hot springs and wiped a bead of per-spiration off her nose. She smiled coldly at them. "Two reasons. The first: The builders around here are a bit of an old-boys club, as I'm sure you're aware. Even with the NDA, I think when my former contractor parted ways, he must have blacklisted me, because now no one will return my phone calls, and even if they did, I'm sure they'd try to gouge me however they could. You know how it goes, gentlemen: ten thou-sand added on to the countertops, fifty grand on the roofing. . . . As I just told you, this isn't the first time I've built a house. They think I won't stand up for myself. They think because I'm a woman I won't put my foot down. But I will, and I *know* you won't cheat me. My mason, Bill, will make sure of that. He's my eyes and ears when I'm not here."

"And the other?" Cole asked. "The other reason?"

"I need this house built before Christmas," she said, dusting off her hands and smiling at them, each in turn.

"Lady, that's, what," Teddy muttered, counting on his fingers, "four months away?" He looked at the building site as if it were a twenty-five-thousand-foot peak they'd been asked to climb in an afternoon's time. "I don't know. . . ."

"No *way*, is what I know," Bart said. "That's fucking impossible."

"Is it?" she asked. "Come, let's eat some lunch and we'll discuss the finer points of my ask."

They shared some disgruntled and disbelieving looks as she led them back down the path toward her Range Rover, where, as its rear hatch lifted on a press of her car key, a gust of cold from the air-conditioning met them, and she revealed a little picnic perfectly curated down to the red-and-white gingham tablecloth everything sat upon: chilled Sancerre and frosty cold bottles of beer, ham and Gruyère sandwiches, fancy potato salad, a jar of cornichons, even a platter of brownies. The three men eyed one another, their hands plunged into pockets, as they peered back to the would-be house site.

Bart shook his head. "Look," he said, accepting a sandwich from Gretchen, "uh . . . thanks. What you're asking, though, I gotta be honest with you—it's no wonder that contractor disappointed you. I've *worked* on sites where we were rushing to hit some deadline. Working basically round-the-clock—which is what you're asking us to do. That's how people get hurt. You end up working in the dark. Working in the elements. You get exhausted. Even the toughest guys get sick. Nail-gun accidents, trips and falls, stupid mistakes and accidents . . . Hell, we saw a guy working in a rainstorm get hit by lightning. Blew him twenty yards off the house, but he was dead before he hit the ground."

"Great sandwich, by the way," Teddy said, smiling, before popping an expensive little pickle into his mouth. Cole and Bart glared at their friend, who seemed quite oblivious to it.

Perched on the bumper of her vehicle, Gretchen neatly polished off her sandwich even as she regarded Bart fixedly. She swallowed, wiped her hands clean, and took a small sip of the cold wine.

"I neglected to mention your bonuses," she said.

The three men all subtly shifted; Bart coughed into his hand, Teddy stretched his arms over his head and then commenced rubbing his newly buzzed pate, and Cole transferred his weight from one foot to the other, one finger pressed to his lips. Had they been sitting around a poker table, their tells would have been well broadcasted.

"One hundred and fifty thousand dollars for *each* of you, if the house is completed before Christmas."

"Holy crap," Teddy said.

"Fuckin' A," murmured Cole.

"And if we can't?" Bart asked, collecting himself. "Finish on time?"

"You'll still be paid, of course, and your builder's fee honored," Gretchen said professionally. "But obviously the bonus itself will have expired."

"Why, though?" Bart said. "Why Christmas? Up here, you'll be snowed in anyway. There's no way you can keep that driveway open all winter."

"What's your last name, Bart?"

"Christianson, ma'am. Bartholomew Christianson. But Bart's all anyone ever calls me."

"That *is* a mouthful. But look, Mr. Christianson, I'd rather not elaborate. Suffice it to say that time happens to be, well, more valuable to me than money. All right? I'm a busy, busy woman. And don't worry about the driveway. That's my business, and I'll be sure to have it plowed, no matter the cost. Having said all that, though: Look, if you and your partners aren't interested in this job, then, please, let's stop wasting each other's time. I'm sure you have gutters to hang somewhere."

With that, she began disassembling the picnic, her back turned to them, as they stood there, looking at one another, the river below them persistently loud, and far overhead one of the buzzards still orbiting on the high thermals.

"Can you give us a minute, Gretchen?" Cole asked. "I think we're in agreement, but obviously your timeline is, uh . . . well, it complicates things a bit, doesn't it?"

"I'll tell you what, Mr. McCourt," she replied. "I'm going to drive back down and check in on the road crew. You can have all the space you need for your little chat. And feel free to go on and look at the site more thoroughly, if you please. As I said, all the preparatory work has been done. I simply need a general contractor to keep things moving along. The question is, are you my men?"

And with that, she slammed the hatch of the vehicle, climbed in, and then pulled away, kicking up a few handfuls of gravel in the process.

They did not deliberate long. Meeting her in the middle of the gravel road below not fifteen minutes later, Cole pressed her to raise their bonus to a quarter million, per. She sighed, and eventually they settled on a hundred and seventy-five thousand per man. A half hour after that, they worked their way back up to the skeletal housing start, where they signed the paperwork she'd arranged beside the hot springs, and where she poured four flutes of very cold, very crisp, very delicious champagne. None of the three men had ever tasted Dom Pérignon before, but without ever so much as discussing it, they all agreed they liked it, very, very much indeed.

It tasted like success.

2

They sat inside Sidewinders Tavern, each of them utterly flabbergasted at the three-hundred-thousand-dollar earnest-money check sitting on the battered old bar before them.

"Britney's gonna be so psyched," Teddy said. "Now we can pay for Kylie's orthodontia, and maybe those baking classes that Kendall and Kelly have been asking about, and still set aside—"

"Shut up, Teddy," Bart growled. "I'm of half a mind to cash this check and skip town. Four months? Impossible. A fucking good way to get killed is what it is. A goddamn honey-trap."

"Now, slow down, Bart," Cole said evenly, running a finger over the rim of his pint glass. "Are we supposed to just go back to unplugging toilets and tearing out piss-stained carpeting? What if we were destined to build this house? 'Cause it sorta feels like that to me. Look, I *want* this project, okay? This is it. This is what we been dreaming of. And she's experienced; she's built houses before. You can bet those blueprints are tight and there won't be two thousand goddamned change orders. The foundation's done, the I-beam work is done, and once we get the box sealed up, once we get the roof on, brothers—we can *crank* on that sumbitch. *I'm* willing to work around the clock for a few months to cash a six-figure bonus. Know what I mean? We can *do* this. I know we can."

"I'm with you." Teddy nodded fervently. "I am one hundred percent with you. Britney can spare me. Sure, she'll have her hands full for a little while with the kids and all, but I mean, when it's done? We can maybe buy our own house, right? No more condos. No more landlords. Come on, Bart. Whaddya say?"

Bart threw down a shot of Jägermeister and shook his head. "I think this is fucking doomed. I really do. There's something off about this whole fuckin' thing, and I don't like it. My daddy always told me, if it looks too good to be true—"

"Geez, Bart," Teddy said, "there's such a thing as a good luck, isn't there? Maybe we just got lucky, huh?"

"—then it probably is," Bart finished. The two friends sipped at their beers and simply stared at each other across the impasse.

"It's gonna be all hands on deck, Bart," Cole said solemnly. "I mean, seven days a week, no doubt. Workin' harder than we've ever worked before. We need you, amigo."

They'd named their little business True Triangle Construction for obvious reasons. There were three partners, sure. And even with their limited educations, they all knew the strength of a triangle. But throughout their lifelong friendship, if that triangle had a weak side, it had been Bart. He was the first to leave Utah, in the wake of a public intoxication charge that utterly embarrassed his parents: caught pissing in an alleyway. He'd been threatened with a charge of indecent exposure, a crime that would have forever marked him as a sex criminal; thankfully his lawyer had finagled a deal whereby the charges would be dropped if Bart left town. So, he had. Less than a year later, Cole and Teddy followed him out to Jackson Hole and an unending string of drunken nights, often culminating in Bart getting tossed in the clink again, this time for a bar fight or possession or whatever the local cops wanted to tag him with.

There were people in the world who seemed plagued by bad luck. The perfectly healthy thirtysomething who suffered a heart attack on a routine jog or at the yoga studio. Or the well-meaning family that lost its life savings to a nefarious evangelist. But there were others who seemed to manufacture their own bad luck, and it was hard not to place Bart in the latter camp. He was not a nihilist, no, because Bart did subscribe to a kind of code that above all prized loyalty, hard work, and determination. Still, it was difficult to imagine him growing old, let alone aging gracefully. The sundown horizon of his life seemed much closer than theirs. *Volatile*, that was how Cole and Teddy tended to think of their friend.

And the drugs, always in the background, like a poorly tuned radio, a fuzz of interference that muddled his days: mostly pot, mushrooms, LSD, a lot of coke, plenty of Molly, and, last but never least, meth. In the summer, Bart was a beer drinker. Fall through spring, he switched to brandy; brandy in his morning coffee, brandy and Coca-Cola in the evening. Throughout, Cole and Teddy were there to prop him up when he fell too hard; ready to carry him into a cold shower, ready with a glass of water and a trio of Tylenol, ready to find ways for him to disappear off the jobsite on some mindless errand if it meant a foreman not discovering his drunkenness. And to Bart's credit, he never forgot their kindness either. Anything they needed, he was right there.

Now Cole rested an arm on Bart's shoulder even as his friend stared down at the bar, at that six-figure check just setting there.

"You with us, buddy? Can we count on you? 'Cause this is it, Bart. This is what we've been working for. Our break. It's right here."

"I'm here, ain't I?" Bart grumbled. And then, "Hell, fine—I'm with you fellas, all right?"

"*Are* you?" Cole badgered. "Because before we talked to Gretchen, you seemed all in. Brother, you were fucking electrified about this project. And Christ, now you're hangdogging it like all we did was score another shitty roofing job or something. I could swear you almost look . . . pissed or something."

"I told you already, there's just something about this whole thing I don't like."

"Is it that I'm the one leading our talks with her?" Cole asked. "Because if that's it, buddy, hey, I'm more than willing to take a backseat." He didn't at all mean what he'd just said, but it was surely the right thing to offer.

Bart turned his head to look at Cole. "Naw, well . . . a little, maybe. Then again," he said, grinning, "you two do seem to have yourselves a budding little rapport."

"C'mon," Cole said with as much conviction as he could muster. "She ain't interested in a mug like me. Gretchen's high-class as hell. There ain't got any room in her world for slumming around with construction workers."

"But I seen you," Bart said as he pointed a finger playfully at Cole, "rushing over there to give her a hand like she was Elizabeth Taylor or something. You like her, don'tcha?"

Cole sipped his beer so as not to dignify the question. "So, what?" he said, circling back. "You with us, amigo?"

"I'm with ya."

After parting ways, Cole found himself driving all the way back to the building site; he couldn't explain it exactly, why he felt so rejuvenated, so *awake*. He drove patiently, and when he came to the gravel back road extending off the highway and leading to Gretchen's driveway, he rolled down his window and moved through the night slowly, that cool, fresh night air rolling over him as he peered up at the stars and down toward the river, where the moonlight quivered and rippled on the moving water.

At the turnaround, he parked the truck, turned off the ignition, and simply sat there in the cab, listening to the slow tick . . . tick . . . . . . tick beneath the truck's oversize hood. He could not remember ever feeling so alone in such a remote place, and yet he didn't feel *lonely*, not like the past few months in his apartment, in his bed.

He got out and walked up to the house, thinking the whole way up about Gretchen. How had she settled on this design? Where was she now? And was she with someone, perhaps out at some trendy restaurant, or even just in her bed, fancy reading glasses perched on her nose as she proofread some important document, her companion lying beside her, reading a folded newspaper or working a crossword puzzle?

He'd joked with Bart that there was no room for a guy like him in this woman's life, but now, standing there beside the house, he wondered, *Why not?* Maybe he could make her *see* him. Maybe he could find some way, some small space, some commonality between them and steal into her days and nights. . . .

An owl hooted somewhere in the canyon, the sound echoing softly. Cole realized dawn was already bluing the horizon, and so he got back into the truck and beat it back to town, slid his key into the apartment's lock, and promptly slumped down onto his bed, where he fell asleep with both boots on.

3

From her office on the twenty-fourth floor of the Century Tower, the hawk's nest in a neighboring building three floors below could be seen with the naked eye as a jumble of debris outside a south-facing apartment window where the bird had chosen a home as much, no doubt, for the generous and predictable warmth of its southeast exposure as its buffered position, a refuge from the howling winds of those concrete canyons. And from the first moment she noticed the Cooper's hawk (*Accipiter cooperii*), it was not an overstatement to say that Gretchen found herself uncharacteristically distracted by the bird, spending long passages of her business day at the window behind her desk, a pair of Vortex binoculars pressed to her eyes. During conference calls and even during proper meetings, she found herself gazing out any given bank of windows, thinking of the raptor and wanting very much simply to observe the creature. When she was lucky enough to spot the hawk transporting bits of urban rubbish back to its nest—a length of yellow police tape, a wheelbarrow's worth of deadwood, and what appeared to be the remnants of a tattered orange windsock—she experienced a sense of mystery she had not known in years. And a sense of true peace. So much of her life was meted out in billable increments; all day long nearly every minute measured and recorded and entirely within this building—her life so predictable and confined. She was a machine when it came to billing, to metering her time, but it also became an obsession, a compulsion, an artificial drive that, increasingly, she wanted to be severed from. Watching the hawk fly from the silence of her office, she often felt as if she were viewing a beautiful film with no soundtrack. At times, the hawk felt like the only real thing in her life, completely ungovernable and wild. Every other component of her existence so rote, so seemingly civilized, so commodified. . . . It was one of the reasons why she could not wait to escape to Wyoming, where she would slough off this life like a carapace.

More than once she realized that she had forgotten to breathe.

She'd taken to visiting a nearby and venerable steakhouse on her lunch hour, a change in routine that was roundly applauded by her male colleagues, who had never invited her to join them for lunch or even for a collegial downtown stroll, leaving her to work through the noon hour at her desk with the sparest consolation of a Tupperware container full of carrot sticks, or maybe a small green salad, with a Thermos of oolong tea. There was a jocular condescension to their approval now, and it was clear to her that their only conceivable explanation for this change was, obviously, some mystery man—a waiter or chef she liked, perhaps some slender young sommelier. She was not unaware that some of her partners at the firm suspected her of being a lesbian, and in fact delighted in their failure to puzzle her out, for there was always an advantage to being slightly unknown, or unknowable.

In the close darkness of the steakhouse dining room, she sat alone at a small two-person booth near the kitchen. Her waiter was the same every day, an older man who initially wrote down her order but, after five meals of selecting the same dishes, began asking, "The usual, sweetheart?"

It pleased her very much that he should call her that—*sweetheart*. He could not have been more than ten or fifteen years her senior, but there was a warm weariness about him that was a comfort to her, and she imagined him a grandfather, a patriarch presiding over a great tumble of grandchildren. She liked that he hummed to himself as he brought her meal: always a Caesar salad, a petite filet mignon (rare), and a glass of the house red, of which she seldomly drank more than a few lingering swallows.

Her lunches were spent reviewing the architect's plans, which, as meticulous as she was exacting, she'd asked to be printed and bound up in a smaller format for easy reading whenever she had a moment—between meetings, say, or on a plane. Having already built three prior houses—the first in Taos, New Mexico; the second on Bainbridge Island in Washington State; and the third in Puerto Rico, an old sugar plantation that she had imagined as a newly remodeled rum distillery; all three now regularly booked as executive retreats or short-term rentals—she'd made enough mistakes not to spend a single dollar on construction until she was absolutely confident in the blueprints. In the past, builders had convinced her to move ahead with a project despite questions in the plans, always citing the importance of getting the foundation laid, a premise that she now realized entrapped and committed *her* to the structure much more than it did the builder, who could simply walk away from a project without owing taxes on a half-built house and site.

Her architect this time was young, freshly graduated from UC Berkeley, and this was no mistake on Gretchen's part, let alone a cost-saving measure. Gretchen had designed much of the house herself, though there were of course countless facets of architecture and engineering she did not know, and this outmatched architect rarely second-guessed her, save in the most critical structural concerns where her own opinions might need to be checked and redirected, if only to stay true to code. They met every week, for twenty minutes over coffee, where the architect reviewed and approved—or helped modify—Gretchen's own alterations and notes.

No one in the office knew of her plans to retire early. They all assumed she was a stoic workhorse, this no-nonsense professional, unburdened by children or a needy spouse, consistently billing over twenty-three hundred hours a year and at a ridiculous hourly to boot. Beyond that, no one really knew what she did with her time outside of work. She was not on Facebook, Instagram, Twitter, or any of the other ubiquitous social media platforms. The younger associates at the firm had made a game of it: trying to find a nonprofessional photograph of her on the Internet. It was impossible. At least Sasquatch had the Patterson–Gimlin film and some hoax plaster footprints to grab on to. But this woman? She was a ghost.

There were just three things she did with her time: 1.) work, 2.) assiduously manage her investments, 3.) build beautiful houses. As a result, her net worth was approximately $66,750,000, at least in part on the strength of seven properties, including her Pacific Heights condo (a 1913 post-earthquake mansion she'd bought and rehabbed during the late eighties); a small but well-run apartment building in Oakland; an office complex in Mountain View, California, bought before the tech boom boomed; and the as-of-yet undeveloped hot springs site outside Jackson, Wyoming. It was true that she'd inherited a tight little fortune from her deceased parents, but she had long since quintupled that in the years since, her market timing always perfect, often eerily so.

"Sweetheart, may I ask you a question?" her waiter asked.

She folded her napkin onto her lap and smiled at him. "Albert, my friend, you can ask me anything you'd like. Fire away."

"It's just that every day you come here for lunch, you order the same thing, and every day, you never, ever touch your steak. Now, why *is* that?"

"I save it for dinner," she replied breezily, taking the smallest sip of her wine.

He raised a finger as if in deduction, or polite declaration. "Gretchen-honey, I think you're fibbin' 'bout that."

"Or maybe"—she smiled—"I'm taking it home for my boyfriend."

He regarded her for a moment, a slow grin breaking across his face. "If I was your boyfriend, I'd never let you eat lunch alone."

Every business day she carried a small plastic clamshell back to her office, where she'd ride the elevator to the very top of the tower and, wrapping her coat around her tightly, step into the daylight, be it a brilliant midday shine or a heavy wool of fog off the bay, all the dozens of neighboring skyscrapers beaming back at her and the wind whirling about, her hair always crazing itself. Then, setting the steak on a squarish HVAC unit, she'd step back some twenty paces, holding the empty container, and sit down on an old rusty folding chair, where she knew the building's janitors came to smoke on their breaks. She'd even begun to keep a pack of American Spirits in her jacket, should she be interrupted by someone. But the top of the tower was almost always abandoned, and for ten minutes she would just sit there and wait, watching for her hawk to come. She had never witnessed the bird accept her offerings, but every day the meat disappeared, and once, from her office window, she watched as the hawk flew down from the many floors above her, a chunk of meat clutched in yellow talons.

4

Every morning Teddy Smythe awoke to a series of happy explosions. Four young girls spilling out of their beds and into his, there to prop open his eyelids with little-girl fingers, there to flop open his covers, there to complain, to cuddle, and to otherwise disturb his last moments of rest. Explosions everywhere: clothes piled on every stick of furniture and spilled to the floor as the girls sifted through their garments, dressing and undressing themselves, leaving the clothes in new piles. Fights over the shower, over the prime real estate in front of a particular mirror, fights for a hair dryer, over the spilled confetti of a box of sugary cereal, spilled milk, spilled orange juice, the blare of a radio, Britney shouting motherly directions, a TV squawking, the minivan outside idling, and now a cavalcade of *I love you, Daddy* and a parade of kisses, and then—perhaps thirty minutes of quiet before he drove to the jobsite.

Teddy loved his life. But as good as things were, he could see a brighter future ahead of him. It was like a glimpse of heaven, glowing white-silver on the horizon, a point on the map he now recognized and would undoubtedly touch. . . .

To start with: Gretchen's house. The night before Teddy had lain in bed, staring at the ceiling, running various iterations of phrasing through his mind: Riverrun, Steam House, Cloud House . . . searching for an elegant name for the project, like Frank Lloyd Wright's Fallingwater or Taliesin. And he imagined finishing the structure on the morning of Christmas Eve, and the following day presenting Gretchen with the keys along with a flute of champagne before walking her through the house, and then: that moment when she'd hand the three men their much-deserved fee, and that sensation he'd have, later, carrying that money home to Britney. . . .

How he longed to see the pride in her face. Pride in the fact that he had changed the fortunes of their family. That finally, after all the years of scraping by, of clawing, they'd *done* it—and as a family. He could practically feel her ex-cheerleader legs squeezing around his waist as they kissed, just like old times.

He had a dream-board in the basement of the condo they rented. A secret grotto that the girls were not likely to discover in the shadowy, dank space smelling of old cat piss and mold. It was where Teddy went to bench-press and jump rope, a quiet place to exercise his frustrations away. And above the laundry sink, there was a cabinet in which he kept his dreams sequestered.

On the inside of the cabinet door was a picture of the body he wanted for himself: a photo of Bruce Lee, circa 1973's *Enter the Dragon*. And there were other pictures, of various heroes: Arnold Schwarzenegger in full Conan regalia; Terry "Hulk" Hogan; Clint Eastwood; Mike Tyson; Teddy Roosevelt; and, in-flight from the free-throw line, Michael Jordan, pink tongue tasting the rarified air of a six-time NBA champion.

There in the basement, headphones shutting off the world, muscles burning, the room dark and somehow womblike, he was free to envision his future. This future where he was a man among men, physically strong, financially assured, and maybe even intellectually surprising. The dream-board was festooned with houses he'd photographed around town: modern ranches with unorthodox angles, big windows, and forever views—views looking all the way out to those big, white-teethed monster mountains amid the clouds, and Valhalla not so far away. He saw a future where his family would own dozens of acres of land and he'd look out in the mornings and see eight or nine horses frolicking in a meadow, his daughters delightedly chasing them or perhaps collecting fistfuls of wildflower bouquets. And back in their bedroom, he and Britney would be as enraptured with each other as ever.

They'd always been good at that—sex—ever since they were teenagers. Soothing each other with their bodies. Whatever was in their way, whatever troubles addled their minds, they were perfectly matched for each other and always would be, he knew. They would grow old, of course, but their love would continue on like an eternal heartbeat, rhythmically pumping on and on into their shared future. In the past he had endeavored to write a poem capturing the intensity of these feelings. A single page. All the heavy words neatly center-aligned and capitalized, but when he sat down to transfer what was in his heart onto a page, he found the task insurmountable.

These were the kinds of things, Teddy had learned, *not* to share with Bart, if he didn't want to suffer through his friend's unyielding harassment. Teddy practically cringed at the thought of Bart's jaundiced worldview, snaking into his own untroubled mind.

After Britney hustled the girls into the minivan for school that morning, Teddy crept down into the basement and jumped rope for fifteen minutes. He needed to steel his mind. Time, he knew, was about to rush forward, as if caught by the shirtsleeve to a locomotive. He would have to be strong of body and strong of brain if they were going to get through this in one piece, the kind of friend and partner Cole and Bart needed. He knew that he wasn't as smart as Cole or as brutally forceful as Bart, but he could be the vitally positive force between the two, the way he'd been as a child, when his parents fought.

He closed his eyes, felt the muscles of his arms strain, felt the callused balls of his feet bounce off the concrete floor, and saw that household, the one he'd grown up in. His father arriving home long after dinner had cooled, his mother by then close to tears, and how, as early as twelve, he'd taken pride in separating them, in placing his body between his father and his mother. Even back then, twenty-odd years ago, he was strong. Strong from emulating Kung Fu movies, action flicks; strong from football and wrestling practice; strong from internalizing all the house's strife, focusing it all into his muscles and diffusing it later, in sport.

It was the same reason he loved construction. After high school, he'd been lost in life, drifting from one dead-end job to the next: stocking shelves at Walmart; flipping burgers or delivering pizzas; working as a night auditor at Motel 6. Cole was the one who'd gotten him his first construction job, and he'd instantly taken to it. The camaraderie of the work crew. The physically demanding work. And, at the end of a job, the satisfaction of looking at a completed project and knowing you'd done something that would stand the test of time, something that might even outlive you. He loved those nights when, after finishing a project, they'd all hit the bars and their foreman would buy them a round or two of beers and thank them for their hard work and he'd go home, exhausted, sunburned, and so utterly thankful for the reassurance of his bed and the cool, soft cup of his pillow.

He showered, quickly ate a bowl of oatmeal, pounded a glass of orange juice, and lit out for True Triangle's last mundane jobsite: a garage teardown-and-rebuild in town. Nothing sexy. An older woman had hired them, and they'd been putzing away, putting in a few focused hours at a time before going off to work other jobs for a week or more. They knew the woman was frustrated, but they'd bid the project too low, and so there was very little profit to be made.

He pulled his truck up in front of the homeowner's house. The morning was bright, and he felt hopeful, happy. A new concrete pad waited for them, and he inspected this. If they busted their butts, they could get all the framing and roofing done in a day or two, and then hanging the garage door would be a piece of cake.

He noticed the front door crack open, and the woman stood there in her nightgown, a TV remote gripped in her hand.

"Well," she said. "I thought you boys had given up on me. Hadn't heard a peep outta you in days now."

Teddy was hardly a masterful actor, but there was one role he could play quite convincingly when called upon—that of a dumbed-down version of himself. Sensing the woman's anger and disappointment, he grinned slowly and rubbed at the top of his head. "Gee, we've just been so busy," he said, walking slowly toward her, "this whole town, there's work everywhere and we're just being run ragged."

"Uh-huh," she said. "You boys were sure hungry for this job two months ago. That sales spiel your friend gave me? About being a small local company. Bootstraps and all that bologna. I'm an old lady, and I about could've built this garage faster'n you three bozos."

Teddy looked at his feet. This was part of the hustle: Line up more work than you could possibly handle, because there was no guarantee there'd be work on the horizon next year, or the year after. And then find ways to manage or ignore your clients' disappointment when you drifted way past the projected deadlines.

"Is there something I can do for you, ma'am? Some gesture to make things right?"

She regarded him coolly. "My furnace has been acting up since May," she admitted. "Nights are getting colder, and I'd like it fixed before the snow flies. Why don't you come on in and give it a look for me?"

Teddy nodded amiably. "I'd be happy to, ma'am. We do aim to please."

The house was perfectly kept, everything in its place. Not even any

of the bric-a-brac so many of their older clients hoarded: the collect-
ible plates hanging on walls, towering stacks of moldering newspaper
and magazines rising from punky warped floors, paperback books,
garbage . . . No, this little house was immaculate.

"You sure keep a tight ship," Teddy said.

"Yes, sir, I do. Which is why that mess out there," she said, pointing to where her garage once stood, "is *killing* me. I know the neighbors are talking. And yesterday a developer was here, wondering if I
was thinking about selling. Let me tell you something, my husband
and I bought this house forty years ago. Nine thousand dollars, it cost
us. Cash on the barrelhead. There were no millionaires here back
then. Just a bunch of ranchers, some cowboys, and a few dusty miners,
hanging on."

He followed her down a set of uncluttered stairs and into the cool,
dry basement.

Teddy walked over and knelt down, studying the furnace.

"Well, ma'am, I don't know how to tell you this, but . . . this thing's
ancient. Anything could be wrong with it at this point."

"I checked the filter already," she put in. "Just like my husband
taught me. Filter's fine. I'd changed it about a month ago." She pointed
an arthritic finger to a meticulously organized log that hung off the
furnace by a loop of twine: Every time the furnace had been serviced,
every filter changed, all neatly recorded over the decades. . . . "I checked
the fuses, too."

Teddy withdrew a pocket flashlight and stared into the furnace.
This sort of chore pleased him; he liked the direct contact with a
homeowner. So much of their time was spent up on a rooftop or bang-
ing away with hammers, covered in dust, loud music playing. Sometimes it felt like their only connection to the homeowners were
arguments about money or timelines. But this was real, tangible.
Something was broken and needed fixing. And the homeowner wasn't
some toxic tech wonder boy, either, some gel-haired sports agent, or
pharmaceutical executive.

"Got it," Teddy said at last, revealing a broken loop of hardened black rubber. "Your blower belt broke."

"Is that bad?" she asked.

"Ma'am, this furnace's older than I am. All things considered, I'd say it's pretty good news. You can get yourself a new one at the hardware store pretty cheap."

She took the broken belt from his hands and looked at him with something like a reserved approval.

"Would you like a cup of coffee?" she asked.

He glanced around the basement at shelves of neatly arranged cans of paint, a work bench and pegboard, an old dartboard, and not far down the wall, a Budweiser calendar still counting the days of December 1999.

"Not much of a coffee drinker, myself," he said. "But I'd take a tall glass of water."

They sat at a small circular table in her cramped kitchen, and she fed him well-buttered white-bread toast with homemade blackberry jam. She talked about her home, about how this place had grown a family of seven children, about how, with just those two tight bedrooms, it had been stuffed with people: kids sleeping in closets, kids sleeping in bunk beds, kids sleeping in the basement, and a single toilet for them all to share. Teddy stared out the window as he chewed his toast. His partners were already late, and he was beginning to wonder if they were coming at all.

"These houses they're building today," the old woman continued, "you could fit ten of mine into any one of them. My lord, you could fit this whole home just in their garage alone. It's an abomination, don't you think?"

He tilted his head, not entirely sure how to respond. "Well, ma'am, the thing is, a big house like you're describing, I mean, that's a lot of jobs for a lot of people. And for a long time, too."

"Honestly, I think it's a big waste," she continued. "All the people out there who are hungry and homeless. Think of the ways that money could be spent."

"Yeah, but this is America, ma'am. People don't like to be told how to spend their money. Even homeless people."

He stood from the table and approached the window, gazing out at the street as he swallowed down the cold tap water. Cole and Bart were nowhere in sight. He checked his phone for messages and immediately spotted a text from Cole:

We're at the house site. Where ARE you?

Teddy quickly texted back:

Thought we were working on the old lady's garage?

Behind him she kept prattling on. "An eight-thousand-square-foot house and they live there, what, maybe two weeks a year? Pushing the taxes up, too. Another five years, I won't be able to afford living here."

His phone vibrated again:

Forget the old lady. We need you out here. PRONTO.

He returned to the table and sat down heavily, felt her eyes on him. "Your partners aren't coming, are they?"

He glanced down at his boots. "The lumber we were expecting didn't arrive," he lied, finishing the glass of water. He rapped his knuckles on the table. "But next week is looking real good."

"I raised seven children," she said quietly. "I know when I'm being lied to. And I don't suffer fools either."

He stood again, placed the glass and plate in the sink. "Tell you what," he said. "Give me twenty minutes. I'll be right back with a new belt. Get that furnace up and running again."

"Son, I'm eighty-two years old. You don't fix that garage soon, I may not be around to pay you for your work, if you catch my drift. My clock is ticking. Loudly."

From the front door he regarded her where she sat at the kitchen table nibbling at her toast. He did not believe her. This was a woman who might outlast the mountains.

5

The house site was still swaddled in morning shadow when Teddy reached the springs. Cole and Bart were flanking Gretchen as they all peered down at a set of blueprints laid out on Cole's open pickup tailgate.

"Mornin'," Teddy called.

"Teddy, hello," Gretchen said. "This is my architect. Elizabeth Crown."

"Miss," Teddy said, shaking her hand.

The architect was a tall, thin woman with long black hair, and stylish eyeglasses she seemed to readjust more or less constantly.

"Miss Crown will not be on the site very much, if at all," Gretchen said. "She's a young hotshot with a new firm in San José. I was lucky to snatch her up for this project. And I wish *I* could linger a bit longer, too, gentlemen, but I've got an early-afternoon flight. So, if you require any specific direction, please don't hesitate to call. No doubt you'll need to make a draw fairly soon. I assume you're familiar with the title company?"

"We know who they are," Cole said. "I'd like to begin framing as soon as we can. Then get a roof on this. Seal up the box so weather isn't a concern."

"Indeed. I'm glad you're on the job."

"Us, too," Teddy put in earnestly.

"Oh, there's one more thing," Gretchen said almost offhandedly, her voice trailing off. "A gentleman I'd like you to meet."

Cole almost smirked; seeing in that casual delivery quite the opposite—a premeditated calculation: What was to follow meant to look like a second thought and had clearly been determined some time earlier. Had they been playing chess, he had no doubt Gretchen could have beaten him nine hundred and ninety-nine times out of a thousand, but on this move, he'd anticipated her, seen her plans well-telegraphed. Or, then again, perhaps that was the point.

"Follow me," she said, and they did.

Near the garage, two men stood leaning against the bed of a Ford pickup. There was something about their quiet discussion, the way their hands and forearms rested on that truck, that Cole recognized immediately as a friendship, a familiarity built over years. The two men were talking, yes, but Cole suspected that even without words they could know each other's minds, or, at the very least, what was required of each other to complete the job ahead of them.

"Bill," Gretchen called out. "Bill, I'd like you to meet these three gentlemen."

Bill said one last thing to the young man, perhaps in his late twenties, before ambling over toward them. He was an extremely robust man, built like the professional wrestlers of yore, a six-foot-tall wedge of day-labor muscle and calluses. When he greeted the three men, it was with a hand as thick as a slab of rough-cut lumber, and about as hard, too. His eyes were clear and intelligent, Cole saw, as he sized them up, assessing the new situation.

"Bill is my stonemason," Gretchen went on. "He's built the fire-places in all my vacation homes. A true master."

At that introduction, Bill directed his eyes toward the gravel at his feet.

"Anyway, Bill and his assistant, José, are the only two contractors left from . . ." Her voice trailed off momentarily. "From the beginning stages of construction. So, Bill, these gentlemen are the new generals: True Triangle Construction."

The men gave death-grip handshakes.

"And now," she said, stepping back down the driveway, her young architect trailing behind her toward the river, "I really must be taking my leave. We'll be in touch."

Bill stood a moment longer, watching her go, then nodded his head silently at the men and, reaching into the bed of his truck, filled his arms with fifty-some pounds of stone before climbing up the stairs to the second story of the still-skeletal structure.

Back down the driveway Gretchen and Elizabeth Crown drove off, leaving the three men standing there, a sweet symphony of sounds all around them: the seep trickling into the hot springs, the hot springs feeding the creek draining down toward the river, and far-ther away, the river itself, rushing always downhill, back toward civilization.

Cole motioned for his partners to follow him down the driveway and then stopped at the middle of the bridge, where the three of them stared back at the house.

"I'm gonna tell you boys something right now," Cole said. "That mason is a goddamn spy."

"She all but told us he was," Bart said. "But my main question re-mains: How the hell are we going to pull this fucking thing off?"

"And what about that old lady's garage project, by the way?" Teddy asked. "We told her we'd be done ages ago. I was there this morning, and she—"

Cole's eyes closed, and his hands framed his temples. "Teddy, forget about the old lady, okay?" he said. "If she wants to fire us, then she should do that. Right now, we got bigger fish to fry."

"But, I mean, we could pound out that garage in two days if—"

"Teddy! Shut the *fuck* up, man," Cole barked. "All right? This is a multimillion-dollar house. How 'bout a little focus, huh?"

"You don't have any qualms about any of this, then, huh, Coley?" Bart asked. "The schedule this lady's imposed is dangerous. Working around the clock maybe seems doable at the onset, but, brother . . . I'm worried. Worried for you two bastards. Worried about us all. And I still think it's fishy as hell about her other contractor. . . ."

"I'm gonna level with you, Bart. I got zero qualms. So the lady's got a tight timeline? At least all our expectations are out in the open, right?" Cole argued. "And, I mean, hell. Look, if we're getting toward the end and we can't make it in time, we sacrifice some of the bottom line to pay some subs for last-minute help. That ain't the end of the world, is it?"

Bart collapsed the distance between himself and Cole, spitting down into the dirt and tipping his chin up. "I'm willing to bet she's the reason they quit, or were fired," he reasoned. "Working after dark on a three-story house ain't exactly a recipe for OSHA-approved safety. You think we can finish what they started, but, bub—I'm worried we could get fired, too."

"Yeah, well, we can't worry about that now, can we?" Cole said. "We can't waste time. So, for the love of Christ, come on you two—*focus.*"

Teddy had grown up inside a house where his parents fought violently, and there was nothing he disliked more than confrontation. "All right, all right," he said, settling his hands on his partners' shoulders. "So how do we get on track here?"

Cole exhaled and offered his hand to Bart, who warily accepted.

"I need a cigarette," Cole admitted, smiling wryly. "You guys want one?"

"Naw," Teddy said, wrinkling his nose.

"Fuck, yeah," Bart said.

Cole shook two cigarettes out of a pack he kept stowed in his glove box and passed one to Bart, lighting it up for his friend. Both men inhaled.

Bart shook his head, snickering to himself almost inaudibly. "Nothing I love more than these mountains," he said, raising his arms. "This fucking project might be crazy as all get-out, and yet . . . here we are. In all this glory."

The cliffs above them were ablaze with light, and the only sounds were the gentle trickling of the mountain seep into the springs, and the creek as it wound downhill to the river's roar. Far off, the plume from the road construction crew could be seen, but the river's steady soundtrack rendered whatever noise they produced soundless.

"I think we move a big shipment of lumber, joists, and plywood here as soon as possible," Cole said. "We can store a lot of it in the garage. I think we move the windows here as soon as possible, too. And the roofing metal. We need to get a plumber and electrician on board. We need to schedule the solar installation. I like the idea of getting that solar up and running on the off-chance that the electricity goes out. Wouldn't be a half-bad idea to get a heavy-duty generator here, too. Just in case."

"Me and Teddy can get a generator," Bart offered.

"Britney's cousin is a plumber and just finished a job," Teddy said helpfully. "You guys remember him? Zach? Just got back from Iraq about a year ago?"

"Yep." Cole nodded. "Good dude. Give him a call, Teddy. Bring him on board. Me, I'll get our supplies rolling. And try to figure out who Gretchen's old general contractor was. He prolly had subs all lined up who might still want the work."

"We're gonna need a trailer or something, too," Bart said. "If we're gonna be stationed up here for the next four months, we're gonna want shelter. Someplace other than that house. A place to cook food, change clothes, get out of the elements. What do you guys say?"

"Sure," Cole agreed. "That's gonna be a chunk of change, but with that earnest money, we can afford something nice. Don't skimp either, Bart. We need to project a sense of professionalism. Hear me?"

"Copy that," Bart said, giving Cole a flippant little salute.

"We can do this," Teddy said.

Cole smiled. "We can definitely do this."

"All right, then, gentlemen," said Bart. "Only way out's through, I guess."

6

There is a unique excitement that imbues the construction of a new house—and a sense of mystery, too. For the person holding the blueprints, yes, they know what the structure they're building *should* look like in the end. But that doesn't always make it so. A homeowner's dream, for one thing, does not always perfectly correspond to a homeowner's checking account. And there are any number of factors that cannot be predicted with real certainty. When drilling a well, for example, what comprises the bedrock beneath the site? A homeowner may have a general sense of the local geology and topography, but they cannot know with precision what strata of stone the drill will discover, or how deep the aquifer may lie waiting underground. Certainly, the homeowner cannot control the weather: howling winds, five-day storms that sock into the landscape like an unwanted houseguest. So much about the actual building of a house cannot be sketched out on a blueprint.

For Cole, Bart, and Teddy, there was an overwhelming sense of satisfaction in watching subcontractors and suppliers slowly pull up the long gravel road toward the job they were overseeing. Grizzled old men would amble onto the site, peer up at the cliff-faces and then down into the hot springs, and rub at their heads or chins before saying something like, *Never seen nothin' like this.*

These men looked at the partners of True Triangle with a mixture of respect and envy, and the effect was intoxicating. It altered the way they spoke, the way they walked, the way they slammed their own truck doors, the confidence and volume with which they spoke on their phones. In a matter of days, they'd gone from living as working-class ghosts to feeling like other men were watching them and marking the things they said, the assuredness with which they executed orders. The day Bart pulled the new camper-trailer near the house, there was a palpable sense of awe in the air. *How the hell did these unknown assholes score a project like this?* And, *Look at the money they're spending already!*

"How much did this thing cost us?" Cole asked Bart, as they parked the trailer on a fairly level area before popping their heads inside for a quick look-see. It certainly was deluxe: a sleeping area, a bathroom, a small kitchen, and even a sort of living and dining space.

"You don't wanna know." Bart grinned, knowing that the final tally was well over a hundred grand. "I put it on the company card. It's all good. Hell, I even stocked the fridge."

"Guess this is our first official office," Teddy quipped. "I like it."

"Yep. This here's our headquarters," Bart said, slapping at a thin wall of fiberglass and vinyl. "The ole HQ."

"And like most houses in America," Cole said, shaking his head, "if it catches fire, it won't burn. It'll melt. A whole lot of plastic went into this."

As if on cue, they all peered out through the windows of the trailer to Gretchen's house, where over a dozen men were scurrying around, performing their various duties.

"*There's* a house that ain't gonna melt at the first errant match-stick," Bart said. "We're building one for the ages, boys."

"You're right about that," Cole agreed as he left the trailer. "So let's get back to work."

n those fast-shortening days of late September and early October, with dusk coming on as quick as an encroaching thunderhead, the men worked long, long hours, arriving in the predawn blue-black of fading night, when the stars over the mountains were so near, so precise as to steal your breath and make you feel for a moment the truth of it all, that you were just a living speck on this great blue-green marble tumbling its way through outer space, beholden to so many invisible laws, and, against that sheer infinitude of blackness and space, alive but an instant. At least that was what Cole felt, as he drove each morning along that gravel road. Sometimes in his rearview mirror he caught a glimpse of his partners rumbling up the same road behind him, their headlights separated by a mile or more, like a poorly strung necklace—Teddy probably checking in with Britney before he lost his cell phone signal; Bart flipping through the FM radio dial while he spit brown, tobacco-flecked Copenhagen-juice into the red Solo cup that would be lodged between his thighs.

The three men worked as hard and as diligently as they could remember, arriving long before their subs came yawning and drag-assing onto the site. Already they'd be laying plywood over the floor joists, the generator howling and their nail guns going *pfffttt, pfffttt, pfffttt*. Their boots pounded the floors almost as loud as the boom box screamed Aerosmith or Metallica or AC/DC, something to keep them moving, moving, moving, something to keep the testosterone pumping, and even if Cole might have occasionally preferred something a little more mellow, *fuck that*: He needed Teddy and Bart flying around the worksite like demons. Needed them jacked-up and empowered and willing to meet the subs on the driveway and point to here or there with total authority.

It took them almost two weeks to complete the roof. They might've been done sooner, but a storm settled over the mountains, thunder booming in the canyon and white-blue lightning piercing down to explode a nearby pine tree. Three full days they spent in their trucks or the trailer, peering at the skies, hoping against hope that the sun would burn a hole through those thick, low-slung banks of fog. But those days were wasted, and by the late afternoon of each day, with no relent in sight, they simply picked up their tools and headed for home.

Eventually the storm passed, and the day broke bright and clear, buoying their spirits. How they ran along those rooflines, like brave-hearted alpinists, like daring funambulists, balancing and tiptoeing as they went, imagining themselves dancing on tightropes, racing along Olympic balance beams. The roofing steel was incredibly high-quality and heavy, and the shifting rooflines demanded intense concentration. A mistake of mere centimeters on the western side of the roofline could mean an error of actual feet over on the eastern side. And of course, there could be *no* mistakes on this house. They knew this, and held this standard in their minds, like a mantra, and reveled in their newfound precision and care.

But the bullshitting! Harassing one another constantly: about their sex lives or lack thereof, about money, about Britney wanting another baby, about Cole rejoining the dating scene, about Bart never ever finding anyone to marry him, and when no subs were on the site, daydreaming about their bonuses, imagining how they'd spend the money. It was just like when they were teenagers, on some backpacking trip, imagining that they'd won the lottery and how they'd spend their imaginary fortune.

For Cole, with no children and a soon-to-be ex-wife, there was nothing much he wanted, just this work, this time with his friends, this pinprick vision of a goal on the far horizon. He could focus on that, and it gave him meaning, something to pull him out of bed in the morning, some place to aim his truck toward, like a compass bearing.

There was just one thing that held his curiosity, one imagined possession that he thought of as a reward, or rather, as a manifestation of his reward, his bonus: a wristwatch; a beautiful wristwatch. In bed at night, peering at his phone, he researched Rolexes and Breitlings, Cartiers and Philippes . . . After this job, he'd be in a position to rent any townhouse or apartment he wanted, wear whatever clothes he wanted, travel wherever; but somehow, what he really fixated on was the idea of this watch. He pictured himself sitting at a bar, his shirt-sleeves rolled up, his forearms tanned and well-muscled, and a woman touching his wrist, his hand, and noticing this watch, seeing him as someone more worldly, more refined. This watch, she would see, was no accident; but rather, a cultivated statement by a man whose time was valuable, who recognized the import of every hour, every minute, every second. He thought of that wristwatch as the perfect symbol for the completion of this house. Thought of himself in bed with a woman, not a stitch of clothing on either of them, as he almost hovered over her, his arms straining, her legs wrapped around his lower back, and clasped about his thickly competent wrist, the watch, the watch, the watch marking all that sweet, sweet time.

But first, with the roof complete, they could seal up the house, framing in the walls, making way for windows. Already, the structure was taking shape; no longer a flashy steel skeleton against the mountain, it was shelter, and soon it would be a house. They stapled Tyvek to the exterior, preparing the house for fiber-cement siding. A subcontractor arrived and hung the copper gutters, all of which led to rain barrels, one of them stationed immediately adjacent to the hot springs, so that a person could leave those steaming waters and plunge their beet-red head into a barrel of clear, cold water. The house was a sharply angular three-layer cake slightly askew, each floor an L, a fold of a fan unfolded, so that against the mountain the house looked native, echoing the bands of rock that were striated and set apart, even as they conformed to the whole. The house was gorgeous, from every angle, in every moment of the day or night, and with the hot springs steaming beside it, and the deep softness of the afternoon shadows . . . Christ, it was sexy. And satisfying. No two ways about it.

The windows were commercial-grade glass and their transportation to the site a real production. The trucks entrusted with safely carrying the windows drove no faster than five miles per hour along the gravel road, the drivers careful to study the way forward for any potholes, dips, or washouts. Cole, Bart, and Teddy held their collective breath as each window was set into place. One mistake here could cost them weeks; these windows were all custom-made and shipped from halfway across the continent. Were only one of them to be cracked, scratched, or otherwise compromised, there would be no choice but to send it back to the factory and insist on a replacement; and of course, there was no guarantee *that* replacement would arrive before the heavy snow. When all the windows were finally and properly installed, there was a collective sigh of relief. The package was finally more or less sealed. The siding would soon be installed, and after that, insulation could be blown into the walls and attic, drywall could be hung inside, then taped and mudded, but from that point on, the house was at the very least watertight. The plumbers, HVAC guys, and electricians would be back sporadically, and as needed. But now, the house was nearly ready for winter.

7

Gretchen stood in the kitchen where the wide farmhouse sink would sit and stared out the window. Steam often condensed on that bank of windows; beads of water running down the glass in serpentine paths. She was aware of the three partners of True Triangle standing off to the side, their arms nervously crossed while they silently watched her. Today, the air was incredibly still, with low clouds socked in tight against the mountains, and the steam roiling off the springs seemed stymied close to the house, rather than wisping off toward the valley.

She nodded to the south, out past the river, to the far ridge east of the huge cliffs.

"You've been on the site for several weeks now," she began. "About how many days has the view been like this? Totally obscured, such as it is."

They glanced at each other like three schoolchildren called on for the answer to a complex mathematical problem.

"I don't know," Cole said, shrugging. "To be honest, we're so damn busy, we don't pay much attention to the weather as long as we can get our work done."

Gretchen gave the men an appreciative smile and chuckle. "Not the information I was seeking, Mr. McCourt," she said, wagging a finger in his direction, "but you couldn't have possibly produced a better answer."

He blushed as she walked past the men, to that landing, where the view again opened wide. She peered intently to the south again.

"This frame," she said, pointing at that huge window, "is much wider than I imagined. Doesn't it seem wide to you?"

"Well, those are enormous windows," Bart offered. "They need a pretty stout frame to hold all that weight, all that glass. And in these elements—"

"But the view," she interrupted. "I mean, looking south, standing right here . . ." She shook her head and then waved a hand toward the window. "The view is obstructed with that frame right there. The frame is all I can see."

The men stood looking at her, wide-eyed and their mouths agape.

"Well, you could always just take a step to the left," Bart offered, "or to the right. There ain't any shortages of views in this house—"

"I fucking know that, Bart," she said, cutting him off. "But this isn't Fenway Park. There shouldn't be *any* obstructed views, now, should there? This is a *new* house. How does this happen?"

She could see on their faces that they were frighteningly confused.

"Get me a chair," she said.

"I'm sorry," Teddy said quietly. "You want a—"

"A fucking chair," she repeated. "Please."

She stood, her back turned to them, staring down into the valley below, the brume obscuring the world beyond. Behind her, she could hear the men quickly disperse, and moments later, Teddy settled a grungy collapsible camping chair on the floor.

"Here you go," he said.

"There's no chance of getting a window with a smaller frame, is there?" she asked him.

He cleared his throat. "Honestly, ma'am, I don't think so. Not under the time constraints we're under. A window like that would have to be specially fabricated and then transported. We'd have to take this window out, which might require taking the neighboring windows out. . . ."

She turned her head just slightly without ever looking at Teddy.

"Any mistake along the way and there'd be no guarantees we'd finish on time."

"And that's not even accounting for costs," Cole put in. "For one thing, this window is custom. You ain't getting your money back on it. And for two, a window with a less conspicuous frame than this one would . . . let's just say, it'll cost you."

"Cole," Gretchen began, "do I seem like a client deterred by cost?"

He shook his head in the negative.

She sighed loudly.

"But, ma'am," Teddy continued, "there ain't a bad view in this house. Hell, where I live, our condo, there's six windows in the whole place. And one of 'em looks out on our garbage cans."

"You can go now," she said.

"Yes, ma'am."

Long after the men retreated downstairs to the garage, she allowed herself to sit in the flimsy chair, the frame of the window directly in her line of sight. Outside, the fog intensified, and yet she remained that way until dusk, when she heard tentative footsteps behind her.

"I was, uh, gonna head into town for some chow," Cole said. "Can I get you anything?"

"Do you have any masking tape, Mr. McCourt? Something colorful?"

"I could probably find you something," he replied. "How much do you need?"

"Not much," she replied.

She heard his footsteps drift away and a moment later, the sound of his return. He held a roll of blue painter's tape out for her.

"Will this do the trick?" he asked quizzically.

"Yes," she said. "I hope I can live with these windows, Mr. Mc-Court. I don't understand how such a critical detail could be so overlooked."

"I'll leave you be," he said quietly.

She waited several minutes before briskly standing from the chair, ripping off two twelve-inch-long strips of tape, and then placing them on the floor, where the chair once sat.

8

The next morning, just before sunrise, they watched as she parked her Range Rover and walked across the bridge, a white paper cup in her hands. The fog was gone, and the morning was crisp and cool, a small assembly of stars in the steadily brightening sky.

"I think I like it better when she ain't around," Bart said as she neared the garage.

She moved wordlessly past them, past some of their subs, up the stairs from the mudroom, and back to that landing area near the kitchen, where she had spent so much time the day prior.

It was Teddy who saw her place the chair over the two strips of blue tape that formed an *X* on the floor.

Just as the sun crested the mountains in the east, she stood from the chair and looked down into the valley. She stepped to either side of the window's frame. She moved around that entire floor, looking down into the valley at *something*. . . . Was it the river? A specific peak or cliff-face? A particular cottonwood, its last remaining leaves like golden spangles in the early-morning light?

A half hour later, she walked out onto the driveway, pulling a pair of gloves on her hands.

"The window and that fat frame will have to do, gentlemen. We'll be in touch."

They watched her retreat to her Range Rover and drive off before they marched up those stairs to the landing. The chair was nowhere in sight, and the blue tape that once made an X on the floor was gone, but Bart could feel some adhesive on the wood. He walked downstairs to the table saw and, reaching below the tool, picked up a handful of fine sawdust and carried it back up the stairs. He knelt again and sprinkled the sawdust on the floor. The fine pale dust settled into place, and he gently blew on it, scattering most of it across the floor but revealing a crude X.

"Get me that tape again," he growled, and before long, there was a new X on the floor, and for the next several days, the men stood there, looking down into the valley for what, they did not know. They sat in the camp-chair and looked. They sat cross-legged on the floor and looked. They stood, they glassed with binoculars, and yet there was nothing of note in all that wild; beauty everywhere, but nothing of particular interest.

One day, Teddy thought he spied something.

"That ridge," he said, pointing at a meadow for Cole. "You see that highest point, at about your one o' clock? Come down to maybe your eight o' clock. Just above the tree line. Sometimes I think I see . . . sort of a light out there."

"A light?" Cole pressed.

"Or, I don't know," Teddy continued. "A flash, a . . . glint."

Cole pressed the binoculars to his eyes and scanned the meadow intently.

"All I see are some shiny rocks," he said dismissively. "Who the hell knows what she's looking at. Anyway, we ain't got time. I need your hand with some siding. C'mon."

9

On a Friday in late October they held a barbecue, the kind of gesture they'd always hoped a general contractor might extend to *them* as subs but never did. Cole pointed out that the barbecue might also help sustain any goodwill they had managed to engender with their subs heading into the first throes of winter. They bought cases and cases of beer, and at five in the evening, they fired up a gas grill to cook up countless hot dogs and cheeseburgers as they stood around with the other men and discussed the house taking shape, and though they were used to second-guessing a homeowner's design decisions, they all agreed this was the finest house any of them had ever worked on: not too big, no, but also not some dinky tiny-house singing of liberal guilt. No, this was a smart house, well thought out, well designed, built of timeless and durable materials so as to disappear into its surroundings.

The cold beer went down easily, and soon Bart was building a bonfire of the scrap lumber lying about the site, and a few of the men were rolling joints, and that was okay, because this was the mountains and they were alone with one another, and their work, at least for today, was complete.

One of the older contractors hauled out a guitar and some other fellows had fiddles and a banjo, and everyone gathered around the campfire, sharing their smoke as the musicians strummed and sang, and deep inside that canyon the music echoed off those faraway cliff walls, and through the last remaining cottonwood and aspen leaves, so citron and gold, clinging to the branches, and dear god, what a beautiful night in America! To have worked so hard alongside your brothers. To have carried great weight without complaint, to have solved problems, to have helped build such a sound and elegant dwelling. Inside Teddy's chest, his heart felt ten feet tall. And though Cole was prone to worrying and did not often relax, he allowed the beer to loosen him up, and he sang along with the subs and drummed his palms against his thighs and tapped his toes, and everything was all right. They'd damn well finish this house before Christmas, and with any luck over the next couple of years, he might just make himself a newly minted millionaire.

When one of the many circulating joints found Bart's fingers, he took a deep, long draw, felt that pungent cloud good and warm in his lungs, felt his muscles relax, and that was when he realized that not only was he feeling mellow, he was *exhausted*. They'd been working fourteen-hour days or more every day since they'd agreed to terms with Gretchen, and he hadn't had a break in over seven weeks.

"Fuck," he said now, and to no one in particular. "I am *beyond* beat."

"Need a bump, man?"

It was Reuben, one of their drywalling subs. He was a dirty sumbitch. Drywall dust in his hair, arms all adorned with fading tattoos of the unprofessional variety, wiry as hell, standing there beside Bart in his bare feet and a Phish T-shirt, gas-station sunglasses hiding his eyes from anything so bright as the campfire crackling before them. He could often be seen around the worksite, bouncing a Hacky Sack on his breaks like he was lounging on a Malibu beach.

"Yeah, I think maybe I do," said Bart. "Let's take a walk."

They strolled along, easy as you please, passing the joint between them as they made their way down to the river.

"Fuckin' beautiful spot here, brah," Reuben said. "No idea how you assholes landed this gig, but shit, brah, I'm happy for you."

"You holding?"

"Always, man. Whatcha need?"

"Just a little coke, maybe. Like a ball."

"You boys been workin' long days, ain't you? Workin' like dogs."

Reuben handed Bart the coke, from which Bart then poured a bit on the back of his hand and snorted it right up.

The rush hit quick, and he was right back where he wanted to be, felt the old power in his muscles, in his hands. *Wwwhhhoooooooo*— that was *nice*. He took another small bump, and then bounced a bit on the balls of his feet, on his toes, like a prizefighter about to enter the fray. Cocked his neck side to side, squinted up at the stars, and somehow they looked *sharper*, like bits of broken, beautiful glass.

"That's better," he said. "Fuck yeah. What do I owe you?"

"You got a hundred?"

"Right here," Bart said. "Hey, buddy?"

"Yeah?"

"I'm going to be in the market, I guess. Least 'til we wind this project down."

"Yeah, well, I'm trying to get out of dealin'," Reuben said. "But you know Jerry in town? He'd help you out."

"I know Jerry," Bart said, nodding. "Sleazeball."

"True, true. But he's got the shit," Reuben said, winking.

The two men turned; Teddy was walking toward them, a can of Bud Light in his hands, a big smile slung across his face. He wasn't much of a drinker. *A damn cheap date*, Bart always joked.

"This looks like trouble," Teddy joked, and then, looking up at the stars, "You believe it out here?"

"Hey, fellas," Reuben said, giving them both fist bumps, "I gotta split, or my old lady'll be on my ass."

"Right on," said Bart, his tone suddenly professional. "We'll see you Monday. Hey, how's the drywall coming?"

Reuben squinted at Bart, like a student considering defying his teacher. "Yeah," Reuben laughed, "now you're all boss-man and serious and shit. Drywall's fucking great, man. We'll be done when we're done." And with that he flicked Bart and Teddy a peace sign and disappeared toward the bridge, his bare feet moving noiselessly in the dark.

"I never liked that guy," Teddy said earnestly. "Real druggie."

Bart was a tall man, about six-three, two hundred and ten pounds and as lean as a panther; shoulder-length black hair, with a sharp jawline and, somehow, perfectly straight white teeth, and in these moments he peered down at Teddy as if his kid brother were part of some anti-drug after-school special. "Naw, Reuben's fine," Bart said. "Come on, guys are gonna start peeling off."

They walked back toward the fire, no music being played now, a few huddles of men smoking as they talked about the house, a handful of men waving as they walked back down toward their trucks, headlights popping on, then tracing the road back down and out. Finally, it was just Cole, Bart, and Teddy standing around the smoldering flames of the fire, Bart bouncing, shadowboxing, throwing rocks out into the darkness.

"Tell you what, boys," Cole said, setting down the beer he'd just opened and removing his shirt, "since the first day we came out here, I've been curious about these hot springs, and right now I believe is a most *opportune* time to test the waters." Shucking off his boots and socks and stripping down to his underwear, he picked up his beer, walked gingerly to the side of the pool, dipped his toes in, then his feet, then his calves.

"How is it?" Teddy asked excitedly.

Cole slipped all the way into the water then, and his head disappeared before bobbing back to the surface. He pushed his hair away from his face and smiled, his short chin whiskers dripping water in the darkness.

"Come on in, boys; the water's fine."

One of life's greatest luxuries was floating in a hot spring, a cold can of beer in one hand and an infinitude of stars scattered across the heavens above. Teddy and Bart joined their friend, and soon the three men were floating, their arms outspread along the lip of the pool, their necks tilted back and up. Only Bart fidgeted, occasionally swimming from one extent of the pool to the other, until at last Cole said, "For Christ's sake, smoke a little more weed, man, and chill out. I can't believe you still have this much energy to burn."

To which Bart did light a little roach, settling down enough so that the pool was again a serene plane of water reflecting the perfect sky, just little burps of bubbles now and again roiling the water, but mostly the night was utterly still, marked only by the yips and singing of far-off coyotes, a shooting star streaking overhead, an owl hooting down by the river.

"Can you imagine actually living here?" Cole said, perhaps to himself.

"Fellas," Teddy chipped in, "I hate to be a party pooper and all, but I really ought to get back on home. Britney's gonna have my head, I know it. I been gone enough as it is."

"I've been thinking about that, actually," Cole said. "And I wonder, you know, especially when the snow starts to fly, if maybe we ought to set up some kind of camp here."

"What do you mean?" Teddy asked. "You mean, like sleeping right here on the site? In the trailer?"

"That's exactly what I mean," Cole said. "Look, instead of spending an hour or more each day driving to and from the site, we could just sleep here. Work until we drop."

"Yeah, but, Cole, when would I see my family?" Teddy asked a bit woefully, his brow a washboard of concern.

"Well, maybe they could come out a weekend or two, when it's just the three of us working, maybe camp here or down by the river. Hell, swim in the hot springs, go fishing, hiking. They'd probably love it. Like a mini-vacation."

"Maybe," Teddy said, swallowing. "Or maybe they've got a dance recital that day. Or horseback riding lessons, or some other kid's birthday party . . . Or, I don't know, Cole, maybe Britney's got laundry to do, or maybe we'd like to go on a date. I mean, we still got more than two months on this house. I can't just check out for that long."

Cole sighed in frustration, rubbed the sweat off his face.

"Just speakin' for myself, but I'm *all for* staying out here," Bart said. "Helluva lot prettier than my apartment. And we're here all the damn time anyway. Certainly paid enough for that trailer. May as well use it. There's just the one bed, but it's probably big enough for two of us. And someone could sleep on the floor or maybe we could rig up a cot or a hammock."

Teddy crawled out of the springs and stood dripping in his boxer shorts. "I suppose we didn't think to bring towels," he said.

More than a little drunk, Bart rode back into town with Cole, and they followed Teddy, who was clearly working hard to keep his truck between the painted lines. Mostly they rode in silence, Cole's heater on full blast to cut the night's chill, the cab otherwise silent. Bart tapped his fingers on any surface he could find: the passenger-side window, his thighs, the dashboard. . . .

"I don't think I saw him drink more'n one beer," Cole said, "but I guarantee he's feeling a little loopy."

"He's a good man," Bart said, searching his pockets, the glove box, and the cab of the truck for his chew. "Can't help picking on

GODSPEED

that simple fucker, but truth is, I love him more than just about anybody."

"I know it," Cole said. "He's been working his ass off back there. 'Course, we all have."

"Listen, Cole," Bart began, "you actually think we can finish this project? 'Fore Christmas, I mean? You think that's even possible?"

Cole kept his eyes on the road.

"Yeah," he answered, "I do. The way we're working, I think we might even have a week or two to spare."

They followed Teddy's truck to his condo and watched their friend shoulder his tool belt up to the front door, where a light was still shining for him. Britney came to the door in a pink bathrobe, but she did not wave at Cole or Bart, just cracked the door open enough for Teddy to slide in, and then the light went out and they drove on.

"Wanna beer at my place?" Bart asked.

"Sure," Cole said. "No reason for me to rush home."

"So, things between you and Cristina are still, uh . . . Look, I'm sorry, man. I been worried about you, but wasn't sure how to ask how things were. . . ."

"She reconnected with someone from high school, I guess. Guy's a fuckin' plastic surgeon down in Las Vegas, I think. She's already posting pictures on the 'Gram. Driving around the desert in a convertible, fruity drinks at a poolside bar, nightclubs . . . Guess that's what she wants. We sure never did any of that shit."

"No wonder you're so gung-ho about camping out at the building site."

Cole thumbed at his phone as he drove and then, upon opening the Instagram account in question, passed it over to Bart.

"Damn, she's looking good, too. Sorry, amigo."

"What do you think of Gretchen? You think she's married?"

Bart sighed deeply. "You gotta abandon that pipe dream, brother. Ain't no way, ain't no how."

65

"Yeah, you're probably right," Cole said. "Better to just keep my eyes on the prize."

Bart's apartment was a dump, really, a simple one-bedroom with a living room, galley kitchen, small "dining room," and one dingy bathroom. Bart threw his keys on the counter, snagged two Coors out of the largely empty refrigerator, and passed one to Cole, who flopped down on the couch.

"How are your knees?" Cole asked. "You ever go to the doc?"

"I'll make it," Bart said, grimacing. "Soon as we get through this project maybe I can get 'em fixed up."

Cole peered around the apartment; it had been months since his last visit there.

"Jesus, this place's a sty."

Bart shrugged. "Don't get too many visitors. I just need a place to crash, you know? A place for my mail to land."

The two men were quiet for a while then, just sipping at their bottles in the close darkness of that sad little apartment.

"You dating anyone, Bart?"

"Buddy, I just wanna get through these next three, four months. I ain't even thinking about women right now. Get through these next four months, and then, I don't give a shit *what* you and Teddy think, I'm taking a nice, long vacation someplace warm. That's pretty much what I'm focusing on."

Cole drained the last of his beer bottle, kicked off his boots, and stretched out on the couch.

"Where would you go?"

Bart sat down heavily in an old, broken La-Z-Boy recliner and propped up his feet.

"Panama," he said at last.

"Panama?"

"Yep."

"How come?"

"I don't know." He yawned. "I like sayin' it."

Cole whispered, *"Panama, Panama, Panama . . .* Good-looking women down there?"

But Bart had drifted off into sleep and, fully reclined in his chair, was already softly snoring. There was nothing to stop Cole from doing the same, and some three hours later, Bart rose from the chair, tried to shake his sleeping friend awake, and finally draped a blanket over Cole, shuffled into his room, closed the door, and fell into his bed, where he slept without any dreams at all.

10

The explosion the next morning at Teddy's house came from Britney herself, who pulled all the sheets off Teddy's sleeping body in a single flourish, like yanking the dining room tablecloth without upsetting any of the silverware or wineglasses. She did likewise with the curtains, and morning greeted him thus—bright and angry.

"You came home last night smelling of beer," she snapped. Then, her voice warming just slightly, "Come on, get up, okay? Help me get the girls ready."

He almost said, *I only had one*, but quickly thought better of it. Rising from bed, he stretched; his body was not as sore as usual and he wondered if the hot springs might have had something to do with that.

"What'd you eat last night?" he asked, scratching at his belly.

"I made chicken," she said.

"Chicken *nuggets*," their eldest specified from the hallway, en route to the shower.

"Hey, tiger," Teddy said, reaching out to give Kelly a hug, only she ducked right beneath his arms and in a single motion managed to shut and lock the bathroom door.

He roused the other three girls and then went down into the kitchen to pour their bowls full of cereal. A few minutes later they were at the table, wordlessly spooning breakfast into their mouths before rushing off, as if the meal had never happened at all.

"What's the hurry?" he asked. "Where's everybody off to? I thought it was Saturday. Don't you guys, you know, just hang out, watch cartoons?"

"We've got swimming lessons at eight," Kendall said. "Then Kylie has Spanish lessons before lunch—"

"And I've got dance this afternoon," Kodi said.

"Where's your sister?" Teddy said. "She still upstairs?"

"*Teddy!*" Britney called. "Get your daughter *out* of the shower!"

He climbed the stairs and moved quickly toward the bathroom, giving the locked door a solid pounding. "Hey," he hollered. "I really wish you wouldn't lock the door."

"I'm almost *done*," Kelly shouted over the shower.

"Yeah, well, you're gonna be late," he yelled back, though he had already forgotten what for, exactly.

Suddenly Britney was at his side, tying her hair back into a ponytail and looking pointedly put out. "We need to talk," she said. "Tonight, okay? And *please* don't be late."

She kissed him on the lips, and he brightened up; she couldn't have been *too* angry.

"Look, I'm sorry about all that," he said. "Bein' late and all."

"It's okay," she said. "We understand. But we've still got a household to run here, you know? And we need your help. *I* need your help."

"I know it."

"Plus, you need to brush your teeth," she said, wrinkling her nose. "Dragon breath."

There was an hour-old text from Cole on Teddy's phone, wondering if he wanted a lift, and Teddy responded that he'd come in on his own and be at the site soon.

He had never developed a taste for coffee but stopped at his favorite gas station for a Mountain Dew and a breakfast sandwich, which he devoured almost immediately. He'd been losing weight, his pants hanging off his body; Cole and Bart could plunge through the day without ever eating, it seemed, maybe just two or three five-minute breaks where they gnawed at some warm jerky, tossed a handful of peanuts at their mouth, and drank ice water as if running a marathon. Then it was right back to it. It was still safely mid-autumn, yes, but this high up in the mountains, winter was always a threat, as if looming in the clouds just over the peaks, ready to descend upon them, sealing off the whole world for good until spring skipped back onto the scene. Cole, who wasn't a religious man, had told Teddy that he'd been praying for this long, mild autumn to continue.

Bill the mason was at the site early that morning. His pickup truck was pulled just outside the garage, a no-nonsense navy-blue Ford, its bed filled to the brim with good-size rocks. José was unloading, carrying as much as he could before pounding slowly up the roughed-in staircase to the second floor, where he made a pile near the hearth. Bill stood near the mass, looking over each rock, as if inspecting a crime scene. His chest seemed nearly as thick as two stacked concrete blocks, his black hair curly and his hands square and dry. Though shorter than Bart, Bill was as broad as a medieval blacksmith, and a jet-black push-broom mustache obscuring the man's mouth, making it impossible to know if he was grinning, or frowning, or neither.

"Mornin'," said the mason, turning to greet the men. Teddy had the sensation of addressing a grizzly bear. He was hardly unaccustomed to meeting physically imposing men in the construction trades, but this Bill was a huge man.

The four men stood in a sort of awkward huddle, brushing their boots against the plywood subfloor. And it seemed that if it were left to Bill, they might well stand there all day in complete silence, just the sound of his assistant plodding up and down the stairs, adding rocks to the pile near the hearth.

"So, sounds like you've known Gretchen awhile . . . ," Cole mustered.

Bill nodded, offering nothing.

The truth was, he'd known her almost twenty years now, dating back to that Taos house. They'd become close after one of the contractors on the job made a habit of hitting on Gretchen long after she'd loudly dropped a hint that she was not interested in him, and never would be. When the man cornered her in a closet of her own house and laid hands on her, she'd dropped him with a well-aimed knee to the groin, and after she called out for help, it was Bill who forcefully removed the man from the worksite, adding a strong right-cross that broke the man's nose, before stuffing him into a truck and telling him to fuck right off.

Not too long after that, they began a friendship that then warmed into something more. They both enjoyed discussing architecture and design, and both had an affection for the wild, for wide-open spaces. But ultimately, their lives were just incongruent. She was more or less wed to her work and San Francisco and he to his home in the desert outside Reno and to far-flung building sites in the American West. More than that, neither was much capable of compromise, so that even though they respected and cared for each other, maintaining both a sexual attraction and a genuine friendship, ultimately, they were both too independent to be suited to long-distance exclusivity, let alone marriage.

"How was it working for her on those other houses?" Bart said.

"Good," Bill replied.

"Sure seems like a nice woman," Teddy said brightly.

Bill peered over his shoulder and outside the window. "Need my tools," he finally said, and nodded at the three men before taking the stairs down into the garage and out of the house.

Cole, Bart, and Teddy stood on the southern edge of the second floor, looking out at the landscape through the impressive wall of floor-to-ceiling windows. They watched Bill walk slowly toward his truck, opening the cab doors and rummaging for what looked like a toolbox full of hammers and chisels.

"He's a fucking monolith," Bart said under his breath.

"Seems nice enough to me," Teddy offered.

"*Everyone* seems nice enough to you," Bart joked.

"Who cares, long as he gets his job done, right?" said Cole. Then, looking at Teddy, "You gonna be able to work next weekend, too?"

"I told Britney I'd go to the girls' soccer games."

"Leave him alone," Bart grumbled. "We'll be fine."

"Sure we will," Cole said. "But we're partners, Bart, remember? Three sides of a triangle. So I ain't gonna be afraid to call either of you out if you're not pullin' your weight."

"Aw, get off it, Cole," said Teddy, his voice rising in volume and pitch as he stepped in front of him. "Huh? I mean, you *know* I've been working my tail off a long time now—long before we even got this gig. I'm barely seeing my kids as is, barely seeing Britney. So I'm gonna take next weekend off to be with my family, okay? And after that, I'll be dialed right in. You can count on it."

"You fuckin' better be," Cole said, knowing that with Teddy, it was often worthwhile to challenge his heart and commitment to extract the best possible effort.

Bart insinuated himself between his two friends. "Knock it off," he said. "All right? Now just stop this bullshit!"

They'd hardly noticed Bill, who was thudding his way up the roughed-in staircase, shouldering two bags of dry cement on one shoulder, his toolbox clutched in the other hand. At the top of the stairs he stopped and looked at the three men for several moments before walking to the center of the house, where the future fireplace would be, its flue already rising up the structure and out into the big, blue sky.

"You think you'll have time to finish that by Christmas?" Bart said, motioning toward the hearth.

Bill lowered the cement to the floor and looked at the concrete hearth as if withholding an opinion about a painting he was staring at. "I listen to the rocks," Bill said flatly. "They tell me where to place them. Sometimes they tell me quickly. . . ." His voice trailed off. ". . . And sometimes they don't. But it's a nine-foot ceiling here, so . . . shouldn't be a problem. I suspect we'll be done around Thanksgiving, give or take."

"I don't know that we've been formally introduced to your co-worker," Cole said.

"José," Bill said. "Been with me since my back went out in Durango. Forty-foot-tall chimney and my back just quit. I was three stories off the ground, up on scaffolding, and my back seized right up. Couldn't work for months. José was working as a bricklayer on that project, and I hired him to help me finish the chimney. Been with me ever since."

It was the most they'd ever heard Bill say.

"How old are you, Bill?" Teddy asked.

"Fifty-one," the mason said. "And them rocks get heavier every year."

"Well, we'll leave you to it," Cole said.

But Bill was already turned away from them, peering into the pile of rocks, his hands turning each rock over and over, looking at them from every conceivable angle.

Cole and Teddy moved on then and took measurements of where the kitchen island would be while Bart stood rooted there, watching Bill. Something about what the mason had said, about the rocks getting heavier, struck a chord that reverberated deep within him. Because what his partners didn't know, couldn't have known, was that Bart wasn't sure he wanted to do this work anymore, wasn't sure that he could keep going even another couple of years.

Five months before, they'd been working on a project, a teardown-rebuild of a deck, when he'd injured not just one but both knees. It had been an icy morning, and he was humping a load of two-by-fours up an asphalt driveway when he lost his footing and, afraid to drop the load or dent one of the nearby vehicles, buckled his knees while his feet skated in opposite directions. He'd felt the tearing, knew that real damage had been done, and was furious with himself. So, he simply lay there, on that icy pavement, embarrassed, as he mentally prepared himself to stand. Only he could not—he could not stand—his knees, sirens of pain.

Eventually, he was able to right himself and, standing gingerly, pick up his fallen load. For the rest of the day, he moved like an invalid, making excuses to stay near the porch and work there, rather than retrieve supplies or even take a break for lunch.

That same night he called an ex-girlfriend, a woman named Margo whom he had actually loved, or nearly loved, but who wisely sensed in him some innate weakness (call it immaturity, perhaps; call it addiction). A nurse who also moonlighted as a Pilates instructor, she found him in his bed.

"Bart, I haven't heard from you for at least a month now," she began, leaning on the doorframe leading into his bedroom. "I thought we weren't even doing this anymore." But he was sweating profusely, and she saw then the pain etched on his face. Bart was many things, but he was not prone to complaint or exaggeration.

"Jesus," she said, approaching the bed, "what's wrong?"

"My knees," he hissed, pulling back the bedsheets.

His legs were grotesquely swollen, the kneecaps hidden under flesh that had puffed up and gone purple.

"Oh, my god," Margo breathed. "Bart, we've got to get you to a hospital."

"No, no, no," he protested. "Can't do that. Please."

"How come?"

"Look, I just fell," he said. "I was wondering if maybe you could look at it, though. Maybe tell me what's wrong?"

"You need to get yourself to a hospital, okay? Look, Bart, don't be stupid. Now, what happened?"

He explained as she rose to get him a glass of cold water and a handful of ibuprofen and then sat with him on the side of the bed.

"Thank you," he said. "I know it's been a while. I didn't mean to bother you, but . . . you were the first person I thought to call."

She sat back, surprised by his last statement, then ran her hands down his knees, applying pressure with her fingertips and watching for his reactions.

"My guess is you tore some ligaments," she said. "Not your ACL, thankfully, but . . . you might have some significant tearing in both MCLs and maybe LCLs."

"Is that bad?"

"Uh, *yeah*, Bart; it is. It'd be one thing if you were a desk jockey shuffling paper for a living, but your line of work? You're going to be in a lot of pain. I mean, your knees *might* heal on their own, but probably not." She sighed. "Let me guess: no insurance?"

He shook his head.

"Obamacare?"

He shot her a look.

"And *that's* why we're not still dating," she said, smirking smartly. "In a nutshell."

She stood up from his bedside.

"What can I do?" he asked.

"I don't know. Rest, maybe? You can ice it. The hippies swear by their CBD oils."

"If I wanted CBD," Bart said, "I'd smoke a joint."

She leaned down and gave his unshaven cheek a slow kiss.

"Too bad," she whispered into his ear. "Other than those knees, you're still looking pretty good. Might have been able to convince me."

But the pain was so sharp, and his body so tired, that this was the single time in his entire life when he had actually chosen not to make love to a woman. Even as she began to kiss her way down his neck, he thought for a moment about making it work, and as she straddled his body and began to pull off her shirt, he tried his level best to ignore the pain and just focus on how good it might feel. But nothing would erase the pain shooting up and down his legs.

He lightly touched her elbows as her fingers worked to remove her bra.

"I'm so sorry," he said. "I can't. I really, really, really wish I could.... But I can't. Sorry, Margo."

She stared down at him. "You're really hurt, aren't you?" she asked.

"Yes, Margo. I'm really fucking hurt."

She shrugged back into her shirt, pecked him again on the cheek, and left.

For the next several weeks he went about his work, hobbled and almost always high; OxyContin helped, but the accompanying nausea was enough to make him swerve back toward weed, which became the only solace he found. Waking early, he would lie in bed, smoking a joint as he watched the weather forecast and dreading the moment he'd slowly swing his beleaguered legs out from beneath the blankets and set his feet on the floor. Simply standing took heroic effort.

Then, come evening, when he returned to the apartment, removing his boots and clothing would take ten or twelve tortured minutes, after which he would plod naked to the bathtub, there to soak for an hour as he puffed away, listening to Bob Marley and dozing off until the sudsy water finally cooled, the joint disappeared into sodden ash, and he roused himself to dry off, shuffled toward the kitchen, and cooked a little pot of Campbell's soup. Sleep, when it came, was like a velvet mallet to the head, an almost instantaneous knockout, like falling down the shaft of a thousand-foot-deep mine into complete darkness. There were nights when Bart's only true experience of happiness was that fraction of a second before his eyes truly drooped shut, when the promise of sleep enveloped him like the dark wings of a gargoyle, sealing off the rest of the world—goodnight.

Christ, the hours and days run together," Bart said, sometime after lunch as they unloaded a truck of its freight of two-by-fours.

"I know it," said Cole. "I've got about four hundred emails stacked up I haven't even glanced at, fucking twenty-four voicemails, and my soon-to-be ex-wife wants to get together for some kind of 'goodbye dinner.' Sent me probably thirty texts before I finally replied."

"When's that?"

"Uh, Saturday night," Cole said. "Wait—isn't that tonight?"

"You're asking the wrong guy."

"*Teddy!*" Cole yelled.

Teddy sat inside the cab of the truck, staring back at them in the rearview mirror. "What?"

"What's today?"

"The twenty-fourth, I think. Kodi's got a 4H meeting tonight."

"Christ, Teddy-Bear, I mean, what day of the fucking week is it?"

"Saturday, remember. You're always busting my ass about working the weekend, and now you can't even recollect that it's a Saturday. Why?"

"Shit," Cole said. "Shit, shit, shit, shit, shit."

"Now who's ducking out early?" Bart asked, smiling devilishly.

They waited for what few subs had reported for work that day to collect their tools before quitting, and then Cole, Bart, and Teddy cleaned up the worksite, locked the temporary "front door" that led into an entryway-mudroom off the garage, and walked on down the slope toward their trucks.

"Bill ever say anything to you guys?" Bart asked Teddy. "I mean, after this morning, when we said hello."

"Not a word," Cole said. "Just kept moving rocks up into the house."

"Goddamn spy," Bart said. "He's keeping an eye on us. Every move we make. Might be worthwhile to whisper something to the subs, case anyone thinks about lighting a joint on the site or, hell, cracking into a damn beer. That barbecue was one thing, but I bet that sumbitch don't approve of fun-loving as a habit."

Cole and Bart slumped into Cole's truck.

"Fuck," Cole said, "I'm really not looking forward to tonight."

"Ah, it'll be great." Bart laughed. "Least there's no pressure to pick up the check, right?"

11

He could not say how long it had been since he'd last seen her, and he'd forgotten how beautiful she was. Half-Mexican, half-Irish, with long black hair and dark, dark eyes, she was sitting on a tall stool by herself when he entered the restaurant's bar. She was compact, a firecracker of a woman, with short, thick legs, wide hips, and an achingly narrow waistline. Twirling an olive in an already empty martini glass, she was decked out in tall leather boots, a short black skirt, and a turquoise sleeveless blouse that showed off her tanned and toned arms. He was unsure if all this was meant to rub his nose in the fact of their impending divorce, or something else. Either way, he was too tired to be played for a fool. He leaned into the bar, leaving a whole stool between them before ordering a beer.

"What's this? Christ, Cole, you don't have to be afraid," she said, patting the empty stool that separated them. "Come on. Come sit next to me like a normal person."

She'd always had that throaty voice that just undid him. He worked hard to pretend that instead of warmly welcoming him, she'd just called him a *shit-for-brains meathead*. The beer arrived, and he raised his glass at her in a bittersweet, half-mocking toast. "To new directions," he said.

"Oh, come *on*," she said, leaning toward him, her cleavage suddenly dominating his field of vision. "Don't be so dramatic."

He took a long swallow of beer.

"What do you want?"

She glanced down at the bar, her hair falling around her face. *Wait a minute*, he thought. *What, is she . . . ? She cannot be crying. Not after all she's put me through. Goddamn it.*

"Cristina?"

"I don't know."

He took another pull of beer. "Don't know *what*?"

"There are moments I miss you, Cole. We had some good times, right?"

He took a long, long drink from his glass of beer and felt the alcohol quickly work its way through his dehydrated system. Felt the sunburn on his nose, neck, and ears.

She glanced up at him, her makeup already gently smudged.

He thought about Bill, how few words the man elected to utter; decided this might be an excellent argumentative tactic to utilize with Cristina. Maybe she'd think he'd matured. And so he focused on that, on simply being quiet, on enjoying his beer. He pretended she wasn't there at all. He glanced outside the bar and grimaced. The darkness out there meant he'd be back at the site soon enough; every minute he spent away from the house felt like a penalty he'd suffer in those December days leading up to their deadline.

"At least we didn't have any kids," she said, offering a small, hopeful laugh.

"I always wanted to make a baby with you, actually," he confessed. "Maybe if we had, things would've been different."

"Oh, Coley," she sighed. "I was never going to have a baby with you. At least, not until you grew up a little bit."

She reached for her purse and collapsed the distance between them, moving onto the stool he'd intended as a kind of barricade. She was wearing a new perfume, one he didn't recognize, all citrus and flowers; it reminded Cole of their honeymoon in Jamaica, and he was suddenly caught up in a spell of memories: fucking in the airplane's bathroom at thirty-two thousand feet, drinking rum-cream out of her tight belly button and sucking her toes while sitting on their hotel room's little porch and looking out at the ocean while it rained, Cristina handing him a hot cup of coffee in nothing but her underwear and then crawling into his lap and reading him her beloved García Márquez....

He took another sip of beer, and then another, and finally drained the glass and threw a twenty-dollar bill on the bar.

"Come on," he said, and took her hand.

"Where are we going?" she asked, more than a touch of curiosity in her voice.

"Out of here."

"Oh," she breathed, grabbing her purse.

Long before they reached the front door, her legs were wrapped around his waist and his hands cupped her breasts. With the keys dangling from the lock, he nudged the door open with his shoulder, and they made it as far as the living room couch, into which he collapsed, Cristina still straddling him while she tore off her blouse. Her breasts were astonishingly pale where the Nevada sun had been blocked by a bikini top, and for a moment, she pressed her arm beneath them, pushing them up high, and tighter together. He pressed his face into her nipples and inhaled. For a moment he was disorientated, felt like he'd returned to their home with a stranger. Then went with it.

"Oh, fuck," she said huskily. "*Ohhh . . . fuck.*" She unzipped his pants.

He went very light-headed for a moment and realized he hadn't had an orgasm in several months . . . maybe half a year. She was bouncing on him now, up and down, and he was simply staring at her tits, his hands fixed on her hips, which he truly did love more than anything else in the world, the way her muscles and flesh swelled out there, so firm and unapologetically curvy.

"No," he said, flipping her onto her stomach, raising her skirt, and moving her underwear to the side.

"Jesus," she sighed. "Oh, Jesus, don't you *ever* fucking stop."

He woke up in the early morning, well before dawn, and walked into the bathroom, where he sat down on the toilet, if for no other reason than to think. He glanced out a little window at the moon, made his hand into the shape of a pistol, and fired a few rounds at the little white bull's-eye up there. His body felt like a frayed electrical wire. Yes, he felt better for the night with Cristina; yes, the sex was welcome; yes, he missed holding her in bed, her face on his chest, his fingers in her hair; and no, he didn't really want to be divorced. . . . But his muscles throbbed, his fingers so sore they were often bunched into painful fists, his head felt blurry, and somewhere out there, miles off beneath that same moon, Gretchen's house waited for them, imperious in its continued demands.

He showered, made a pot of coffee, and saw on the kitchen table the divorce papers, a little yellow Post-it note reading: *Please sign these? XOXO, C.* He looked back into their bedroom, taking her in, unsure whether a future with Gretchen was a complete daydream, the fantasy of a blue-collar roughneck trying to climb his way up an impossibly high ladder.

He signed the papers where they were marked for him, all at once feeling officially untethered and very, very desolate. After all those years, he was single again. And that was that.

The mountains made the night darker, blocked even the starlight, hid the moon and the coming dawn, and in that deep, nestled darkness Cole left his truck parked beside Bart's, trudging toward the house with his tool belt draped over one shoulder, a Thermos of coffee thumbed from the hand supporting it, and in the other, a bag of quickly cooling McDonald's.

The house was already partially lit, and as he crossed the bridge, he recognized the sound of Jimi Hendrix on guitar: the first few licks of "Hey Joe." He could see shadows in the house moving, *dancing*, and Bart's voice was there, too, singing—all of that sound echoing off the cliffs.

Inside the house Cole called out, "Bart? Bart, you here?"

He found his friend carrying lumber from the first floor to the second, big armfuls of lumber, his eyes and muscles bulging, sweat pouring off his reddened face. Clearly the guy was amped up and hearing nothing but Jimi.

"Bart!" Cole yelled.

His friend startled, losing his grip on the lumber, which then spilled out of his cradling arms and went clunking down the makeshift stairs in an avalanche of two-by-fours.

"Jesus," Bart said, "didn't even hear you. Scared the *shit* out of me."

"You okay?" Cole yelled. The music was rising to a crescendo of wild guitar and vocals; for a moment, Cole recollected an image of Hendrix lighting his Fender Strat on fire.

"Yeah," said Bart a little shakily. "I guess it's the moon or something. Just couldn't get to sleep to save my life."

But of course, it wasn't the moon. It was the vial of cocaine back in Bart's truck. Or maybe it was the shabby solitude of his squalid little apartment. Or there again, that Lonely Planet guide to Panama and the promise of never-ending sun, rarely visited crescent moon–shaped beaches, and the Atlantic Ocean showing every shade of green-in-blue. Bart had nothing else in the world but this house and the money they had been promised—one narrow way out of this mundane, haggard life of his. And he was willing to work himself down to the bone to grab that golden ring.

12

The protocol is this: Materials need to be bought; subcontractors need to be paid; and of course, the general contractor needs to be paid. So, the general writes up what is known as a *draw*, basically a bill, an invoice. The homeowner okays the draw, and the draw is then examined by a title company before the bank releases the money to that title company, which then in turn passes it to the general contractor for disbursement. In this way, there is oversight, checks and balances. Theoretically, no one is gouging anyone.

The day after Halloween, Gretchen flew back to monitor progress on the house. The roof was on, the outer shell of the house had been wrapped in Tyvek and sided, windows had been installed, the drywall was up and waiting to be taped and mudded, and in that first week of November, the electricians and plumbers would begin their work.

The house had not only taken form but was somehow nearing the early phases of completion. The work that remained was in the details: trim, painting, tiles, cabinetry, countertops, fixtures, appliances, lighting, sinks, toilets, faucets, carpeting. . . . Hundreds of moving parts to be sure, but by god, the building was sealed; a person could live there if they needed to. The space wasn't yet luxurious, but it was more or less habitable.

Cole, Bart, and Teddy met her where the road ended and walked her over the bridge and up the driveway to the house, pausing meaningfully to take in the structure.

"That was—pardon me, ma'am—a helluva roof to install," Cole said to her. "That there is high-quality standing-seam metal, the best we've ever worked with, heavier than shit, and it should last fifty—who knows?—seventy-five, maybe a hundred years. And because you've got a smart, south-facing alignment for this house, the snow just ain't gonna build up on that sumbitch either. I can't wait to see it, to be honest. This house is gonna shrug off the snow like a fuckin' afterthought."

For the first time that they could remember, they heard Gretchen laugh.

"I'm sorry, ma'am," Cole apologized. "Our language out here can . . . deteriorate. Beg your pardon."

She touched his forearm to let him know it was okay, lightly, like a butterfly landing on a flower, and he felt the pads of her fingers graze his arm hair. He peered surreptiously at her; not squarely, not directly in the eyes, but just a stealing glance as he continued talking about the roof and pointing to how the gutters would run. On this day, she looked closer to fifty, he had to admit, or fifty-five, though beautiful, of course. But there was something about her skin that struck him as . . . less vital. Maybe it was the change in seasons; they were all seeing much less of the sun now, all of them slowly growing paler. Or maybe it was just the stress of building the house. All that money spent, the extra phone calls, and the travel time between there and her home in California.

"Gentlemen, you can *relax*. Not my first time at the rodeo."

They moved closer to the house.

"So, your garage doors should arrive any day. Real dandies. That nice semi-industrial look you wanted. Quiet and dependable. There won't be another garage with a better view than yours, especially with all that glass in them doors. And the entryway-mudroom is going to be a stunner. Very utilitarian, but I think that west-facing window is going to make a statement that you're not entering any old house."

They walked through the garage and up a flight of roughed-in stairs to the first floor.

"A person could damn near use an elevator in this house," Bart joked.

"It's funny, actually," Gretchen said as they reached the first floor. "I've always thought of stairs as a form of life insurance."

Oh, but the house was beautiful. And the men could see by the look on her face that she was delighted. Even such as it was, still lacking finished flooring, paint, lighting, appliances, furniture, the space *sang*. This first floor was long and open and inviting, and those stairs that led up from the garage deposited you smack in the middle of the floor plan, presenting a breathtaking view of the land south: to the left, the hot springs; directly in front, the driveway leading to the bridge and river, and beyond that, mountains; and, finally, to the right, one of the huge cliff-faces, always shining, generously sharing its refracted light with the rest of the house.

Gretchen covered her mouth with one hand.

"Ma'am," Teddy said, "you all right? Everything okay?"

"Oh, my," she breathed. "It's just—this is what I've always wanted. Just . . . This view, right here, going on forever."

"So those windows will work for you? Them frames will be okay?" Teddy asked. "You sure had us worried a few weeks back."

"No, no, no." She laughed breezily. "The windows are magnificent. I don't know what came over me. You gentlemen were right, there isn't a bad view in the house."

They walked to the would-be kitchen area, practically hanging over the hot springs, and Bart very professionally outlined where the counters would be, where the twelve-by-four island would be stationed, the refrigerator, and so on. They'd marked spaces for everything on the floor in pink-colored masking tape.

"There's still plenty to do," Bart said, "but at this point, it's more like air-traffic control. It's managing all the subs. Making sure we get the right timing. We ain't gonna lie to you, Gretchen. It's gonna be close. But we think we can make it."

Turning toward the center of the house, they interrupted Bill, who was busy grouting stones into place around the hearth. He stood up, and before he could even clean off his hands, Gretchen had given him a short hug. The big man blushed and continued wiping his hands with a wet cloth.

The hearth was dramatic, a work of art in the making, no doubt about it, and Cole had to admit he could understand Gretchen's loyalty to this man. Bill was a true craftsman, and as they stood there, Gretchen touching a rock here or there, he described how he'd alternated the placement of different rocks, some standing upright, others lying down; how he'd created an exhibition of sorts to let the hearth display the *personalities* of the rocks.

"*Look*," he went on, "this is greenstone, from Michigan's Upper Peninsula. And this is Baraboo quartzite from north of Madison, Wisconsin. Beautiful, huh? I collect these stones from my travels. Road trips I take, here and there. Actually got a dinosaur fossil encased in some stone from Montana . . . Nothing crazy, just a prehistoric fish, but . . ."

"Bill," Bart said, "we've been working on this site for six weeks now and we ain't heard you say *shit*, and now you're gushing on and on about *prehistoric fish*?"

The mason blushed again and peered down at his boots.

"When Bill has something to say," Gretchen put in, as she slid her arm around his elbow, linking them together, "he says it."

She moved toward the living room, and the men followed, leaving Bill to return to his work. Now she stood at the center window, holding her elbows and looking south. Cole, Bart, and Teddy simply watched her expectantly. She coughed into a small fist. "So," she said at length, "are we still on schedule, gentlemen?"

Cole glanced at his partners and then nodded. "We think so, ma'am," he said. "Yes. Barring anything totally unexpected."

"Magnificent," she said. "Well, you've done incredible work, I have to say, and not just in terms of the tempo either. Very impressive. Now, why don't you show me to the third floor."

They marched up another flight of roughed-in stairs to the top floor of the house, and in the space where the master bedroom would soon be, Gretchen stood quietly, leaning against the window, her breath fogging the glass.

"Would you give me a moment?" she said.

"Uh, of course," Cole said. "We'll be just down on the driveway. Take your time."

Fifteen minutes later she met them outside the garage, her demeanor once more all-business. "Gentlemen, you've done superb work here. As I've told you before, Bill has worked on some of my other properties, and he confirms what I'm observing today. You're as good as your word. Just to say, I am more than happy to sign your draw."

"Wonderful," Cole breathed. Each draw amounted to over two million dollars, and each time he organized the invoices and tallied their own labor, the sums had simply stupefied him. He'd never been so close to such deep wealth. In fact, he found the ledger-balance of his own life completely incongruent with the work he was performing there. How was it possible, he wondered, to own no house, to have no savings, no college education, no art, nothing, really—not a single artifact to mark his nearly forty years on the planet—and yet find himself here, building this shrine in the mountains? The sheer disconnect of it sometimes left him dumbfounded and the only solace he took was that this house, in some small way, was also *his* impression, his legacy, even if his name was not etched on any surface, any stone.

Even now, he could hardly say he really *knew* Gretchen. He had no idea what her job was, whether her money was actually earned or just accumulated through the generations proceeding her, as a birthright. There were so many days when he stood up to stretch his back, and looked over the other men on the site, marveling at how each moved as if on some predetermined track: pouring concrete or running a bulldozer, driving a semitruck or carrying loads of rock up to Bill for the fireplace. . . . Of course, this was just the way of things, he had reasoned, the way it had always been, perhaps, for time immemorial. Right here, right now, these men were busy building this latter-day "enlightened" palace for someone clearly beyond wealthy, where thousands of years earlier it would have been the same story, only multiplied by many hundreds, constructing a pyramid for some man who fancied himself a god. There were those who *built* and those who did the building. Just as there were those who got on with it and those who didn't.

Still, it unnerved Cole. And after Gretchen signed the paperwork, shook their hands, and walked back to her vehicle, Cole's head throbbed with something like resentment. Yes, he loved construction; he was proud of the company he'd formed with his friends and appreciated being his own boss; yes, he liked working outside in the elements, the caress of the sun on his neck, the early-morning fog that made his morning coffee taste better, or the heat of a cigarette in the dampness after an afternoon rain squall. He knew he was probably unfit to do anything else, too, and yet . . . His vocation, he now better understood, was essentially the very same thing it had been back on those ski lifts or working as a bartender: He was in the business of providing pleasure to the top tenth of one percent of the population. It was as simple as that.

Dust rose in the air from Gretchen's vehicle as it retreated down the mountain. Cole looked again at the check in his dirty hand: $2,427,750.00. Jesus Christ.

13

The following day, the men were gathered in the garage, eating their lunches, a light rain falling outside, when they watched with curiosity as a sheriff's truck pulled across the bridge, up the driveway, and parked twenty paces away from the house.

"Now what the hell is this about?" Bart asked in a low voice.

"Beats me," Cole said. "I ain't done anything wrong. How about you, Teddy?"

"No way. Never had so much as a speeding ticket. In my life. Anyway, I don't think I've done anything wrong," Teddy said, a hint of guilt in his voice. "I mean, I hope not."

The sheriff stepped out of the truck, and a moment later, a fellow in his early thirties opened the passenger door and climbed out into the drizzle.

"Afternoon," said the sheriff.

The men stood and wiped their hands on their pants, on pieces of paper towel.

"Oh, I don't mean to bother you none. This here feller just forgot a tool and given the stipulations of that NDA your boss had him sign, he felt like it was the proper thing to have an escort up here. I don't blame him."

"Sure as hell glad to be done with this place," the man said.

"A tool?" Cole said softly.

"Any of you guys see a Milwaukee cordless drill and two batteries?" the sheriff called out.

"Yeah," Bart said. "Funny you should ask. We got it right here. Wondered who'd left such a nice tool up here."

He stood from the pile of lumber he'd been sitting on, and after retrieving a small cardboard box, he handed it to the man.

"Hey," Cole said, "maybe—if you wouldn't mind—uh, is there any possibility you could tell us what happened here? Why you fellows had to walk off the job?"

The man scoffed. "What is this, a trick? I tell you what happened, and you scabs go back and tell her and get our deals ixnayed. No dice, assholes. I appreciate you keepin' my drill safe, but I ain't spillin' no beans."

And with that, he tipped a dusty baseball hat in their direction and climbed back into the truck. Then the door opened again, and the man climbed out, leaning against the truck.

"Actually," the man said, "I'll say this much. I don't envy you sumbitches one bit. You're doing the devil's work, and you don't even know it."

And with that, he slammed the door.

"Gentlemen," the sheriff said, turning his back to them and walking to his truck.

"Wait a minute," Cole said. "That fella might've signed an NDA, but you haven't. Clue us in, Sheriff. Don't you think we got a right to know?"

The officer stopped, turned on his heels, and looked back at the house for a long time before addressing Cole. "You fellers really don't know, do ya?"

They shook their heads in the negative.

"A worker died here," the sheriff began. "They was working round-the-clock, and a feller was up on them top I-beams after dark and toppled off." The lawman made a motion with his hand, like a bird falling out of the sky, and then hitting ground. "Broke his back in multiple places. He was more or less dead on impact; skull fracture, massive bleeding. I came out the following day to talk to witnesses, but it didn't much matter. No one was directly responsible. We ruled it an accident. A stupid, preventable accident. Wasn't like anyone could press charges, so there's nothing on the record. I guess your boss talked to the man's family and paid off the rest of the crew for their silence."

"Where'd he fall?" Teddy asked.

"Over yonder," the sheriff said, pointing near the hot springs.

"Sonuvabitch," Bart said. "Son of a bitch."

"You boys be careful," the sheriff warned. "That man died because he was being *worked*. The word around the campfire was that he hadn't slept in three days. Now, good day to you."

They watched the sheriff's truck reverse, and then pull back down the road.

"You gonna call her?" Bart asked Cole. "Or should I?"

"Oh, I'll call her," Cole said. "I say we call her right now."

They piled into Cole's truck—all three of them—and rode out to the highway, where the cell reception was good enough for Cole's phone to find a signal. He dialed Gretchen's number and then turned the phone's speaker on for all to listen.

"Cole," she said warmly enough, "what news from Wyoming?"

He laughed darkly and looked at his friends. "What news, Gretchen? Well, a little bird just told us what went down at your house before we were hired on. You got any comment on that? Any comment on working a man until he fucking died?"

There was a brief pause, and the men looked at one another and out the rain-slicked windshield as a logging truck rushed by on the highway.

"That man," Gretchen said, "was notoriously noncompliant with standard safety protocol. He didn't care to, for example, wear a helmet. And the day he died, he was not strapped into a harness, which would have certainly saved his life. He was also known to begin drinking at five in the evening whether he was done working or not. He fell about twenty feet away from his last can of Steel Reserve. . . . Not that it really matters, but I also examined his criminal records, where I discovered that he had been arrested for three incidents of drunken driving and two instances of not paying child support. Those details are not necessarily germane to the question you are asking, but they illustrate that this man was no saint. . . . So, Mr. McCourt, would you like to rephrase your question?"

The men stared at one another, the cab of the truck filled with a strange combination of dread, remorse, and anger.

"Well, a little honesty would have been appreciated," Cole said. "We don't care for being called scabs, ma'am, and it does make a little more sense now, why that crew walked off the job such as they did. One of their guys died, and from what we heard, he'd been working for days on end."

"Am I on speakerphone?" Gretchen asked coolly.

"You are," Cole said. "It's me, Bart, and Teddy."

"Good. Gentlemen, you've been offered an opportunity. An opportunity to change your own lives and the fortunes of your families. Don't find excuses to fail. Just do your jobs. Do your jobs, and the cosmos will smile upon you. I promise."

The men knew not what to do with this advice; it was not what they had expected her to say.

"Now then, if you'll excuse me, I have another call," she said. "Good day."

They heard her hang up and then stared at one another, each offering deep exhales.

"What about that mug who died?" Bart asked. "The cosmos sure as shit didn't smile on him."

14

After a series of voicemails and texts, Bart's new dealer, Jerry, had sent him an address for a party he was working; an address Bart didn't recognize. That was no real surprise. So many new houses were being built these days, so many new developments plotted along the valleys, the GPS programming couldn't possibly keep up, let alone the battered gazetteer in the backseat of Bart's truck. So he drove through the night, his left elbow resting on the door, a cigarette burning between his fingers. On a hunch he headed toward the golf course south of town.

There wasn't much keeping him at his apartment, and now that Margo seemed more or less out of the picture, the place felt lonelier than ever. Flush with cash, tired as shit, and sort of itching for a fight, Bart had put on his best cowboy boots, some tight Wranglers, and a black button-down shirt, with the bad intention of getting straight-up *lit*. He was looking to score, looking to fuck, or looking to knock someone's teeth out—and any old combination of those options would do just fine.

Slamming the door of his truck, Bart felt the adrenaline surge along with his testosterone. There was something powerful about walking into a party uninvited and doing so with the knowledge that your day-to-day job prepared you in a way to win just about any physical confrontation. He rolled up his sleeves, the veins of his arms like pythons pulsing beneath his sunburned and tattooed skin.

The notion of building a house on a golf course represented everything Bart loathed about the construction business. Golf, in and of itself, did not bother Bart; fact of the matter was, he never really thought about golf. Thought about golf as much as he considered the politics of mainland China, say, or the rainfall in Belize. There was nothing necessarily *objectionable* about spending a Saturday morning outside, after all, with a cooler full of beer, maybe, taking your workaday frustrations out on a tiny Titleist ball; motoring around in a cart and talking to your buddies. But when you factored in the breathable collared shirts, the fancy spiked shoes, the *performance* visor hats, and the aerodynamic beta titanium alloy drivers, golf quickly became rather easy to hate. To say nothing of its worship of *grass*. That perfectly preened, chemically laden carpeting of fescue. And to build a multimillion-dollar house on a private golf club betrayed so much about the homeowners—gauche, look-at-me-and-my-money types needing to be in close proximity to other awkwardly loud rich people, all of them staring at one another from infrequently used outdoor furniture, or through the dusty lens of a decorative telescope never once aimed at the sky.

Walking into the house, Bart felt even stronger, because *this* wasn't the house they were building, and Gretchen sure *wasn't* this kind of homeowner. She was a classy broad, and he meant that with profound respect. Never would she be caught dead building a home on the sixteenth hole just to make stupid small talk with people she didn't even like, or to be seen grilling chicken breasts while sipping a glass of prosecco. She'd chosen to build her house alone, in the mountains, with a view of heaven, in a place where no one would ever find her. She might be some kind of plutocrat, sure, but Bart respected the hell out of this lady for her sense of aesthetics at least. And maybe even her priorities.

As for this monstrosity . . . probably over seven thousand square feet, he guessed, with catalog furniture that could not help but be thoroughly intimidated by all that vacuous space, the art offloaded by some insurance company trying to update their office space with "fresh" wall hangings. Bart was no art major, but he knew when someone had taste or not. Gretchen had taste. Whoever owned this place had money, yes, but not enough to own the house outright, he guessed, much less properly furnish or decorate it.

He passed through the entryway, where a hideous copper sculpture of a horse greeted him, then through the crowded kitchen and living room until finally he stepped out onto a back porch. A bartender stood vigil behind an outdoor bar, and Bart ordered a double Maker's Mark neat, then, wielding a two-dollar tip in his right hand, asked the barkeep if he knew Jerry Swanson. Tweezing the tip from between Bart's fingers, the bartender nodded in the direction of an outdoor propane fireplace. That always irked Bart: If you want to have a campfire, burn wood, not gas, for Christ's sake.

Jerry was in his mid-fifties, with a big gut and a penchant for gold necklaces, pinky rings, and exotic pets. A relic of the eighties, he seemed to have honed his fashion choices on popular Michael Douglas movies of that era, maintaining a meticulously trimmed stubble-beard and a single diamond-stud earring. His hair had long ago receded, but, as if in protest, Jerry had grown what remained into a rather desperate ponytail that he kept either wet or so laden with product that it appeared so. Jerry's jeans, miraculously, were always stone-washed and held tight with a braided belt, his feet jammed into loafers, except during winter, when he preferred oversize UGGs.

"I take it this is someone else's place?" Bart asked.

"Sure as hell ain't mine," Jerry replied, "but I'm thinking of tonight as sort of a pop-up shop. Isn't that what you kids call it? Spontaneous retail."

"What?"

"Anyway," Jerry growled around a fat Rocky Patel cigar, "take a load off. I hear you boys have been working around the clock." He smiled mischievously. "Tell me all about it."

The house may have been gauche, but in the darkness, Bart could see neither the golf course nor the neighbors' houses. There was just the easy champagne laughter of women, the jocular arguments of a few drunken men, and the rustling of the aspen leaves above. It might have been worse. A light mist had begun to descend, but Bart hardly noticed it; the fire was hot against his kneecaps and his face, and the whisky felt wonderful in his chest. The chair he was sitting on might have been cheaper than its rather grand aspirations, but somehow it was far more comfortable than any stick of furniture *he* happened to own, and reclined there, telling Jerry about Gretchen's house, he felt entirely apart from the party, and for the first time in several weeks, relaxed.

"And the thing is, Jerry," Bart said, "we get it finished before Christmas, there's a huge bonus in it for us. Huge. I mean, real money."

Jerry leaned toward the fire that separated them. "*Christmas*," he spat. "Brother, you couldn't finish that house before Christmas if you were smoking all the meth in the world. That's craziness. The heavy snow could start flying any day now. Hell, you're lucky it hasn't *already*. Then what? You gonna live out there? And even if you do, what about the finish work? How you gonna get your subs up there? You gonna pay to keep miles of road and driveway open? The fuck's wrong with you?"

"*You're* wrong, Jerr," Bart said confidently. "We are fucking *cranking* on this project. Morale's high, the subs are really coming through for us, and we've just been working our tails off, man." Having reassured himself, Bart eased back in his chair and took a final rip of his whisky. The mist had developed into something closer to a light rain, each drop of precipitation hissing in the flames.

Across the fire, Jerry looked like an aged cherub, his face glossy with the mist and shining bronze and gold in the light of the fire. Over in the Jacuzzi, women were laughing loudly now as the rain began to intensify; he even thought he heard sex-type sounds, rhythmic thrashing and moaning. Glancing over his shoulder, Bart saw what appeared to be an ad-hoc orgy as some others among the party were already beginning to depart with the rain.

"Well, Bart," Jerry said as he stood from the chair, "let's go chat in my office, how 'bout?"

Following him past the Jacuzzi, Bart snagged a bottle of whisky as he drifted by the bar and then trailed Jerry through the house, its tiled floor a mess of dirty footprints. The kitchen island was piled with dirty plates, empty bottles, and discarded napkins. A middle-aged Mexican woman stood at the sink filling a dishwasher. Bart waved at her on his way out the front door.

She gave him a dour little nod as she reached for the next plate.

Out in Jerry's new yellow Dodge Charger, the rain drumming against the roof and running down the windshield, they got down to business.

"So, you lookin' for something along the lines of recreation," Jerry asked, "or maybe a little more practical?"

"I love coke," Bart said, "but I can't afford the comedown. And I fucking hate the idea of meth, but . . ."

"It's a rocket ship," Jerry finished. "Nothin' better if you find yourself needin' to build a cathedral in all of a month."

Bart had been down this road before, and he knew what it meant. He loved meth, loved being strapped to that chemical missile and whizzing through the days. He was lucky, he supposed, because in the past, he'd managed to stop every time. Something had always scared him off at a critical point—the way a kid on the street would stare at the skin of his face; or a hallucination wild enough to make him quit, make him crawl into a hole and let the meth trickle its evil way out of his system.

But right then, he knew no other answer. He saw the weeks stretching out ahead of him, endless and yet totally insufficient, and as weary as he was now . . . Gretchen had talked about climbing stairs, about how she thought of that as an insurance policy. Well, maybe a little meth now and again would be *his* insurance of sorts. He knew, even in the abstract, how ridiculous that sounded, but . . . it was energy, wasn't it? *However* you got there. And he knew there'd be mornings ahead when he'd *need* that energy, need it to fly through the backbreaking days and bleary nights. There was just so much work ahead of them. All the flooring, all the trim, all the painting, all the cabinets, all the lighting, the exterior porches, the doors, the closet systems . . . And not just all that work, but the added pressure of getting it done *perfectly*. This lady had standards. She wasn't your average homeowner, who would tolerate a poorly hung door or window trim that wasn't perfectly snug. Everything had to be just so. Perfectly so.

"I need an ounce," Bart said, exhaling, his wallet well-bulging in his back pocket, flush from the draw money.

"The fuck, man? You gonna start dealing?" Jerry asked, startled. "Put me out of business! What d'you need an ounce for?"

"This house," Bart explained, "it's tucked way back into the mountains. If we get stuck back up in there, I ain't gonna find any reinforcements, man. May as well have a little inventory, you know?"

Jerry reached into the backseat for a gym bag.

"I don't just keep an ounce on me, man," Jerry said. "The ski bunnies and frat bros are more into Molly or coke or weed . . . but I can hook you up with maybe four, five grams for now. . . . Call me back in a week or two and we can get you the rest."

"Works for me," Bart said, handing Jerry the cash.

They exchanged: a fat wad of dampened twenties for five little plastic baggies of beautiful translucent crystals.

"Appreciate it, Jerry."

"I'll send you a text in a week when I get the rest of your shit."

Bart opened the passenger-side door. The rain was falling hard and cold now, and he couldn't help feeling he tasted a hint of winter in the wind.

"Hey, Bart," Jerry said, rolling down his window a crack. "Watch yourself, hombre." And then the dealer drove off into the night.

15

No one could remember such rain. Down it came, for days on end. Late in the evenings the rain became snow, and on the fifth morning, with just a light drizzle coming down, Cole exited the highway onto Gretchen's road and stared with dismay at the once rather tame river, now raging up and over its banks. It was almost unrecognizable. And the road had been ravaged. Because it had been built in haste, and because the summer had been remarkably dry and mild, the roadbuilders did not think to install many culverts, and now, where water coursed down off the mountains and foothills and swept over the road, some stretches were nearly impassable. Cole thumped along the road at a cautious crawl, the coffee in his travel mug sloshing everywhere.

The bridge itself was destroyed, he now saw, lying in the river beneath a giant boulder, which must have somehow come down off the mountain in the night, miraculously missing the house at least, and the hot springs. Now it sat there, in the middle of the river, hulking there on the broken bridge like a drunken ogre, water angrily frothing all around it, the banks on either side of the river thoroughly chewed apart.

"Fuck," Cole yelled. "Fuck, fuck, *fuck!*"

Cell phone reception in the canyon was hit-or-miss, so he backed the truck down the road to the first spot where he could actually turn around, then floored it almost all the way back out to the highway, where he finally dialed Gretchen. The call went straight to voicemail, and Cole left a message, doing his best to sound both at once professional and sufficiently urgent.

None of the subs had come to work the day before due to the road conditions, and now they were looking at a delay that could stretch on for days, certainly, and maybe weeks. . . . Indeed, it was entirely possible the project would now have to be shelved until the following spring or summer. Removing the broken bridge would take a day or two at the very least, to say nothing of constructing a new one. He didn't know the first thing about how bridges were put into place and could not imagine the profound amount of forethought and engineering involved before you even *began* site excavation. To say nothing of the fabrication of a goddamned steel bridge! Cole felt his heart thumping inside his ribs, felt sweat beading on his forehead and trickling down his back.

Teddy's truck pulled up beside Cole's, and they both rolled down their windows.

"You're not even gonna believe it," Cole said, motioning up the road. "But we are royally *fucked.*"

Teddy rubbed at his face and absentmindedly tugged at an ear. "Tell me the bridge's still there," he said quietly.

"The bridge is *fucked*, is what it is," Cole said, slamming his hands against his steering wheel. "*Fucked!*"

"So . . . Crap . . . What are we gonna do, Cole?"

Cole shook his head, then threw up his hands in defeat. "I have no idea, Teddy. Never needed to build a bridge before."

They sat there in their idling trucks, the mist slowly alleviating, and finally, for what felt like the first time in weeks, the sun began to burn a hole through the cloud cover, some of the higher peaks now shining white with freshly fallen snow.

Cole rubbed at this jawline, trying to piece together their strategy.

"All right," he said, "you text the subs. Tell 'em we're gonna have a few days' delay. Blame it on the road—they'll swallow that easily enough. But don't feed 'em too much information. If you tell 'em about the bridge, they might just move on to the next project, figuring we'll never get this thing untangled. Right now, I need to get a hold of Gretchen." He took a long gulp of coffee. "You seen Bart?"

"Not yet," Teddy said. "Reckon he's on his way."

"Why don't you text him and tell him to save his gas. Explain about the bridge. We're all going to be a lot more valuable today in town, sad to say."

"You want to make phone calls from my place this morning? I'm sure Britney would make us breakfast. We got plenty of juice and some doughnuts from the grocery store. . . ."

It was several hours before Gretchen called back; she'd been in a meeting. Her voice sounded slightly different over the telephone—more tired, perhaps—but she was as professional as could be; she wanted photographs of the bridge for her insurance people and assured Cole that help was on its way and coming as quickly as possible.

It was left to Cole to address the elephant in the room, the notion that they'd lost time due to an act of God.

"I hear you," she said evenly. "And yet the deadline, I'm afraid, remains the same. It may be that you cannot finish the house before Christmas and, well, that is something I will simply have to accept.

But that is still our goal. So, all I can tell you is: Find a way, all right? Find a way. And know that I'll do everything on my end that I possibly can to help you in doing that."

Two days later they stood at the end of the road, watching an excavator reach its steel teeth into the river and remove the boulder and what was left of the bridge, setting them off to the side.

"Save that boulder," Cole ordered. "Christ, has to be the most expensive rock in the world. Maybe Gretchen will have some use for it."

The road crew was back now, constructing new culverts in the washed-out areas and regrading the surface with fresh gravel. There was talk of paving certain stretches of the road, not least on either side of the new bridge, if and when it arrived.

And so they waited, checking their phones every other minute for a message from Gretchen, checking the calendar and the time, even as December 25 inched closer and closer with nothing for them to do but wait—wait for the insurance adjustor to visit the site and okay a new bridge; wait for the bridge-building company to show up and build it; and hope against hope that when all those factors aligned, everyone would be ready to snap back into action.

It took Bart a few hours to gather his things: an aluminum cot, a sleeping bag, his toiletries, food, his tools, spare clothing, extra blankets. From his underwear drawer he found and packed the meth and his old glass pipe, both of which he wrapped in clothing and packed in the center of a big backpack. It felt like he was essentially moving out of the apartment for good. He thought about that for a moment. What difference did it make? His lease was month-to-month, and he had no nostalgia for the apartment—none. On a whim, he gave notice to his landlord, dragged all his furniture to the curb, and on a piece of cardboard scrawled, *FREE*, leaving this placard on the couch, mist already beading on the tired old Naugahyde and velour.

He filled the bed of his truck with these supplies, along with a collapsible thirty-five-foot extension ladder he had very specific plans for, and not simply for changing a lightbulb or accessing the roof. Before driving off, he texted Cole that he was en route to the jobsite. Cole texted back a moment later,

Not sure why, but good luck . . .

Bart finally managed to reach the end of Gretchen's road. The remains of the broken bridge sat on the turnaround side of the river, and beside that wreckage, the boulder. The river was running roughshod, and looking out over it all, Bart knew their chances of meeting the Christmas deadline were pretty well shot. He wondered if they'd even be able to complete the house now before next summer. Still, they had to at least *try*. Sitting around, he felt, was no option at all. They would certainly run out of time if that was their only tack. And he had a plan.

Kneeling beside the river, he ran his hands through the turbid, icy water. The house was a scant hundred and fifty yards away; looking through the rubble of the bridge he could see it plainly. And the river wasn't *that* wide. Maybe here, at this transect, his little plan wouldn't work; the banks were disintegrating with every passing minute, and the channel was fairly wide. And farther downstream, the mountain rose too precipitously on the construction side of the river. But upriver, there might just be a place friendly enough for a crossing. A narrow distance between rock-solid banks to jury-rig a solution . . . And wouldn't Cole shit a brick if somehow, Bart could find a way? If he could get over there and make himself useful somehow, maybe cutting and painting trim, or laying some of the flooring while they waited for the cavalry to arrive?

He walked north, up the river, picking his way among huge boulders and occasionally sliding down the steeply pitched slope and then scrambling back up. A quarter mile upriver the channel narrowed tightly between two near-vertical rock faces rising some thirty feet up from the water it so rigidly constrained. The river here was no more than twenty or twenty-two feet wide. Bart grinned and walked back to the truck.

The extension ladder weighed just forty-five pounds, but it was unwieldly enough to feel like he was carrying a baby giraffe through the thickly clumped pine trees and alder. It was hard to know how to move its long bulk most efficiently; Bart alternated between a side carry and humping it along awkwardly on his back. Soon enough his face was cut in multiple places from sharply broken tree branches, his arms marred by scratches and gouges. Sweating profusely, he reached the river's bottleneck and simply dropped the ladder on the ground.

The mist had stopped, and the sun shone weakly. Bart sat on a thick bedding of moss and regarded the river below and the mountain-sides above. Then, from upriver, he heard a noise.

He didn't immediately identify the sound as a bear, but when the creature came closer, there wasn't any doubt. It was a mature black bear, a boar, weighing upwards of five hundred pounds. Bart couldn't be sure that the bear had either smelled or seen him, so he stood on a nearby fallen tree and shouted, "Hey, bear! Yo! Hey, bear!"

The beast stopped, lifted its head into the air, and then, as if to match Bart, rose up on its hind legs.

He knew there was no outrunning the bear. And as exhausted as he was, there really weren't many other options. So he simply stood his ground, shouting at the animal. He had no idea whether this was help-ing the situation or worsening it. Once, the bear charged toward him, leveling a small aspen, but he yelled again and again and clapped his hands and even shook a nearby tree before tossing a few small rocks in the bear's direction. Eventually the animal wandered off, leaving Bart to collapse with relief into the cool, thick moss.

It was a strange thing, but just then, Bart thought of Panama, of the guidebook he'd bought years earlier with its brightly colored pictures: a wildly graffitied bus in Panama City, toucans in the branches of a banana tree, a coffee plantation high in the mountains. He had no wife, no children that he knew of; his parents were serenely retired and pre-ferred to see him but once a year, his sister somewhat ashamed of him and his very evident lack of education or ambition. The only thing that drew him through his days now was the notion of finishing this house, of seeing the pleasure on Gretchen's face and handing her the keys. And then he'd promised himself two things: The first was that he would take a long dip in those hot springs, a wish he was positive Gretchen would grant him—hell, maybe she would even join him—and the second was to buy himself a first-class ticket to Panama City. He was thirty-nine years old and he had never flown in an airplane, and this he desperately wanted to do. And he did not care to sit in the back of the plane with the rest of the cattle, no. Bart wanted his first flight to be like the movies from his childhood: wide seats, warm and generous flight attendants, and enough room to recline and stretch his long legs.

Suddenly, in a strange burst of practical lucidity, he realized he did not have a passport. *But there is time to deal with that, right?* Because he'd just managed to avoid being mauled by a bear. He allowed himself to lie in the moss, watching clouds drift through the heavens. He realized his body was throbbing with adrenaline, and what he really wanted, what he needed, was a cigarette and a moment to catch his breath, to chill the fuck out. He studied the clouds for several moments, focusing on his breathing, laying a hand over his heart. He picked out a single cloud that looked like an anvil and thought, *Please don't fall on me.*

Spanning the river with the ladder was more of a production than Bart had imagined. His nerves were fried, and the effort of carrying the ladder upriver had left him exhausted and likely dehydrated. Still, with great concentration, and all his muscles trembling, he managed to expand the ladder up, and up, to its full thirty-five feet, using a nearby lodgepole pine as a kind of brace for balance. Then, moving ever so slowly, he walked the ladder over to the high bank and, as carefully as possible, guided the ladder's descent all the way to the far side of the river. This was a loud and inelegant operation, but the ladder landed successfully in its place, and Bart allowed himself a moment of celebration, even as he reckoned that hours had by then scudded by. Retreating back to the truck, he took several long swigs off a canteen of cold water and bit into a granola bar before lighting a richly deserved cigarette. He stared across the river at the house, where it peered patiently back down at him. He loaded a backpack with clothes, food, a few tools, the pipe, and the meth, and locked up the truck.

Then he worked his way back upriver. At the ladder, he sunk to his knees and began to slowly ease his full weight onto the ladder, which shuddered unevenly below him. The moment he was fully suspended out and above the river, his hands tightly clenching the rails of the ladder, every muscle in his body desperately flexing, he realized what a goddamn foolish thing this was to do. A surefire way to die, to spill off the jostling aluminum ladder, falling dozens of feet down onto the sharp awaiting rocks, his limp corpse swept downstream, possibly to feed the very same bear who had just antagonized him. A genius plan, really.

He inched backward, but that was no good either; if anything, that felt more uncertain than simply plodding forward. So he pressed on, lowering closer to the ladder and essentially dragging his cowering body to the far bank.

When he finally shimmied onto solid ground, he was both exhilarated and jangly, shivering with disbelieving relief. He walked slowly to the trailer and, opening the refrigerator, quickly polished off a cold Coors, which, in that moment, tasted like the best bottle of beer in the world. He then drank a second beer, before exhaling deeply and giving himself the goal of measuring and cutting out trim; but in a thirty-eight-hundred-square-foot house, there would be damn near a country mile's worth of trim. Maybe a couple of miles' worth of decorative wood to accent the floor and ceilings, each piece to be cut precisely to adjoin its neighbor, no seams or rough edges. It was a putzy job, one that a more established builder would give to some lackey on the crew. But Bart was beginning to wonder how many subcontractors they could even count on for the homestretch of this project. There was something about the place that seemed to exude bad luck. First, the death of that previous worker. Now the bridge. And looming over all of it, Gretchen's ludicrous deadline.

Inside the house, Bart sat on the hearth and sifted through his bag, collecting his pipe, the bag of meth, and a lighter. He needed to know that he could handle this, and the empty house, well, it provided the perfect trial run.

He flicked the lighter and was about to touch flame to pipe when he considered the building—the home—he was sitting in. He looked out the wide, thick windows to the countryside below. Looked down at those streamers of steam billowing up from the spring. Felt the stones beneath him. This house stood for something more than what he was about to get back into, so much more, that he couldn't abide himself smoking inside. Couldn't taint it. And so he left the house, walked down the path to the river, and stood on the bank, looking out over the wrecked bridge. That was more like it. The lighter sparked and caught, and he held the flame beneath the glass bowl of the pipe.

He inhaled—

To a **RRRRRUUUUUSSSSSSHHHHHHHHHHH!** There it was—the rush! Like, like, like fucking grabbing the tail of a **COMET**, like traveling at *light speed* even as he stood s . . . t . . . i . . . l . . . l, like diving from the tallest mountain and discovering that you're a platinum fucking *falcon* falling from the highest reaches of heaven. Oh, *fuck*, the ecstatic **RUSH**.

He pressed his hands to his face and felt his cheeks compressed by the gravity of the drug, the speed of the drug; *he was flying*. Oh, his face, he felt his skin, felt *every* **ONE** of his pores . . . felt every **ONE** of his whiskers, felt his hair, felt his teeth, touched his skin. *Ohhhhh* . . . Now his fingers explored the wood grain of an old, washed-up log and yes, yes, yes, that was something smooth, yes, smooth, though not as smooth as it would be in five years, or ten years, or twenty years, after the rain and wind had buffed it down, yes, rounded its corners, yes, sanded it smoother still, and . . . still . . . and still. . . .

The river beside him! Look at the **light** on the river, the light, all that light, the last light of the day, and the stones beneath that cold water—they would be smooth and cold, and the water would be cold. . . . He fell to his knees and then to his stomach and stretched his arms down and thrashed in the water. Oh, that felt good, that felt *real good*, that felt like living inside a damn beer commercial. Yes, the total nirvana of those beer commercials of yore. Mountain streams and golden meadows, trout leaping into wicker creels and canoes plunging into V-shaped rapids . . .

He laughed and laughed and laughed, and then he felt something, felt eyes upon him, a look, someone looking at him, watching him. Was it the bear? The bear he'd seen earlier? Could that be? No, no, no. That wasn't it. He stood and fidgeted there beside the remains of the bridge, clutched that log and held on to it as if at the bow of some speeding boat crashing through an endless ocean of breaking waves at a speed surely meant to tear the boat to smithereens.

Grab a hold of yourself now, he thought, gritting his teeth. *No one here but us, but me, but the house over there. All alone now. Harness it now, Bart—harness it. And get down to work.*

As he walked back up toward the house, there was no exhaustion in his body any longer. Only fuel and fire, electricity that felt like it was sizzling his very synapses. *SSSizzzzzzle*. **YESSS! All right now.**

16

The house was bleeding her, and there was no tourniquet to quell the loss. In truth, it wasn't even the house, the structure, that was the source of the hemorrhage. At the moment, it was the seven miles of partially ruined road and the mangled bridge that would end up costing her hundreds of thousands of additional dollars, if not millions. In building a house, there were costs that eventually provided pleasure, like a beautiful fireplace or a luxurious bathtub. But there were also costs that provided no gratification, really, none at all. And this road was one of those costs that only provided her pain. She sat behind her desk, listening to the joints of the high-rise around her sigh and murmur.

In the hallway beyond her closed door she heard two partners talking about a forthcoming fishing trip to the Caribbean. The men in the firm seemed to have so much more time for such kibitzing, these jovial moments of hallway bullshitting, while the more senior women in the firm stayed behind closed office doors, rarely engaging in gossip or camaraderie, rarely displaying any personality, in fact, any individual-ity, save perhaps in the judicious flourishes of their appropriately sub-dued fashion: a pair of red Jimmy Choo pumps or a thousand-dollar scarf from a weekend jaunt to Paris.

In a rare moment of real irritation, she slammed her hands against her desk and swiped the telephone base onto the floor. She heard the hallway conversation stop, then the dim sound of footsteps moving in opposite directions.

She'd sell the other houses. She should have done so before, any-way. But there was the sense that liquidating them all at once or in succession might smack of some kind of signal. It was a fact: The wealthiest of the world's population notice that kind of thing; they just did. *So-and-so is off-loading that wonderful Schiele—but why? Why would they do that? And at auction! Does this mean a divorce? Or maybe that son of theirs is in legal trouble yet again....*

Gretchen had always prided herself on maintaining a private life, a life of secrecy. She rarely consorted with the other partners and had never invited anyone from work to her home. She knew what they'd say, how they'd appraise the stillness, the cleanliness, and the order of her space. Rather than seeing her interior life as a testament to her commitment to the firm, they would simply come to look at her with sadness, even pity. A beautiful woman "wasted"—no husband, no children; no warm, brightly decorated suburban house. There really was no way to win. The firm asked only this: Eat what you kill—and kill everything you possibly can. So she had. She'd brought back tens upon tens of millions of dollars to the firm's coffers. Her billables were obscene. And wasn't that enough for everyone?

Standing abruptly from her chair, she stepped around the desk and righted the telephone, then glanced outside the window. Selling the properties so abruptly would certainly cost her. But if the houses were to sell quickly, she'd be flush by January. And, as she reminded herself, she was only doing what would have had to happen anyway. This was just speeding things up a bit. A kick in the pants, really.

She returned to her desk and exhaled slowly three times, then picked up the phone and dialed a Salt Lake City area code. She heard the phone ring four times and then the sound of wind riding over flat terrain and whiskers rubbing against some distant iPhone.

"Well, now," came a deep, gravelly voice, all familiarity and self-assurance. "What a pleasure. My favorite woman-attorney in the world. How can I help you, Gretchen? You ready to run away with me yet? 'Cause I can charter my plane to get you. We could go off to Tahiti, rub suntan lo—"

"Look, Wally, I really don't have time for niceties, I'm afraid. Right now, I just need your help."

"Well, darlin', now you caught me on the third green here, and I'm looking down the barrel of about a twenty-foot putt, so—"

"I need a bridge."

She heard the man laugh, heard him readjust the phone in his huge, swollen hands.

"Okay," he said. "I reckon this ain't foreplay, now, is it, Gretchen? Tell me more."

"I need a bridge built. And now, Wally."

"Darlin', I don't hear from you in four years and now you call me up outta the blue to ask for a bridge?" He laughed. "You got some kind of—"

"Remember those projects of yours in Uzbekistan? The money you made there? How I helped you, ahh"—she paused—"*compartmentalize* those assets, so your wife would never know? And what was our favorite word for those kickbacks you were getting at the time—I can't quite remember. . . ."

"*Enticements*," Wally finished.

She heard him cough and spit. "Right," she continued, "enticements. What a sexy way to say *bribe*."

"So, you want a bridge?" he said. "Where?"

"I'm texting you the location right now," she said, typing on her phone.

There was a pause in their conversation and then a *ding* as her message found its way into his hands.

"Hold on," he said. "I gotta put on my cheaters."

She spun her office chair around to consider the view. The day was leaden, and below her, the city went about its business, brake lights glowing red, and far off, a crane swinging smoothly through the sky. Now she stared out the window, looking for her hawk, its nest. She could not see it, and the day was clear. The nest was gone. She stood from her chair and moved closer to the window, disbelieving the nest's absence.

"Middle of nowhere," Wally grumbled. "The hell you need a bridge *there* for? Better off gettin' yourself a mule."

"How soon can you help me?" she purred.

She heard him sigh, imagined his big lungs and swollen gut expanding as he wiped his brow and inhaled again, considering the golf course in front of him, the secrets buried in certain bank accounts in the Caymans and Switzerland, the nights in a Tashkent hotel when he'd been blackmailed, two prostitutes tying him to a bed while they rode him—one on his delighted face, and the other on his pharmaceutically assisted penis—occasionally breaking to snap photos of their shenanigans on their cell phones. *Too bad*, he'd later tell his old college frat brothers. *It was the best night of my life. Felt like a king.*

"How wide is that river?" he asked.

"About forty, fifty feet."

"Shit," he growled. "All right. Let me make a few calls."

"Thank you," she exhaled.

"But, Gretch," he said, "understand—we're even now, ain't we?"

"Yes," she admitted. "After this, we're even. Only, Wally? How long, Wally?"

"I'll have to send a few guys out there," he said. "They'll look over the site, do a quick survey. Then we'll fabricate your bridge as quick as we can. But, Gretch, it's gonna be a miracle if this can get done before Thanksgiving. And that's me pulling every string I can 'cause you *know* I'm in love with you." *Not to mention under your damn thumb,* he thought.

"I'll give you ten days," she countered, hunching forward on her desk.

"Not possible," he said.

"November twentieth. I can't give you a day more, Wally."

"I'll do what I can," he sighed.

"Thank you, Wally," she said sincerely.

"You drive a hard bargain, woman," he said, and she could almost hear his big, wide smile. "Good thing I'm so attracted to smart broads like you. Fact of the matter is, I actually feel my pecker getting—"

"Keep me in the loop," she said quickly, and then hung up. She exhaled deeply and stared across the expanse between her building and where the nest once was, against that residential tower perhaps two blocks away. She stood, donned a jacket, rode the elevator down to street level, and walked briskly to the tower in question.

Inside the lobby, she asked a man in a pair of one-piece navy-blue overalls if he knew anything about a hawk's nest on one of the upper floors of the building.

"Oh that." He laughed. "Yeah, we pulled that down this morning. Started to be a nuisance. Bird shit everywhere."

"You did what?" she asked.

"Well, I didn't do anything, lady," the man explained. "It was the window-cleaning crew. They pulled it apart, put everything in a garbage bag. I mean, it wasn't like there were any eggs in there, if that makes you feel better. We're not monsters."

She left the building, pulling her jacket tightly shut, a strong wind swirling her hair.

17

The ladder became a makeshift bridge, the men doing what they could to solidify it, improve it. They brought two more extension ladders and set these beside the original. They laid sheets of cut plywood over the ladders and on either side of the riverbank erected two sets of poles with rope running from one side of the river to the other, like handrails. Of all the subcontractors, only Bill and José would brave the jury-rigged bridge; everyone else was beginning to peel away from the project, providing Cole with whatever lame excuses they could conjure up. And every day, the sun gave off less light; every day, the mountains seemed to loom larger; and the temperatures were beginning to fall.

Their work became so much harder then. It was an education, a reminder of how things had once been built. Without their trucks, they had to carry everything. Up the river, across the river, and then down the river, then finally up to the house. The going was slow. They'd made a path to their ladder-bridge, using machetes to cut back the thick stands of willow and dogwood, but the way was still rocky and uneven. One morning, when the ground was slick with a thin layer of snow, Bart slipped and crumpled to the ground. A share of the flooring he'd been carrying fell on his back, and he lay there, groaning, his breath rising in the wet morning air.

Teddy set down his end of the load and went to his friend. "You okay, buddy?"

Teddy noticed that Bart seemed both more energized of late, and more fragile. He'd lost weight. Then again, they all had. It was a joke between the three of them. Measuring their waistlines. Teddy had even gotten a picture of Cole and Bart on his phone: holding their shirts up to show yellow tape measures circled above their pale bony hips. Bart claimed to have dropped from a thirty-eight-inch waist to a thirty-two. Cole from a thirty-six to a thirty. Teddy was embarrassed to admit that his jeans were so loose that he'd had his mom mail some of his old high school clothes to him.

Bart pushed himself off the ground and stood there, the knees of his pants muddy, his hands bloodied.

"Let's keep going," he said.

"Bart?" Teddy said quietly. "Are you sure you're okay?"

"Yeah, buddy," Bart said, bending down to restack the boards. "Fit as a fiddle."

"You look . . ."

Bart held his end of the stack of boards near his waist and stared at Teddy, hard. "Yeah?" he growled.

Bart's face had grown gaunter since earlier in the summer, his skin less sun-browned, but it was his eyes that bothered Teddy. There was something numb about his eyes, something faraway that Teddy couldn't quite place . . . a darkness, a vacancy . . . like one of those abandoned houses or trailers you see off the highway, half-camouflaged in overgrown brush, the front door kicked in and hanging off its hinges, all the windows broken by vandal stone-throwers and the ragged curtains blowing in the breeze. . . .

"Nothing," Teddy said. Then, affecting that air of never-mind indifference that always seemed to do the trick, "Come on. Let's get this over with."

They'd been working this way for days. Spending four, five, six hours at a time transporting materials across the river like laborers from some bygone time. Cole had even contacted a company about renting a crane-truck, but with the road still largely in disrepair, there was no getting big machinery back up to the house.

Teddy had always stood in awe of Bart, who was in so many ways his opposite: a self-confident brute of a man, unattached to anything and living day-to-day like a wild animal. But in those days of dwindling light, he was astonished at Bart's sheer capacity for labor. It was true that Bart had begun living in their company trailer, but even still, he was up before dawn every day, working on trim or laying flooring, music pounding, and practically running around the site.

Bart's single-mindedness had at first invigorated Cole, and they seemed to be almost in competition, burning the midnight oil, yelling at each other, pushing each other, like two athletes halfway through a marathon. But as the days wore on, Cole was breaking down; Teddy could see it. Could see him sitting on a cooler, his head in his hands or even just staring off at the wrecked remains of the old bridge. In so many ways, Cole was their leader, even as Teddy and Bart resisted that outsize role. He was steady, whereas Bart was bullishly impulsive, and Teddy, too quick to please. Moreover, Cole was ambitious enough for all three of them: He was the one who had talked Britney into the bookkeeping role of the company; he was the one who attended Chamber of Commerce meetings, networking and schmoozing with business leaders Bart wouldn't have the patience for and Teddy would be intimidated by. And yet it seemed that Cole's reserves were fading, that what he needed was a long weekend away from the site—several days of rest and relaxation. Surely that would reenergize his batteries.

Teddy sat down on the cooler beside Cole.

"You should take a day off," Teddy offered. "We can hold down the fort here."

Cole just shook his head no.

"Come on, man. Go on. Get yourself on one of those dating websites. Go out to a bar. Heck, stay in bed for two days and catch up on your sleep."

"There's no way," Cole scoffed quietly. "There's just no way."

They sat quietly for a moment, then both looked up at the house in time to see Bart pop down into the garage for several cartons of tiles that he balanced on a shoulder.

"Where does he even get the energy?" Teddy laughed.

Cole glanced down at his feet. "You really don't know?"

Teddy peered at Cole, feeling once more like a younger brother left out of a joke. "What do you mean?"

"He's on something, Teddy. I don't know what. Some kind of upper, though, I imagine."

"You mean like, drugs?"

Cole rubbed his eyes. "Yeah, Teddy, drugs."

"That's horrible. We have to help him, Cole."

Cole stood from the cooler and stretched his back.

"Cole? Don't we? Don't we have to help him?"

"Teddy, I'm about out of magic, amigo. Like the sands of the hourglass, bud. . . . You want that paycheck, you better figure out a way to stay lively for the next what, fifty or so days? Because I don't know about you, but the last thing I want to do is wake up on Christmas morning *without* that paycheck in my stocking. Know what I mean?"

Teddy frowned.

That night, Britney was waiting for him at the kitchen table, an array of home listings neatly arranged. When he shambled into the kitchen, sweaty and filthy from a sixteen-hour day, she seemed to hardly even notice, launching into a soliloquy that she had no doubt rehearsed all day long in preparation for his arrival.

"I've got ten showings scheduled for Sunday," she began. "The earliest is at eight in the morning." She motioned to a two-page listing on the far left of the table. "It's a bit out of town on a larger lot, and the price is beyond what we could afford now. . . . But when your bonus comes in December, the mortgage wouldn't be a stretch. Can you imagine?" She smiled. "I mean—our own place? After so long? Teddy, I'm so excited!"

He reached into the refrigerator, his hand diving instinctively toward a bottle of Coors. Without turning to face her, he twisted off the cap, pressed the cold brown glass to his lips, and pulled a long, contented swig. It felt delicious to stand there, in front of the refrigerator, cold air gasping out. Even as the days were shortening, even as the mornings and evenings were growing colder, Teddy was often sunburnt from crawling carefully along and across the river, a hundred pounds of materials strapped to his back, and even when he wasn't, his body felt like an engine in overdrive. He took another deep swallow from the bottle and turned to face Britney.

"That sounds great, baby," he said, "but I'm not sure I can get outta work on Sunday. . . ."

"Theodore," she began, flummoxed, "first of all—church."

"I know, I know, I know," he replied, "but it's like you just said: When that bonus comes in, everything's gonna change. But that's only *if* I can get that bonus. Right? I mean, you understand that, don't you, baby?"

He'd sunk into a chair at their kitchen table and was absent-mindedly peering at the listings, one moment reaching for a stapled sheath of papers all adorned with carefully staged photos, and the next, setting it aside to run a hand over his forehead. The bottle now empty, Britney had gently plucked it out of his hand and installed herself in his lap. He flinched as she set her entire weight on his thighs.

Not because she was heavy—she wasn't—but because he hadn't anticipated her touch, and more than that, he was just so, so sore.

"Well, I know I'm not as skinny as *you* are," she said with a laugh, "but I can't be that big, can I?"

He reached out and tucked some of her hair behind her ears.

"You're beautiful," he said, and then, from somewhere unexpected, somewhere near his guts, he felt a question arise, a question he could never vocalize, but a feeling, a sense of foreboding. *What if this bonus isn't worth it?* he wanted very badly to ask. And, *What if we can't make the deadline?*

The words had escaped his mouth before he could retrieve them, before he could even consider their import.

She tilted away from him, studied his face.

"I mean, our builder's fees are steep enough as is, right? What do our books look like? This has to be our best year, right? Isn't that enough?"

"Well, sure," she began. "It's been a real good year. Even before this big project. But if True Triangle wants to take that next step, you can't just bleed all the profits into our own pockets. You have to invest. Get a proper office, for one thing. Actually hire an accountant and a secretary. Get a foreman you can trust. I can't keep doing this forever. At some point, you're going to need someone who can handle a serious payroll."

"That makes sense," Teddy agreed.

"That bonus," she said, touching the tip of his nose, "that's our nest egg. It's just for us. Earned by *you*."

"Thing is, I'm really worried about Bart," Teddy said quietly.

"If there's one fella you don't have to worry about," she said wryly, "it's Bart."

"No," Teddy continued, "you haven't seen him. I don't know what he's doing, but I think he's on somethin'. Least, that's what Cole says. He's like a demon. Working eighteen-hour, twenty-hour, twenty-two-hour days, I think. He's even sleeping out there now, in our trailer. Did

I tell you that? At least, I think he's sleeping. He's on somethin', Brit. Some kind of drug, I can't figure it out."

"Probably just some kind of speed, you know? Like what truckers take to stay awake? Or what those country singers used back in the seventies?"

"Maybe you're right," Teddy conceded, though he suspected it was much worse than all that.

"Come on," she said, standing. "Let's get you into the shower."

He stood creakily, as if his joints were badly rusted. By the time he stood from the chair, she was already upstairs. A few seconds later, he could hear the shower running. He shuffled toward the refrigerator, snagged another bottle of Coors, and plodded up the stairs to the bathroom.

Inside the shower, the bottle felt so cold against his cramped fingers while he watched the day's grit and filth wash off his hands and arms, funneling down the drain. Leaning his head against the tiled wall, he closed his eyes and might have fallen asleep for a moment or two, water pounding off his swollen shoulders.

18

Leaning against the bed of the truck, as the gas pumped rhythmically into its tank, Bart rolled up a sleeve and worried the skin on his arms, picking, pinching, and digging with his nails. His eyes flashed over the parking lot and up to the bowl of mountains above, where the snowline crept farther down every day, then back over the parking lot, as restless as a plastic bag in the wind. He ground his teeth and picked, picked, picked. The pump clicked off, and he peered at his arm, where a new sore oozed blood. He glanced around quickly and saw only an old rancher staring at him from another pump. Bart raised his hand to tip his cap in the man's direction and realized only after the man had turned away without acknowledging him that his own fingers were sticky with blood. Then, noticing a smear of his blood on the gas pump, he spit on a paper towel and wiped it away.

A text rattled Bart's phone in his pocket as he slung back into the truck.

LUNCH?

Margo. He hadn't seen Margo in many months and wasn't sure he wanted her to see him this way. But just like that, a wave of hunger broke inside him and he realized that he hadn't eaten in ... had it really been two days? Just a tin of Pringles chips, several plastic bottles of Mountain Dew, and a can of peanuts. He could hear his stomach growling, even over the late-autumn wind rustling the garbage cans.

They met at a little roadside Mexican restaurant, as unpretentious as could be around Jackson Hole. Margo was already ensconced in a booth, typing away at her phone, and before sitting down, he slowly took off his jacket to regard her. She glanced up at him with a quick, polite smile, only to aim her eyes back down at her phone.

As he slid into the booth, she said, "Sorry, fella, seat's taken. I'm waiting for someone."

He touched her wrist lightly. "Margo, it's *me*. Bart."

She set down the phone, then covered her mouth for a moment before pretending to glance for a waitress, her eyes landing everywhere but on him.

"I mean, I know I've lost some weight," he admitted, "but ... Christ, Margo. I don't look *that* bad, do I?"

Finally, she exhaled and looked him fully in the face. "I really didn't recognize you," she said quietly.

"Yeah, I got that."

"Bart, are you okay?"

"Yeah, yeah. I'm fine, Margo. We've just been, you know, workin' around the clock. What can I say?"

"You must've lost twenty, thirty pounds."

"Well," he said, smiling gamely, "then let's eat."

Every time she returned to his health, he dodged her questions and concerns; this was practically a game with them and had been when they'd dated as well. She'd ask about his drinking or cigarette habit, and he'd simply make a joke or point out that he never much questioned *her* choices. When the check came, she quickly handed the waitress a credit card and, placing both hands on the table, stared at him.

"Heard you gave up your apartment, too," she said. "Seriously, what gives?"

He shrugged. "Didn't see the point anymore. Barely ever slept there. Never ate there. No visitors."

"So, where have you been living?"

"Out at the site. We bought ourselves a brand-new RV trailer. It's pretty nice, actually. Bigger than my apartment, maybe. Definitely newer and a helluva lot cleaner. Or at least it was a lot cleaner. A month ago."

"And what are you going to do when the cold comes?"

"Oh, I don't know. It stays plenty warm. There's a little heater in there connected to a propane tank. I mean, people live in those things, Margo. I ain't bivouacked under a tree or nothin'."

"What about the snow? Bart, this isn't a joke. You could get stuck up there. People die."

He waved a hand dismissively.

"Are you okay, Bart? You'd tell me if there was something going on, wouldn't you?"

He shook his head in the negative. "Honestly, Margo, I probably wouldn't."

The waitress returned to the table with Margo's credit card and a pitcher of cold water. The former couple was quiet while the waitress refilled their water glasses and then collected their dirty plates and utensils.

"Here's a thought," she said, flipping her hair and glancing out the window. "What happens if you don't make the deadline?"

"We will."

"Yeah, but what if you don't? Or what if you do, and she refuses to pay you? Did you ever think of that? What if she never expected you to finish? What if she wants the house done by February first, and all this was just some kind of charade? A carrot on a stick. What then?"

He had in fact considered many of these questions, but the one that troubled him the most, the one question of Margo's that he *hadn't* considered, was the notion that the deadline was something of a red herring, a bright and promising enticement meant only to lure three rubes onto an unfinished worksite, to entice them to work themselves to death when no other crews would, in what promised to be the worst weather possible. He ran his right hand up and under his left sleeve and began picking the scab that had formed on his forearm.

"We've got a contract," he said, though that fact gave him little assurance.

"Oh, I'm sure you read every word, too." Margo laughed. "Did you have a lawyer look it over? Do you even know what you signed? For all you know, you might've just signed a contract that ensures *her* a grievance if the house *isn't* finished by Christmas. Or—who knows?— maybe it indemnifies her if you're injured on the site. Did you think of that?"

The wound on his arm was bleeding freely now, and he began to dig at a new spot.

"She's not that kind of person," he murmured.

"Oh," Margo said, leaning back against the cushions of the booth. "Oh, well, that's good. Because I heard a rumor you're working on a house where a guy got killed. The whole crew quit, and then True Triangle moves in, like a bunch of scabs."

Bart winced at that last word.

"You guys might find other projects after this one, other big houses, even, but you might also have a hard time finding workers. From what I hear, that place is bad luck. Maybe not 'haunted,' but, you know, something closer to cursed."

"That's a bunch of bullshit," Bart hissed, sliding out of the booth to stand. He shook his jacket over his shoulders. "I don't have to sit here and take this. Look, I just thought we'd have a nice lunch and, whatever, catch up. I sure as hell don't need to be lectured. Christ, Margo."

"Sit down," she said quietly. "Please."

He stood there, his knees jittering, his eyes sweeping around the restaurant. Without a word, he sat back down.

"What are you using?" she asked.

He looked her hard in the eyes. "Meth," he admitted. "A little coke, here and there."

"Jesus," she sighed.

"It's the only way we'll make it," he reasoned. "The only way."

"Please, please, *please* do me a favor?" she asked.

"I don't know, maybe."

"Quit that shit, Bart. Okay? For me?"

He was aware at that moment of mutilating himself, could feel the slick warmth of his own blood under his fingertips and knew he'd have to hide his hand from her, knew she'd be appalled to see his arms, his fingernails, let alone his teeth, the enamel of which had already begun to degenerate significantly over these past few frenzied weeks. He looked at the table, allowed himself to look at her hands, strong, sun-tanned, and well-veined.

He nodded his head, though what was he really agreeing to? Nothing. All he knew was that he had no clue how they'd make it otherwise, without the help, how they'd ever drag themselves over that finish line on time. Still, he understood in that moment that her concern was for him, not for their goal, and certainly not for Gretchen's house.

As if on cue Margo stood and said, "Don't be fooled, Bart. She's just another rich asshole with too much money to burn."

And then she was gone.

Back at the house, Bill and José were wrapping up their work, José cleaning off their tools, while Bill sat near the hearth, scribbling out what appeared to be a to-do list.

"You fellas almost done?" Bart asked.

"Not long," Bill said without looking up. "Maybe we'll wrap up just after Thanksgiving."

"Lucky you."

"Yeah, well, last thing I want is to be up here when the snow really starts to fly. Hard for me to believe Gretchen is going to be able to keep that road plowed and open."

"I know it. Everyone says we'll be snowed in."

"How about you boys?" Bill asked. "You gonna make it?"

Bart was silent for a moment, not exactly digging the mason's superior tone.

"We'll make it," Bart said, glancing at his boots. "We'll make it."

"Well, it ain't any of my business," Bill said, "but to me, it seems like you could be hiring on a few more subs. Soon as we get that bridge back, anyway. You boys are taking too much on your shoulders."

"Ah . . . Bill, you know as well as I do what we're up against. Nobody wants to work on this job. They don't know me and my partners, and most of 'em don't trust us. They don't much like the homeowner either, and they think the house is cursed. And who knows? Maybe they're right."

Bill shifted his weight slightly. "Gretchen's the finest woman I ever met," he offered. "Never worked for a homeowner who was fairer or had better judgment or taste. Helluva woman, you ask me."

Bart was surprised by Bill's candor.

"You sweet on her, too, Bill?" Bart asked. "You two got a history together or somethin'?"

Bill stared at him with no hostility, but no warmth either. "Good day to you," he said to Bart, tipping his baseball cap and collecting his tools to go.

19

art was laying tile in the master bathroom. He'd bought three Sonos speakers that connected to his phone, and in this way, he kept music throbbing through the empty house at almost every hour of the day or night. Sure, he was partial to his old boombox, but there was something about *sprinkling* speakers throughout a house, and moving room to room, just as the music flowed. Anyway, when Teddy and Cole were gone, it made the structure feel less cold, alone.

Oh, but the meth, *that* was what really helped for jobs like this— for the tiling, placing each one, getting zoned out on the geometric patterns that kept multiplying, like a grid. Instead of picking at scabs, he was *placing* them, on and on and on—little work, putzy work, work that he otherwise wouldn't enjoy, but there in the early morning, an hour or so before dawn, he could listen to the entirety of a band's work, an entire oeuvre, could begin with Nirvana's *Bleach* and before midnight, complete *Unplugged in New York*, then shift into something altogether different, like the Beatles, or, when his partners weren't around, as they were not just then, jazz—especially Miles Davis, which Margo had introduced him to. *Goddamnit*, he thought, *that woman was a keeper. Maybe it's not too late to win her back....*

Today it was in fact Miles Davis's *In a Silent Way*, a dreamy sound-world that filled the house, a sonic wave he could lazily ride any which way he wanted. During the day, when other subs were around, he tried to keep the meth under wraps. He wasn't sure what Cole and Teddy knew or didn't know, and so it was easier to hit the pipe late at night or just before dawn, and damn, did he love that feeling—of strutting around the site, the house, just all jacked-up, fueled on crank, flying around and showing Cole what he was able to accomplish in the wee hours. His goal was to complete this bathroom before the end of the day. Think: the money he'd saved them, and the *time*. The tiling guys in the area were notoriously finicky, as temperamental as the winter weather, prone to not showing up for work or showing up only to ask for a cash advance on their wages.... Cole had gotten in touch with a tiler who'd originally signed on with the first general contractor, but he wasn't about to carry tile and grout across a river, and certainly not for what he'd originally bid out the work. When he told Cole that his fee would have to quadruple, Cole had essentially told the fellow to kiss his ass, and that was that.

Even protected by heavy-duty professional-grade kneepads, Bart's knees were screaming. He placed several tile sheets before standing and stretching his back. The rush had long since subsided, and he'd been powering through on the shoulder of that high, only then feeling the downslope. He walked out of the house, into the last hour before dawn, the starlight still bright enough to leave the mountains shining like crystalline castles.

He dragged himself into the trailer, considered flopping down on the narrow bed, but thought better of it. The pipe and meth were hidden in a hollowed-out hardcover copy of Stephen King's *Needful Things*. Bart suspected Cole was on to him by now but didn't care to know the particulars. But if Teddy ever caught on to the extent of things . . . Luckily, Teddy wasn't much of a reader. In fact, Bart had once heard him launch into a diatribe about how King was part of a larger cabal of liberal intellects attempting to rot American culture from the inside out with his "devil books." There wasn't a chance in hell Teddy would touch that novel or the evil things inside it.

Bart took the pipe and meth out to the springs and lowered himself to the rock, the steam warming him in the early-morning chill. He touched the flame of his lighter to the bowl and inhaled.

Oooooooohhhhhh . . . and there he was again . . . the veins in this neck, surging, each of them, and the veins in his tired arms, *no longer the least bit tired*. His knees, which had been so close to betraying him, now felt like iron wheels, like he was the **LITTLE ENGINE THAT COULD**, *powering right up to the peaks of those mountains* ^^^ . . . He shook his head. *Oooooooohhhhhh* . . . Pressed his hands against his eyelids, felt that his eyeballs were about to ***POP*** out of his skull. His tongue felt hot, as if he'd licked battery acid.

He walked down to the river, feeling for the first time since he'd begun using again . . . afraid. Yes, he was afraid. Afraid he was trapped. There was no time to quit the stuff, and the crash he'd be facing now, he knew, would be epic and torturous. He'd have to sink deep into a horrific hole, a deep mineshaft of pain, and then the withdrawal, months of desperately seeking that high again. . . . It had been years since he'd used anything this religiously, rode a high this hard . . . But: *Oooooooohhhhhh* . . . His body felt so hot he began shedding clothes: his shirt, his pants, a sock, until he found himself sitting in the cool of the river, weeping, splashing those scarred arms of his.

And that was when he saw it, far off at first, lights flashing a sickly yellow and white, and then that beeping drone, and he was filled with terror. A huge noise was filling the valley now, ringing in his ears, monstrous in its rising volume as that accompanying light blotted out all the stars.

He scrambled up the bank of the creek and ran naked from it, a single sodden sock still on one foot, and, once inside the trailer, hastily locked the door, searching that small space for something to block the doorway; he wrenched the miniature refrigerator from its spot and lodged it in front of the door, then began stacking whatever he could on top of the refrigerator: a case of beer, books, blueprints, clothes.

Oooooooohhhhhh Christ!!!!!! The light and sound were growing steadily closer, and his fevered mind was of two theories: one, aliens. He was alone, and this was it. They'd beam him up into their ship, and he'd suffer all manner of indignity before they released him hours later, no one the wiser, the only proof a little chip implanted just below the surface of his scalp, so that they could track him through the universe. Or, two: The federales were after him. Of course they were. Someone on the crew must have ratted him out, wanted the project to fail. Maybe it was Bill; yes, it fucking had to be Bill. Who else could it have been? Or Gretchen herself? What a way to put the kibosh on those hefty bonuses. They were close to the finish line now, and with the house sealed up, she could just wait out the winter and rehire a crew of subs with the goal of moving into the house on July 4. No, no, no . . . He was right the first time; it had to be the federales, the feds, ATF, FBI, or some yahoo local sheriff. They'd heard about drugs up at the new house site, heard about a crew of guys likely on meth, and . . . **WAIT!!!** Where was the pipe and the meth?

"The pipe! The pipe! The *pipe*! The pipe and the crystal, the pipe and the *crystal*!" he roared, scrambling toward the ad-hoc barricade he'd assembled in front of the trailer's door and now ripping it apart, tossing the case of beer, tearing at the blueprints, and all but throwing the mini fridge, then blasting out the door and into the cold, naked still, save for that single wet sock, and without a light, too, and on his hands and knees, feeling blindly around the rim of the springs, the rock there, the gravel below, until he stood and just about as he was ready to run downhill toward the river, he felt something crack below his heel, and then a sharp pain. The pipe! *The pipe, the pipe, the pipe.* He knelt down and collected the little glass pieces as best he could, cupped them in his hands, and, finding the baggie of meth, too, retreated back to the trailer, where he built the barricade anew, hiding what remained of the pipe and meth in *Needful Things*, then diving onto the bed and covering himself in blankets, there to cower as much out of fear as from the cold. And all the while the distant lights and noises crept closer and closer, like an encroaching army. He heard men's voices and the crunch of tires on gravel, and eventually, the lights were so close they strobed over the windows of the trailer. He waited for the inevitable: knocking fists on the trailer's door, the cry of *We've got a warrant!* or even the metallic *chick-chick* of guns locked and loaded.

It was incredibly difficult to measure time. Bart was terrified to look out the windows, for fear of giving himself away. Eventually, more and more light did seem to creep through the shutters, and then there was intermittent birdsong. He thought he could hear truck doors slamming and the laughter of men, no doubt peering at the trailer through binoculars or the scopes of their sniper rifles.

More time passed until, at last, he heard the approach of footfalls.

"Hey, Bart!" The voice was familiar; it sounded like Cole, but how could Bart know for sure? "Bart, you in there?" How could he know for sure whether they were just holding his friend, a pistol pressed between his shoulder blades or against the back of his skull?

"Bart, look, buddy, I'm coming in. You better be decent."

Bart shrank beneath the blankets. He might've ground his teeth together, but lately they hadn't been feeling quite right; mushy, somehow.

The trailer began to shake, and the door handle groaned but would not give.

"Open up, Bart! You okay in there, buddy? Hey, hang on now! We'll get you! Hold tight now."

Bart sensed an apprehension outside the trailer, heard the sound of two men talking, two distinct voices, and then a key in the lock of the door, and suddenly, morning light spilling in, as someone began pulling all of Bart's makeshift barricade away from the doorway. Bart screamed.

"Hey, buddy," came a quiet voice. "Come on—calm down. It's just us."

It was Cole and Teddy, standing in the doorway, looking extremely concerned, if not terrified. Cole was crouched on his knees, holding out his hands, the way you might coax a dog back toward the leash, while Teddy just stood there, both hands resting on top of his head, staring around the wrecked trailer and blowing out a defeated sort of sigh.

"Bart," Cole said. "Bart, it's just us. You must've had a bad dream or something, buddy. All right? A nightmare. Hell, man, your clothes are all over the place outside."

"Blood, too," Teddy whispered, pointing down at the floor of the Airstream, and then to the bedsheets wrapped around Bart.

"You're awake now, buddy," Cole said. "It's okay. We're here. And we got good news, too."

"Look at all the blood," Teddy said.

Cole smiled extravagantly at Bart, inching forward until he could rest a hand on his friend's shoulder.

"Wha—what news?" Bart asked.

"We got ourselves a new bridge," Cole said, smiling.

"A new bridge?" Bart almost laughed.

"Yeah, some big-deal boys out of Salt Lake City. The whole bridge is right out there," Cole said, standing. "Down there right now! You gotta see it, buddy. They've got it out on a giant flatbed truck. Three days, and they'll be done, and then we'll be back in business. A crane-truck, floodlights—the whole shebang. You believe it?"

Bart rubbed at his face, his eyes.

"What happened to your arms?" Teddy asked, pointing to the scabs and open sores adorning Bart's arms from his wrists all the way to his shoulders. "Dear god, Bart."

"He's just a little beat-up, aren't you, buddy?" Cole said, gathering some clothes and helping Bart into a T-shirt. "Come on, let's—"

"No," Teddy said firmly, then, "*No!* Now, damn it, Cole, just *stop*."

"What?" Cole asked. "There's work to do, Teddy." He drew back all the curtains, and light blasted into the trailer. "Look, it's a beautiful day out there, am I right?" Cole went on. "We can't . . . Teddy-Bear, we just can't . . . We gotta keep moving forward! The clock is ticking, and we can't just—"

"No!" Teddy said, pushing Cole out of the way and sitting down beside Bart. "No, this ain't right. We've got to take him to a hospital, Cole. Look at him. Look at him!"

But Cole would not look at his friend, just rubbed at his jaw and at the back of his skull, and occasionally stared at the windows, at the bridge-building crew, how efficient they were, how, at that very moment, they were cleaning the landing on the far side of the river, readying it for what the foreman assured Cole was a reliable if temporary fix. Then, in the spring, they'd return to lift the bridge off its temporary footings, pouring proper new concrete pilings that would withstand most anything. The important thing was, in three days, they'd have a functioning bridge again, and with any luck, at least most of their subs would return to the site.

"We're almost there," Cole said quietly. "Just a matter of weeks now. We're weeks away, boys. Weeks!"

"I don't care," Teddy said. "I'm takin' him to the hospital."

"And then what?" Cole roared. "You see his arms! Those ain't bug bites, Teddy. He's on *meth*. Okay? You want to get him arrested? You know how long it's gonna take him to dry out?"

"I don't care, Cole. He's my friend, and right now he needs our help."

Teddy took one of Bart's arms and draped it over his own shoulder, then, standing, took his friend's weight, which, to his surprise, was frighteningly reduced from even a month or two earlier.

"Sit. The. Fuck. *Down*," said Cole.

Teddy stood there, beside the bed, Bart leaning into him like he was a broken fencepost.

"This is a partnership, amigo," Cole said sternly. "Or was. 'Cause you go through that door, we ain't partners anymore."

"He needs help," Teddy pleaded. "He's working himself to death."

Cole bobbed his head and cracked his knuckles, glancing at Bart.

"All right," he said. "What if we meet in the middle? That bridge is gonna take three days. So maybe everyone goes home, gets some sleep."

"What about Bart?" Teddy asked. "He doesn't even have a place anymore."

"You mean you don't want to take him home?" Cole laughed. "And here, a minute ago, you were talking about taking him to the hospital."

"Fine," Teddy said. "He can come home with me."

"No," Bart croaked. "I don't want Britney seeing me this way. Or your girls."

Cole shook his head. "I'd take him, but . . ." He sighed. "I don't even know what furniture's left at my place."

"Yeah, well, we can't leave him here," said Teddy.

"I'll be fine," Bart said, slumping onto the bed.

"No, you won't." It was true. Cole knew it. And then there was the fear that if Bill found him this way . . . "We gotta get you out of here." He glanced at the open door.

"I ain't goin' out there," Bart mumbled. "How do I know this ain't some kind of ruse?"

"A what?" Teddy asked.

"A goddamn act. The feds out there, pretending they're our bridge builders. How do I know what to believe?"

Cole sighed, stared at his recalcitrant friend, this man who, now that he studied him hard, looked very unwell indeed. Not just exhausted but gruesomely transformed, the kind of strung-out junkie you could push over with a pinky finger, if he didn't stab you first.

"Tell you what," Cole said. "If those mugs out there are the feds, you can have my bonus. I swear to god."

"Have your bonus?" Bart repeated, arching his eyebrows and probing his arms with twitchy fingers.

"Come on," Cole ordered, picking up his friend by the elbow. "Trust me, amigo. I got an idea."

They helped Bart dress and then tossed his toiletries and some clean clothes into a duffel bag and led him upriver along a newly beaten path to their jury-rigged bridge. Bart seemed to have shrunken overnight, moving about as feebly as an old man. When they neared the bridge-building crew, he gamely put on a good face, straightened his posture, and moved briskly past the workers, even as Cole slapped a couple of backs and shot the shit for a few moments, before catching back up to Bart as he and Teddy stood near their trucks.

"I don't know, Cole," Teddy said. "Maybe this ain't worth it. Maybe we ought to just . . . I don't know. . . . Look, there'll be other great projects. Maybe this one is just doomed. Even if we were to walk away now, we still would've made a bundle of money."

"No way," Cole said. He opened the passenger-side door of his truck, and without having to say anything to Bart, his friend ducked into the cab and sat motionless, his eyes closed. "Take three days off, Teddy. All right? Relax. Have fun with your family. We'll all come back better for this break. Ready for the home stretch."

Teddy leaned through the window of Cole's truck and extended his hand to Bart.

"Take care of yourself," Teddy said firmly. "I got your back, no matter what. Far as I'm concerned, we can walk away at any time. You just say the word."

Bart gave a little grin and waved his hand in the air.

As Teddy walked away, Cole caught up to him.

"By the way, this notion you've got that we've made all this money?" Cole said. "That ain't exactly true."

"What do you mean?"

"I mean," Cole continued, "we bought a brand-new trailer, generators, tools. Teddy, we've spent easily over a hundred and fifty grand, already. And the thing is, if we don't get our bonuses, it ain't like we're millionaires. Not even remotely. Sure, we would've made some decent bread, but it ain't life-changing money. You know that, right? We need to finish the job, and on time. It's nonnegotiable, far as I'm concerned."

Teddy stood silently, unable to meet Cole's eyes. "Take care of him," he said finally. "He's our friend."

"I will," Cole said. "I promise. And I'll see you in a few days."

Cole drove them to the finest hotel in town and, parking his muddy pickup in the valet line, said to Bart, "Wait right here."

"Don't you worry about me," Bart said, staring down at his dirty, disheveled clothes. He glanced at himself in the mirror, grimaced, then aimed the mirror away. "I ain't going anywhere."

Cole walked casually into the hotel lobby, aware that he was still in his work clothes, his boots grimy, on the thick, cream-colored carpeting. The lighting in this lobby was golden and intimate, the walls decorated with tasteful black-and-white prints of the surrounding landscape. Behind the front desk was a fantastic European mount of a massive elk, looming like a crown above the head of a wisp-thin female clerk. He had given some thought to checking into much cheaper accommodations, but then again, what he wanted most was relaxation. He did not want scratchy bedsheets, a tired mattress, or eighteen-wheelers idling outside the window.

"I'd like a room, please," Cole said. "And I don't have a reservation."

The clerk typed away at her computer and then, after frowning at the screen, looked back to Cole, with a barely camouflaged look of contempt. "Unfortunately, the only room we have available is our largest suite."

"Perfect," Cole said, slapping his credit card on the counter. "I'll take it. Three nights."

"Three nights?" she repeated.

"Yep," he said, glancing back at the pickup truck, where he imagined Bart sat, picking at his arms.

"Two beds, right?" Cole confirmed.

The clerk looked at him, confused. "Sir?"

"There's two of us. We're, uh, friends."

"That room has only a king-size bed, sir. But we have had guests sleep on the couch, which is lovely. I've heard."

"Fine," Cole said. He nodded, signed her forms, and placed his credit card in his wallet.

"Two keys?" she asked.

"How about just one," he said.

Cole settled Bart into the suite; pushed him into the bathroom and threw his clothes into a garbage can. Then he ordered two hundred and fifty dollars in room service—salads, steaks, a few appetizers, and a bottle of very good wine—and then slumped back into a comfortable, overstuffed leather chair to think. He had to get Bart back on track, get him eating again, figure out how to nurse him through the end of the year.

Assuming he was able to persuade their subs to return, he did not doubt they could finish before Christmas. But if the subs would not come back to Gretchen's house, that was another matter entirely. There'd be at least a week of trim work, followed by a week of painting. The countertops were on order, and all the natural stone Gretchen had selected was sitting in a warehouse and needed to be installed before the plumber could install the sinks and faucets. He needed to get the appliances moved, and there was no time to spare. He only hoped their cabinetmaker was on schedule; he'd need to get him on the telephone, and pronto. So much depended on an order of operation, and he needed these subs to work in concert, to follow his directions, and to be flexible. What was more, he needed all this to happen *despite* the fact that some of them had been thrown off the project when Gretchen's first crew quit, and *despite* the delays incurred by the broken bridge. He was prepared to pay these guys premiums, too, even as he tallied the cost for this three-day break likely in the low thousands.

Cole felt a wave of anxiety pass over him. He began dialing numbers.

20

Britney led Teddy from house to house, each one more overpriced than the last. A three-bedroom for seven hundred and fifty thousand in need of a new furnace, a new roof, a kitchen that would have to be completely remodeled, and a radical overhaul of at least one bathroom carpeted in dandelion yellow shag circa 1976. Every time he pointed to something that was hopelessly outdated, broken, or hastily and only impermanently repaired, she scoffed, folding her arms defensively across her chest.

"But that's the thing, Teddy: *You* can do all those things. We don't have to *pay* to fix those things."

All he wanted to do was sleep. Or work at his own leisurely pace on Gretchen's house. Perhaps roll onto the worksite around noon and kick off at five. *That* would seem like a vacation.

Now they stood inside a nondescript 1960s-era rambler, and the sound of Britney's voice comingled with the real estate agent's, a white noise he ignored as he stared out into the backyard, pretending to imagine some future fire pit, or the herb garden Britney was always talking about.

"Isn't it great?" Britney asked. "Some TLC, some elbow grease, a little attention to the curb appeal, and we can turn this place around. I mean, the bones are good, right?"

He absent-mindedly rapped his knuckles against some faux wood-paneling; the hollow sound that returned to his ears betraying a lack of insulation. He imagined exorbitant winter heating bills, especially since the girls complained anytime he turned the thermostat below their requisite seventy-five degrees.

"Yeah," he said, "great bones."

"And honestly," the real estate agent said, a prodigious keychain dangling off her index finger, "the price is right. You just can't get into this market for any less than this. It is an *impossibility* at this point. Trust me."

Teddy stared hard at the agent, a woman in her fifties with a Jane Fonda aerobics body, platinum blond hair, and the ridiculous name of Shelley Winterbottom.

"We've looked at twelve houses, honey," Britney said. "And I really think this is the one. This *has* to be the one. Don't you think?"

But the only house he could think about was Gretchen's, out there in the mountains, the hot springs steaming up into the blue late-autumn sky, the last of the yellow cottonwood leaves falling into the river, the house's sleek lines and beautifully wide windows staring out, searching for the builders, looking for him.

Britney was standing beside him then, holding his arm gently in both of her hands.

"Teddy?" she whispered. "I know you're tired, baby, but help me out here. This is so important. If we don't make an offer, this house could be gone by tomorrow. Or even tonight. We don't have time to hem and haw."

Winterbottom made a point of looking at her watch. "Tell you what," she said, her heels clicking loudly on the wood floors in all that unoccupied space. "I'm going to be at the office the rest of this afternoon and evening until six. If you want to write up an offer, just shoot me a text and I'll get your paperwork started, m'kay?"

After escorting them out of the house, they shook hands all around, and the agent drove off in a black Audi R8, leaving the Smythes on the driveway, both with their arms crossed and rather troubled looks on their faces.

"Teddy," Britney began, "what's your head at?"

He didn't even know where to begin. Perhaps by explaining that working on Gretchen's house had pretty much ruined him for any other house, or that he found this endless tour of the town's less desirable real estate to be something of a death march, that everything about this property they now stood upon depressed him, that he could spend the next twenty years remodeling and troubleshooting this house and it would never, *never* approach even a fraction of the beauty of Gretchen's house—not its quality of materials, not its breathtaking vistas, not the time and thought that had gone into every inch of those blueprints. He thought of Gretchen's kitchen. Of the deep sink that would soon be installed and the beautiful farmhouse faucet. Of the Wolf range and Sub-Zero appliances. Of the hood so powerful it would practically suck a sparrow out of the kitchen and up into the mountain air. Of the giant island of Italian marble and the skillfully made cabinets. The granite countertops. And that was just the kitchen; never mind the fireplace, the space-age mechanicals, the solar array and geothermal heating, the triple-glazed, ultra-efficient windows . . . And all of that was before he even got to the really troubling stuff, to the subject of Bart, or their deadline, or the fact that December was no longer so very far away.

He reached for her hand. "I really like this house," he said at last, looking into her eyes. "I think it's the one. You're right."

He could *see* her heart leap. Could see her eyes brighten and her shoulders rise before she came to him, kissing him hard and squeezing him with all her might, smothering him with happiness.

"Oh, Teddy, you really think so?"

He smiled. "I do," he said. "This is it. It feels right."

"Oh, baby," she purred. "*Finally*. Finally we have ourselves a *home*."

She snapped out her phone and shot a text to Winterbottom before they'd even crawled into the car. A few blocks down the road Britney directed him down a new cul-de-sac, no houses yet built, and only after she'd told him to park the car did he understand, just as she pulled down her underwear and moved over to his side to straddle him. He closed his eyes and allowed himself to forget everything, felt her hand freeing his belt, and then her hand on him, and he pushed into her and felt an incredible relief and a sort of healing, and they kissed and kissed and then, just before she was finished, she arced her body backward, pressing into the steering wheel and the horn, and both of them collapsing into giggles, because he thought, *Fuck it. It's just money. That's all it is. I'll just work harder.*

They drove on to the agent's office, holding hands. Teddy glanced over at his wife to see her wipe away several tears. "You all right?" he asked, pulling the car to the side of the road. "Baby?"

"No, no, no!" she said, smiling through tears, and laughing. "You don't have to stop. Please—keep going."

"What's wrong?"

"I'm just so *happy*," she explained, new trails of mascara now streaking down her cheeks. "I'm just so, so excited, Teddy, is all."

He couldn't help grinning as he pressed down on the accelerator.

They'd scratched and saved for years, but these past few months, with all the work on Gretchen's house, they had just enough for a down payment. Of course, Teddy's heart had fairly stopped when they talked to the bank and calculated their monthly mortgage payments. The debt they were assuming was colossal. But if they could finish Gretchen's house on time, the bonus would go a long way toward paying off the principal. But without it . . .

For the first time he understood that this town did not want people like him and his family. As laborers, yes, but . . . could they just please live as far out of sight as possible? Or, better yet, strive for invisibility altogether. This town did not want rusted, old minivans on driveways, plastic toys in the front yard, or loud music and smoky charcoal grills, true townie bars or mom-and-pop greasy spoons. No, everything was becoming polished and perfectly clean. The town wanted houses like this to be razed, torn down and rebuilt five times larger. A few of his ranch-hand friends never even came into town anymore; they'd come to hate the looks they got for chewing tobacco, smoking a Marlboro, or ordering a Bud Light.

And yet, he felt a growing wave of excitement at the notion of being a homeowner. All right, the place wasn't perfect. But Britney was right. Bart and Cole would gladly help him out, and starting with the roof, they could work their way down: gut the kitchen and bathrooms first, then finish the basement. Maybe the girls would even pitch in, help paint the house, have the opportunity to know the pride in improving something. Heck, in ten years, maybe they could flip the house for double what they'd paid and start a new project—maybe even get some acreage outside town.

Whenever he thought about the mortgage, his chest tightened, so he put that out of mind. *America is the greatest country in the world*, his father always used to tell him, *as long as you don't run out of money*. Now those words rang in his head. The only solution was to work harder, harder, and then harder still.

If he hadn't already been committed to that deadline, he sure as heck was now.

Teddy held the door for Britney as they walked into the agent's office, a small street-level space with brick walls and wide Doug fir flooring. As soon as Shelley Winterbottom saw the Smythes she held out a hand, as if to stop them perhaps, or warn them, and then, showily pantomimed zipping her lips shut. It appeared Winterbottom was in conversation with someone over the speakerphone.

"Well, you'd be stupid to take that offer," she said rather loudly, a cross look etched across her face. "My buyers are preapproved and can make a down payment as early as tomorrow morning. They're a beautiful family with four young girls in the local school system."

"Yeah?" a man's voice boomed out from the phone set. "Well, look here, Shell, 'cause I got another buyer who'll pay *fifty more* than asking with a cash deposit *tonight*—"

Winterbottom shot them both cold looks and yanked the receiver off its cradle. Teddy and Britney sat down heavily in two chairs opposite her. After some time, she said, "All right. Yeah, okay—just hang on, all right, Royce?"

She sighed, pressed her thumb and forefinger against the bridge of her nose.

"I hate to say I told you so," she began, "but if we'd just made an offer on this house yesterday, or even four hours ago . . ."

"What's the matter?" Teddy said. "Where do we stand?"

"Another offer. Came in *simultaneous* to yours. And the seller's agent says this other party will go fifty more than asking—well, you heard."

"Wait a minute, what do you mean *simultaneous* to our offer? How's that even possible? One of the offers must have come in first. I mean, why would they pay fifty more if *their* offer was first?"

Winterbottom shrugged. "That's what the seller's agent is telling me. The question is, can you go another seventy-five grand higher?"

"No!" Teddy said. "No. And that *isn't* the question. The question is, who was first? The question is, what is *right*? We texted you immediately. Couldn't been five minutes after you left. There's gotta be time stamps on those emails. When'd you put in our offer?"

Now it was Winterbottom's turn to stare coldly at Teddy.

"Let me call you right back, okay, Royce?" she said, hanging up the telephone and exhaling loudly. She then reached into a desk drawer and appeared to pop a piece of Nicorette into her mouth. "Mr. Smythe, what would you prefer I do? Impugn Royce Hollister's integrity and destroy my relationship with him, and, in doing so, muddy your name,

your wife's, and, by the way, the good name of your construction business? *Or*, would you like me to call my friend Royce back and tell him
we're willing to go another seventy-five over asking—or, if you're serious, a full hundred—and that you'll get him a cashier's check tonight,
or at the very least, no later than tomorrow morning? Because, um,
those are really your two choices here."

"A hundred thousand dollars?" Britney asked, her voice atremble.
"But that's . . ."

How many times had Teddy lost? How many times had some customer belittled him, talked down to him, skipped a payment, or argued an invoice? How many times had some tenant in some shitty
apartment talked to him like he was a servant? How many years had
he struggled to keep food on the table, to buy new clothes for the girls,
to occasionally splurge on Britney? Never, *never* before had he complained or even expected anything. And now, he could see that the
house was lost, and he sighed deeply. Without turning to look at Britney he took her hand and could feel her body wracking with what he
knew was a different sort of crying, a different kind of tears.

Teddy knew his own limitations; knew he wasn't as smart or clever
as Cole, or as strong and relentless as Bart. And yet, surveying his
future in this town, he knew that he would need Winterbottom. Knew
he'd need her to sell houses they might build in the future. Knew he'd
need Royce Hollister, too. Knew that these real estate agents had last
names as recognizable as the area mountains or rivers dominating the
local maps; heck, in a few cases, the creeks and basins carried their
names. These were people he'd need as friendly business acquaintances for the next three or four decades. He was in no position to
make an enemy here, let alone two of them.

And so, he glanced down at his boots, rubbed at the stubble of his
head, squeezed Britney's hand, then slowly stood. He wanted very
badly to pick up Winterbottom's desk and, in one heroic moment of
defiance, send that bulky furniture through the office's expansive

front window. That was what the heroes on his dream-board would have done. But instead, he offered Winterbottom a tightly apologetic smile, squeezed his wife's shoulder, and just said quietly, "Let's go."

Britney did not so much as look at the agent, nor did she say goodnight or waste time with any of the pleasantries Teddy was so accustomed to hearing her chirp out at people. She simply moved slowly toward the front door, leaving him there, beside their agent's desk.

"I'll keep you posted," Winterbottom said. "Look, sometimes things fall through. We wrote a good, clean offer. Sometimes . . . sometimes you just get bested. Especially in this market. Anyhow, we'll be in touch."

"Right," Teddy murmured. "Goodnight, then."

Out in the car, Britney came fully apart. Teddy hadn't seen her so disappointed in many years, and he did his best to comfort her.

"It wasn't meant to be, I guess," he said quietly, "and I'll tell you something, Brit: That house was a money pit. It would've been a boondoggle, baby. We would've paid way too much to begin with. Who knows? We may've just dodged a real bullet."

"I want *more*," she said at last. "I want us to *build* something. I don't want to just keep renting. Our parents owned their houses. Why can't we?"

"We will," he said, kissing the top of her head. "We will."

He dearly hoped that his words weren't empty, that they could complete Gretchen's house on time, that Gretchen was true to her word, and that he would have the stamina to finish the job, to stand there on Christmas morning and receive his award, like some kneeling knight waiting for the shoulder-kiss of a ceremonial sword. But the closer they moved toward that impossible goal, the more the whole deal felt like a cursed bargain; even this town had begun to feel like a mirage, an illusion of what once was possible in America, rather than what it was—a tony playground for the richest of the planet's rich.

21

Gretchen's father had bought the land for twenty-five thousand dollars in the days just after the Korean War. A corn-fed kid from Decorah, Iowa, he knew not a thing about the West. But when a friend from the Marines told him about a thousand-odd acres out in the mountains with good hunting, some hot springs, and a river running through it, the flatlander was charmed.

Every summer they packed up the station wagon and lit out west. She'd stare out those wide rear windows at the vistas of, at first, nothing. Just fields and fields of near endless corn and then wheat, the land rising by degrees until finally, deep into Colorado, the Rockies suddenly thrust themselves up to the heavens as the air grew cool and dry. She remembered how slowly, how carefully, her father took those mountain roads even as cars honked and swerved around him, his forehead sweating with concentration.

Back then, of course, there was no road to the hot springs. Her father would write a letter in March to an old rancher named Samuel

Wilkins, and in April, his reply would arrive, promising to meet them beside the gravel county highway on the appointed day and hour in early June. He would meet their Conestoga of a station wagon, packed with dry goods and books, transferring it all to the several horses and pack mules he'd brought.

Oh, the adventure! The uncertainty! To think: How much depended on those letters, and on a person's word—that they would actually show up by the side of the road in an area that was otherwise total wilderness. Gretchen's father would shake the rancher's hand with a fifty-dollar bill neatly packaged in his palm. Then, when everything was secure, they would mount the horses and the rancher would lead them along the river and up into the clouds.

The first time they visited the land, she was nine years old and had never ridden a horse before. She was delighted in every way, as if her parents had just presented her with the world itself, granting her every wish. She could hardly stop grinning at the old rancher as he lifted her up into the saddle that first time and adjusted her stirrups just so.

"These are called *reins*," Samuel explained, handing her two softened thick strips of leather, "though you ain't gonna need 'em. Your horse here is called Lightning, but all his stormy days are behind him, I assure you. And you're gonna ride right behind me, so he'll know just where to go."

She beamed down at him. Nearly forty years later she could still draw a picture of his face. Every kind wrinkle, every little scar, every white hair. Every sweat stain on that battered old Stetson of his.

"You afraid?" he asked, though he was fairly certain this little girl was nothing of the kind, that the only emotion overcoming her at that moment was extreme happiness—elation. That little smile seemed unbreakable. And so he found himself smiling, too; he liked this girl who was immediately unafraid of horses and willing to ride up into some of the most challenging terrain he'd ever seen. He'd never had a daughter and secretly always wanted one.

"No, sir," she said.

"Glad to hear it," he said. "You'll do fine."

They rode up into the mountains under a pouring sun along that narrow, sunbaked, dusty little trail. The journey took several hours, longer than normal, given how unaccustomed they were to the saddles and the elevation. Every hour or so, the rancher stopped to water the horses, though in truth he was more concerned about the family he happened to be shepherding.

It was dusk when they arrived at the springs, as she remembered it, though she'd happily admit that first memory had been enshrouded by an almost mystical sentimentality. Certainly, it felt as if they had entered another reality—an enchanted mountain was how she thought of it, as the horses crossed the river at that ford and trotted up the slope toward the hot springs, where Samuel had already set up three canvas wall-tents: one for her, one for her parents, and a mess kitchen.

How many nights had there been when she could not even bring herself to close her eyes, when the natural world was just too beautiful to say goodnight to? When she'd lain in her cot, listening to the coyotes yip, howl, and sing. When she'd watched the stars wheel and shimmer. When she'd read by the holy light of a Coleman lantern, while low and mysterious sounds emanated from her parents' tent . . .

And all those blissful days spent planning a more permanent structure. Not a house, no. The way her father described it, nothing more than a one-room log cabin with a south-facing porch where they could sit in rocking chairs and read. Perhaps a roughhewn table, too. A place to play cards on rainy days. Someday, her father laughed, maybe even an outhouse with a crescent moon carved through the door to let in the sunshine and starlight.

Days spent panning for gold in the creek, collecting beautiful river stones, staring at mountain goats through binoculars, fishing in the river, or stalking deer. The mountains were said to hide lost hard-rock mines, and she imagined herself discovering some long-forgotten motherlode, or the macabre skeletons of doomed miners, their tattered clothing still clinging to white bone, pickaxes lying askew beside them.

What she discovered in that wilderness, in all that space and silence, was herself. Time to read hundreds of books, anything she desired, from Rumi and Shakespeare to Charles Portis and Wallace Stegner. Candy books, too: Louis L'Amour and Zane Grey. But there was also the time and space to learn and care for horses, to range freely, learning the names of the area flora and fauna. To know the constellations and to gaze at the formations of the clouds. In her later teenage years, to meet one of Samuel's nephews, a young man named Loney Wilkins, and ride with him through the mountains, stopping to spread a blanket among the sage and learn each other's bodies, from the first electric touches of their fingertips to the later wild swirling of tongues and then: one inevitable day, the frantic bucking of hips, the knots of lean legs, and this new forbidden language they seemed to have taught each other.

It was not just herself she began to know and trust and gain confidence in, or the natural world. But her parents, too, her family, and her place in that family, an inheritance of shared history and ambition and love. As an only child, her little family of three moved easily, and there was no drama when it came to the dispersal of parental attention, for she received as much of it as she needed. Later, in college and law school, she would quietly observe that most of the world was not afforded this luxury, the time and space to ask your parents about their lives and their dreams, and to in turn receive their questions, without embarrassment or impatience, but with warmth, as if two great teachers were preparing her for the unseen path before her.

They celebrated Gretchen's seventeenth birthday there, in the log cabin her parents had built with the help of Samuel and Loney Wilkins the summer before. They roasted a lamb, cooked vegetables in aluminum "hobo" packets, drank beer kept cold in the river, and enjoyed an apple cobbler in a heavy Dutch oven set directly in the fire's coals. She could think of nothing better, the faces of those she loved burnished by firelight and alcohol, her parents nuzzling each other discreetly, Samuel telling epic stories of his own childhood in these mountains, when there were still gunfighters and grizzly bears, when the land was so wild you could barely comprehend "settling" it. And in some small moment, stealing away to the shadows with Loney, though not so long as to openly disrespect the rancher, who she could sense by then knew about them, who, she knew, subscribed to an older code of honor, for he had once gently pulled her aside and said, "The world is harder for a woman, Gretchen. It shouldn't be, but it is. The world wants to imagine you in certain ways, wants to see you just so. . . . Don't make it easy for them."

"I don't understand," she had said, though she could guess he was talking about impropriety, about her dalliances with the nephew, most likely. Surely that was what he was circling around so cryptically.

"You're better than the rabble," he said, then hesitated, turning his face away from her. "My god, you're already a beautiful young woman."

After midnight, the rancher and his nephew laid down their bedrolls and slept near the campfire, and she stayed up all night long, with the precious knowledge that summer was even now slipping away from them, and wanting so much to wake the boy and slip into the hot springs and press her wet skin against his, glossy with starlight and steam, love and passion. But there was the thought of the rancher, and his sad, old blue eyes, and she knew damn well that he'd know if she took her lover's hand to draw him away from the fire, and the disappointment that would cause the old man, who lived by the principles of some bygone time and morality, and that was why it wasn't until the middle of the night, a few hours before sunrise, that she crept barefoot through the dust and gravel and stood as silent and still as a deer, listened to Samuel's breathing, watched his eyelids not so much as twitch before she took her boy's hand and led him to the springs and they did make love, too afraid to make even the slightest of sounds. The whole furtive liaison probably took less than five minutes, she would later reflect.

When she woke in the morning and went outside the cabin to greet Samuel and Loney, the old man would not meet her eyes, and without ever being rude, exactly, he ordered his nephew to saddle up their horses, and they rode off down the valley and away. She knew the boy was oblivious about his uncle's disappointment, just as she knew the old man's heart was broken, because all that he had asked was for her to wait, and she couldn't, and in her weakness, she'd showed him that she was less virtuous than he imagined, or, worse yet, like any other young person he'd ever met.

The next summer, Samuel did not meet them with horses. It was Loney who aided them up the mountains, and Loney who appeared newly sullen and detached, at once older and somehow more childlike. Samuel Sampson Wilkins had passed on, having suffered a heart attack that spring. Something had changed in the nephew, too, Gretchen felt, and after they made love the first time that June, he confessed to being engaged to a young woman from town, a young woman who was pregnant with his child.

Now she understood. Understood that Samuel had been telling her about the world, yes, but also about the fault in his nephew; telling her that his nephew was unworthy of her affection.

The world darkened for her that summer. She was less open with her parents, less patient, and at times their days together in the mountains felt almost tedious. Instead of feeling as if she were home in this great range of peaks, she felt suffocated by their refuge, the springs' very steam like a curtain drawn around her. She found no solace in her books either. For the first time in her life, she wanted the city, and told her parents so. Told them she would apply for college in New York City.

It was also during those years—her late teens and early twenties—when her mother confessed that she had cancer. At the time, the news was so monumental, so life-altering, that Gretchen could hardly digest what she'd been told. But the evidence was clear. Her mother was more frail-looking, brittle, almost, and she was easily exhausted. Still, this wouldn't keep her from their place in the mountains, even as her husband pleaded with her to stay in Iowa, where they were close to her doctors.

"I won't let this disease deprive me of what I love," she declared. "I wouldn't trade ten years in a hospital for a single summer out west." Then she'd pointed a finger at Gretchen. "You mark those words, young woman. Don't you dare mourn me before I'm gone. Don't pity me. That is *not* how I want to be remembered."

How she wanted to be remembered was riding horses and swimming in those hot springs, hiking the high ridgelines and peaks, and exploring caves and canyons. And as such, Gretchen had no gray memories of her mother dying. Only a bright slideshow of an adventurous childhood; her parents with the crystalline focus of those who know their time is short.

She had started college at Barnard, later transferring across Broadway to Columbia as soon as it went co-ed. She was invigorated by Manhattan, walking the streets arm in arm with girlfriends and feeling so much more worldly, so much more complicated. She could be sharply rude and flippant to people she would have been kind to even two years before, people she recognized as country folk, slow-talkers who, depending on how you saw it, were either admirably or tragically sincere. Oh, but those people reminded her of her Midwestern parents, and of that sad old rancher. The world was streaking right past them at the speed of light while they clung on to some antiquated code of conduct. How quaint, she thought. All the while trying to put the thought of her mother's cancer out of her mind.

It took her three years to weary of the city, the alienation she felt riding the subway, the masks people wore on their commutes to camouflage their emotions, their very humanity. Her apartment was robbed three times within the span of a month, the last incident while she was asleep; she woke in the night to the sound of the robber closing her bedroom door and slipping away like a wraith.

She never felt homesick for Iowa, knew in her heart she was not destined for Des Moines or Dubuque, Sioux City or Cedar Rapids. But Wyoming... The more time she spent in the metropolis, the more she hungered for nature, and entering her fourth year of college, she was ravenous. Desperate to encounter some form of wildlife other than a rat or squirrel, a pigeon or starling.

She began calling her parents once a week and writing them letters. She imagined graduating that spring and dedicating herself to her mother; taking her to doctor's appointments and cooking for her. She would lie in her narrow single bed, envisioning every line of topography on that Wyoming property. She could *feel* her horse below her, as they moved beside the river and up, up, up into the mountains. In that claustrophobic apartment, she imagined the smell of pine and sage, woodsmoke and horse sweat.

Then, a week before her graduation, not long after she'd spoken to her mother on the phone and promised her that she would in fact be spending the whole summer at the hot springs, her parents died in a car crash. An eighteen-wheeler lost control on one of the mountain roads near their cabin, killing them instantly.

Borrowing money from a friend, she flew to Salt Lake City, then hitchhiked east, arriving in Jackson and the mortician's office.

"I'm so sorry, darling," the undertaker said, running his hands through long white-yellow hair and then smoothing his mustache. "I don't know how to say this delicately, but the accident your parents had ... was ... horrific. We did the best we could to, ah, reassemble their bodies, but ..."

She watched as this old man turned his back to her, reached into his back pocket for a handkerchief, blew his nose before collecting himself, and turned back to her.

"I've been in this business for forty years," he said, "and I've never seen such a terrible accident. Truth be told, I haven't been able to sleep a whole lot since." He shook his head as if to dislodge the memories of the aftermath of the accident; dislodge and dispose of his nightmare visions.

"There was nothing to do but cremate them," he explained, his eyes red with sadness. "In good conscience, I could never allow you to see . . . I'm so sorry, darling."

Her grief in that moment was overwhelming. All the months and months of homesickness and worry, all the days she had denied her mother's diagnosis, the inevitability of her condition . . . and now, the great exhaustion of traveling cross-country on a shoestring, only to arrive at this funeral home with this sad old man, who offered such paltry consolation.

She collapsed into the thick carpeting of the funeral home, weeping uncontrollably. *Too late, too late, too late*, she thought. *I'm too late, and they are gone. Gone, gone, gone—forever gone.* The old man knelt and gathered her into his arms, brushing hair away from her tear-streaked face.

"Oh, darling," he said. "Oh, sweetheart."

They stayed that way for a long time, her body shuddering while she released her sorrow, and the mortician said not a word, simply humming "I'll Fly Away."

When she finally wiped the tears away from her face, and they stood up, his warm hands on her shoulders, he said, "You must be hungry."

She nodded, could not recall the last meal she'd eaten.

"Please," he offered, "let me buy you supper."

At a small café in downtown Jackson, the mortician sipped from a cup of black coffee and watched her circulate a spoon through a bowl of chicken noodle soup.

"Do you have siblings?" he asked.

She shook her head.

"Aunts and uncles?"

"I haven't had time to tell anyone."

"Shall I arrange a funeral?"

The spoon fell out of her hand, and she covered her eyes.

"I will handle it all," he said, as a waitress arrived at the table, handing her a fresh white napkin with which to wipe her face.

When she had suitably settled down, she took a long drink of water and peered out the window at the failing early-evening light.

"I have a favor to ask you," she said.

"Anything," he sighed.

She slept that night in a small roadside motel and in the morning, the undertaker arrived, loading her two bags lovingly into the trunk of his pristine black Cadillac. Stretching to buckle herself in the passenger seat, she peered over her shoulder into the expansive backseat, where she saw a cardboard box carrying her parents' urns and, on the floor, a long-handled shovel. They drove out to the property in silence, and upon reaching the cattle-gate that marked the entry to those hallowed acres, he placed the automobile into park.

"Your supplies ought to be here soon," he said quietly, then, "You're sure you don't need any help? I could ride up there with you? Make sure you get settled in."

"No," she said, "you've done enough already."

They sat in silence, watching the sun break over those eastern peaks, illuminating the sagebrush and grasses of the meadows before them. Minutes passed before she heard the sound of another vehicle pull in behind them.

Loney Wilkins slung out of the cab of a truck in cowboy boots, Wrangler blue jeans, a chambray shirt, and a barn jacket. His shoulders slumped, as if he expected to be scolded, but she was relieved to see him just the same.

"I called him up last night," the mortician said, "just like you wanted. I didn't realize you two were acquainted."

She slid out of the car, then opened the back door and collected the shovel and box of urns.

"I'm sorry about your parents," Loney said, removing his cowboy hat and looking at her dolefully.

"We ought to get moving," she replied. "It'll be dark soon."

"They were always very good to me, and my uncle," Loney said. "Christ, he woulda been all broke-up about this."

The mortician stood beside the open trunk, her two bags of clothing and toiletries sitting on the gravel.

"Well," he drawled, "you need anything, anything at all, you come find me."

They watched the mortician drive off, and then they went about the work of saddling their horses and packing supplies.

The ride up into the mountains was quiet, and at the hot springs, they carried her effects into the little cabin before building a small cook-fire outside.

"My wife sent along some chili and corn bread," Loney offered. "Why don't I get some heated up."

"I'm not hungry," she replied, thinking, *For your wife's cooking.*

"You have to eat something, Gretch. You look exhausted."

She turned on him. "I loved you," she said. "I was in love with you, and you ruined everything."

He was silent just then, and the canyon was very quiet, only the small popping sounds of their campfire.

"Don't you even have anything to say for yourself?" she demanded.

"I'm sorry," he said at last, though there was so much he might have added, so much he wanted to tell her, to share with her: the stress of being a young parent, the adoration his uncle Samuel had for her, the many nights he imagined another path for his life, moving out to New York City to find whatever work he might in the hopes of supporting her. . . . Now, standing on the other side of the flames from her, he saw the fire kindling her eyes with rage and sorrow.

"I don't want to see you again, after tomorrow," she declared. "Take your horses and get out of here, and don't come back."

"I'll help you bury them," he said. "Allow me that much. More than one person should know where they're buried. 'Sides, I can help you carry everything."

She remained quiet while she recognized the wisdom in his words. The last thing she wanted to do was desecrate their remains in an ill-conceived funeral.

"Fine," she allowed. "Tomorrow morning."

J ust after dawn, they rode over the river and up into an alpine meadow. Every hundred yards or so, she would turn in her saddle to look back toward the springs, and though he was curious, he did not ask any questions. They rode until the sun was nearly directly overhead in the sky, and then, after peering back to see the steam of the springs rising softly against the stone backdrop of the mountain , she dismounted into a small patch of wildflowers.

"Here," she declared. "We once had a picnic up here."

She dug the shovel into the rocky, unyielding soil, uprooting a few pasqueflowers and some hardy grass. He watched her from off to the side.

"This is a good place," he said. "They'll have a good view."

She was already sweating from the effort of digging, and after their long ride.

"It might have been a blessing," she said. "She'd been battling so long, and . . . I can't imagine my dad living without her."

She stopped digging and leaned on the shovel. "You want to help?" she asked.

He straightened right up, walking toward her with an arm reaching for that shovel.

"No," she said. "I'll dig the hole myself. But we're going to need two stones. Or at least two cairns. Can you start collecting rocks?"

He smiled, slid on a pair of calfskin gloves, and got to work.

Several hours later, with the sun sliding toward the mountains, they finished stacking the cairns that would mark her parents' graves. Both of them caked in dirt, streaked with sweat, and sunburned. She turned to glance toward the springs, then began searching their saddlebags, riffling through his effects.

"What are you looking for?" he asked.

"I'll know when I find it," she replied.

"Can I help?"

She relented. "Something reflective." She motioned back toward the hot springs. "I want to be able to see them."

They settled on two objects, one for each cairn: Loney's belt buckle for her father's grave and his small shaving mirror for her mother's. They aimed those objects in the rough direction of the hot springs.

"If we were gonna do this right," Loney said, "we'd have walkie-talkies, and you'd be back at the springs, telling me when I got the angle just right."

"This will have to do," she said. "I'll come back. Maybe stack some quartz on top of their cairns."

She dusted off her hands.

"Thank you, Loney," she said.

"I'm just so sorry for you," he replied. "I really am. I'm sorry about everything. About the way things turned out."

She peered down at her boots.

"Let's get back," she could only say simply.

They rode down into the valley, and she turned to glance over her shoulder just once, as if leaving behind all the happiness she had ever known.

For the next several years, she returned to the hot springs, backpacking alone all the way from the county highway up to their spare little cabin, where she sat in desolate mourning, struggling to untangle herself—who she was and what it was she valued. She was alone now, a sobering thought. She had relatives, yes, but they were scattered across the country, folks who came into her life only for a matter of days at a time, at family reunions or the rare holiday. No, the only thing she had left in the world was this land.

Every summer she rode up to those two cairns, decorating their graves with bouquets of wildflowers—monkshood, aster, windflower—and leaving some bright and shining object on their cairns, some memento from her parents' lives: a piece of her mother's jewelry, her father's straightedge razor, some rock they'd collected from a trip, a handful of coins, or a pair of glasses.

For the next twenty-odd years, she went there at least twice a year—in the summer, backpacking up to the old log cabin, and in winter, skiing the nearby mountains—until three years earlier, when she discovered the log cabin had burned down, likely the result of a lightning strike. And she determined then to build something that would endure, a house to enshrine the memories of her parents, of Samuel Wilkins, and all those wondrous days in these mountains. This was who she was. She felt confident of that now.

22

ole woke in the early morning to the sound of retching and stumbled toward the bathroom to find Bart wrapped around the toilet, a bedsheet draped over his shoulders, his skin sickly pale and shining with sweat.

"I'm really hurtin'," he groaned.

"What do I do?" Cole asked.

"Call Jerry. Get him down here."

"I don't know how this works, Bart," Cole said. "I've never used meth before. You can't just, you know, kick the stuff cold turkey?"

Bart began chuckling until the laughter became violent coughing, then more heaving.

Cole frowned in horror. "All right, I'll call Jerry."

An hour later the dealer knocked on the door. Brushing past Cole, he slipped into the suite like a specter, a black nylon gym bag slung behind him. Bart had cleaned himself up by then and was nonchalantly watching the third stringers of early-morning cable news, his hands folded across his flat stomach. Only his feet were in motion, tapping at the thick carpeting like he was keeping time to his own tortured heartbeat. Jerry sat down in an overstuffed chair beside him.

"Anyone gonna offer me a drink?" he groused.

Without asking what he preferred, Cole riffled through the mini-bar and poured a small bottle of Johnnie Walker Blue over a glassful of ice cubes, then passed it over to Jerry.

"You assholes *do* know I don't generally make house calls," Jerry said, tossing back the whisky and holding the glass out for Cole to refill. "I ain't a damn physician. And this hotel, by the way, fucking hates me. I had a client check in here, but, uh . . . well, you get the picture. Nineteen years old. Pretty young thing, too."

"We need two ounces," Bart said, even as his feet hopped around the carpet.

"Two ounces, huh," Jerry said. "So it's damn the torpedoes, then?"

He searched around through his bag and produced two plastic bags, tossing them at Bart.

"This is the best stuff I've seen in a while," he pronounced. "There's a lot of Mexican garbage floating around right now. Shipped across the border in gasoline tanks and then reconstituted. I never liked that idea. This shit is cooked right here in the U-S-of-A. Some fellas I know north of Vegas. They don't put none of that food coloring in it neither, or any of that other bullshit to dress it up. Pure as pure."

"We'll take it," Bart said, nodding at Cole, who passed him a roll of cash. "Two other things. I lost my pipe. You think you can get me another? Oh, and we need a little coke, too. Maybe a coupla eight balls."

"Anything else?" Jerry asked, rooting around in his pharmacopeia for the cocaine. "Want me to pick up some groceries? Get you boys some ice cream cones, maybe?"

"Fuck you, Jerry," Bart replied coldly, and then, perhaps to remind the older man of his still imposing physique and his formidable bar-fighting record. "Come January, I'm sure as shit gonna dry out and kick this stuff. We're almost there."

"I'm gonna level with you, Bart," Jerry said. "You don't look like you're gonna make it, bub. You look like a zombie, is what you look like. I told you that house was a bad, bad idea. But guess what?"

"What?" Bart said.

"Nobody comes to their dealer for advice, now, do they?"

With that, Jerry patted the armrests of the chair and stood, pushing the cash deep into the wells of his pockets. "Also, this may come as a surprise to you," he said, "but I don't have an inventory of fucking crank pipes on hand. Might take me a day. I'll bring it by tomorrow around lunch."

On his way out the door, Jerry reached into the mini fridge and grabbed a handful of bottles, cramming them into his gym bag as well.

"*Vaya con dios*, amigos," the dealer said before leaving.

Bart and Cole sat for some time in the half-dark of the suite, the television's volume on low, Cole peering at the translucent crystals of meth like they were shattered treasure.

"I've never tried meth," Cole said at last.

Bart shook his head wearily. "Yeah, well, I wouldn't if I was you."

"You think we'll finish on time?" Cole asked.

"I do," Bart said quietly.

"What's the weather look like for next week?" Cole asked.

Bart scanned through dozens of stations until he settled on the Weather Channel. They watched without exchanging a word. The five-day forecast looked mild for late November, but on that final, fifth day, the forecast showed a huge blizzard moving into the mountains, with nothing but heavy snow behind it for the following several days. The meteorologist smiled as he swept his arms across the weather map, pointing to locations expected to receive extremely high amounts of snow.

"Folks," he said with a grin, "after an exceedingly warm and dry early autumn, ski resorts around these parts will be rejoicing soon, because the real powder's on its way. If you're a skier, then you're about to be in heaven."

Bart shut off the TV. Now his feet were tapping, yes, but his fingers were clawing at his arms, too.

"Dude," Cole said, "*stop* it, man. Your poor arms. They're gonna be all scarred after this."

Bart snorted.

"What?" Cole asked.

"You," Bart said. "We been buddies a long time, Cole, but let's face it, you don't give a shit about my health. All you care about is this fucking house. And if we're near the finish line, it's because of me, okay? It's because I been out there, day and night, busting my hump. Yeah, I'm gonna have scars after this house. Show me *yours*, huh? Show me your fucking scars. What the hell have you given?"

"You need to eat something, brother. You're tweaking. We need to get you some food and some sleeping pills. Something to chill you out."

And then Bart started crying, rocking back and forth in his chair, like a little boy. "I can't stop moving," he said. "My body won't stop moving. Feels like I'm fuckin' shaking apart."

"What can I do, buddy?" Cole said. "Just tell me. Tell me how I can help you."

Bart stood and began pacing around the room. Then he all but leapt toward a lamp standing beside his bed and frantically removed its shade, began unscrewing the bulb.

"What the hell are you doing?" Cole asked, but he knew the answer as soon as the question had left his lips: Bart was looking for a way to make a pipe, any pipe he could, as he now explained, and there was a trick he'd once seen performed at a party where someone jury-rigged a lightbulb into a makeshift pipe by removing the metal base and filament and then placing meth into the remaining glass.

"Come on—*stop* it," Cole said, reaching for his friend's hands.

The bulb dropped, paper-thin glass exploding all across the parquet floors.

"Get the fuck away from me," Bart snarled. "I ain't your damn prisoner."

But Cole seized Bart in a bear hug and in that moment felt his friend's fragility, the muscle and brawn he'd melted away as the drug sizzled his every last synapse, his very veins on fire, this state of habdabs. He squeezed Bart all the tighter, and felt his friend fall apart again, relenting, wrapping his arms around Cole now and giving in to that tough love gripping him.

"I wish we hadn't done this," Bart said. "I mean, we were doing all right. Weren't we?"

"We're almost there," Cole whispered, rubbing Bart's back and shoulders. "You just—can't give into this. We're so close now."

"Yeah? 'Cept I'm afraid I might not make it," Bart said. "I'm so afraid of letting everyone down."

"You won't," Cole said gently. "You *can't*."

Cole gently pushed Bart away, but he stayed right there with him, stayed close to him. Close enough to let Bart know for sure he wasn't alone.

"I hate this fucking drug," Bart sighed roughly. "But I love it so much, too. I love it so damn bad."

Finally, Bart's body began to calm just a little.

"I'm going to order us some more food, okay?" Cole said. "And I might step out real quick and go back to my apartment. Get you some sleeping pills. You need to rest if we're gonna finish this house. I know I'm tired. We just need to close our eyes a little while."

Cole called down to the front desk, placed another extravagant order of food, and then, before leaving, collected all the drugs, stowing them in a garbage bag he held on to tightly. Finally, on the off-chance Bart was still holding, he went through the room and unscrewed the remaining lightbulbs, placing those in the bag, too. He also searched the suite for any lighters or matches but found none, and then, satisfied, prepared to leave.

"You're literally leaving me in the dark," Bart said.

"Yeah, well, I just don't want you to make a mistake. You just need to relax for a little while. You need to get your strength back."

"Well, man, kinda hard to make a mistake with no crystal to make a mistake with, you know?"

Cole stared at him. "I'll be right back," he said, his fingers on the doorknob. "You gonna be okay?"

Bart waved him away. "I'll make it," he said, one hand buried in a pocket where a single piece of glassy meth seemed to burn against his palm like a lethal promise. He'd snatched it while Cole was paying attention to Jerry.

Cole closed the door and walked slowly down the hallway toward the elevator, and then, just as he was about to press the down button, he turned and slowly padded back toward the room, pressing his ear against the door to listen. Another thought rose in his mind then, like a bubble of crude oil, bursting black and toxic, and he felt somewhat sick the moment the thought expanded, its conclusions and repercussions taking form: Were Bart to die, say, from an overdose, or even sheer exhaustion, it would stand to reason that Teddy and he might well be able to split his bonus, and certainly that much more of the builder's fee. He shook the thought away; just a moment of morbidity, a moment of human frailty and greed. Of *course* he didn't want his friend to die.

Hearing nothing inside the room except the steady babbling of the TV, Cole walked back down the hall, took the elevator to the lobby, hopped in his truck, and drove the several miles to his apartment, where he quickly snatched up some sleeping pills, some junk food, and toiletries: a couple of unused toothbrushes, mouthwash, floss, deodorant, soap. Then, considering Bart's rapidly deteriorating teeth, he grabbed some apple sauce, pudding cups, ramen noodles, and a container of gummy multivitamins.

Back inside the hotel suite, Bart paced the floor plan like a panther. He had, what? Ten, fifteen minutes at the most. Grinding up the crystal seemed risky; he didn't need Cole finding any residual powder, and he also didn't need his nose on fire, that feeling of a particularly hot crank burning your nasal tissues like you'd just snorted napalm.

Soon his pacing brought him into the bathroom. He closed and locked the door, avoided looking at his reflection in the mirror, not wanting to see what he already felt. Sitting down on the toilet, he thought of a guy he'd known years earlier who liked, above all, to *parachute* his crystal—to wrap the meth in toilet paper and then eat it. Bart broke his only piece in half and swaddled the crystal in the soft tissue to his right. Something about putting the little package in his mouth reminded him of communion. He closed his eyes and took it, ate it.

When Cole returned, Bart was sitting at the desk in the bedroom, a pad of paper before him, working out a list of their remaining tasks.

Cole clasped a hand on his friend's shoulder. "You actually seem a little better, buddy."

"Yeah," Bart said, feeling the magic course through his body again, like a supernatural power. "It's not easy being without the stuff, but I figure if I can just cut back a little, I'll be okay. Maybe come out on the other side, same as I ever was."

"Getting hungry?"

"I could eat a little."

And so they passed the balance of the night as they would have almost twenty years earlier, eating food and watching TV and occasionally talking about issues of some import, but mostly just bullshitting, content in each other's company. And yet, beneath the surface, always was the bleak anxiety that they were two men on a runaway train steaming toward a broken bridge, and below it, a canyon deep and dark enough to wreck their lives forever.

23

The falconer came down from Northern California grudgingly, and only, Gretchen suspected, because she was being paid a thousand dollars, plus lunch and mileage. She was a young woman, not that far removed from her college years, and Gretchen would have thought her thrilled to be in the city, thrilled to be the object of an older woman's respect, or at least curiosity, thrilled to be paid for her time, like a seasoned expert. But this young woman, Abby Saunders, just seemed on edge, suspicious, even.

"Here's your fee," Gretchen said at lunch, handing the young woman an unsealed envelope with two thousand dollars in it.

"This is too much," Abby said, running her fingers through the bills. "Lady, this is way too much. We talked about one thousand, plus mileage."

"No, keep it," Gretchen insisted. "I'm so grateful you're here."

The young woman held the envelope up and in front of her, as if it were a bribe she wanted out in the open, dirty money she made a point of not caring to touch. After several moments, she shrugged and slid the envelope into the backpack slung off her chair.

No purse, Gretchen thought. *Delightful.*

"Would you mind if we ordered?" Abby asked. "I haven't eaten anything today."

Gretchen studied the young woman's wide, sunburned face, the thick, brown braid of hair swept onto her left shoulder, the peculiar vest she wore, her worn blue jeans, and the hiking boots she'd proudly trekked into this upscale downtown dining room. Already, she had scarfed down two rolls laden with butter and gulped a Coca-Cola Classic, even as Gretchen sipped her obligatory pinot.

"By all means," Gretchen agreed. "Whatever you'd like."

Albert took their orders, hardly suppressing his upraised eyebrows and the curious expression on his old face. Gretchen returned his look with amusement. *And what must he be thinking now?* she wondered. That she had a mysterious daughter—a young woman who must look much more like her father, because where was the striking red hair or green eyes? Where was the thin build and sophisticated countenance? And, frankly, where was her father? Or . . . was this a young lover? No, no, no . . . That couldn't be right. And yet, one of the waiters had whispered to Albert that money had traded hands. . . .

Forty-five minutes later, after the young woman's dessert course of Bavarian chocolate cake, Gretchen sipped an espresso, watching Abby fidget in her seat and work at her teeth with a plastic pick she extracted from a pocket Swiss Army knife.

"The bird is with you?" Gretchen asked.

Abby nodded. "Yeah, in my car."

"And you parked where I told you to?"

Abby nodded again.

"Let's go, then," Gretchen said.

They stood on the top floor of the Century Building, where Abby set a three-foot-tall metal cage on the green metal of the HVAC unit. Abby donned a long, thick pair of leather gauntlets that stretched past her elbows before pulling a thick navy-blue blanket off the cage to reveal the falcon, blinking out at the bright, late-fall afternoon.

Gretchen stood off to the side in a long camel-hair coat, a turquoise-colored scarf wrapped around her neck and oversize sunglasses hiding her eyes. She felt incredibly vital today, and strong, and she was grateful for the young woman's presence when just about everything in her life had become more difficult: rising up and out of bed in the morning; toweling off after a shower; her commute to work.

Abby removed the falcon from its cage, settling the bird on her forearm and immediately rewarding it with a scrap of meat.

"What is that?" Gretchen asked.

"What? The meat? Roadkill. Saw an opossum last night on the side of the road near my house. No sense paying for meat when I can get it for free."

Then, almost as if she were throwing the bird into the sky, Abby loosed the falcon in a single, smooth movement, and they watched it circle the tower and the spires of other downtown skyscrapers.

"Say that I wanted to learn how to become a falconer," Gretchen said after a few moments. "How long would it take?"

Abby followed the bird's flight.

"Depends," she said. "Is it just gonna be a weekend thing? 'Cause this is a lifestyle for me, lady. In the summer, I'm working my falcons ten, twelve hours a day. Protecting orchards and vineyards from birds stealing those crops. But I been at this since I was twelve years old. My daddy was a pheasant hunter and liked to work a bird dog and a hawk on his hunts. So, falconry's my whole life, you know? I think if you're just doing it part time, I dunno, might take you years, if at all."

"Years?" Gretchen asked.

"Sure," Abby said. "This bird and I have a relationship. We trust each other. You can't just buy that or get it overnight."

The young woman suddenly wondered if she had not inadvertently offended Gretchen.

"I mean, no offense, lady," Abby went on. "You could totally do it. But it'd probably take you two years, minimal, working with a bird every night, and hard on the weekends. You'd also need a mentor, probably. Someone to show you the ropes. And it helps to live in the country, too. Let's face it, you need a place to keep the birds."

Gretchen glanced down at the hem of her coat, lifting on the swirling wind. She was crying, stoically; no sounds, no drama, just the overwhelming realization that there wouldn't be enough time for everything she wanted to do, all the things she still wanted to learn.

Just then the rooftop door swung open, and two young male attorneys spilled out onto the roof, vape pens in their gloved hands. They came toward the two women, squinting through the sunlight just as the falcon returned to Abby's arm and she commenced feeding him another scrap of roadkill.

"Whoa!" one of the men said. "Check it out. An eagle."

Abby rolled her eyes, while Gretchen coughed into her fist and wiped away the tears that Abby had not even seen, so engrossed was she with her charge.

"This is an American kestrel, actually," Abby explained. "A member of the falcon family."

"That's awesome," the taller of the two men said, and then, "I'm Ed, by the way. This is Cory. We're both in Litigation."

Abby shifted the bird to her left fist and shook their hands.

"You work here?" Cory asked the falconer. "Haven't seen you around before . . ."

Abby snorted, startling the bird, then offered it another small bit of the dead opossum. "No," she answered. Then, pointing at Gretchen, said, "*She* does."

Gretchen's coughing had not abated, and she held up a hand, half in greeting, half in pardon.

"That's so frickin' cool," Ed said as he drew on his vape pen, a vanilla-scented cloud drifting over his shoulder like a strange white cape. "I wonder if we could do something like that . . . Up here, on the roof. Build a little enclosure for the birds. Come up on lunches. Before and after work. Train 'em to go after pigeons." He slapped Cory on the meat of the man's biceps. "We could do that, right, bro?"

Gretchen's cough intensified then, to the point that she was bent over, her shoulders wracked, and the tears of disappointment she'd just shed comingled with tears of actual pain.

"Hey, assholes," Abby said, "why don't you ask your co-worker if she's okay?"

They both glanced at Gretchen, as if noticing her for the very first time.

"I'll get some water from the break room on twenty," Cory volunteered.

"About time," Abby muttered, as she and Ed approached Gretchen.

"You okay?" Abby asked.

Ed bent down on one knee, his right hand on Gretchen's left shoulder, peering into the older lady's face.

"I'm fine," Gretchen said finally, bringing herself up to full height.

But a moment later, she felt as if a wind had caught her up and sent her toppling over the tower, because she fell into Ed's startled arms.

She awoke in St. Francis Memorial in a room without a view. No vistas of the Pacific Ocean, the Golden Gate Bridge, or the skyline. With the IV drip in her thin arm, the incessant beeping and humming of medical devices, the pale, institutional look of her bed and room, and the only half-muffled sounds of traffic, jackhammers, and sirens outside her bleak little window, she wanted only to travel to Wyoming as quickly as possible.

"You're dying," Abby said, from a chair opposite the bed.

"Yes," Gretchen admitted, "I am."

"They thought I was your daughter, so . . . ," the young woman said, "they told me everything."

Gretchen pushed herself up in bed.

"I'm sorry," Abby offered.

"Not your fault," Gretchen wheezed.

"Okay, maybe I kind of pretended to be your daughter," Abby admitted.

Gretchen gave her a sidelong look of mild disapproval. "What did they say?"

"They want to keep you here. The doctors were saying at least a week. Maybe more."

Gretchen shook her head. "A week, a month. What does it matter?"

"Don't you have anyone?" Abby asked.

"No," Gretchen said at last. "Look, you've done more than enough. You don't have to stay here. I can take care of myself."

But Gretchen knew that this was not true. As her condition worsened, she would *not* be able to take care of herself. There would come a point when she would be too weak to prepare her own meals or to fetch her own medications; too weak, she feared, even to find the toilet in a timely manner, or to get herself dressed. She wondered if she could even summon up the necessary strength to visit her house out west, her last and final destination, as she'd so assiduously planned these last few years, ever since learning of her diagnosis, if not the cancer's swiftness.

"How old are you?" she asked Abby.

"Twenty-nine."

"Are you married?"

Abby crossed her arms. "No. Like that matters."

"Kids? A partner? Family?"

Abby shook her head. "Just the birds."

"Birds? Plural?"

"I have six. I only brought the one here."

"Oh."

Gretchen began violently coughing, tiny polka dots of blood coloring her palm and fingers. Abby stood from her chair hesitantly, uncertain what to do—go to Gretchen and help her, or stay where she was, out of respect for the older woman's privacy, for the strength she had remaining. She decided to pretend to stare out the window.

"Get me a Kleenex, would you?" Gretchen asked. "And a cup of water, please?"

Abby did as she was told, and then they were quiet for several minutes.

"What if I hired you?" Gretchen asked.

"For what?"

"To help me."

"I thought you didn't need help."

Gretchen stared at her.

Abby sat down again, her chin resting in her hands, her fingers obscuring her lips. "Lady, I'm not a nurse."

Gretchen looked out the window. It was two days before Thanksgiving. True Triangle had about a month in which to finish her house.

"I could hire you to teach me falconry." Gretchen sighed. "And you could stay on at my home, while I tie up some loose ends. Then, if I'm feeling weak or need something . . . you could act as my assistant. Not like skilled nursing, necessarily . . . just the occasional small task."

Abby was quiet. A monetary offer was imminent, and already she'd seen the depth of this woman's pocketbook: the two-thousand-dollar envelope, the lunch, her clothing, her law firm . . . She waited.

"I don't know . . . ," she demurred. "Why me, huh? I mean, why not a real nurse? Or even a doctor? Obviously you've got the dough."

Gretchen sat up in her bed, presenting her strongest self, as if she were about to commence a legal argument.

"Because you remind me of me," Gretchen said, "and because I don't *want* someone around who's going to try to simply keep me alive. I want someone who will listen to me and do what I ask."

Gretchen continued staring at the young woman.

"Please," she said calmly, without a hint of desperation. "I'll pay you a hundred thousand dollars for one year. And a ten-thousand-dollar sign-on bonus. I'll write the check this instant. Is my purse here?"

"Yeah," Abby said. "I grabbed it before the ambulance came."

Abby sat very still. Her "home," forty minutes south of Eugene, was a ramshackle house she rented for nine hundred dollars a month. She held over seventy thousand dollars in student loans, and she'd rattled down into the city in a 1991 Chevy Suburban with almost three hundred thousand miles on the odometer, four bald tires, and a windshield so fractured it was like looking out through a spider's web. Her diet consisted largely of ramen noodles she fancied up with peanut butter, green onions, eggs, and the bottle of Sriracha she'd stolen from a Thai restaurant. Her checking account balance at that very moment stood at just under forty dollars.

"Are you fucking with me?" she said at last.

Gretchen coughed into her fist and said, "Where's my purse? And my phone?"

Abby stood and collected Gretchen's purse from the closet, brought it to her. She watched Gretchen write the check and hand it to her, and then the money was in her hand, just like that, like it was the easiest thing in the world. She backpedaled away from the bed and sat down heavily in a chair beneath the hanging TV set to mute. Holding that check in both hands, she wanted to weep with joy. She looked up at Gretchen.

"How can you not have anyone?" she asked.

Gretchen shook her head. "I don't know," she said.

Though, in fact, she did; she did know. Knew she'd spent years and years of her life in that skyscraper she could now see from this very hospital window, the sun setting behind its tower, to leave it in dark silhouette. The years she'd spent behind that desk, working and working, billing and billing, pushing hard for partner and eventually earning that, and in a time when she was one of just a handful of female attorneys in that whole building. It was something. She often felt that at the very least, it was an example, a path forward for some other woman to follow; she had blazed the trail, and now it was for others to follow her. And yet—the years and years of her life she'd spent accumulating hundreds of thousands, then millions, and finally tens of millions of dollars, investing and reinvesting, left her really no time of her own even to spend it, except on those houses, on the architecture she researched in the minutes and hours while she lay in bed before sleep found her.

"Sit closer," Gretchen urged.

Abby dragged a chair closer to her new employer.

"There is something else I need to tell you," Gretchen said. "I'm building a house. Outside of Jackson, Wyoming. You and I will be traveling there on Christmas Eve. You need not worry about your ticket. I'll handle all of that. But it is important for you to know that for the next month, we'll be here, in California, putting my affairs in order. And then from Christmas on . . . we'll be up in the mountains. Is that agreeable to you?"

Abby had not even considered Christmas. And why would she have? She had no money to buy any presents, owned not a single Christmas tree ornament, and had no real interest in returning to her parents' home back in Grosse Pointe only to be judged and condescended to by both her father and mother, two exceedingly successful corporate executives who described her vocation as a falconer by simply telling their friends, "She's still somewhat in search of herself."

"Can we bring my birds?" Abby asked.

"Oh, I'm counting on it," Gretchen said.

Gretchen extended her hand to Abby, who took it, and then they shook, both of their grips very strong indeed.

24

Teddy woke well before dawn, padded softly down into the basement, and jumped rope for a half hour. Later, after a quick shower, he kissed Britney and each of his girls on the forehead before shutting the front door behind him.

For the past two days he'd worked dawn to dusk on the old lady's garage, assembling a crew of relatives, acquaintances, and friends from his congregation. No one expected or desired a thing from him; it was enough that Britney arrived at the little house at noon with slow cookers full of hot food and coolers full of soda. The fellowship on the worksite was beautiful, everyone slipping into a role, with more hands than were even needed, so that all the framing and roofing—two onerous jobs indeed—took hours instead of days.

For her part, Penny Abrams invited Britney into the house at the end of both days, and they sat at the old woman's kitchen table, looking through her shoe boxes full of photographs. The children knew more than a few kids in the neighborhood and were content to run from yard to yard, playing tag or watching videos on one another's phones. The town was relatively quiet, and the street had a decidedly blue-collar feeling, especially this time of year. Tourists, for the most part, did not spend their Thanksgivings in the mountains, preferring to stay back home in November before the big snow arrived, at which point they'd descend en masse for Christmas and New Year's, skiing the area mountains and traipsing through town with their rarely worn Stetsons, sheepskin jackets, and cowboy boots. But for the moment, the town belonged to the townies, and that felt just about right.

At four in the afternoon on the last day of the Triangle's self-imposed three-day break, Teddy finished Penny Abrams's garage, and after sending his crew home with a series of hearty hugs, jovial back-slaps, and Tupperware containers full of leftovers, he tasked his four daughters with surveying the site for any errant nails, scrap lumber, or other detritus. Finally, Teddy went inside the little house, where he found Britney and Penny at the sink washing dishes, the smell of pumpkin pies baking in the oven.

"May I get you a cup of coffee?" Penny asked.

Outside, the temperature hovered just above freezing, and it was true that Teddy's fingers were numb and chapped with cold. A mug of coffee inside the cove of his hand sounded incredibly soothing, the steam of it rising up into his raw face, the hot, black liquid warming him from the inside out.

"That sounds great, actually," he said. "Thank you."

Britney turned from the sink, raising her eyebrows. "Since when do you drink coffee?" she asked, smiling.

"My husband used to drink about two pots a day," Penny said breezily, setting a cup in front of Teddy and lightly touching his shoulder. "That was our ritual. I'd get the coffee on while he dressed, and then we'd sit here, talk about what the day held. I'd hand him his lunch and his Thermos, and then I'd even have a little time to read one of my novels before I got the kids ready for school."

"Right here, huh?" Teddy asked.

"You're sitting in his very chair," Penny said, returning to the sink. "That was his favorite coffee mug, actually, the one in your hands."

Teddy raised the mug to his lips, took a testing sip. It tasted atrocious, but he put on a brave face as he took another drink. He could like coffee, he decided; it was like jumping rope, really, or push-ups—a little punishment, yes, but also the reward of a jolt of energy. And while you were just *sitting* there, too. There was something very adult, very civilized, about this ritual, he decided, as he peered around the kitchen: the old wood floors, the wallpaper, the clock above the sink, the aged cabinets and antique-like pulls.

"Say, Mrs. Abrams," he ventured, "you have any cream and sugar?"

She turned and faced him, a look of pleased surprise lighting her face; he realized he'd asked the question with a note of confidence in his voice.

"Of course," she said, fetching a white porcelain bowl and spoon for him, and then a little can of sweetened condensed milk from the refrigerator. "Would you like a few cookies, sweetheart? My husband always used to like some cookies with his coffee."

"I think I would, yes," Teddy said, pouring about four tablespoons of sugar and a long syrupy flow of thickened milk into the mug until his coffee was a color closer to pale khaki.

"Anyhow, we're all finished, ma'am," he said. "I apologize for taking as long as we did, but, well . . . I sure appreciate your patience."

Penny dried her hands on a dish towel. "Let me get my checkbook," she said to Teddy. "I'm sure you and your family have your own matters to attend to."

"Ma'am, that's not necessary," Teddy said casually, sipping his coffee.

Britney shut off the tap and shot him a look over her shoulder.

"No, I'm serious," he insisted. "We took too long on this project, and I apologize about that. Please, let me do this for you."

He'd planned this for days and thought about it from dozens of different perspectives. He knew Britney would not understand, that she'd be pissed, and that he might well take some heat for it. He also knew his partners wouldn't agree with his decision, but that was a risk he was more than willing to take; he had done the work on his own time, using his own resources; it wouldn't have cost True Triangle a dime.

The thing was, they needed a *break*; they needed some good luck, and though Teddy didn't know precisely what karma was, he understood the merit of doing the occasional good turn, and that was how he thought of this project. And maybe, just maybe, if he could shine a little light now, the good Lord would look favorably on them as they hustled to finish Gretchen's house. He hoped that wasn't too selfish, thinking that way, but he truly felt that in his own life he'd almost always thought of others first: Britney certainly, their girls, and, of course, his business partners.

Penny Abrams stood in her kitchen, her mouth agape, her hands limply holding the dish towel. "I think it *is* necessary," she said.

He finished his coffee and stood, saying, "Please—it would be my pleasure, Mrs. Abrams. It truly would."

The coffee, the cool confidence, the words leaving his mouth, all of it seemed like new terrain to Teddy, like the actions of a man much more like Cole than himself. But he liked it. Liked this new Teddy. He felt light, free.

"Come on, babe," he said to Britney. "Let's get on home."

Penny Abrams followed them out of the house and into the cold, where she stood before her newly built garage. The girls were just across the street and quickly piled into the minivan. Just before Teddy shut the driver-side door, he walked back to the old woman.

"I do have one small favor to ask, though," Teddy said. "If you're ever thinking about selling this house, please give me a call, okay? I'll make you a more-than-fair offer, and we can cut the Realtors right out of the whole deal."

She presented her hand to him, and they shook.

"You can count on it," she said.

25

They stood outside the house, a slow, steady snow sifting down on their shoulders. Cole had stopped them there, on the driveway. Behind them, the bridge spanned the river, awaiting final touches. And above them, the three stories of horizontal glass and steel loomed like a latter-day house of the holy.

"We made that, fellas," he said. "Yeah, we might have inherited a little head start, but then again, we got handed more than a few shit-storms, too. And look what we've done so far."

By god, it was beautiful. From the outside, the structure looked complete. The driveway leading up to that tucked-in garage on the lower-left-hand corner of the house and alongside the entryway-mudroom, and to the right, a little workshop and storage. Up the central stairs to that wide first floor (or second floor; the men were always arguing how to count the garage level—was it a lower level or the first floor?) with its expansive living room, kitchen, fireplace, and dining room. Then up one more flight of stairs to the four bedrooms on the top floor, with commanding views of the river valley below, and all around them the teeth of the Tetons. An architectural gem, hidden here at the terminus of that godforsaken road. It was a house to die for.

Bill and José were finishing their work, painting a kind of gentle varnish over the fieldstones so that the whole hearth would shine under the floodlights directed at the mantle itself, a thick slab of old oak that Bill had been saving for just this kind of house. Walking up the lower staircase onto the first floor, Cole, Bart, and Teddy simply gaped at the fireplace for a moment. They'd seen it slowly come together, of course, but viewing it anew after three days away, three days of critical last touches, this was different; finally complete, the hearth was nothing less than magnificent, and each of them imagined living in that house, spending a winter there, and rising from their morning bed to build or restoke the fire, and how it would be impossible to be lonely there with a fire in that hearth, with a fire to cut wood for, a fire that needed a dry cache of wood, a fire that would need feeding and care. Each of them had the sensation of wanting nothing more than to feed that fire for the rest of their days.

"Well done," Cole said to Bill, near breathless in his admiration. "I've never seen anything like it. It truly is the heart of the building."

Bill wiped his hands on the thighs of his jeans, and in a rare moment of relaxation, he smiled shyly at Cole, Bart, and Teddy, shaking their hands, one by one.

"I gotta hand it to you boys," he said. "I didn't know if you could do it. But it looks like you might actually pull it off. Like you might just land this plane."

They all glanced around that first floor; there was no shortage of tasks still to be done, and the month of December would be busy, but it no longer seemed insurmountable. The towering peak they'd visited back in August was now perhaps within reach, just a few hundred feet above them, and all the time and effort that had brought them this far, even that now seemed like a memory from ages ago. An unspoken agreement had coalesced between the three friends with Bart back on the jobsite, even as Teddy tried his level best to monitor his friend's erratic behavior. They simply could not do without Bart's energy and brawn; he had thrown himself relentlessly at the house, like a berserker foot soldier gone battle-mad.

"We got plenty left to do," Cole confessed. "No doubt about it. Gotta install all the cabinetry, for one thing. And there's more trim to cut. A few more rooms to floor. Painting, of course. Light fixtures to hang. I don't know how we're going to get the appliances up here, and apparently Gretchen is going to have new furniture delivered any day, but . . . we're almost there."

"Well," Bill said, "I suppose we'll start cleaning up, then. Be out of your hair in the next coupla days, I reckon."

Cole, Bart, and Teddy huddled up around the kitchen's grand marble island, the steam rising up outside its great, wide windows. Three of the upstairs bedrooms still needed flooring and trim, and it was decided that Cole and Teddy would team up and bang out those tasks. Bart volunteered to cut trim in the garage.

After plodding down the stairs into the garage, Bart opened the garage doors and cranked some Led Zeppelin on the ancient paint-spattered boombox he'd owned long before the fancy new Sonos speakers. He stretched his back, tried to bend down to touch his toes, which he couldn't quite do, and so pulled his stiff arms across his chest instead. Just shy of forty, his body already felt as rusted and cranky as if he were seventy. He could feel the absence of meth in his system, as if his veins themselves had hardened, the blood within darkly coagulated, his brain sluggish and short-circuited. Nothing that couldn't be rectified with the right help, though. He walked down the driveway to the trailer, found his stash along with a new pipe, and then walked up the river and out of sight, where he could smoke in peace. It was only a matter of minutes before he returned to the site.

Only, now he felt like a ballet dancer, a matador, a goddamn iron butterfly! Now he bounced on the balls of his feet like a prizefighter, shadowboxing and weaving around the garage, as if waiting for his opponent to step through the ropes and enter the ring.

Ooooooohhhhhhh . . . They were actually going to finish this house—finish it. *Ooooooohhhhhhh* . . . That would mean he could walk into an airport, Denver's airport, perhaps, the one with that crazy white tent-roof, could stroll through security wearing a pair of Lucchese wild-caught gator cowboy boots, a real fresh pair of tight designer blue jeans, a white dress shirt, a dark blue blazer, and maybe a garnet bolo tie. He'd strut right into that airport like he'd flown a thousand times before, like he was the sort of man who'd bought his very own airplane. A nice pair of mirrored Ray-Bans, a sharp haircut, a spritz of cologne, and a wallet full of five thousand dollars cash. Nothing much to weigh him down but a leather tote bag with three pairs of underwear, two bathing trunks, a pair of flip-flops, a few T-shirts, and a toothbrush.

Bart smiled broadly as he hopped around the garage, sorting through the lengths of trim wood. But if he could have seen himself, he would have known that the smile on his face right then looked nothing like those dream-images playing inside his own mind, the ones in which he looked like a 1980s Robert De Niro, all thick long hair, suntanned skin, and smoldering charisma. No, Bart's teeth were quickly dissolving, while his skin had grayed and become dotted with septic sores. No longer the muscular man he'd started this project as back in August, he was reduced now to mere sinew and bone, a shade in clothes billowing off his frame, his strangely pronounced cheek-bones looking vulnerable and too large for his face. But he couldn't see that, and now, now he was *flying* around, marking a ten-foot piece of trim for a future cut even as his mind was elsewhere, half-focused on slinging himself into a first-class seat, and the cool press of a glass whisky tumbler nestled in his palm, and then what he imagined as the magical moment of *wheels up*, when speed and gravity would press him back into his oversize leather chair and for an instant or two, he'd feel like an astronaut, and he would have to play things cool, like he'd done this so many times before it was actually boring.

He could hardly even imagine it. Being so wealthy that flying in an airplane was *nothing*—like driving to work. And then he imagined Panama, focused on those beaches he'd fantasized about for so, so long. He saw his legs stretched out ahead of him on some chaise and iguanas racing along the sand. Those sunglasses would come in handy, too, because he hoped to find a woman to flirt with, a woman he could ask out to dinner. *Wait*—he'd need another jacket—a linen one. Yes, and perhaps a pink dress shirt. And she would wear a beautiful dress, a floral-print dress, and she would smell like wet orchids, too, and they'd sit at a small table, the sound of the surf pounding, and light music wafting through the thick, tropical air, and he'd reach for her hand, and she'd reach for his, and she would not see him as the working stiff he was now but as a mysterious wayfaring stranger, a man of means and sophistication. Would he be smart enough for her? he wondered. Maybe he ought to read a book or two. . . . No! No, no, no, no, no. He was plenty sophisticated. He'd helped build this house, hadn't he? He was a business owner, an *entrepreneur*. Soon, he would have over a hundred and fifty thousand dollars in his bank account, and perhaps after True Triangle sorted through their costs, a lot more than that—*hundreds of thousands of dollars*.

Ooooooohhhhhhh but did Bart feel energized—and not just energized, but *electrified*, amplified, felt like his brain was *a-sizzle*, and with the cold and the swirling snow and Led Zeppelin playing "When the Levee Breaks" . . . he laid the piece of wood on the table, grooving to the bassline, and started the saw spinning.

Maybe it was because of John Bonham's crashing, sludgy tsunami of percussion, or Robert Plant's wailing freight-train harmonica, or maybe it was just because of the meth blistering every inch of Bart's body by then, but he did not even hear Bill pounding down the stairs into the garage, an eight-foot ladder under his arm. Because if Bart had heard Bill, he no doubt would have shut off the saw and offered to help the hirsute mason. At the very least, he would have moved the small stack of boards that he had dragged over near the saw and sloppily left lengthwise across the garage floor.

New table saws often come equipped with sensors that identified the difference between wood and flesh, instantly terminating the saw's spin and preventing horrendous accidents. But the decades-old table saw owned by True Triangle had been given to the three business owners by Cole's father, and they were overjoyed to receive the saw as a tried-and-true heirloom gift not only because it saved them money but also because it seemed like the kind of tool, endowed with decades of goodwill and craftsmanship, that might just bring them some good luck; Cole's father had been an accomplished woodworker himself, after all, and—who knew?—with his saw in their possession, perhaps some of that expertise would rub off, like osmosis. They never thought for a second about its dearth of safety features.

Had Bill actually stood on those stairs for some length of time, frustratingly calling out, in fact, shouting at Bart to shut off the saw and move the boards? No one could say for sure, after it was all over. But one thing was for sure: A doggedly proud man, he wouldn't have sought help from anyone but his old friend José, who, at that moment, was painting a layer of clear veneer on a corner of the fireplace and certainly would not have been able to hear Bill over the screaming Led Zeppelin. So maybe Bill slipped on that pile of lumber, or maybe Bill accidentally brushed Bart with the ladder . . . Or perhaps it was just Bart himself—Bart who was startled, Bart who wasn't paying goddamn attention. . . .

Indisputable, though, was the fact that *something* caused Bart to lose both his focus and his balance, prompting him to arrest his fall into the sawblade by bracing for impact with his left hand. And, because of Bart's abrupt forward momentum, the saw easily sliced off all his fingers on that left hand, thumb included, spraying a curtain of blood across the garage's ceiling, floor, and staircase wall.

Bart did not respond with shock. Did not stand still like a victim, no—filled with meth-fueled rage and paranoia, he saw Bill standing before him, looking horrified, maybe even guilty, and for the first time since they'd met him, vulnerable, and in all of Bart's rage, all that miscalculated rage, he reached with his undamaged hand for a framing hammer and swung at Bill, swung at his head—not once, but two, then three times . . . *This goddamn mason was not just Gretchen's spy—he was an assassin, a fucking stone-cold KILLER.*

Bart's wretched screams certainly *did* carry up the stairs, and all through that empty house; just as they carried out through the snowy canyon itself, startling the ravens sitting at the apex of an old cottonwood tree and sending them flying through the storm like messengers of doom.

At that moment, Cole, Teddy, and José all dropped their work and thundered down the stairs to discover a phantasmagoria of blood. In his right hand, Bart still held that huge framing hammer, and just inside the garage, in a crumpled heap over the fallen ladder, lay Bill, his head stove-in, a growing puddle of blood seeping out into the snow. Certain details burned into their memories in that moment: tufts of Bill's dark hair on the hammer, the shrieking, whining music still playing for several seconds until Cole finally bent down to shut it off, Bart's chest heaving so violently it seemed his heart might explode, and of course the blood, all that blood still pumping out of his mangled hand onto the floor even as Bill's body convulsed where it lay, bleeding out fast. And the snow, falling down so heavily and white, so very beautiful over it all.

Taking all of this horror in then, José ran off, screaming, into the snow.

"Get a fucking tourniquet on that arm!" Cole yelled at Teddy. "And get him down to the truck!" Cole raced off after José, pleading for the man to stop.

With Bart now collapsed onto the concrete floor, Teddy glanced around the garage and spotted a bungee cord.

"Oh my god, oh my god, oh my god," he said, holding his friend's arm, so sticky and wet with blood. "Oh my god, Bart. Hold on, okay? Just hold on, buddy."

Teddy tied the cord around Bart's elbow until the lower half of his arm turned purple, then pulled his injured friend off the floor and dragged him out into the cold.

"Brother, you gotta keep that arm up," Teddy said, wanting very much to vomit but aware that Bart might die if they didn't get him to the hospital and fast.

"That fucker tried to kill me," Bart said hoarsely. His eyelids closed, and he slumped into the snow. "He just pushed me . . . pushed me right into the damn saw."

Teddy stood helplessly, watching as Cole raced downhill toward José, who, still screaming, turned backward to gauge his pursuer's distance and tripped, falling just shy of the bridge. Teddy glanced down at Bart; there was no time to get him to the hospital. At least not a proper one. The little hospital in town wasn't equipped for this kind of carnage and would fly him immediately to the closest metropolitan hospital they could, likely Denver or Salt Lake.

He reached for his phone: no signal. And so, summoning something like superhero strength and imagining his heroes in this position, he squatted down beside Bart, draped his friend over his back, and then, in one jerk, surged upwards, his thighs trembling, the blood vessels in his neck and face popping. He let out a yell and started downhill with Bart motionless on his back, morbidly thankful his friend had recently lost so much weight. Within several seconds, he was charging past Cole and José, to his pickup truck, into which he threw Bart before blasting back down the mountain, cell phone in his hand, frantically searching for a signal that he knew would not appear until he got down to the entrance to Gretchen's property and the paved highway just beyond it.

Beside the bridge, Cole had leapt on top of José and was struggling with the man, urging him to calm down, *calm down*—that it was all just a terrible accident.

"*Cálmate! Cálmate!*" he kept frantically repeating, trying to pin down the younger man. "It was an accident! Okay? Please!"

This was before José rolled over, a fist-size rock in his hands, which he now swung at Cole. The rock hit Cole's shoulder with an audible popping sound. No longer trying to subdue the man beneath him, Cole intuited in a rush of animal clarity that he was in a real fight, a fight for his own life.

They rolled across the graveled ground, struggling to gain position, tearing at each other's shirts, occasionally landing a poorly placed punch that skimmed off the other man's chin, ear, or forehead. But neither one finding a sure advantage, they rolled down the slope of the riverbank and landed in the water, gasping, out of breath. There was a reason most fights took only a matter of seconds, and at most, a few minutes; the most harrowing competition, it was also the most exhausting, with the difference between first prize and runner-up . . . everything. Now the two men stood in knee-deep freezing water, snow falling all around them.

"*No me mates,*" José said, shaking his head. "*No me mates.*"

"I don't want to kill you, bud," Cole said, "but I ain't lettin' you go like this. Look, we ain't bad men."

"*Déjame ir, por favor,*" José said, backing slowly away from Cole and downriver.

This time, Cole did not reply, and José knew to run, though it was already too late. Cole caught the man and shoved him down into the water, then stood over his body and, with one knee on his back, circled his hands around José's neck, until the man stopped struggling—a gruesome process that seemed to take forever—until José's body finally relaxed. As Cole stood up from this, José's body washed a few feet downstream before his clothing caught on a fallen cottonwood, where he came to a stop, the current rippling around his prone form.

Cole stood there, panting, the river running around his calves, snow steadily falling. He was freezing, he realized, and if he didn't leave the river now, he would rapidly become hypothermic. Glancing once more at José's body, he decided that the corpse wasn't going anywhere, and so he picked his way back up the slope of the riverbank and, shivering uncontrollably, pulled off his torn clothing and slipped down into the hot springs to recover.

What a profoundly incongruous swirl of emotions overtook him then. At the very basest, utter relief and animal comfort in the hot water all around him. He ducked his head under the surface and rubbed at his face. Then, rising back up, he glanced toward Gretchen's house. Through the open garage door, Cole could see the ladder all akimbo and a puddle of blood slowly draining downhill.

He looked back toward the river. He had killed a man. Christ, did that make him a *killer*?

Cole leaned toward the lip of the pool and vomited out into the inch or so of snow that had collected. Then he dipped his head back into the pool and washed off his mouth and face, focused on steadying his breathing. Surely, this was all just a very vivid nightmare, the by-product of sleeplessness and stress; surely, this was in no way . . . real.

Then, from far off, he heard the *whup-whup-whup* of a helicopter's blades.

The second Teddy's phone had shown a signal, still on Gretchen's dirt road, he dialed 911, explaining that his friend had suffered a gruesome injury and was in desperate need of immediate medical attention.

"He's lost a lot of blood," Teddy said, peering over at Bart, whose slumped head bounced off the passenger-side window with every pothole, dip, and rise in the road. "And he passed out." Bart's skin was a ghostly white, and despite the tourniquet, his mangled hand slowly dripped blood down onto the floor of Teddy's truck. "There might not be time for an ambulance."

The helicopter landed on the state highway, right at the mouth of Gretchen's road. The paramedics grimly loaded and secured Bart after peppering Teddy with the requisite questions as to how the accident happened, how long he'd been bleeding, and whether Bart had any family.

"Not much room in the copter," a paramedic explained, "but you can ride along if you want. We'll be takin' him over to Salt Lake."

"I'm coming," Teddy said, wedging himself into the helicopter.

"Hey, wait! You got the fingers?" one of the paramedics asked.

Not immediately understanding the question, Teddy blinked big and slow.

"Your friend's fingers? You got 'em? They close by?"

The helicopter's rotors created a furious blur of the snow.

Teddy thought back to the scene at Gretchen's house: the horrific spray of Bart's blood, Bill's dead body, and José racing toward the river with Cole in close pursuit. He hadn't even considered Bart's fingers; couldn't remember seeing the digits on the garage floor amid the sawdust and offcuts. The crushing reality of what had just happened suddenly hit him like an avalanche.

Teddy shook his head. "No," was all he could manage.

With an abrupt shudder, the helicopter pulled up into the air, awkward at first, and then more assured—away from Teddy's truck, from Gretchen's road, over the smallish mountains of the immediate area, and on toward Salt Lake City. Midway through the flight, one of the paramedics noticed that Teddy himself appeared to be in shock and draped an emergency blanket over his shoulders, passing him a bottle of water and a sedative.

26

There was no explanation for what had happened that could plausibly exonerate them. Bill's skull had been crushed from behind, and José had been killed either by strangling or drowning or both. Bill's truck was sitting damningly on the driveway turnaround as dusk crept over the mountain. Cole sat in the trailer, trying to puzzle out how any of this could be handled. He needed to somehow move the bodies, though he could not at first bring himself to think of doing so as *disposing* of them. But the more he turned their situation over and over in his mind, the clearer it became that, yes, in fact, that was exactly what he needed to do. He needed to dispose of both men, and Bill's truck, too. And he needed to do this quickly, before any other subcontractor returned to the site. He gave himself until dawn.

The idea of burying them on or near the building site seemed foolish, obviously pointing to True Triangle. He had considered digging a deep, deep hole, covering the bodies with lime (*wasn't that supposed to rush decomposition?*), and then burying them, even going to the trouble of paving over the spot, perhaps with concrete, calling it an additional parking spot or some such. But that wouldn't change the fact that two men had disappeared from this very spot, and the last people to see them were Cole, Bart, and Teddy. . . . If the police came, they'd spread out everywhere on the premises, and a freshly paved patch of earth would seem more than a little suspicious. To say nothing of the fact that Gretchen had a very specific vision for this place, with every foot of the immediate property accounted for. The added "parking pad" would draw not only her curiosity but also her ire.

He thought about bringing the bodies up into the mountains, thought about disassembling the men, *butchering* them, and either burying the pieces in some remote grave or leaving their broken bodies to the buzzards, mountain lions, and bears. But there was sure to be an investigation, and any detective glancing from the driveway up the mountains only to spy dozens of vultures wheeling over a spot less than a mile away . . .

The truth was, Cole was no criminal, and this was all simply beyond him; he could think of no way out. No matter how long he wrestled with various solutions, they came up short, every one of them.

And so, in the end, he had but one very unsavory choice.

First, he changed into his worst clothing, garments that could be burned without a second thought. Next, he dragged Bill's heavy, heavy body into the woods about a hundred yards from the house. It was taxing work, and Cole was sweating heavily within minutes. The body kept catching on low-hanging branches and cumbersome rocks. Once Cole was satisfied that the body was no longer visible from the house, he noticed that the corpse had created a trail as it was dragged. He snapped a branch off a pine tree and walking backward along this trail, did his best to obscure the gruesome passage before walking to the river with a flashlight and peering down at José. He would never be able to carry the dead man out of the water and up that steep bank. Cole glanced at his truck. Perhaps he could tie a rope around José and, with the aid of the truck, tow the man not only up and out of the river but all the way over to Bill's body. Then both men would be out of sight, at least for a little while. The cold would be helpful, he imagined; for there would be no smell, and maybe the snow would cover them.

He slid down the riverbank in the dark, snow still landing in his hair, on his shoulders. In the river, he secured a thick towrope under José's arms and around his back, then wrestled the man's body so his head was positioned toward the truck. The cold water was crippling. He looked again at the body and decided he did not want to spend his night in this river, retying knots and grappling with a corpse. It began to sink in again, the horror of what he'd done, of what he was doing right now, José's lifeless head lolling this way and that, so that Cole noticed certain details he hadn't before: an earring hole, a tattoo of the Virgin Mary just above his heart, and those sad, generic, brutalized sneakers. Cole would disappear this man, and if he had any family, they'd never see him again; never know where he'd gone, how he'd spent his last days, or even if he was still alive somewhere and had simply chosen some new and unimaginable course. Cole realized he knew nothing about the man at all, and yet, there he was, struggling to tie a sort of harness around his midsection, weaving the rope through his lean legs and around his narrow waist.

Once the harness was secure, Cole ran back to the truck and sat in the cab, the heater blasting so as to thaw out his frozen feet and legs. Then he put the truck in reverse and began to steadily pull away from the river until he could feel the towline growing taut. He kept a steady pressure, slowly, slowly pulling, until in one ghastly moment, he saw José's head bob over the top of the bank in the cones of the headlights, through the slowly falling snow, and then his two arms, like a zombie miserably crawling out of his watery grave.

But the knots held. Cole almost smiled with relief. An hour before midnight, he untied the ropes, dragged José beside Bill, and then snapped off several pine boughs and stacked them on the bodies in a crude sort of camouflage. Then he rushed back to the house to collect two large plastic buckets and poured water from the hot springs over the garage floor where Bill had fallen, washing away the coagulated blood. And now he crept slowly around, the flashlight directed toward the snowy ground just outside the garage door, desperately searching for the hammer. It wasn't long before he found it, and he was just about to grab it before he realized he needed a pair of work gloves. Locating those easily enough, he picked up the hammer, placing it in a thick black plastic bag.

Now he stood back, away from the scene of all that carnage. One of the garage doors was still open, and there was blood spattered all over the garage walls, ceiling, and floor. As horrific as the garage looked, *that* at least could be explained away. After all, Bart had suffered a horrendous but hardly unprecedented accident. They could even admit to any inquiring investigators that indeed Bart, the poor soul, had begun using meth as a means for working those hundreds of dogged hours on the house. All of that was true.

But the cleanup would cost them a day, for sure, and they'd have to do the work themselves. Between the rapidly accumulating snow and this house's known track record for bad luck, Cole could not plan on finding a cleaning crew to erase this horror and, even if he could, the cost. . . .

So, the final stages of construction would fall entirely on Cole and Teddy. As for Bart, his career was likely finished. Had they been three men climbing a mountain, one of their team would have just fallen into a chasm, placing the summit once more in doubt.

Cole would need to drive Bill's truck up to the house. He'd need to collect all the masonry tools and the ladder and stow all that in the bed of Bill's Ford. He collected another two pails of water and carefully rinsed any blood off the ladder. Then he walked back to where Bill and José rested, their limbs contorted unnaturally but their eyes at least closed and their heads arched back as if in deep slumber. Cole fumbled through Bill's pockets and collected his wallet and keys, then bent down and did likewise with José.

He drove the stonemason's truck up to the house, those old

headlights shining like two dirty, golden lanterns. He stowed the ladder and all their tools in the back and then drove to the turnaround across the river, taking care to park out of the way—not hidden, exactly—but certainly under the overhanging branches of a big pine, the passenger-side wheels off the asphalt entirely.

It was after midnight. Cole's adrenaline jolted through him like electricity. Stripping off his clothes, he made a small pile where they normally burned scraps and offcuts. He doused the clothing with a bottle of lighter fluid from their barbecue back in October, when everything felt so different, when it seemed like they would easily make their deadline, all of them together, happy, and healthy, their business fortified and now endorsed by this elegant, high-net-worth customer. True Triangle had been on its way to such great good things.

Now Cole stood naked in front of the little fire, steam drifting off his pale body even as the snow kept falling down.

There was someone he needed to call.

Jerry met him at the Rose. The bar was almost empty, and Cole sat in a booth, half-hidden by after-midnight shadows, a chandelier glowing against the bar's close darkness. Jerry ordered a drink from the rather blasé waitress and slumped against the Naugahyde.

"I gotta tell ya, I'm gettin' a little tired of your late-night phone calls," Jerry grumbled. "And 'sides, where's Bart? You ain't a customer of mine."

Even in the gloom, Cole could see something crystallize in the dealer's widening eyes. "Well, Jerry," Cole began, "see, that's sort of why I called you."

Jerry stood abruptly and seemed ready to split, but he leaned down toward Cole, pointing a trembling finger in the younger man's face.

"I ain't in *any* way responsible for him," Jerry hissed. "You hear me? That's the fuckin' social contract between dealer and customer! I mean, what the fuck—"

Just then the waitress arrived at the booth with Jerry's drink, what looked to be a screwdriver.

"Gonna be last call soon," the bartender said. "Can I get you fellas anything else?"

The two men glanced at each other, shaking their heads, allowing the waitress to drift away.

"Sit down," Cole said evenly.

"Fuck you," Jerry replied as he stood there defiantly, sipping his drink.

"Sit down," Cole repeated, "or I will most definitely rat you the fuck out."

Jerry hesitated a moment, then slid back into the booth and listened intently as Cole told him the entire story, leaving nothing out.

"I need help," Cole said. "*Bart* needs your help."

"Why should I?" Jerry said.

Cole leaned forward. "Because you're old, Jerry. And you don't want to go to jail. We get caught for this thing—guess what?—I'll have nothing to lose. No wife, no kids. So, I'm asking you to help us out here, okay? Let's just help each other out."

Jerry sat back, sipped his drink.

The bartender flashed the lights. "You don't have to go home," he sang out, "but you can't stay here."

"I want a hundred grand," Jerry said. "That's what I'll need, if you want my help."

Cole shook his head.

"Well, then," Jerry said, rising from the table, "as the Mexicans say, *Buenos suerte, pendejo.*" He pounded the last of his drink and started out of the bar.

Cole sucked in a tortured breath, threw some money down on the table, and rushed out into the night after the dealer. "Fifty!" he yelled.

The door to Jerry's Charger was open, and he stood there, dragging on a cigarette in the wan light of the bar's front windows as he exhaled a great plume of smoke, flicked the butt out into the snow, and collapsed the distance between them.

"Look, I can have your whole mess cleaned up before lunch," he whispered. "But it's gonna cost you a hundred, bub. And you can try to rat me out, by the way, but I hope you got at least a million to pay those hotshot attorneys you're gonna need."

"Seventy-five," Cole spat.

"Tell you what," Jerry said with a grin, extending his hand, "because I *like* you, I'll do it for a hundred. Final offer."

Cole could practically feel his heart fall out of his chest and plunk down in the dirty snow amid the cigarette butts, plugs of discarded chew, and spent matchbooks. He could see it down there, beating slowly and sadly, new, pure snow melting on the defeated organ. *Oh, my lord*, he thought, *what have we done?*

He shook Jerry's hand.

"Don't take it so hard." Jerry smiled darkly. "Just think of it as fifty per body."

The dealer reached into his car, retrieving something from the passenger seat, and then, taking Cole by the arm, pushed him back toward his truck.

"We've got to hurry now," Jerry said. "We can leave my car right here. So now, how 'bout you take me to your little cemetery."

About forty minutes later they stood over the bodies of Bill and José, which were now entirely covered in snow. They might have been a load of firewood under a white tarpaulin.

"You got any big trash bags?" Jerry asked. "Like, heavy-duty ones? No cheap-ass generic bags—you know, the real deal."

Cole nodded.

"How about a handsaw? And don't give me a dull blade either; it's gotta be sharp."

Cole nodded again.

"Good, go get all that shit. The more you help me with this, the sooner we'll be done with the whole thing."

It took about an hour for them to finish their grisly work and load the bags into the back of Bill's truck. Jerry hastily threw some scrap lumber and two spare tires onto the bodies.

"Now what?" Cole asked. "We only have a few hours."

"They have cell phones?" Jerry asked.

"Yeah," Cole asked, "I found 'em in the house."

"Good," Jerry said, "you gotta smash them all to pieces. Then, be sure you put 'em in a bag with the bodies. We'll destroy them, too."

"Understood," Cole said.

"We're fine," Jerry said. He yawned into his fist. "Now here's the thing: You drive the stiff's truck. We'll dispose of the bodies, then get my car. When we get into town, I'm gonna need you to stop at a café so we can get a cup of coffee and some breakfast. I ain't used to this graveyard-shift bullshit."

He slapped Cole's arm. "Get it?"

At the highway, Jerry asked Cole to put Bill's truck into park, and the dealer made a call, speaking calmly and cryptically into his cell phone.

"Hey, Birdie," Jerry said, "sorry about the hour. Listen, remember that problem you helped me out with a few years ago?" He lit a cigarette. "Yeah, well, I got two more problems I could use you for."

Cole stared at Jerry's face through the darkness, hoping that no traffic would pass on the highway.

"I'll do my best to get you the cash this morning, yep, you bet. And listen, sure do appreciate the help, Birdie." He hung up, blew out a jet of smoke.

"What are you gonna do with the truck?" Cole asked.

"My parents left me a little land, outside town about fifty miles. We'll remove the plates, scrape off the VIN, and just park her in the barn. Padlock the sumbitch up. My guess is that I'll croak before you do, and at that point, you may have a concern." He drew on his cigarette. "At that point, you could do a coupla things: Try torching it, or you could move it again. But who knows? We might not even have a planet by then. . . . And one other thing, Cole. I'm gonna need ten grand up front to get those bodies disappeared."

"Jerry," Cole said. "I don't just *have* ten grand on me."

"Yeah, so, when your bank opens this morning," Jerry continued, unfazed, "I'm gonna need you to make a rather large withdrawal. You probably can't get your hands on all hundred grand. But the ten'll do for now. After that, I can put you on a payment plan until that big bonus of yours lands. Think about it like layaway. If that ain't amenable to you, I can start spilling Hefty trash bags in front of the cop shop. Now, let's get going. There's a little café on the other side of town. You can buy us breakfast."

"You have to be fucking kidding me," Cole moaned.

They drove into town, the black plastic bags in the bed of the truck rustling with the wind. At the café, they were clearly the first two customers, and the waitress seemed to know Jerry, slapping him playfully on the arm before leading them to a booth in the corner of the restaurant surrounded by wide windows offering up a commanding view of the coming day. Cole sat opposite Jerry, watching the dealer eat his breakfast, a huge platter of pancakes, bacon, sausage, two eggs over easy, and sliced orange alongside a cup of coffee and a tall glass of cranberry juice.

"I like ketchup on my eggs," Jerry offered. "Some people think that's crude. But the lycopene's good for my prostate. I think it's my prostate. The juice, too, though that's probably mostly sugar. Thing is, just about everything worth eatin'll kill you."

"I can't believe we're doing this," Cole whispered, leaning across the table. "I mean, Christ, Jerry—they're right out there." He pointed to the parking lot.

Jerry waved a piece of bacon in the air, dismissing him. "They ain't going anywhere."

Cole put his head in his hands. He was so tired right then, with no idea whether Bart was dead or alive, or Teddy's whereabouts, for that matter. He didn't know what day it was or where his phone was—probably in Gretchen's house, he guessed. He sat back in the booth and breathed deeply, the thick, embedded smells of the café almost too much for him. He felt at once nauseated and claustrophobic, his own life closing in around him like a black velvet hood cinched about the neck.

"You boys got greedy, didn't ya?" Jerry said. "I told your buddy Bart, right from the start. Not with all the meth in the fucking world could you build that house. It was a farce, Cole—a complete and utter boondoggle. She used you boys right up."

"We'll complete the house," Cole said sternly. "We *have* to."

"Why?" Jerry asked. "I bet you've made your money off builder's fees, haven't you? Enough already." He forked a great serving of pancake into his mouth, maple syrup dripping onto his chin. "No one's gonna blame you, Cole. One of your partners lost his goddamn *fingers,* all right? Quit, regroup. Hell, people might respect you more for telling this lady to *fuck off.*"

Oh, but how Cole wished he could quit. Wished he could call Gretchen and tell her in the most sincere and sorrowful voice that they simply could not bring it all home. But that was just it, really: One of the very things drawing him forward was the thought of Gretchen's face as they walked her around the house, as they watched her reactions, as she presented them with their checks. And even more than that: to complete something grand, this palace in the mountains, amid the steam of those hot springs; this house of grandeur, so well imagined in its blueprints, so timeless in its materials. And now, *their* blood and sweat and tears embedded in its very drywall and studs.

He thought of Bart's fingers, lying somewhere on the garage floor. If they didn't press forward, what would all of it have been for? And how could they let another builder, some group of strangers, move in, with just a few days to go now, and finish their work for them? It would be like another man up and marrying your wife, raising your child as his own, while you slumped through life, receiving their beautiful Christmas cards in the mail and visiting on weekends, some schlub, some secondhand parent. No. They had to finish this. Especially now, with Jerry taking *a hundred thousand* of Cole's dollars, *two-thirds* of his bonus. How could he possibly quit? There was no choice.

"You boys were doing *fine*," Jerry continued. "You were amigos, three young bucks. You owned a goddamned company together. How many guys your age can brag about that? And people knew who you were, too. You were on the cusp, on the make. Another five years, you would have been getting them glamourous jobs all the time, I guarantee it. But now . . ."

His voice trailed off, and he pushed back from the table and took a big swallow of coffee.

"Hell, Bart is finished. I don't know too many one-handed builders. And sweet Jesus, the amount of meth he did . . . coulda killed a buffalo. That motherfucker has a *looonnnggg* road ahead of him 'fore he's clean. And you're never really clean again, now, are you?"

Cole looked out the window at the pickup truck.

"Happy Thanksgiving," Jerry said.

An hour later they pulled into a veterinary office down a quiet little road a ways out of Jackson. The world was just beginning to stir, sporadic traffic here and there, but the little parking lot was empty, save for Bill's truck. Jerry strolled up to the front door and knocked on the glass. Within moments, an extremely tall woman answered the door. She looked to be about six-foot-three, including the hairdo piled on the top of her head, and towered over both Jerry and Cole with oversize glasses that magnified her eyes

"Mornin', Birdie." Jerry smiled. "Thanks for helping us out."

"You have my money?" she asked in a deep voice, blinking at him from behind those thick lenses.

"Got your money right here," Jerry answered, reaching into his bloated pocket for a fat roll of hundred-dollar bills. He turned back to Cole. "I'm in the cash money business, son. See? Never have to wait for a bank to open. I *am* the bank."

Birdie took her time counting the money and then scanned the parking lot and glanced up and down the street.

"All right," she said, "there's a loading dock in the back. Pull around. Quick. I've got an eight o'clock with a patient who had a pretty major disagreement with a porcupine."

They did as they were told, Cole standing in the bed of the truck and passing the heavy plastic bags out to Jerry. There was a tense moment when a corner of one bag caught on a doorknob, ripping open to reveal a stiff, pale hand, but Birdie was there to calmly stop Jerry and free the bag. In a few minutes the truck bed was empty and they stood in the back of the veterinary's building.

"Now what?" Cole asked.

Birdie pointed to a large contraption that looked like a steam engine.

"I'll cremate them," she explained. "And poof—they'll disappear." She blew at her fingers, as if to make a wish on a dandelion's fluff.

"Come on, Cole," Jerry said. "Time to go visit your banker."

"No," Cole said firmly. "I want to see it done. This is my money."

Birdie glanced at Jerry, who shrugged and yawned.

"Take a seat, then," Birdie advised. "It'll be a bit. We're not nearly up to the proper temperature yet."

Not long after nine o'clock that morning, Cole left the bank with a ten-thousand-dollar cashier's check. He slung wearily into Bill's truck and passed the check to Jerry, who quickly examined it. He pointed at the memo line.

"Nice. I like that touch. 'Consulting.'"

At the Rose, Jerry climbed out of the truck and back into his car. They drove far out of town to the southeast, where the landscape was slightly less rugged, more rolling foothills and arroyos than mountains. Off a gravel road and past a cattle-guard and -gate that Jerry unlocked, they drove toward what was obviously an abandoned ranch: a barn, a metal toolshed, and a clapboard two-story house whose windows were mostly broken, the front door hanging on by a single hinge.

They parked the truck in the barn, removed the license plates and VIN number, and then padlocked the old weathered building.

"Throw those plates in the garbage," Jerry advised, dusting off his hands. "At a gas station or something. And make sure your prints aren't on 'em either. I scrubbed that truck as best I could. You get real twitchy, we can always come out here at some point and torch the vehicle, but . . . I suspect you're in the clear. And don't forget, I want another check in a week, and that final payment's due the first of the year. If you don't—I'll be leaving an anonymous tip for the local *policía*. *Capiche?*"

Jerry drove them back toward Gretchen's house, leaving Cole just off the highway.

"You can't take me up to the house?" Cole snapped.

"And get a flat tire on that shitty road? Go to hell, Cole. Have yourself a nice walk back, and hey, try not to kill anybody else for a little while, huh?"

Then Jerry drove off into the steadily brightening morning, and Cole was left in the cold, his hands trembling, a sickly-smelling sweat trickling down his forehead and back. There was something like seven miles ahead of him, all of it uphill.

27

A doctor roused Teddy from where he slept in a waiting room, just outside the Intensive Care Unit. The Wasatch mountains outside the hospital's smoky black windows were smaller and farther away than what he was used to back home, the landscape somewhat drier and flatter. The doctor was an older woman, heavyset, with a broad, sun-tanned face; her hand on Teddy's shoulder felt uncommonly kind, and he almost leaned his cheek into that touch.

"Your friend is very, very lucky to be alive," she said.

Teddy exhaled a deep sigh of relief.

"But Mr. Christianson's far from being in the clear," she continued, sitting down beside Teddy. She studied his face for a moment. "Were you aware of the fact that your friend is a heavy crystal meth user?"

At first, Teddy shook his head. *No, that wasn't quite true,* he thought. *I mean, yeah, he might use it a little, but he's not a "user."* Not Bart.

"Well," Teddy began, "he was under a lot of stress. We're building a house, and I think he was sort of using—sort of—you know, smoking a little meth to stay awake, to keep going. . . ." Even Teddy didn't believe what he was saying.

"What is your name, sir?"

"Teddy Smythe, ma'am. Bart and I are business partners." He swallowed, bit his lip. "And we're buddies, ma'am. Known him all my life. There's nothin' he wouldn't do for me. Or my family. He's a good man."

She nodded. "Mr. Smythe," she began.

"Teddy," he put in.

"Teddy," she said, smiling gravely, "your friend has a serious septic infection stemming from sores all over his body. His immune system is . . . frankly, Teddy, it's wasted. Right now, I am extremely concerned that he's susceptible to further infections. He's also going through withdrawals, and to be honest, the poor man looks not only malnourished but physically exhausted. This is to say nothing of his severed fingers, of course."

She placed a hand on Teddy's back.

"I need to prepare you for the fact that your friend is in an incredibly delicate, even dangerous position. There is a not-insignificant chance that we may still lose him. He lost almost a *half-gallon* of blood, Teddy. Most people with his injuries . . . They'd be dead."

Teddy worried his hands, rubbed his shaved head, and tried with great difficulty not to cry.

"Does he have a partner, or family?" the doctor asked.

Teddy shook his head.

"Well, we're going to have to keep him here for quite some time," she said softly. "He could be in Intensive Care for weeks before we can release him to another room, and *even* then," she continued, "he's going to need to find a treatment center and also look into physical therapy for his arm and hand. For one thing, he's going to need to think about whether or not he wants a prosthetic."

Teddy was overwhelmed with the scope of his friend's needs; his future; *their* future.

"You said you and your friend were working on a house? I take it you work for a construction business together."

"We own our company," Teddy explained. "We're partners."

After listening to Teddy, the doctor breathed a forlorn sigh of sadness before clasping her hands together. She hardly even needed to say it, that Bart's construction days were likely over. He knew.

"How long can you stay with him?" the doctor asked.

Teddy shook his head. "I have to get back, I think," he said. "We've got to finish this house. Thanksgiving is . . ."

"Today, as a matter of fact."

"Shit," he said. "I need to call my wife."

The doctor smiled. "The good news is that your friend is alive, and we're going to do our level best to get him healed and strong again. And you know what?"

Teddy glanced up at her.

"He owes his life to you. Most of the time, we don't advise tourniquets. But in *this* case, you saved his life. Just so you know, you did everything right."

She stood up.

"Now go call your wife," she said. "And please, do get some sleep. I don't care what you say, that house can wait."

28

ole picked up Teddy from the Jackson airport. It was midafternoon when Teddy finally walked out of the terminal and he looked like a much older man. Bags of exhaustion sagged below his eyes, and his clothes hung off his body, wrinkled, dirty, and spotted in places with blood. Cole gave his friend a long bear hug.

"How's Bart?" he asked.

Teddy shook his head and blew out a sigh of sadness. "He's back there all alone," Teddy said. "I just— Poor guy."

"Yeah, well, let's get you back to your family," Cole said. "Britney'll be worried sick."

"She's super-pissed is what she is," Teddy replied. "And can't say I blame her. Didn't know where my phone was. I guess I left it in the house. She couldn't get a hold of me. And man, I didn't even know what day it was. That's how much I've lost track of things."

They drove in thick silence, neither of the men ready to speak of the horror they had participated in.

f Britney was angry, she put on a good face. The Smythe family condo smelled of Thanksgiving, and the girls seemed unaware of their father's emergency trip to Salt Lake City. Soon, Cole and Teddy were slumped into chairs in the family's living room, sipping boxed wine in front of a football game they could barely care about. Two of the older girls were in the kitchen with their mother, making final preparations, while the younger two seemed to orbit around Teddy, taking turns climbing into his lap for a short cuddle or telling him about the previous day's doings. He listened intently, or at least made a sincere production of pretending to.

"You mind if we step outside for a minute?" Cole asked after a while. "There's something I want to show you in my truck."

Teddy eyed him suspiciously.

"Britney!" he called out. "Me and Cole are gonna go look at something outside. Back in five minutes."

"Okay, well, dinner's almost ready," she replied. "So . . . hurry up, all right?"

The two men hustled out to the truck and stood around the bed, as if looking for some tool. Cole glanced back over his shoulder to find one of the girls staring out at them through parted drapes.

"Makes me want to throw up," Teddy began, "just thinking about it. I mean, dear god, what happened, Cole?"

Cole recounted the night in the vaguest of details, and he did so to protect his friend, to keep from further incriminating him. For if there was one bona fide blessing to emerge from that gruesome night, it was this: Teddy had done nothing wrong. Teddy had harmed no one and seen no violence directly. So when Cole laid out their shared narrative, he did his level best to paint only the most general picture, figuring that Teddy could wade through his omissions and half-truths in the way a bloodhound captures a scent: not out of any great intellect, just intuition.

"And José?"

Cole shook his head.

"My lord," Teddy murmured.

"Yeah."

"Huh," said Teddy when Cole was all through. "The only loose end, then, is Jerry, I guess. And the vet, maybe—and the truck."

"Yeah, that's how it looks to me. But the way I see it, we each got dirt on the other, and at this point, hell, Jerry's already hidden the truck and helped with the bodies. And the vet, too. Ain't like anyone's hands are clean. The fact of the matter, Teddy, is that it was all a horrible accident . . . and there's no sense in getting taken down for it."

"But we sure do owe Jerry a shitload of money."

"I couldn't think of another way out, Teddy. You were gone, Bart was gone, and I had two bodies on my hands. Blood everywhere."

Cole had left out the gory details of dispatching José but could easily recall with haunting clarity their struggle: the freezing water, the younger man's wet black hair, and then, not long after, tying those knots around the already stiffening corpse. In a way, that was another accident. Cole hadn't *meant* to kill him. And in the end, hadn't he just defended himself?

Just then the front door opened and one of Teddy's girls called out, "Dinner's ready!"

They held hands and said a prayer before the meal: turkey, cranberry sauce, stuffing, gravy, mashed potatoes, a green-bean casserole, rolls, and both pecan and pumpkin pie. Cole hadn't eaten in about two, almost three days, and he began loading his plate with a ludicrous amount of food. Teddy's girls laughed at these two men, who you would have thought were starving, shoveling all that food into their mouths with a strange sort of sadness in their eyes, as if they weren't actually sitting down for a holiday meal—with all the time in the world before them—but just rushing this food down their gullets before running off into the night.

Cole was aware of it, aware of how he couldn't quite stop himself; this food was the best thing he'd ever tasted, and he could feel tears in the corners of his eyes at the thought of what they'd done, at the thought of Bart, and the reminder of all that was yet undone. If he could have, he might have thrown that November feast right into a dozen Tupperware containers and lit out for the jobsite, worked through the night, until the thing was done.

But he forced himself to relax, if only a bit, engaging the girls in conversation and making harmless jokes at Teddy's expense, jokes designed to ensnare the whole table in the kind of laughter you'd expect on a holiday. Jokes designed to detour his mind away from the light smoke he'd seen rising out of that veterinary office's smokestack that morning. Or the bats swooping around Bill's truck in that darkened barn. Or Gretchen's house and the bloody mess he'd still have to clean up the next morning.

Cole slept on Teddy's couch that night after several slices of pie and a cup of decaf coffee. It was the kind of sleep so dense and deep that his mind went blank a second after his head touched the pillow. And morning itself came all too soon. Even though it wasn't a school day, he heard the tumble of dry cereal landing in ceramic bowls and hairdryers blowing upstairs and the soft sounds of television talking heads chattering away. He lay on the couch, and the first thought that took shape in his mind was that there were now fewer than thirty days before Christmas. A stab of anxiety and fear caused him instantly to sit up and rub his eyes. He had to get dressed and make for the building site.

In the kitchen, Britney poured him a glass of orange juice and then went back to wiping down the counter with a dish towel. "Too bad Bart couldn't join us last night," she said, looking at Cole curiously.

"Yeah," he responded, "too bad."

He knew then that Teddy must not have told her everything, though he *had* to have told her about Bart and why it was he had disappeared for a day. She clearly had no idea about Bill or José; but, then, there was no reason for Teddy to tell her. And she would only have blamed Cole for everything, because she saw him as their leader, even if he wasn't that, exactly, even if they were technically equal partners. Britney, Cole understood, was the kind of wife who, clear-eyed about her husband's weaknesses and limitations, looked at everyone in his life as someone who would either help or hinder him.

Just out of town Cole stopped at a Walmart and bought a six-pack of Mason jars and a gallon-size plastic jug of vinegar.

Back at Gretchen's house he scoured the garage floor for Bart's fingers, which he found, half-buried in a drift of sawdust, and deposited them in the vinegar-filled jar. He was not sure what else to do with the digits and could not see throwing them in the garbage or out into the forest for the ravens and crows. . . . He walked the jar to their trailer and placed it into their dorm-size refrigerator.

29

The day after Thanksgiving was the best day of her life. She could not remember another day in recent memory and maybe not since her childhood when she'd felt so free, even as her body felt ever more fragile, even as the pain intensified, localized. Somehow, she felt incredibly light. After calling for a meeting with those senior partners of her firm, who, like her, would actually bill for at least a few hours, even on a holiday Friday, she submitted a no-nonsense, one-paragraph-long letter of resignation, effective two weeks from that day. The partners present roundly thanked her for her enduring service to the firm and even offered up a standing ovation, something no one could remember ever having happened before. A firm-wide email was immediately circulated promoting a retirement cocktail party at a trendy subterranean speakeasy a block away, where she was sure to be given a ridiculously expensive token of their corporate affection and no doubt some sort of plaque or piece of engraved glass.

Back at Gretchen's Pacific Heights penthouse, Abby was handling various facets of the move out to Wyoming: the purchase and delivery of furniture Gretchen had already picked out for the new house, a moving truck to pack and relocate certain effects inside the penthouse, and more practical details as well: a new pharmacy and oncologist, the transferring of bills, and the collecting of updates from Gretchen's various real estate brokers, scattered, it seemed, all across the western hemisphere.

When Gretchen came home that evening, it was as if they were longtime roommates. Gretchen felt so relieved to have crossed all these obligations off her list, she actually flung her heels in the air, startling Abby's raptor in its cage. She reached into the refrigerator for a bottle of Dom Pérignon, quickly poured two flutes of champagne, and, passing one to Abby, cried, "I'm done! I can't *believe* it! I'm actually *done*!" And then, after two glasses each, Abby ordered a Lyft and they rode to the downtown steakhouse, where they sat at the bar, looking at men and laughing.

"I can't wait for you to see it," Gretchen said, the happiness in her voice like the seconds before an unexpected present is unwrapped. "It is unlike anything, Abby, really—any place you've ever been. The hot springs, the creek, the river, the mountains . . ." She shook her head, wishing they could be there now, wondering how the men were progressing. "Have we heard anything yet from Bill?" she asked.

"No," Abby said. "I actually called him *twice* today. Once in the morning, and then again just before you came home. Emailed him, too."

Gretchen's mood darkened ever so slightly. She'd known Bill over a dozen years by then, and while he could of course be laconic, in her experience he was also unfailingly considerate, returning phone calls and emails the same day, often within hours. They were friends, after all, and once, very briefly, lovers. In her gut, she feared something was wrong, a chill passing over her, as when a thick, dark cloud suddenly blotted out the sun, with no sign of dissipating.

"Try him again tomorrow morning. A phone call *and* an email. And please do me another favor?"

"Of course," Abby said. "Anything."

Gretchen worried a few strands of hair between her fingers. "If you don't get Bill, I want you to check in with Cole—Cole McCourt of True Triangle Construction? Remember, I gave you his card? Shake his tree, will you? He should know where Bill is, or, at the very least, when he completed the fireplace, what his plans were. And don't let them brush you off either. Be firm with them. I want to know what's going on out there."

"Got it," Abby said. The young woman was gaining an affection for her new employer, this older woman so incredibly confident and direct. "Done." She jotted herself a note on a paper bar napkin and tucked it into the pocket of her blue jeans.

And then the maître d' appeared to escort them to Gretchen's table, where Albert, as usual, greeted them warmly. It was clear from the light in his eyes that he was pleased to see one of his favorite customers, and at a time other than her usual. After noting the drinks they had carried over from the bar, he hastened away from the table, offering them time to glance over the menu.

This was pleasing to Gretchen. Sitting at a table with Abby at this steakhouse so familiar to her. And why on earth hadn't she done so many of these things years ago? Quitting the firm, learning falconry, mentoring a younger person . . . She watched Abby's face as the younger woman read through the menu, her eyes widening at the prices only to yield a quiet smile as she no doubt reminded herself that she could choose whatever she wanted here—that this was real, this world was possible; that it wasn't all thirty-nine-cent ramen noodles, shitty apartments, and endless student debt.

They ordered another round of drinks with their entrées and then sat comfortably in the warm dining room. Abby was the first to break the silence.

"Was the firm, uh, understanding about your retiring?"

Touching the rim of her wineglass, Gretchen considered her earliest days as an attorney, when the firm she now worked at had been called Sherman & Perkins, a classy, old-school assemblage of about three dozen attorneys. She actually knew both Sherman and Perkins; they had personally hired her, and even though they'd made a big show out of taking on a woman, and certainly slapped each other on the back for doing so, they were in every other regard regal, both of them, fantastic legal minds who felt that an attorney's legal education really came on the job, not in some oak-paneled law school lecture hall. She could not recall ever reading a memo about her billables back in those days; the focus was on advocating for their clients and "doing good work." But both Sherman and Perkins had long since died, following which the firm was sold and then consolidated into no fewer than four multinational factories of law. Soon there were skyrise offices in London and Dubai, Sydney and Shanghai. Partners were annually making well into seven figures, and it was not unheard of for the real rainmakers to pull down *eight* figures, including generous bonuses, of course. And Gretchen, well, she was a rainmaker, an ever-reliable money-making machine, like a tractor that just never breaks down, never quits, only demands a quart or two of oil every now and again. Turnover, always considerable, had become much more regular, especially among female associates; they would put in four to six years of dedicated work and then, like clockwork, quit in favor of starting a family. Committees were formed and hands were wrung, but really, nothing changed; men were allowed to grow old behind their desks, while women were presented two choices: become mothers, or not.

In those early years, Gretchen was the only female face in the yearly firm photo. Once, she had been standing beside the elevator bank when she watched a client point at her name on the Sherman & Perkins roster of attorneys (magnetic stainless-steel letters on a framed black felt background). "Didn't know there even were lady lawyers," the man said, laughing gruffly. Gretchen had ridden the elevator up those many floors, standing right beside that idiot, knowing full well that he'd taken her for some compliant secretary, the kind of woman who would fetch his coffee with a "yes sir" and a smile. Oh, the pleasure she took, when, some ten minutes later, he was ushered into a meeting room where she introduced herself as his attorney. How he had foundered in that moment, as she stuck out her hand in confident greeting.

She knew no one would miss her—oh, her billables, sure, but not *her*—and that blunt fact stung. She imagined being married to a man for decades and then, one day, simply disappearing from his life, but with the ability to spy on him, to become invisible, and watch how he responded. . . . And what if, instead of immediately calling the police, instead of xeroxing thousands of posters with her image and stapling them to telephone poles across town, instead of offering a reward, instead of scouring the world for her, instead of losing sleep and slipping into a desperate depression, he did . . . *nothing*. His life went on without a hitch, and then, in two or three or four weeks, having found a suitable replacement, he simply continued on, undeterred. How was her commitment to the firm any less serious than a commitment within a marriage, especially when she'd spent more time in the office than in her home?

She took a long swallow of her Bordeaux and braved a smile.

"Of course," she replied. "They were great about it, actually." Then, clapping her hands to project a lighter mood, she asked, "So, tell me. What is it you want for your life?"

Hours later they returned to the penthouse. Gretchen felt wiped out, exhausted. But after bidding Abby goodnight, she made a point of sending Bill a quick text:

> EVERYTHING OK? PLEASE RESPOND.

Then she held the phone against her chest and listened to the great prewar building creak and hum under louder punctuations of traffic below, and she could hardly wait to abandon her life here, hardly wait to begin what time she had left out in the mountains.

And then, unable to sleep for all her exhaustion and excitement, she sat up and began answering farewell emails.

30

I t was two days after Thanksgiving when the sheriff ambled up the driveway, both gloved hands resting on his belt, snow collecting on the brim of his brown cowboy hat. Cole and Teddy hadn't even noticed him, so engrossed were they in the work of cleaning up the garage. Already they'd swept the bloody sawdust out the wide-open aperture and into the snow beyond, and later, mopped and bleached the floors. Now they were just applying a second coat of industrial primer over the bloodstains on the walls when the old lawman came calling.

"Funny thing," he yelled over the blare of their music. "This is the third time I've visited this house already, and nobody's even moved in yet. That don't strike me as a good omen."

Cole dropped his paintbrush, nearly jumping out of his own skin. They'd put off some appliance deliveries for that day just to clean up the site and to be sure there was no evidence of their crimes. They could certainly explain Bart's blood, but if there was any other sign left over, some clue pointing toward their involvement in Bill's or José's disappearances . . . Cole hustled over to the stereo to turn down the volume.

"First, it was that contractor," the sheriff continued, pointing toward the second floor cantilevered out over part of the hot springs. "Took himself a swan dive offa that corner of the house. Then coming back for that drill and filling you fellas in on all that preceded you . . . And now . . ."

He peered around the site and sucked cold air over his old, yellow teeth.

"To me," the sheriff went on, "I just dunno. A place this damn beautiful being gated up and hid away? I ain't no big government type, but . . . this oughta belong to everyone, seems to me." He shook his head. "Can you imagine? Having all this to yerself? Like owning a piece of heaven. And I ain't sure that's even allowed."

The garage door was still open in order to let the fumes from the primer escape, and the sheriff moved in, examining their work.

"And now, what in the world is that?" he asked, pointing to the floor by the table saw, which they had made a point of *not* cleaning entirely. "That looks like blood, there. Boys, is that blood?"

Cole felt Teddy's eyes burning into him. But he forced himself to relax. They'd gone over everything. They had their story down. Now he would demonstrate for Teddy how easy it was to simply stick to that narrative. Hell, the fact of Bart's blood might actually work to their advantage; his injury was well-documented, after all; had been from the moment that rescue helicopter landed.

Cole blew out a cold jet of air as he reached down for the fallen paintbrush. "It is," he admitted. "Maybe you heard about the medivac that came out here Wednesday?"

The sheriff removed his hat and scratched at the back of his skull. He was a big man, with shortly cropped white hair and a salt-and-pepper goatee. He was tall to begin with, but taller still in his cowboy boots, and his hands had the wide spread of a former athlete. He snapped his fingers as if remembering a bit of long forgotten trivia.

"I do remember that," he murmured. "That was you fellas, now, was it?"

Cole nodded his head gravely. "Our partner nearly cut his hand off," he explained, gesturing toward the table saw. "Lost every finger on his left hand. As you can imagine, he lost a lot of blood, too. A half-gallon or more, the doctors said. Teddy here drove him out to the highway, where the helicopter picked him up to fly them to Salt Lake City. We've been cleaning up all day."

The sheriff squinted in sympathetic agony and walked over to the table saw, touching its sharp steel teeth with his fingertips.

"Well, boys," he said, "I am awfully sorry about your partner, but I'm out here today on other business."

"Oh?" Cole said, wiping his hands on a rag.

"See, a feller—or maybe *two* fellers—haven't been seen in about three days, and I got word they were working as subcontractors for your company. A stonemason, by the name of Bill Hardy. That name ring any bells? And his assistant, some Mexican—name of José somethingorother?"

Cole nodded his head. "Two fine workers," he put in eagerly. "Beautiful craftsmen. Finished up their work a few days ago, in fact—same day our buddy was hurt—I remember that. Left the site that afternoon, I think it was. Before the accident. Figured they were on to their next job, or maybe headed home for the holidays. They pretty much kept to themselves."

The sheriff spun the saw blade the way a child might spin the wheel of a downed bicycle.

"Well, now," the lawman said, "I called up a friend in the Nevada Highway Patrol, had him make a visit to Bill Hardy's home, actually, about two hours northeast of Reno. No truck in the driveway or garage. The back door was open, so I looked around and . . . no sign of him. No tools, no dirty clothes . . . Other fella was known to rent a room in Bill Hardy's house, I guess. Least, that's what he was doing before they took on this job. Both men were lodged in a nice Airbnb while staying in Jackson Hole. The owner said they were ideal tenants. Found that Mexican's truck at that property. All their stuff there. No sign of 'em leaving in a hurry. No signs of any struggle. Nothing illegal. And still no sign of the stone-mason's truck . . . Both of those men, like they just up and disappeared."

He let those words hang in the air like huge red snowflakes suspended between the three men.

"So, I guess you all were the last ones to see those men," he continued. He let that sit a moment. "Any idea where they might be?"

Cole looked at Teddy, and they both shrugged their shoulders.

"Can't say we do," Cole said evenly.

"What about your buddy there," said the sheriff with a sly sort of grin. "He talk, too? Or cat got his tongue?"

"I can talk," Teddy said.

"Well, boy?" the sheriff said, his smile nowhere to be seen. "Where'd them men disappear to?"

"José told me he was headed back to Mexico," Teddy offered brightly, "for Christmas. I remember that. Told me the city, too. Santa María Tonameca. Made me pronounce that part about a hundred times: *Ton-a-me-ca.*"

The sheriff stared at him. "Tonameca, huh?"

Teddy swallowed and nodded. "That's right."

"Ton-a-me-ca?"

"Swear to god," Teddy said.

The sheriff laughed. "Don't worry, son. I believe you. Just tryin' to remember the name for my own sake. Ton-a-me-ca, Ton-a-me-ca, Ton-a . . ."

He wandered in little circles around the garage, peering at their tools and running a hand along a wall.

"Mind if I look around?" he asked. "I got a little woodshop, m'self. Down in the basement."

"Please," Cole said. "Be our guest."

The sheriff was making his way up the stairs when he stopped and, leaning down, said, "Your boss called me the other day. Real nice woman. Wondered why you haven't been returning her calls." He stared at both of the men.

Cole threw his hands up in the air. "Sheriff, I could talk to that woman on the phone every fifteen minutes and she wouldn't be satisfied," he scoffed. "It's like with Bill and José. We just saw them a few ago, couldn't've been happier. You know how it is."

The sheriff squinted hard at Cole. "Know how *what* is?"

Cole laughed. "Women."

The old lawman's face was implacable for several seconds before he shook his head and offered a wistful smile. "I hear you, brother," he said. "Been married thirty-one years this spring." And then he continued pounding up the stairs. "My wife's still a mystery to me. A mystery I ain't likely to solve neither."

Ten minutes later he returned to the garage, still glancing all around, as if he'd lost his billfold or perhaps a trusty pocketknife, before offering Cole his business card and then trudging down the hill toward his SUV. About halfway to the vehicle, Cole and Teddy watched him pause to light a cheroot and stand there, absorbing the mountains, before he drifted back to them. Cole felt his throat constrict.

"I'm gonna tell you the god's honest truth," the sheriff said, drawing deeply on the cheroot and exhaling a cloud of smoke. "Something happened to them men. And as much as I don't want to come back here, I may have to. May have to do a proper search of this property. And another thing: Don't neither of you men leave town without giving my office a call, you hear?"

"We hear you," Teddy said, his voice noticeably shaky.

"Ten-four," Cole said.

"All right," the sheriff said stiffly. "Good day, then, gentlemen. And you hear anything from them men, you let me know."

Cole watched the lawman move down the hill toward his truck.

"I better call Gretchen," Cole said quietly.

"Cole," Teddy said nervously, "I don't know how else to say it—I'm scared."

"It's gonna be okay," Cole said reassuringly. "Look, it was all just a terrible accident. Every horrible part of it. Now that's the god's honest truth of it. Bart didn't mean to kill that man, and neither did I intend to harm José. But they're gone now, and that's all there is to it. We just need to . . . we need to focus now, Teddy. That's all. Focus on what we've done right, not the accidents we've had to clean up."

Teddy neither nodded nor shook his head. He simply wandered back into the house and plodded up the stairs.

Cole sat in his truck on the side of the highway, watching a snow-plow curl an endless tube of powder into the ditch while Gretchen lit into him so fiercely that at times he simply set the phone on the dashboard and listened, impressed, while she rained down insult after insult upon him in a veritable avalanche of fury. He'd known it was coming. In the past, he'd been more or less instantaneously responsive, getting back to her just as soon as he could find a cellular signal. But things were different now, and inasmuch as he could, he used that to his advantage.

When she seemed finished haranguing him, he calmly said, "Well, ma'am, no doubt you heard about Bart?"

There was a resonant pause on the other end of the line. The very pause he'd counted on.

"No," she said. "Why? What?"

He explained Bart's injury in great detail, omitting nothing, including the gory scene in the garage and Bart's present location in a Salt Lake City hospital.

"So, you see," he continued, letting a certain indignation rise in his voice, "you'll *excuse* us if we don't answer each and every one of your phone calls immediately. One of my partners is basically crippled for life, ma'am, and as you can imagine, there ain't too many one-handed builders out there." He decided to press what advantage he might have. "To be honest, ma'am, we're of half a mind to walk off the site and call ole Bart a personal injury attorney."

There was a longish pause before he heard her sigh deeply, like a mother annoyed by her son's childish ways.

"Don't be foolish," she said. "First of all, you'd lose any chance you might still have of securing your bonuses, and with less than a month away."

"Yeah, well, the situation's changed, now, hasn't it?" he found himself saying. "So we're gonna need another hundred thousand dollars on top of that bonus if it's gonna mean a damn thing."

He hadn't premeditated this demand. The words just leapt out of his mouth. But he did not regret them. What did he have to lose? What did any of them have to lose? Bart's fingers were surely worth more than a hundred thousand dollars, weren't they? And what about those dirty deeds, drowning José in the river, or the fear that clawed around his heart upon finally inspecting Bill's dead body? What was *that* worth?

He heard Gretchen cluck her tongue against the roof of her mouth.

"Fine," she said breezily. "You get the house done by Christmas morning, I have no problem paying your firm an extra hundred thousand."

"Per," he found himself saying. "Per man."

Now she outright laughed.

He didn't wait to hear more, just hung up his phone and set it on the dashboard, wondering if he'd just made an incredible blunder. He was almost panting for breath, his fingers wrapped tight around the wheel, his chest practically heaving. But he had sensed weakness in her, and on the off-chance that this deadline was actually meaningful— seriously meaningful—he figured he might as well capitalize on that timing. He reached into the glove box to shake out a cigarette, light it, and cradle its warm ember of temporary solace.

The minutes ticked by. . . . Five, ten, then fifteen . . . Twenty minutes later his phone rang.

"Fine," she said quietly. "But know this: I will be standing in that house on Christmas morning, and if one fucking outlet cover is missing or a door isn't hung properly, I'm going to have your balls, do you understand me? Your fucking balls, Cole."

"Yeah," he replied flatly, understanding in that moment that any delusions of romance he had once harbored were like the cigarette smoke drifting away from him out into the mountain air.

"*Yeah?*" she repeated. "Are you taking my food order at a McDonald's, Cole?"

He actually straightened up in his chair and took a last drag of his cigarette, flicking it out the truck window.

"Yes, *ma'am*," he offered with more conviction. "You bet, Gretchen."

"Do *not* play fucking games with me," she said. "Do you understand me? And don't talk to me about personal injury attorneys, you moron. Bill told me about Bart, about his meth use. I could destroy your pissant little firm. I could bring power raining down on you like you couldn't imagine. Bleed you to death with countersuits or crush you under the weight of thousands of letters and petitions. I do hope you can grasp that, Cole. Threatening me . . . Finish my house and finish it well, you fucking nitwit. Good day, sir."

And with that, the line went dead.

31

When the garage was finally cleaned and there was no sign of any carnage whatsoever, Cole began frantically calling subs, namely the cabinetmaker, the countertop installer, the tile fitter, and the plumber. The painters would no longer take his calls, claiming to have moved on to other jobs. But so much was already now done: the flooring, the electrical, heating and cooling, most of the plumbing. The appliances were en route: the Sub-Zero refrigerator and Wolf range, hood, and double oven; the microwave. Teddy would meet the delivery trucks at the highway and usher them up the driveway. He and Cole had gone so far as to borrow a pair of snowmobiles, in case the driveway became impassable, so they could load the appliances onto sledges and haul them all the way up to the house.

And so, while they waited for their subs, Teddy and Cole painted. They began on the top floor, by painting the bedrooms; first coating the ceilings white, and then the window trims and baseboards. Then they taped all the trim and baseboards and painted the walls in the warm and subtle spectrum of grays and off-whites Gretchen had laid out for them.

It was true, neither of the men liked painting—not one bit. It was the sort of job, like drywalling, that they were happy to farm out to some crew of trustworthy if fume-damaged men, all clad in paint-spattered white jumpsuits and well-worn Converse sneakers. There is a pecking order in construction, with painters ranking toward the bottom. The thing is, if an electrician fails at his profession, a house may catch fire; a homeowner might be electrocuted. If a plumber makes a mistake, a house may flood, causing hundreds of thousands of dollars of damage. But if a painter is sloppy, well, the worst that can happen is that a room looks poorly finished, slapdash and amateurish. And *that* can always be fixed by someone even just slightly more competent.

But under the circumstances, Cole and Teddy could not risk the appearance of slovenliness, and so they moved very slowly. Now that the calendar had flipped to December, the days were shortening, the sun mostly stuck behind the mountains, and the men were exhausted. It wasn't just the pace and precision of their work either, though that would have exhausted any builder; it was the weight of their crimes.

Cole had begun to wake up in the middle of the night, thrashing and screaming inside the trailer where he bunked each evening. And sleeping did not come easy to begin with. He was having a difficult time coming to grips with the deaths of Bill and José. He could still feel the young man's dead weight in his arms, in that frigid river, as he tried to knot the ropes around his corpse; these brute physical facts of the murders were something he just could not push away. Surely the sheriff could feel it, too. Surely it was only a matter of time before they were arrested.

And yet, he knew the bodies were gone, that they were free and clear—*weren't they?* There were only three people who knew the whole truth: Teddy, Bart, and himself, and they were all implicated, weren't they? Of course, Jerry knew plenty, and the veterinarian knew enough. . . . But really, it was Bart and Cole who were most imperiled. Bart had killed Bill, and Cole had killed José. . . . As for Teddy, well, he hadn't done anything wrong. All he'd done was save Bart's life; he hadn't harmed anyone; hadn't directly hidden anything either; hadn't paid off Jerry or transported the bodies. Most everything was Cole's doing.

When they finally retired every day around eleven at night, he'd lie in bed for a couple of hours before popping an Ambien and then crashing. Only the sleeping pills made him sluggish in the morning; once, he spilled a nearly full can of paint on a bedroom floor. Another morning he fell asleep inside the Porta Potty for a full forty-five minutes, and, despite the cold, waking only when Teddy pounded on the door.

Late one evening, after tossing and turning in his bed for hours, Cole stood and shuffled over to the dresser, where he supposed Bart kept his meth stash. After rummaging around in the drawers for several seconds, his hands brushed a fat hardcover book; Bart didn't read. Sure enough, it felt suspiciously light when he lifted it, and when he cracked it open, there it all was: Bart's pipe and meth. He cradled the pipe in his hands as if examining some alien artifact. Simply holding it felt . . . dirty, forbidden. He didn't really want to hold it, but he couldn't quite put it down either, and turning toward the house, there was the sense that he sure as hell couldn't sleep, and maybe he ought to be back up there, working. . . . His life was like an eighteen-wheeler barreling down a mountainside with bankrupt brakes and bald tires nearly on fire. Holding the pipe in his hands, he saw it all—the bottom of the mountain, his life come completely off the rails, lying in some obscure valley, smoldering and broken. Or was that fear? They had just three weeks now.

Cole had begun to feel Teddy looking at him with suspicion. *Or was it concern? Something like sympathy?* One afternoon, when Cole surprised his partner, coming up behind him after several hours of patient detailing, Teddy had taken three quick steps backward, as if

Cole were some deranged jack-in-the-box, and he supposed he looked that way, too: sunken eyes, pallid skin, scratches and bruises lining his arms. Because of course he'd earned those.

Sitting on the tiny bed, he loaded the pipe, touched the lighter beneath the glass bowl, watched the crystal begin to smoke . . . then brought the pipe to his lips and . . . inhaled—

FFFFFFuuuuuucccccccKKKKKKKKKKKKKK!!!!!!

His skull, for a moment, felt as if it might, might, might *flee* his shoulders, like a **ROCKET**, like a **blasting ROCKET**, like a **SATURN** *fucking* missile! Oh!!!!!! His bones—could feel every one, every one of them, every *one* of his bones, like they were people in a village that was *him*, and his hairs, each of those, the hairs, like trees in a forest, for example, or individual—*FUCK*—individual—**FUCK**—individual strands of grass, fucking *beautiful* blades of grass—*FUCK!*—swords of grass, on the prairie, but his skin was the prairie and his hair, see, his hair was the grass on the prairie.

He stopped. *Blllllleeeeeewwwwww* on his right forearm.

Now he felt the wind coming down from the Rocky Mountains, coming down from the Rocky Mountains, *racing* down from the Rocky Mountains, down over the foothills, and through the cities, down through the wide avenues and canyons of steel and glass, out onto the prairie and *caressing, caressing, caressing* those leaves of grass, those prairie grasses, hundreds of miles—**HIS** body—could it be that **HIS** body was the prairie, this biome, this prairie, all *kkkkkkiiiiiissssssssssssed* by stormy lightning, and then erased by wildfire? But he itched those fires. **ITCHED!** Itched those fires right out. **OUT.**

He stopped. Breathed. Felt like the trailer was the *Millennium Falcon*, looked out into the inky night and at Gretchen's house, out there, like a gigantic spaceship, the falling snow in between like stars, racing, like this was what TV shows and movies all agreed was "hyperspace," whatever the fuck that meant. OR—maybe that was *it*! He was *flying* in hyperspace!

He sat down, he sat down. Held his elbows in his hands. No, no, no. He shook his head. Closed his eyes. His eyeballs felt on fire, like two egg yolks in a Chinese hot pot. *Oh, oh, oh. No, no, no.*

How did Bart, did Bart—**HOW** *did* Bart {corral} this? Bart! *How, how, how, how, how?*

He steadied his breathing, even as his heart felt like, felt like, inside his ribs, *behind* his ribs, like a separate caged animal, a frightened rabbit, a flopping fish, his heart—*calm the fuck down. . . .*

"Channel this," he whispered to himself, his eyes still closed. "Ride this lightning."

He looked at the house, took a deep breath, and walked back to it all, to the work still awaiting them. Three more weeks.

Now the painting was like playing music and he could feel each stroke, could *feel* the silkiness of the paint upon his brush as it slicked across the wall. He stuck out his dry tongue, wedged between his teeth, and tasted the paint fumes in the air. *Sweet, sweet fumes.* The house was filled with jazz: *In a Silent Way* by Miles Davis. *And where has this album been my whole life?* With a brush he trimmed around the ceiling and his strokes were surgical and clean, and afterward he took up a rolling brush and painted the room in wide swaths, imagining the paint as the progress of a great harvester, making whole tracts of wheat fields *disappear.*

Teddy arrived just before dawn, holding two cups of coffee and a bag of doughnuts. Cole had already finished the top floor and begun taping around the trim and baseboards. Teddy said nothing as he stood in the doorway, and it took everything in his being for Cole to restrain a flood of words, all of which would certainly betray the fact that he was high as a kite.

"All-nighter, huh?" Teddy asked, his brow furrowed in wonder.

It was with some difficulty that Cole met his friend's gaze, and with even greater difficulty that he nodded his head once, rather than a thousand times, the way he used to flick a door stopper in his childhood room, that spring that would accept the sometime violence of a door with nothing more than mute acceptance.

32

Even as she tried to slink out of her office, even as she so desperately tried to pass on file folders and forward client emails and phone calls, her decades of work, her matrix of thousands of clients, began to take on the quality of an elaborate net, each client a strong knot, in a great circuitry of unbreakable fibers that would not release her. Some of those same partners who just two weeks prior had applauded her now dropped *new* work on her desk with all the fanfare they might have offered a summer intern. She even opened her sent-email folder to verify that she *had* in fact sent her resignation letter, that it *had* in fact been received and even responded to many dozens of times over.

"We could use your eyeballs on this," one of them would say, dropping a two-hundred-page contract on her desk calendar.

Or, "The Zabriskie deal closes in March . . . any chance you could mentor your replacement in the new year? Just, like, a day or two in the office each week? Or even just a few conference calls? Look, Gretchen, nobody knows this material the way *you* do."

No one ever seemed to notice that she was fading away, that she often winced in pain, or that her clothes no longer even fit her.

Still, she attacked this work just as she always had: by arriving at the office early and staying late, closing file folder after file folder, resolving issue after issue, and then sternly directing her paralegal to stop all incoming matters and close whatever it was she was wrapping up.

Christmas was two weeks away, and though she was communicating much less with Cole by telephone, she had signed off on the penultimate draw, pleased to see that despite Bart's apparently awful injury, they appeared both on schedule and on budget. Cole had even texted her a half-dozen photos of finished rooms before she politely asked him to stop; she wanted to save all that—the sensation of stepping into the completed house for the very first time, like experiencing the grandeur of an ancient cathedral, or the awe of spelunking into a vast cave network, a new hidden and wondrous world. . . . She wanted to be able to feel it all in situ—the early-morning light of that house— how it danced through the windows and onto the walls; how the hot springs would condense on certain glass or siding; she wanted to have the pleasure of wondering where she would keep her future falcons. In the garage? Or perhaps she would need a new outbuilding or shed? It was not something she wished to rush. Least of all over the very medium she was trying so desperately to shake as she counted the days until she could leave this firm for good.

And then her collapsing body would remind her of time, of how little time was likely left. Pain had begun to inhabit her now, and she often found herself grimacing under its pincers. Her appetite was gone, her clothing looser than ever. *This is a marathon*, she'd tell herself. *Just get to Christmas.*

Abby was a godsend, and the more time Gretchen spent with her, the more forthcoming and candid the young woman grew. She fixed dinner in the evening and prepared a hippie-dippy breakfast of instant oats that she packed into a Mason jar for Gretchen to take with her to work, oatmeal loaded up with butter and cream and laden with organic berries and maple syrup and flaxseed. It was tasty. Tasty enough that Gretchen could actually finish half the jar.

One night at the steakhouse, Gretchen was pushing her food around a plate when Abby asked, "Uh, I don't know how to say this, but . . ."

"Go on," Gretchen said.

"Do you think maybe you need to visit the hospital again?"

"I'm not going to back to the hospital," Gretchen said flatly.

"But last night," Abby almost pleaded, "you were groaning in your sleep, and—"

"And *what*?"

"It, well . . . it sounded like you were . . . god, Gretchen, I don't know if—"

"Spit it out, child," Gretchen said.

"It sounded like you were crying. Like you were whimpering."

Gretchen nodded her head and sipped at her wine, felt the alcohol blossoming in her chest like a dark purple dahlia.

"Does it hurt?" Abby asked, leaning forward.

"Of *course* it hurts," Gretchen spat. "It's cancer."

"You have to stop going to work," Abby whispered, leaning farther across the table. "There's no point. We have to get you to your house. *That's* where you should be."

"I can't," Gretchen breathed.

"Why not?"

"Because this is who I am," she said simply.

"What do you mean?" Abby asked, leaning back against the leather of their booth.

"It's impossible to explain," Gretchen said, making a deliberate effort to lean into her salad and fill her mouth with food, despite lacking the slightest appetite. How could she convey the fact that for her, work was a compulsion, a craft, even sort of a religion; a kind of code that she had committed her life to, even as she understood that the firm promised nothing but money as a reward, no afterlife, no moral legacy, not even much in the way of comfort or community. Still, there was pride in doing a job in an exemplary fashion, in rising each morning and donning one's suit, looking trim and polished and professional, ready once more to accomplish high-level work. Surely this meant something.

"I'd like dessert," Abby said.

"Of course—whatever you'd like," Gretchen said. "You know that, I hope."

"You should order something, too, though."

"Abby," Gretchen began, "I'm just . . . not that hungry, I'm sad to say."

"Trust me," Abby said. "Please. Just order something. Anything. We'll take it to-go."

An hour later they sat on the narrow terrace of Gretchen's penthouse, wrapped in Hudson blankets, their feet tucked under them, passing a fat joint, sipping hot tea, and eating from their takeaway containers of decadent dessert: an apricot cheesecake for Abby; and for Gretchen, a chocolate ganache. Ella Fitzgerald crooned out of a cordless speaker as they stared over the shimmering city and the foggy bay beyond.

"Oh." Gretchen giggled. "I'm out of practice."

"Is it helping with your pain?" Abby asked.

"Umm . . . ," she said, closing her eyes and humming to the music, "not really."

"Can you at least work from home?" Abby asked gently.

Without opening her eyes Gretchen said, "I might have to consider that. There will still be meetings I can't avoid, though. Signings. That kind of thing."

"I'll take care of you," Abby said, reaching out to touch Gretchen's shoulder. "I'll have breakfast and coffee ready, and if you just, you know, tell me what to do, maybe I can help out. Like your assistant at the office."

Gretchen's white plastic fork fell to the bluestone floor, but she did not even startle, her head resting on her shoulder, her mouth slightly agape. Abby rose to check on her employer, initially fearing the worst but quickly establishing that she was merely asleep. Abby took a final toke, pinched off the ashy tip, slid the joint into her pocket, then collected their food and utensils and brought them into the kitchen. Returning to the porch a few moments later, she surprised herself by lifting Gretchen up off her chair, a feat that caused her to feel at once incredibly empowered, deeply trusted, and thoroughly heartbroken. Gretchen could not have weighed more than a hundred pounds, Abby thought as she carried her employer into the master bedroom and guided her gently beneath the covers. Probably less.

The next morning, Gretchen did not stir until after nine thirty, waking with something like a panicked shriek and then scampering into the bathroom.

"I'm late!" she yelled.

"Gretchen," Abby said evenly, knocking lightly on the bathroom door, "I already called your assistant. Told her you were working from home, at least for this morning. It's *okay*."

The door cracked less than an inch, revealing Gretchen's sharp naked shoulder leaning into the frame, her back turned to Abby and the shower already running, steam slowly billowing up to fill the little room.

"Abby," Gretchen said firmly, finally turning around to meet the young woman's gaze, "let me clarify something: *You* work for *me*. Do you understand?"

"Yes," Abby uttered.

"In thirty-odd years of working as an attorney, how many days do you suppose I've worked from home?"

Abby knew well enough to stay silent.

"Zero," Gretchen said, closing the door. "Not one."

33

Teddy was on the telephone with Bart, giving him an update of their progress, when the cabinets arrived, and he let out an unrestrained and triumphant howl before telling Bart he'd call him back. Now the kitchen would finally take form, and with less than ten full days until their deadline. Once the cabinets were installed, why, if he desperately had to, Teddy could damn well drive to Denver or Salt Lake City, physically load the appliances into a trailer, and then haul them up the driveway with a snowmobile, if that was what it took. Hell, he'd get a pack of sled dogs or eight magic reindeer. If push came to shove, he would drink six pots of bittersweet coffee and physically *drag* them up the driveway himself. And what a punctuation mark *that* would make at the end of this whole enterprise.

The cabinetmaker left the warmth of his truck and then stood for some time in the driveway, simply marveling at the house, his breath clouding up into the low-slung sky.

"Holy shit," he said as Teddy all but raced out of the garage to shake his hand. "Gorgeous. Just freaking gorgeous."

"Boy, are we glad to see you!" Teddy said.

The cabinetmaker, Jedd, a wiry man about their age, just stood there in his faded blue jeans, Adidas soccer shoes, and an oversize insulated plaid shirt. He lit a cigarette and continued peering up at the house. "That road's a fucking nightmare, though, brah," he finally said, blowing out a cloud of smoke. "Thought I was driving the Khyber Pass."

Teddy bit his lip, unfamiliar with that last reference.

"Almost lost it," Jedd said, pointing a finger toward the truck. "Came to a corner there and felt the back tires fishtail on me. Jesus, brah. I was shittin' a fucking brick there for a second. There's no way you can keep that driveway open all winter. No way."

Teddy was hardly listening; all he wanted to do was fling the back door of the truck wide open and load some cabinets on his back like a Sherpa ready to summit the nearest mountain.

"Look at my fucking hands," Jedd said, holding them out so Teddy could see them still trembling, two pale aspen leaves in a gale that would not relent. "You guys gotta get some sand on that road. Or a goddamn metal guardrail."

"How long you think installation will take?" Teddy put in. "Can we bang this out today?"

Jedd frowned. "Brah, I just about *died* back there. Lemme at least finish my smoke here. These hands can't install shit right now."

Teddy paced. Their deadline loomed, like a clockface on the cliffs opposite the house; he could practically hear the seconds ticking.

At last, Jedd flicked the cigarette butt down the driveway and popped a piece of gum into his mouth. "All right, brah," he said. "Let's rock 'n' roll."

The two of them brought in the cabinets, and when it was finally time to hang them in their appointed places, Cole quit painting to help hold steady all that wood and glass. He seemed to struggle with that task, though, his hands juttering, feet tapping, and more than once he almost walked away completely, threatening the safety of all those beautiful cabinets. Teddy yelled at him to focus, and when they did take breaks, he later inspected Cole's painting to find that he had attacked the job the way a hypercaffeinated kid might: some walls were painted well, yes. But others were slapdash, the corners unpainted, with drips of paint even beading on the trim. When Teddy pointed out these mistakes to Cole, his partner grew agitated, slapping at his own head or biting his fingernails.

"Hey," Teddy said quietly, consoling his friend with a half hug, "hang in there, bud. We're almost there. You need to take a little break? Maybe a nap in the office?"

"Naw, man," Cole murmured. "I'm good, Teddy. It's fine. I'm golden."

"Okay," Teddy said, studying his friend's face. "You *sure* you're okay?"

Cole wouldn't meet Teddy's eyes. His whole body seemed electrified, shivering with voltage under a sheen of sweat, his skin an unnaturally waxy color.

"Brother," Cole all but whispered then, "I don't know how much longer I can push like this."

"Me, too," Teddy said, "but, Cole—we're so, *so* close."

Now Teddy gave his friend a full-force hug, the sort of embrace shared by two men at the finale of an epic accomplishment with no regard for who might see them or what the hell anyone else thought about anything.

Cole began quietly sobbing. "I haven't slept in a fuckin' week," he cried. "I can't even tell what's real and what's not. I forgot about the hot springs yesterday, you know? Thought the house was on fire. Sometimes, I'm painting, and the walls look like they're rippling, like someone just dropped a stone in a pond. Little ripples everywhere, you know? And I try, Teddy, try to smooth out those ripples, but they just keep coming. . . ."

Teddy held his friend, held his sweaty head in his hands, and rocked back and forth, the way he might have comforted one of his daughters. But mentally, he was doing the math. Could he finish the house without Cole's help in the time that remained? What was left to do? The painting. There was a significant amount of painting left to do. And the appliances. And then there was also the shipment of furniture.

"Take the rest of the day off," Teddy told his friend. "Jedd and I can handle the cabinets. And I'll figure out the painting. Just, you know, go out to dinner or something, okay?"

"Dinner," Cole mumbled. "Yeah, maybe some dinner . . ."

"Go on," Teddy said. "Get some sleep."

"All right," Cole said weakly. "Hey, thanks, Teddy."

"Okay," Teddy said, laying a hand on his friend's shoulder. "I have to help with the cabinets now. Get some sleep."

Jedd was a gifted craftsman, no doubt about that; the cabinets had already been painted white with glass doors, and for certain smaller nooks of the kitchen, he'd sourced some character-rich hickory and created open shelving with walnut pegs that affixed the shelves to the walls. This was a one-of-a-kind kitchen. Everything a gourmand might ever need would be visible and easily accessible on shelves and in cabinets that could never be duplicated, no matter what design magazine someday featured the house.

A new tension arose, though: how to race against the clock without sacrificing quality. On other jobs, they might have trusted everything to the subs, but mistakes could not be tolerated on this project; there was no room for error. If a single cabinet was damaged in transit, all their efforts would be in vain. And so, transporting the cabinetry into the house became something of a religious endeavor, like two men entrusted with carrying the Ark of the Covenant. Despite the cold, sweat poured off the men's faces as they concentrated; no walls could be scraped, no floors gouged.

Teddy had begun to view the house as a temple, though he could not pinpoint what faith it aspired to celebrate. The most obvious religion seemed to be money, but this unsettled him in unexpected ways. How could this beautiful house he had spent so many mornings staring at—the sunrise gleaming golden off the windows and roof, as the hot springs steamed the cool air—how could this structure be nothing more than a homage to wealth? And, if it was, what did that say of *their* efforts—of them?

34

ole did not take himself into town, did not dine at some fancy restaurant. He did not get any farther than their office trailer, in fact; could not even remember crawling into the narrow bed, after turning on the tiny space heater and simply worming beneath the layers of blankets to shut his bloodshot eyes.

He woke up two days later in a tangle of foul bedsheets and sleeping bags. Peering over the edge of the bed, he saw what looked like a plastic gallon milk jug half full of bright yellow urine, the smell unmistakable.

His first thought was not the house, or Teddy, or even poor Bart, out in some Utah hospital. His first thought, his first impulse, was just how to find his next high. His body was rebelling against him, he could feel that, like a sickness, not so much coursing through his veins as *squatting* inside him, like a ghost dwelling inside his skin, urging him to find more, more, more.

He stood shakily from the bed and wobbled toward the dresser, where Bart had stashed his supply in that thick Stephen King book. He rummaged through the drawers with greater and greater ferocity. Nothing. The fuck? No pipe, no crystal, *nothing*! He looked in the mini fridge—nothing. He tore out of the trailer and into the cold night, snow swirling over the ground. The house was lit up, every window aglow, and even from the trailer he could hear the sounds of laughter inside, joyous laughter, of music and playful conversation.

Now Cole was unsure if he was still sleeping, caught in some dream. The golden cast of the light from the house and the steam rising up the face of the mountain . . . all of it was the stuff of hallucination. Only the realization that he was standing in the snow in his icily soggy socks, the fact that he was shivering against the freezing air—only those sensations grounded him to this reality. He hugged his elbows, blinking against the snow and cold.

There were children running through the house, too, laughing and dancing. He could see their little heads at the bottoms of some of the windows. It took him a moment to place the music trickling out through an open garage door: fucking Bing Crosby.

He glanced down the driveway, past the bridge to the parking lot and turnaround, and thought he could see the shapes of several vehicles, slightly obscured by a thick layer of snow. He picked his way up toward the house, gritting his teeth against the cold and the toxic turmoil boiling beneath his skin. The ghost inside him felt like it was beginning to burn now; his flesh felt like paper on fire, his skeleton a brittle wick dipped in jet fuel.

Inside the garage, at least thirty pairs of shoes were neatly lined up, like the entrance to a Japanese shrine, and nearby a potluck had been arranged on folding tables: containers of pulled pork, baked beans, and macaroni and cheese, bowls of potato salad and coleslaw, bags of chips, jars of pickles, and long coolers filled with bottles of water and soda. A few women who had been merrily engaged in conversation suddenly stopped talking, as if their throats had been cut, and they stood perfectly still, their eyes wide, staring at Cole as he wordlessly trudged past the food, offering a weak smile, and a half-hearted wave. He plodded up the stairs and upon reaching the main floor saw that Teddy must have invited about half of his Mormon congregation to the house in what was surely a painting party, the kind of thing a young couple does upon moving into a new house in order to finish a monumental amount of painting.

The children were well-behaved, sliding across the slick new wood floors in their stockinged feet, though their fun came to an abrupt halt as soon as they noticed Cole, standing in front of the fireplace, his socks wet, his clothes filthy, his slack face covered by days' worth of stubble, his hair totally bedraggled.

Cole continued slowly exploring the house. In the expansive first-floor living room, three women were dressing a seven-foot-tall Christmas tree with white decorative lights and what must have been ornaments from their own home. A baby sat on the wood floor, playing with a wooden star, all painted yellow. Now the stereo played Nat King Cole, crooning out familiar Christmas carols. The women at the Christmas tree stopped their work and looked at Cole. He could see in their eyes something like fear.

"Teddy?" he managed to croak, trying to tamp down the volatile mix of anxiety, intense craving, and anger. *Be cool*, he thought to himself. *For fuck's sake, be cool.* He felt his fists clenching.

One of the women pointed upstairs.

He tried to smooth his shirt, straighten his posture; looked behind him at his own filthy footprints. One of the women was on her hands and knees with a paper towel, doing her best to erase his grimy path.

Upon reaching the second floor, he followed the jocular laughter of several grown men, thought he could pick out Teddy's voice among the others. He stood in the doorway and realized with a start that they'd finished painting everything. It was . . . perfect, the house. And essentially *done*. The final touches would just be the appliances, which, they had been told, were to be delivered the morning of Christmas Eve.

"Hey," Cole said, greeting the men somewhat meekly.

"Cole!" Teddy cried out, before truly registering his friend's sorrowful state. For a moment, his face fell, his smile retreated, and there was a palpable tension in the room; these friends of Teddy's were sun-kissed, fit, wholesome family men who enjoyed diversions such as mountain biking and trail running in their spare time, men who had certainly never touched drugs of any kind; a few of them had somehow completely avoided tasting so much as a light beer or coughing on a pilfered cigarette. The silence and tension lasted less than two seconds, but it was real and heavy, before finally, some inner light within Teddy overpowered whatever trepidations he was feeling, and he collapsed the distance between himself and Cole, giving his friend a huge, hearty hug.

"We *made* it," he said, his lips close to Cole's ear. "We made it, brother."

Cole stood there limply, absorbed in his friend's embrace. He had come into the house looking for more crystal, for his pipe, for the next rush, and now, there he was, surrounded by unfamiliar faces, faces that looked at him with if not half-concealed disgust, then cringing sympathy. The house was warm, the lighting perfect. He looked at the gleaming trim, at the expanse of unblemished walls, through the vast windows, out into the total darkness of the night. Below them was the sound of children's laughter, and women in gleeful conversation. The Christmas carols on the sound system seemed to swirl the fragrance of the freshly cut balsam fir and the lovingly prepared food.

Cole collapsed into Teddy's arms, sobbing. There was nothing for him to say, nothing more for him to do. If this was closure, it felt at once like all-encompassing relief and a total void of meaning. For the past four months, he had done nothing but live and breathe this house. He had *killed* for this house. Lost himself to a drug for this house, and now, all of that came caroming down the mountain on top of him in a great landslide, a great avalanche of emotion. He could not stop sobbing, even as his body ached and burned, twitched and screamed out for more crystal.

"Come on," Teddy said. "Lemme show you around."

"Hold on," Cole whispered. "Let me just, you know, get myself together. I'm all—fucked up."

"I know it," Teddy said. "We got to get you some help."

"Can we just stand this way for a minute, please?" Cole asked. "Just to let me . . . you know . . . stop fucking blubbering."

"Sure," Teddy said quietly. "Take your time."

Cole wiped his nose on his own forearm, took several long, deep breaths, and then gave Teddy a little nod to indicate he was composed, or at least as composed as he was going to manage in that moment.

Now the two men moved from room to room, astonished at what True Triangle had created, at how this vision had finally crystallized. Teddy's friends were clearly also astounded, snapping photos for their Instagram or Facebook accounts, many of them posing in the tiled shower stalls with views of the hot springs or mountains. Teddy didn't have the heart to warn them against posting the images; besides, Gretchen and these folks were unlikely to have too many social media overlaps.

"I was worried we wouldn't make it," Teddy explained, "so I called in some favors. We banged out all the painting today. At one point, we had *sixty* people here."

They walked to the master bathroom, leaned against the threshold.

"All the fixtures came yesterday, and the plumber was right here, first thing in the morning."

They stared down at a squat little white toilet.

"That commode there? Seven *thousand* dollars," Teddy sighed. "She has three of them. Over twenty grand in privies. The mirror cost three grand, plus shipping from Italy. The stone in here is from Turkey. Haven't even *seen* the invoice for that yet. The sink: another five grand. This bathroom, all the tiling and cabinetry—heck, this room alone probably cost . . ." He paused, glancing at the ceiling, tabulating the long list of expenditures. "I don't know. Sixty thousand dollars? Maybe eighty."

"For one person," Cole said quietly. His body still screeched out, still pled for the meth, but he held his shoulders tightly, rolled his shoulders over, and focused on staying small, on containing himself.

They stood there, marveling at the sleek elegance of the little room.

"The first time I saw her," Cole managed, "I think I was in love. No woman that smart, that beautiful, had ever so much as"—his body trembled uncontrollably—"you know, given me the time of day."

Cole ran his hands over the tiling. "But now I see that . . . that she was always just stringing us along, you know? Using us."

"You think she ever figured we'd actually finish on time?" Teddy asked.

"I don't know," Cole croaked. He realized he hadn't had a drink of water in days, and his body felt as dry as kindling. As far back as mid-October he'd wondered what her urgency stemmed from. He couldn't be for certain, but somehow he sensed that she had no husband, no partner, no children. She had the air of a queen without a kingdom, and this house was her impenetrable citadel, an impossible aerie. An isolated fiefdom she was content to lord over. "Sometimes I think she just wanted to see how hard she could push. What would happen. Who'd be left standing. Other than her."

Teddy put a hand on Cole's shoulder. "Well, she didn't burn us up, did she? We were like horses that just kept galloping, weren't we, buddy?"

Cole looked down at his filthy, wet sopping socks. "She burned up our friend pretty good, though. Wouldn't you say?"

Teddy nodded gravely. "Day after Christmas I'm headed over to Salt Lake City to visit him," he said. "I promised him I'd be back."

"You're a good man," Cole said. His body felt more and more like that of an insect, just before a molt, felt like he could burst out of his flesh, both reborn and raw. He could take it no longer. "All this philosophizing is great," Cole whispered, "but what'd you do with my shit, Teddy? I'm serious now."

"Threw it away," Teddy said plainly. "Two days ago."

"That was my *stuff*," Cole hissed. "Cost me a lot of money, Teddy...."

Though never a tall man, Teddy now stopped leaning in the doorway and stood to his full height, his body tensed and muscular. He had lost weight, too, over the past four months, but Teddy had never stopped eating or exercising, and his body now had the definition of an Olympic gymnast or a yoga instructor. Something had changed in his character, too, especially since Bart's injury. He wasn't afraid to lead this company. It was as simple as that. And he could not allow them to fail, because if they did, it would affect his wife and his children, and he could not abide by that. He had ideas and opinions, too. They were a triangle, after all, and he was one whole corner of that shape.

He'd actually created a contest among his daughters: The girl who designed the best logo for True Triangle would win a hundred dollars cash, right out of his wallet.

He'd given them some basic parameters:

1. Instead of a single triangle, he wanted three;
2. He wanted each triangle to look like a mountain;
3. They needed to create a corporate slogan to accompany the logo.

With Bart injured and Cole lost in the shadow of meth, Teddy had needed to step up to lead their fledgling company, and in the past two weeks or so he certainly had, because even if at first he couldn't be certain that Cole was using, he began watching his friend more and more closely, especially during his breaks, when he would offhandedly mention going to their trailer for a catnap. Teddy began following him, peering in through a small window, there to see Cole smoking that clear glass pipe; the acrid, toxic smoke like some demon he inhaled that imparted supernatural energy, keeping his friend active for days at a time.

Except, while Cole could focus on the painting or trim with

superhuman precision, other facets of the business were slipping through the cracks: He wasn't staying up-to-date with their subs, for one thing; wasn't returning phone calls; wasn't making sure that shipments would arrive in a timely manner. And so it was that Teddy picked up that slack, ensuring that their impossible timeline could be maintained.

"It was not *your* stuff," Teddy said firmly. "It was Bart's, and it almost cost him his life."

Teddy's rebuttal stunned Cole, as if Teddy had just flicked him with a finger in the forehead. But he was not done yet. Not by a long shot.

"Where'd you throw it, Ted?"

"You need help, buddy. All right? Let me help you out. I can take you to the hospit—"

"Fuck off, you stupid, simple, Mormon *prick*."

The words left Cole's mouth before he could think about them or take them back.

"Cole."

There was no way back but through. "You're a knob, Teddy. A little boy. Grow the fuck up and get the hell out of my way."

"You're not yourself, Cole. I know you don't mean any of that."

Cole pushed Teddy in the chest, and somewhere behind him a chorus of gasps sounded out. Cole knew that there were women and small children in the house—that likely Teddy's family was present—but he could no longer restrain himself.

"I love you, buddy," Teddy said evenly, moving toward Cole with his arms spread as if to embrace him in a hug.

Cole telegraphed the punch he was about to throw; Teddy could almost see it taking shape, originating palpable moments before the fist even came close to making contact. And so, channeling many of his own heroes, Teddy deftly deflected the blow with a hand that sent Cole's forward momentum away from its target and straight into the drywall to the left of the doorway.

For a moment, Cole's fist was awkwardly caught in the wall before he was able to pull it back, his knuckles leaving blotches of blood on that newly painted surface.

"Fuck this house," he said, spitting on the floor. "And fuck you, Teddy." Then he whirled around and punched the wall behind him, too, leaving another ugly hole. He turned and stared at Teddy. "I'm coming back," he said, pointing a finger at Teddy's chest. "I promise you. Christmas morning."

Two of Teddy's largest friends were now at Cole's side.

"Get him out of here," Teddy ordered.

"Touch me," Cole snarled, "and I'll ruin every wall and window between here and my goddamn way out."

Teddy's friends parted to make way for Cole as if the very air he exhaled were noxious, as if, in brushing his skin or grubby clothes, they might contract some horrendous disease.

From those grand south-facing windows in the living room and in the warm glow of the Christmas tree, Teddy watched Cole walk down the driveway in his ragged socks, past the trailer, over the bridge, and into his truck, the brake lights glowing red as the headlights popped on, and he tore off into the night.

"Who was *that*?" Teddy's youngest daughter, Kylie, asked, as she reached out a little hand for Teddy's trembling fingers.

"You know who it was," Teddy said quietly. "That was Uncle Cole."

"It *was*?" she asked. "He didn't *look* like Uncle Cole."

"He's just . . . very, very tired," Teddy said, squeezing her hand.

"He wasn't even wearing any shoes," she said, tilting her head to look at her father.

"Maybe his feet were too hot," Teddy said.

She scrunched her nose and giggled.

35

For months, Bart hadn't had a second to so much as daydream or kick back with a cold beer and watch a meaningless baseball or football game. There had been no time for anything other than Gretchen's house. Even on the rare occasions when they'd rewarded themselves with a one- or two-day hiatus, he'd felt so guilty about the time away that he hadn't left the site, or else suffered an ever-building sense of guilt every minute away from the house. It was as if he were just delaying some inevitable torture that became more painful by the frittered minute.

But then, there in this hospital, with its view of the mountains, time stretched out before him like a near endless plain. There was time to think of his friends, for one thing, to wonder how they were doing, and if his absence had cost them, had made their deadline impossible. Teddy called him each day at lunch, like clockwork, and gave him a rundown of their progress. If they'd suffered any setbacks, he omitted those, painting the most optimistic picture of the project. And it was good to hear that simple bastard's voice, even if at times he droned on and on about his girls, their Christmas lists, and the presents he was planning to buy Britney.

But man, Bart wanted to be right there alongside them, cranking on that house.

He'd always loved that aspect of construction: the definable beginning and end and that steady stretch of labor in between when the demons he'd always fought—alcohol and drugs, namely—were kept at bay by incessant work. He was his own boss, and that was priceless. Not every mug in America could lay claim to being a business owner, with two partners he'd known more or less his whole life. He could listen to his own music, smoke cigarettes without someone giving him a dirty look, and hell, dress exactly as he pleased. He was, in so many ways, free.

Or, he had been. Now he could hardly even piece back together in his mind how it had all fallen apart. He remembered the meth. Just like he remembered the crazy deadline that had sent him back to it. But so damn much of it was a haze. He'd been fully alert for more than two weeks now, sitting up in a bed, flicking through the television stations, flirting occasionally with the female nurses and doctors, and doing his level best to battle the tedium. He was still in the same standard bed he had occupied since arriving there, but he figured it was just a matter of time before they'd need to shift him to some rehab unit or nursing home. Or, then again, maybe he could simply walk out the front door on his own recognizance.

Trouble was, his future was blurrier than ever. What good was he to his partners anymore? And what else besides building could he even do? He could not see his own mangled left hand, but he knew the damage was ugly and profound. All the fingers of that hand were gone now, leaving what would be little more than a club. He could swing a hammer with his good hand, yes, and maybe carry some boards in the crook of his right arm, if the load was well enough balanced, but he understood that his future as a manual laborer was essentially kaput. If he found work on a jobsite, it would be only as some sort of charity case. He thought of the hunchbacks and clubfoots of yesteryear. He shook his head; didn't much care of thinking of himself in those terms—and before even reaching his fortieth birthday.

Bart clenched his eyes shut and yawned, then tried to rub his hands over his eyelids and forehead, but he realized that even familiar movements like that one, like pulling on his socks or pants, say, or, turning the wheel of his truck, hell, grabbing food from the drive-up of a fast-food restaurant—all of that would be difficult now.

"Mr. Christianson," a nurse called, popping her head into the room. "There's a visitor here to see you."

She smiled at him and then opened the door, allowing Margo to slip past her, holding a cooler in one hand and a small vase of garish grocery-store carnations in the other.

"Hey, big guy," she said gamely. "How're you doing?"

Her face almost brought him to tears, crystallizing something in his mind right then: Aside from Cole and Teddy, he was more or less alone in the world.

"You're a sight for sore eyes," he said, pushing himself up in the bed.

"Well," she said, setting down the flowers on the windowsill and then producing a cold Coors from the cooler and opening it for him, before sitting down on the bed and passing him the bottle, "I haven't forgotten about you, if that's what you're worried about. Teddy told me you might want a visitor."

He accepted the beer, despite not really craving the alcohol, happy for the cold, wet glass against his hand and the familiar feeling of the beer slipping down his parched throat. He stared at her for a moment and then aimed his eyes down into his lap.

"I truly have no idea why you're so nice to me," he murmured, "but . . . I *am* really glad to see you."

She smiled at him, reached for his beer, and took a sip herself.

"Me neither," she allowed. "You're certainly not the smartest guy I ever dated."

"No argument there."

"But," she continued, pointing a finger in his direction, "you do happen to be one of the hardest-working men I've ever known, and you take care of the people you love."

No one had ever really acknowledged these traits, but they were qualities he privately regarded as something like guiding principles. And it was powerful to hear her recognize in him those virtues he held so dear. It was like forgetting your own name, only to have someone greet you, call out your name, understanding even better than you ever did yourself who you'd always been.

"Why are you here?" he asked.

"I wanted to know that you're okay."

"You could've just called," he said.

She sighed. "I've dated a few guys since we broke up," she began. "You knew that. But I'll admit it, they were all douchebags. Every last one of them. Rich, conceited, arrogant douchebags. And the more I thought about it . . . about you . . ." Her voice trailed off, and she turned her head, glancing out the window toward the mountains.

"The more you realized what a catch I am?" Bart said, grinning rakishly.

"Shut up," she said. "And don't get cocky."

He nodded. "Fair enough."

"I want to take you home with me," she said. "All right? And then I want you to clean up. For good. I want you to quit your job. I'll help you find something different. I work at a hospital. We'll find you some rehab. Help you get a prosthetic, if you want."

She took a sip from his bottle, then passed it back to him, and he took a greedy swig as he considered what that would even be like: wearing a plastic hand, or maybe one of those silver hooks. He'd heard of this chef, Eduardo Garcia, up in Montana, who wore a metal hook like that, and *he* was a cool dude. Maybe Bart could pull it off, too.

"I'll think about that," he said.

"So, then . . . what about us?" she asked, moving closer to him. "Would you think about that? About giving us another shot?"

He looked down at the stump of his left hand.

"Margo," he sighed, smoothing the bedsheets once more, "you deserve better than me."

Now she pushed him to one side of the bed and tucked herself in the space under his left arm.

"Maybe let *me* decide what I deserve?" she said. "Besides, I gotta feeling about you. That your best days are still ahead of you."

He set down the bottle of beer on the bedside table and shut off the television.

"You can't say I didn't warn you," he said, pulling her closer to him. "*Repeatedly.*"

"Nevertheless," she said, smiling, "she persisted. Right?"

"Oh, Jesus," he moaned, rolling his eyes.

And so they spent the day together, as if on a date, walking around the hospital, drinking weak coffee, and holding hands, talking about their lives, their goals and dreams; those sort of games like imagining what you would do if you received an unexpected and vast inheritance, if you could start all over. Margo liked her work but hated the new money infiltrating their town. Every year her nurse's salary went a little less far, and the idea of buying a house or maybe starting a family ended up getting pushed off further and further, a sensation she resented more and more.

Bart felt her squeeze his hand when she shared all of this with him, and in earlier years, some prickly part of his nature might have succumbed to the urge to make the kind of flip joke that would deflate her excitement, but now, he simply squeezed her hand right back.

The next morning, she ventured into some hip men's store in

downtown Salt Lake and bought him a fresh pair of blue jeans, new boots, underwear, warm socks, undershirts, a flannel shirt, a beautiful barn jacket, along with a cowboy hat.

She closed the door of his hospital room, undressed him, and sponged off his skinny body—for he was no longer even lean, but some measure less than that, his long frame weathered down to the bones by the meth and the work and the stress.

"Just relax," she said, taking his cock in her hand and stroking him gently, firmly. "Just . . . lay back and close your eyes, huh?"

He hadn't been touched in many long months, and her caress felt like a fucking rainbow boa of the softest feathers. "Oh, my god," he gasped.

Then she took him into her mouth. He reached down with his one good hand and took a fistful of her soft, silky black hair and pressed himself deeper inside her. Her fingers ran down through the line of hair dividing his stomach and chest, and she lightly pinched and pulled his nipple and moaned, even as her mouth was full of him.

Sometimes, he reflected later, an orgasm could be as good a marker to measure one's life as anything else.

They walked out of the hospital just before lunch. She leaned her weight against him, and he slung an arm around her as they made their way through the parking lot toward her old Ford Bronco.

It was two days before Christmas, and the day was dark, the light scant.

"Look," he began, "I'm through with the meth, and I can't do much in the way of work, but I do have to get back to the site. The deadline's Christmas morning. And if I can help out—even a *little* bit—I ought to. I *need* to."

She knew that arguing would be useless; one thing she loved about Bart was that he didn't *do* drama. When he spoke, it was economically, with real thought.

"I'll take you out there, then," she offered. "I'm on vacation until after Christmas anyway."

They drove east through one drowsy little town after another. Main streets not more than two blocks long. Old brick buildings lined with pickup trucks. Store windows lit with Christmas lights. Doors decorated in pine wreaths.

On the plains below the mountains, horses and antelope watched them as they passed. Higher up, the temperatures dropped, and a light snow fell. By the time they reached the high passes, even the highway felt claustrophobic.

"I've already decided that I'm retiring after this house is done," he said to her at one point, after a long silence.

He had not yet told her about the bonus, because he couldn't be sure there *would be* a bonus. But if there was, if his partners had managed to pick up the slack for him, and if they could drag themselves over the finish line with the job done and done well, then . . . his life would be forever changed.

"It's not just—not just *this*," he said, indicating his left arm. "Hell, it's my knees, too. I'm in too much pain these days. I've gotta find something else, something new. Some new way. I'd sure as hell like to be able to get out of bed when I'm fifty."

Now he was almost talking to himself. He thought about Bill, about killing Bill, and ran a hand through his hair, wincing with regret and horror.

"What I really want is to go someplace warm," he confessed, drawing a little triangle in the fog on the window. "Someplace where I'll feel, I don't know, loose. Disconnected. Away from all the crap these days."

"What will you do when you get there?" she asked softly.

"I could tend bar," he said almost naturally, and though he hadn't in fact given it a great deal of thought, those words seemed true enough. He could envision that: A Hawaiian shirt, flip-flops, shorts, looming large behind a rickety, sticky tiki bar, chatting up the tourist wives and bullshitting with their husbands—it wouldn't be so different from the world of high-end construction. Walk home at the end of the night with a pocketful of bread and wake in the morning to putz around town; maybe do yoga three or four days a week, or swim. Paddleboard up and down the cerulean coast. Something to limber up those joints of his. To say nothing of putting some distance between himself and that sheriff, who would no doubt be sniffing around Gretchen's house for clues, some explanation for the disappearance of two men . . .

"I like dreaming with you," she said.

"Yeah," he said, forcing a smile. "Margo, seriously—thank you. Thanks for coming out to get me. The taxicab fare back home would have been a real bitch."

"You moron," she said playfully, "no one takes a cab anymore."

36

Of all her years at one of the nation's most prestigious law firms, those first twenty-three days of December marked the most hours she'd ever billed. She took not one day off, working nearly twenty hours a day, even as her body cannibalized itself, the stage IV cancer wasting her away. And yet, on Christmas Eve she awoke, retired. She lay in bed, long before dawn, listening to Abby's gentle snores over in the guest bedroom. Only, Gretchen did not feel free then, released of whatever burden she'd felt the need to shake; she just felt . . . rudderless. The way a dinghy out in the open ocean is at once utterly independent and entirely vulnerable—vulnerable from every direction, including below, where a leviathan, say, might explode up from the bottomless depths and swallow the little craft whole.

With great effort, she sat up then and dragged her skinny legs over the side of the bed, setting her feet down on the plush Afghan rug. She had hoped to wake up on this day, finally headed back to the mountains, with the energy she once enjoyed as a girl. She had hoped to *bound* out of bed, excitedly wake Abby, cook a hearty breakfast, and then rush them to the Learjet waiting at SFO for their flight east and into the mountains. Only now, she felt like simply falling back into bed, doing nothing more arduous than focusing on her breathing.

Had she been alone, she might have just given up, might have made peace with the idea of spending her final days here, lamenting her end, coming to grips with the fact that she'd never even see her new house in the mountains, never experience retirement, the third and final act of her life, when, had things gone just a little differently, she might have finally met a partner, or even a husband, someone to spend time with, to travel with. . . . This realization frightened her—that the only thing separating her from giving up, quitting, was this young woman a room over, a young woman she barely even knew, though she certainly liked, perhaps even respected; a young woman who had performed a yeoman's work these past several weeks: filing and mailing paperwork, packing bags, cleaning the penthouse, cooking, organizing shipments of furniture and personal goods, so the new house would be something more than just an elegant empty shell when they arrived, and, when they had a spare moment, sharing a meal or working her falcon together.

Gretchen pulled herself back out of bed again and with great effort walked to the bathroom, where even the task of relieving herself felt monumental. Then she padded into the kitchen, made a pot of coffee, checked her email, and finally knocked on Abby's door.

"Good morning," she said softly.

Abby sat up and called her in, perhaps slightly embarrassed that this older, severely weakened woman had managed to wake before her.

Gretchen handed her a mug of black coffee. "Today is the day," she said. "Christmas Eve."

"How are you feeling?"

"All right, I guess, all things considered."

"Lady, you don't have to go *anywhere* if you're not feeling up to this. It'll all still be there tomorrow, I promise."

"I've been dreaming of this house since I was a little girl, Abby. It's the only place I ever wanted to live. I've . . . well, I've made mistakes in my life, and when I think about it, that's *one* thing I wish I had back. I should have figured out a way to make a living there. I could have been an attorney there, could've found my niche."

Aware that this bleak last-minute reflection was painted black, that in her final days, she was no font of gratitude or joy but only this rather weak trickle of regret, Gretchen shook her head as if to tell herself, *No*. The house, she hoped, would do something to change her mind-set, she was sure of that. That the house might be enough to put it all right.

"It's wheels up at noon," Gretchen said, feeling a new vigor in her voice. "We land in the early afternoon. I have a reservation lined up at a beautiful boutique hotel in downtown Jackson and then dinner reservations at one of my favorite restaurants. Have you ever tasted Rocky Mountain oysters?"

Abby shook her head, perplexed.

"Everyone should try them at least once in their lives. And then . . . perhaps never again."

Abby rubbed her eyes and yawned.

Gretchen smiled at the younger woman. "Oh, and look in that closet, will you? I bought you a little Christmas present."

Abby flopped the bedsheets away from her and walked over to the closet. How Gretchen could have had the time to buy *anything* for Christmas, especially without Abby's knowledge, she had no idea, and yet, there hung a brand-new, knee-length camel hair coat, a Burberry scarf, a pair of Frye boots, tight burgundy pants, and a chunky gray turtleneck sweater.

"Jesus," Abby sighed.

"Hurry up," Gretchen called on her way out of the room. "I'm making bacon, eggs, sausage, and toast. Something of a cowboy breakfast. Then I need you to call the car service and make sure everything is in order. I want our bags beside the door. And your hawk!

Don't forget that sweet dear. Take a shower, put your face on, and then come eat."

Abby hustled into the shower, thrilled by the expectation of flying on a private jet, of finally glimpsing this other side of her employer. Not that she hadn't already seen plenty. Still, it was all so unreal.

This bathroom in particular had spoiled her. The floor was heated, and inside the shower stall were eight separate jets that sprayed her body from every conceivable angle. The tilework had a playful luxe, with several shades of blue and green, mottled by whites and grays, and then the occasional pale orange, for effect. Gretchen's soaps and shampoos, too, were themselves luxurious; the first time she'd taken a shower in Gretchen's apartment, it all felt about as opulent as a free vacation at a four-star resort. The towels, the lighting, the big, wide mirror . . . Just standing in that space Abby felt more beautiful. Wrapped tightly in a towel, brushing out her hair, she noticed that her skin seemed more golden, luminous, even. She had never considered herself particularly attractive, had never been on more than a handful of dates in her life, but standing there, she caught herself wondering, maybe . . . Maybe she'd been too hard on herself. The steam filled the room, and she could not help but smile; her life just then seemed like a straight shot of good fortune.

As she shut off the water and reached for a towel, the fire alarms began chirping loudly. She hadn't smelled smoke, not with the perfumed scents of shampoo, conditioner, and soap filling the bathroom. But there it was, as she rushed to dry herself off—bacon left in the pan too long and burnt.

"Gretchen!" she yelled out. "Hang on, I'll be right there."

A moment later she opened the bathroom door to find the apartment filled with smoke. She quickly rushed to the windows and flung them open, letting in the December cold. She slung wide the sliding porch doors to the terrace and then, dashing to the kitchen island, found Gretchen on the floor, blood issuing from a wound on her forehead, the breakfast, in two different pans, burnt and ruined and smoking, the bread in the toaster suddenly popping up.

"Gretchen," she said, leaning close to her employer. "Gretchen, can you hear me? *Gretchen!*"

She reached for her phone and dialed 911, but when the operator asked Abby where the emergency was, the young woman suddenly realized she had never properly learned Gretchen's address.

By then, the falcon was screeching in its cage and someone was pounding away at the door.

"Hold on," she told the operator, realizing the words could just as well be directed at Gretchen. "Just a second. Someone's at the door!"

She ran to the entryway, where a silver-haired man dressed in navy-blue silk pajamas stood, a phone in his hand. Beginning to tear up in fright, Abby shook her head and led him out of the foyer and into the kitchen.

"Everything okay?" he asked, bending his neck to peer around Abby to where Gretchen lay on the floor. "Jesus!" he shouted, pushing past Abby and quickly locating a kitchen towel, which he then held against Gretchen's bleeding forehead.

"Call an ambulance!" he cried.

"I *did*," she said, realizing the phone was still in her hand. "What's the address here?"

"The Newman. Laguna and Jackson."

He knelt close to Gretchen, his ear directly over her mouth, one of his great, soft hands encircling her frail little wrists. As Abby looked on, she realized just how fragile Gretchen was, how much weight she'd lost this past month, how pale her skin had become.

"Who the hell are you?" the man asked Abby. "I mean, have you even taken a look at her lately?"

Abby took a step back.

"Christ, she looks half-dead!" he yelled. "Must've lost forty pounds."

"She has cancer," Abby said quietly. "I'm her caretaker." She clutched the bath towel around her tighter, feeling incredibly vulnerable.

The man shook his head. "She's breathing, but . . . I can barely find a pulse."

He peered around the apartment before his eyes stopped on the cage, where Abby's falcon nervously moved from roost to roost, bobbing its head, its eyes blinded behind a hood.

"What the hell is that? A fucking eagle?"

Gretchen's eyes opened as the gurney she lay on was wheeled swiftly through the halls of the hospital. Abby walked alongside, holding Gretchen's hand and peering down at her.

"Oh, thank god," Abby said. "I was so scared."

"Thanks," Gretchen whispered.

"You don't have to thank me," Abby said. "Just—relax and *hold on.* You're in good hands." She squeezed Gretchen's hand.

"Get . . . my . . . checkbook," Gretchen managed quietly.

The gurney moved on down the hallway, through the din of nurses and doctors loudly talking, through doors shutting, past vending machines rattling out cans of soda or bags of potato chips. . . .

"Gretchen, I—"

"You . . . *have* . . . to . . . ," Gretchen continued, "get . . . out . . . there. . . ."

"Gretchen, I can hardly hear you," Abby said, leaning closer to the older woman's lips. "Please, just relax now, okay?"

"Get . . . on . . . that . . . plane . . . ," Gretchen said, reaching up for a fistful of Abby's hair.

"*Stop!*" Abby shouted at the EMTs.

And with that, the gurney came to an abrupt halt. Abby pressed her left ear just above Gretchen's mouth.

"Go home . . . get my checkbook," she began. "Get the plane . . . and fly . . . out . . . there. . . ."

Gretchen gasped for a breath, writhing slightly.

"Okay, I'll head back to your apartment, I'll get your checkbook, and yes, I'll fly out there."

Gretchen nodded, then motioned with a thin index finger for Abby to lower her ear again.

"You . . . pay . . . those men," she said hoarsely. "They'll . . . be . . . waiting . . . for . . . you." Then Gretchen relaxed her grip of Abby's hair and instead gently caressed her face.

"I will," Abby promised. "I'll pay them. But they're waiting for *you*, Gret—"

"Directions," Gretchen croaked, "in . . . a drawer . . . by . . . my bed. Amounts . . . to . . . pay . . . them. And . . . my . . . attorney . . ."

But she said no more. And in that instant, the EMTs sprang back into action, one of them ushering Gretchen down that long, cool tiled hallway while the other began jogging in earnest toward the Intensive Care Unit.

Three hours later, Abby sat on that time-share jet, so discombobulated and frenzied and, yes, sad that she barely took a single sip from the flute of champagne she was offered. Instead, she spent the entire trip reading and rereading the note her employer had kept in the top drawer of her bedside table, sealed in an envelope that was itself notarized and signed by Gretchen across its sealed flap.

The note read:

Dear Abigail,

In the event that I am unable to travel in order to oversee the final inspection of my new house at 1 Granite Peak Road, Jackson, Wyoming 83001, I have with sound mind written the following instructions for you.

Please make your way to my new house on the morning of December 25. Acting as my proxy, you will inspect the construction. Pay close attention to detail. If the house was built to the standards that I have demanded from the builders, then you are empowered to deliver the principle partners of True Triangle Construction two (2) checks.

The first check is for meeting their deadline. In appreciation for each partner's extraordinary hard work under time constraints and great duress, you are empowered to deliver a check for $525,000.00 to True Triangle Construction, LLC.

The second check is a bonus based on my own goodwill. Please deliver a check for $300,000.00 to True Triangle Construction, LLC.

Both of these aforementioned checks are in this envelope, already signed and dated.

Upon completing the inspection, I encourage you to spend a week residing in the house. This will allow you the time to detect any more significant mechanical errors that the contractors should immediately remedy.

Should I die before I can travel to the house, please immediately call my attorney, Aarav Reddy, of the firm Cross + Spence, based out of San Francisco, CA.

Thank you very much for your service, Abigail. You have been a fine employee and companion to me these past several weeks.

Sincerely,
Your friend,
Gretchen

The plane landed on a small runway in a wide, snow-cloaked valley. The pilots and flight attendant carried Abby's two bags across the tarmac and into the terminal, where they shook hands and said their *Merry Christmas*es. A driver stood holding a placard with Gretchen's name. Once Abby introduced herself, he shouldered her bags and escorted her toward an idling black Cadillac Escalade. They drove wordlessly toward town.

Inside the hotel, she tipped the driver as he handed her the rather light luggage she'd brought and showed him the address for the following morning. He did not seem to care that this would be Christmas morning, and if the location of the new house was incredibly remote or unknown to him, it did not register on his face; they shook hands, and after a slight bow, he walked out of the lobby, back into the cold.

The hotel staff expressed disappointment that Gretchen would not "be joining us" but a young woman walked Abby briskly enough to the elevator and then showed her to her suite on the third floor. It was breathtaking, with clear views of the Jackson town square. Before Gretchen's abrupt decline, she had been worried that spending Christmas in this unknown place might make her feel melancholy—that she'd pine for her parents' cozy, well-feathered house in Grosse Pointe. That she'd want to wake up on Christmas morning as she had almost every other year of life and drowsily drift down the grand staircase toward the sitting room, where a Fraser fir would sag beneath the weight of its dozens and dozens of accumulated ornaments and hundreds of feet of garish lights, a small collection of wrapped presents scattered beneath, and just outside the French doors—a birdbath, its tiny pool of water long since frozen over beneath the ancient oaks. She had thought she'd miss all that. And of course, driving into the countryside with her father and the falcons, watching the raptors work an early-afternoon sky.

Just then she realized with a start that she'd forgotten her falcon inside the doorway of Gretchen's apartment, and so, after tipping the hotel staff, she immediately went to work locating the contact information for the doorman at Gretchen's building.

"Chicken will work," Abby advised, running her nails anxiously through her hair. "Just give him a bowl of cut-up chicken breasts. And make sure he has water." She could have kicked herself. Never had she ever been so careless with one of her birds.

"In all my years . . . ," the doorman said. "I mean, I've done a lot of favors in my time here, and Ms. Gretchen never asked for much, but . . . now I'm opening her apartment to feed a *bird*?"

Abby stared out the window as the sky darkened into a deep blue.

She ate alone in an eerily quiet dining room, the taxidermy on the walls staring down at her as if these stilled creatures had something important to say, the votive candle stationed at the center of her table more like emergency heat rather than decoration. A handful of diners sat sprinkled throughout the restaurant and at the bar: a young family of out-of-towners at a six-top, with two aging grandparents in full-on Western wear; a few empty-nest couples; two tables of tourists, likely in town for the skiing; and at the bar, a man in his fifties, wearing a black-and-white track suit, gold chains heavy on his neck, more rings on his fingers than would be advisable. He kept staring at her as if there might be a future love connection, until she finally asked her waiter to be moved out of his line of sight. She would have preferred an evening of room service and *It's a Wonderful Life* for the umpteenth holiday viewing, but Gretchen had wanted to share a meal here, at this restaurant, so she stayed on to honor her. It just didn't feel right not to.

When the Rocky Mountain oysters arrived, the serving size was grotesque for a single person, and though she didn't entirely dislike the dish, the more she thought about what they *were*, where they came from, and the longer that sizable mound of testicles sat there on that serving dish, the queasier she became, until finally she spit the one she was chewing into a napkin and pushed the dish away.

The elk medallions were more enjoyable, served on a plate with spaetzle and pickled beets in a rich pan sauce. The accompanying Brunello di Montalcino warmed her, and she longed only for a good novel, something she could return to her room with, hunkering down under a bedside lamp for a couple of hours until sleep came for her. Only then it would be morning, and she would have to rise to the occasion, acting out this uncomfortable role as a dying woman's proxy.

37

Where *were* you?" Cole asked. "I stopped by earlier and the place was dark."

"Out to dinner," Jerry replied. "Had my eyes on a good-looking piece, but she ducked out before I could so much as buy her a drink. Anyway, merry fucking Christmas. You got more of my money? 'Cause that's the only present *I* want this year."

Jerry lived in a chalet-style three-bedroom on the edge of town in a neighborhood built onto the lower elevations of a larger foothill. The house had never been updated, which seemed fitting, because neither, really, had Jerry. The walls were decorated in sun-faded ski posters from the early eighties and amateurish nude photographs of some woman Cole imagined to be an ex-girlfriend of Jerry's. The carpeting was avocado green here, goldenrod there, and behind the posters and nudes was diagonally laid pine paneling. The fragrance of vanilla vape hung in the air, mingled with Old Spice cologne and head-shop sandalwood incense. Aquariums bubbled throughout the house, displaying various exotic-colored fish, and Cole had already seen two large iguanas parade around the living room. The house was kept at a toasty eighty degrees, and the south-facing windows, foggy with condensation, presented a view of a wide deck where a hot tub sat prominently above the view of town, now nestled in the snow, just a little collection of white and gold lights from here, glowing softly in the night.

"Yeah, I got your money," Cole said, passing him a cashier's check for twenty thousand dollars that had all but depleted his checking account. Any of the money he'd set aside as a nest egg from their builder's fee so far had been given to Jerry, and what little else he'd saved through the years was now well and fully wiped out. He had no idea how he'd explain any of this to Cristina in the official aftermath of their divorce. He saw no way out any longer, no escape. What did Cole want for Christmas? Meth, only meth. Even as he watched his life spinning ever further out of control, the filthy euphoria that little glass pipe could give him had become everything. There really was nothing else. Nothing else that mattered because at this point, he'd lost everything he'd ever had. And everyone. He'd alienated Teddy, and likely Bart, for that matter. For Christ's sake, he was now a murderer, and the kind of man who might visit his dealer on Christmas Eve, rather than being with his parents or siblings, or some family he should have long ago started with the woman who was now officially his ex-wife.

"I'd also like to, uh . . . ," Cole began, unaccustomed to the protocol here. "Could I maybe get a little crystal off you?"

Jerry sat sprawled on a leather couch, the yellowy soles of his feet propped up on a glass coffee table, his arms outstretched like an aged condor. "How much?" Jerry groaned as he reached a hand under the elastic waistband of his jogging pants to satisfy an itch.

"Quarter of an ounce," Cole suggested.

"Thousand bucks," Jerry replied.

"That's more than last time," Cole said, but he could hear it in his own voice—there was no strength behind his objection, no force. He'd practically whined.

"Yeah? Then fuck you," Jerry guffawed. "Wake up some other dealer the night before Christmas and haggle with him on prices." He flicked on a brand-new sixty-inch high-definition plasma TV, apparently the only thing in the house originating from the twenty-first century. "Now leave me alone. I got a basketball game to ignore."

"Can I write you a check?" Cole asked.

Jerry stopped staring at the TV and glowered at Cole. "Motherfucker," he said, "we need to have a talk, all right? Sit down."

Cole did as directed. He was tweaking now, bugs under his skin, his eyes bouncing around his skull.

"I heard the sheriff's been sniffing around town for those two missing bodies," Jerry said. "Frankly, I'm a little surprised you didn't think to give me a heads-up about his visit to that house you're building."

Were *building*, Cole thought darkly.

"Me and Teddy handled it," Cole said confidently. "Look, we had it covered. He came, asked his questions, and left." He threw his hands up in the air. "Do I seem worried?"

"And what if that sheriff connects the dots between those checks you're cutting and *me*," Jerry asked, leaning forward, pointing a finger in Cole's face. "Then what?"

"So, make up some bullshit invoices," Cole said evenly, "and we'll say you were doing labor for us. Carrying drywall, painting, whatever. I already thought about all this." He worked so hard to keep calm even as he wanted to scream, *Where's my goddamn meth!*

Jerry smiled and nodded his approval. "That's not half bad, Cole," he admitted. "You know, I did work a little construction back in my day." It was true. Back more than thirty years earlier, Jerry had been a skinny eighteen-year-old with weed connections, and after providing the other guys on his crew with whatever vice they needed, he decided to ditch the manual labor for something a little less strenuous.

Jerry reached behind the couch he was installed on, producing that black nylon gym bag. After fishing around for a few moments, he tossed four small plastic bags at Cole.

"I'll take a check tonight, dipshit," he said, "but in the future, you gotta start bringin' cash, all right? Now get the fuck outta here, huh?"

That night, Cole checked into a dodgy little motel, its lobby smeared in the afterglow of a neon VACANCY sign. He locked the flimsy door and propped a chair under its cheap brass knob. He turned on the TV, as much for companionship as for entertainment, then bolstered himself up in the bed and lit that little glass pipe.

38

The porchlight of Teddy's condo cast a glow over Bart and Margo where they stood in the cold, Margo's arms stacked with presents, Bart's one good arm slung over her shoulder. They looked like rediscovered love, like a winning lottery ticket plucked right out of the garbage.

Teddy held open the door for them, and as soon as Bart was through the threshold, he gave his friend a viselike hug.

"Merry Christmas, buddy," Teddy said, his eyes glistening.

"I didn't know Mormons celebrated Christmas," Bart replied, a grin on his face. "Don't you guys worship some sacred prophet's dirty underwear or something?"

"Come on in!" Teddy said, chuckling good-naturedly and ignoring the barb.

"We brought presents," Margo said, giving Teddy a chaste kiss on the cheek and then offering a hug to Britney. "Don't worry, though. We won't stay long or anything."

At the kitchen table, the adults sipped eggnog and watched the girls open their presents. Then the children drifted off to their bedrooms, leaving wads of wrapping paper on the worn carpeting.

"You guys mind if Bart and I go for a little walk?" Teddy asked, already rising from his seat to kiss the top of Britney's head.

Bart and Margo exchanged a glance; it hadn't really been posed as a question. Something in Teddy had changed, and for the better, too. It wasn't something a person could squarely place their finger on, but . . . the guy had toughened somehow, his confidence expanding.

The two men donned their jackets and walked out onto the cleanly shoveled driveway. A silver sliver of a moon hung over those mountains of darkest black; the stars a million tiny sugar crystals spilled above.

"I've been texting Cole for the past two days," Teddy said. "Haven't heard back from him."

"Well, I expect we'll see him there tomorrow morning," Bart said, rubbing at his jaw. "He's not going to miss out on that bonus, for one thing. And hey, we're still a triangle, right? Still three partners. Without any one of us, that project would never have gotten done."

"Amen," Teddy said, nodding. "You clean again?"

"Yeah, tryin' to be," Bart said, glancing at his boots. "Don't ever, *ever* pick up that shit. I've always been able to climb out of the hole, but . . . I ain't gonna lie . . ." He thought back to Bill, to what he was pretty sure he'd done. "Without going to that hospital, I might not have actually managed to clean up there. Fact is, amigo . . . I prolly ought to skip town sometime soon. Put some distance between me and this place. If I was you, I wouldn't ask where I'm headed either. I'll find a way somehow to send word."

Teddy nodded gravely. Then both men stood in the cold, blowing into their hands.

"So, tomorrow is sort of the end, then, of our company?" Teddy asked.

"No, I wouldn't say that," Bart replied. "I think the way you brought this project home, the way you shepherded it from start to finish . . . Hell, Teddy, either you can do this by yourself, or maybe you and Cole can give it a go if he's up to it. You'll have this house under your belt and maybe a little publicity, plus Gretchen's recommendation and all that bonus money . . . I mean, you grabbed the golden ring, Ted. You got it."

"Couldn't a done it without you," Teddy demurred.

"So where is Cole?" Bart asked.

"Honestly," Teddy began, "I'm not sure. I tried a few likely places. No dice."

"Well, maybe we should go find him, after all," Bart said. "I don't trust Gretchen. I don't want to give her *any* reason to hold back that bonus, and if he ain't there, holding his hand out, too . . . Yeah, come to think of it, let's not leave it up to chance. We gotta git him. And another thing, Teddy-Bear. If he's out of his mind, we can't have him getting picked up by the cops and flapping his gums. We're so close to the finish line, amigo. But if we were to get so much as pulled in for questioning, let alone arrested . . . All that money we made . . . It wouldn't take long for a team of attorneys to burn through that. . . ."

Teddy whistled low. "Every morning," he said, "I wake up and I imagine that everything I saw was gone, erased. And I try to build a new memory. A memory where we're waving goodbye to them, watching them walk down the driveway to Bill's truck. We make plans to visit José down in Mexico." He shook his head, as if to discard the reality of what happened, then covered his mouth with a hand. "But it's hard, Bart. Those men are gone."

Bart placed a hand on Teddy's shoulder.

"You need to think of your girls," Bart said quietly. "Do whatever you need to do to make that story true, because, brother, the alternative is . . . monstrous. We'll be seen as monsters."

Teddy nodded.

"You understand me?" Bart asked.

"Yeah," Teddy mumbled. "I got you. Guess I oughta tell Britney we're headed out for a bit."

"Good idea," Bart agreed. "I may have just got back together with Margo, so maybe I oughta check in, too. . . . Probably shouldn't screw that up already."

Maybe if they lived in a metropolis, Cole could have disappeared for days, sunk into the fabric of the city unnoticed by anyone. But all it took was an hour of calling the hotels and motels around town before they found him at a Motel 6.

The manager hesitated to cooperate, but when they explained that Cole was likely holed up, doing drugs, he quickly acquiesced, providing them with the room number.

"Cole!" Bart shouted. "Open this fucking door, or I'll bust it down!"

"Go away!" Cole shouted back. "I'm not here."

"I hate to break down a good door on Christmas Eve," Bart sighed. "Seems like bad karma."

Teddy leaned against the door. "Buddy," he began, "it's us. Okay? We're here to get you. We've got just one more thing to do and then we're free and clean. Listen to me: *I promise you*—we'll get you some help. Some serious help. 'Cause, listen, this ain't who you are. All right? Now let us in and we can talk. But if Bart has to break down the door, you know the cops'll be here in a second. And none of us want that, now, do we?"

When the door opened, Bart hardly recognized his friend. His eyes were huge and rolling around in his skull like two loose eight balls. He wore only a pair of dingy blue jeans, no shirt or socks. The television blared behind him, glowing blue.

"Merry Christmas, fellas," he said with some effort.

"Get some clothes on, buddy," Teddy said to Cole. "Warm clothes."

Cole slunk back into the motel room, wandering around the bed in search of his socks.

"You get him into your truck," Bart said, "and I'll gather his stuff and drive his vehicle."

"*What* stuff?" Teddy asked, almost laughing. "He can barely find his boots."

"The drugs, he means," Cole said.

"Oh, right," Teddy said. "Wait, we're not taking him to my place, are we?"

"No," Bart sighed. "Let's go back to where it all started."

They drove slowly southeast out of town, following the snaking road along river bottoms, past mountains hulking up high, and obscuring the heavens where they rose up into the night like sharp white teeth. Then the two trucks left the county highway, as they made their way up that familiar gravel road, Cole in the passenger seat of Teddy's truck, peering out the window like a meek little boy. Up, up, up they rode, cautious on the icy surface and for once in no particular hurry. They wended farther and farther up, until finally, in the distance, they began to glimpse a pale glow.

A quarter mile before they reached that final turnaround, just before the river and the bridge, they caught a proper view of the house in all its glory. Teddy stopped the truck, and they sat there, more or less motionless, save for Cole, whose tweaking body vibrated as if a current of electricity ran humming through him.

"Jesus," he mumbled. "Would you look at what we . . . at what we *did*."

Most of the houses and apartments that True Triangle had worked on, the condominiums and retail spaces, were instantly forgettable, identifiable only in their banality or neglect. The hoarder's house that they'd been hired to empty, for instance—the ten dumpsters they filled with moldering stuffed animals and dolls before discovering that the basement was a repository for years', perhaps decades', worth of the man's urine, all safely stored in hundreds upon hundreds of recorked wine bottles. Or the apartment where they found a brick of cocaine when a sodden drop-tile ceiling collapsed. Or the condominium where Teddy happened into a couple's private dungeon, not much larger than a crawlspace, all lined with mirrors, ropes, gags, and whips.

Light was not generally something those buildings accounted for. And there was a simple reason for this: Windows are expensive. When you are constructing a building on a tight budget, the first line item to be shrunk is the windows. A roof cannot be skimped on. Nor can the foundation, the electricity, the plumbing, or the studs that hold the whole works in place. But windows, windows are a luxury. And natural light, therefore, is a luxury. Think of the shabbiest, poorest domicile you've ever visited, and what you'll often notice is how dark the space is. The trailer park, shantytown, or tenement rarely offers a space with a view.

Glass is nothing more than melted sand, cooled in just such a way as to render the liquid transparent. The larger the window, the more care is required for that pane of glass. Not just in its manufacture, but in its every leg of transport. And its storage. A piece of lumber might have an imperfection, some knot or twist, but these imperfections can be cut away and the wood used elsewhere; in the construction of a house, there is need for all sizes of lumber. But a window has only one acceptable condition: perfect. Anything less, and the window is useless. To a homeowner, one minuscule crack is the same as a million shards of broken glass. Unacceptable.

Cole liked to think of the *time* that went into each window. And not just the labor of crafting the window or transporting and installing it at a building site. But *all* the molecules of sand, all the billions and billions of particles that had once been the proud shoulders of mountains, tumbled down in avalanches and deposited into rivers, only to be broken down into smaller and smaller stones, until, after countless millennia, those mountains were nothing more than pinprick-size crystals.

Sitting there, in that idling truck, looking at those great, wide plate-glass windows and the golden light they now sent forth into the night, Cole was reminded of his grandmother taking him to some country church, and while she chatted with other cottontops, how he touched the stained glass on the church's windows, how he ran his fingers right over Jesus's face, and over the disciples' feet, across the brown wood of the cross, and into the very blood of the chalice.

"To me," Cole said, "this will al-al-always be, the Cr-Cr-Crystal House. For better or worse."

"Come on," Teddy said. "I'll drive you up there."

"Naw," Cole put in. "Leave me here. You get on home to your family. We'll see you tomorrow morning. Meantime, enjoy your Christmas Eve. Have fun with those kids."

They shook hands, and then Teddy turned his truck around, leaving Cole there in the immense darkness, as Bart slammed the door of his own truck and walked over to join his friend.

"You can lean on me if you need to," Bart told Cole, and as the two friends began walking toward the house, Cole leaned into his shoulder, not so much because his footing was poor but because it felt good to press against something warm and solid. The driveway gleamed white-blue under the moon's light, all blanketed with newly fallen snow, and the air was crisp and cold, the faintest scent of pine boughs on the wind mixing with a slight sulfurous tang blowing down off the hot springs.

"I don't know how you handled that stuff," Cole said. "I feel . . . swallowed. Like the only thing I can see is darkness, and somehow, it's all I *want* to see."

"We'll get you back," Bart promised. "It ain't easy going back, but it can be done."

Before reaching the house, Bart ducked into their trailer and came back out into the cold with a small backpack, before leading Cole up toward the house itself, struck by how docile Cole seemed now, as gentle as a lamb. Then, bathed in the light of the moon, and the light issuing out of Gretchen's house, Bart shucked off his clothes—all of them—right down to his newly skinny white ass, before stepping gingerly into those hot springs. Cole watched him, not so much seeing his nudity as registering the delight in his friend's face—the sheer delight—at finally actualizing a dream.

"Come on in, buddy," Bart sang. "Take a load off."

Bart leaned over the rim of the hot springs to reach into the backpack, and he produced two bottles of ice-cold Coors Light, which he then sunk into the yielding snowbank just behind him.

" 'Fraid you're gonna need to help me open these," Bart said with a sad smile. "This one-handed man needs to work on his beer-opening technique."

Cole quickly shed his clothes, unaware of the fact that Bart may have lured him into the hot springs as much to ensure that his buddy's rank body was clean before Gretchen's arrival as out of any sense of celebration. He opened the two bottles and passed one back to Bart.

Bart set down his bottle near the backpack and reached into the sack once more to produce a bar of Dr. Bronner's peppermint soap. He proceeded to lather himself up before throwing the bar at Cole, who clumsily caught it.

"Gotta smell good for the boss tomorrow, right?" Bart said, averting his eyes from Cole.

"Yeah, I suppose so. Hey, keep that stump out of the water, huh? Last thing you need's any infections."

Good point, Bart thought, before dunking his head under the water, one arm upraised. When he resurfaced, Cole was staring blankly at the house.

"You suppose if I told Gretchen about . . . you know, about what we'd done . . . do you suppose she'd help us out, Bart?"

Bart took a sip from the bottle, then set it down and wiped the water off his face and waded over to Cole.

"Buddy," he began, "you need to go to a place in your head where all that never happened. All right? Their bodies are gone. Totally gone. There is no evidence of anything. You did what you had to do because *I* put us in a . . . in a terrible, terrible position. It is truly my fault. But, Cole—you can't tell *anyone* about what we did, ever."

Bart saw that Cole was crying; he looked like a frightened child. "They didn't deserve what we did to them," Cole said. "Burnt up like that, so their families'll never find them. Killed like damn dogs; like two dogs we couldn't suffer anymore. Like two dogs barking too loud!" Cole let loose with a series of crazed barks and howls.

"Stop it," Bart said, trying to cover his friend's bellowing mouth. "Shut your mouth, Cole. Knock that shit off."

He splashed water at Cole's face until his friend finally stopped.

Then, from far down the valley and out toward the highway, came a chorus of coyote cries: barking and yipping and long prolonged howls.

"Jesus, this is a godforsaken place," Cole said, his tears subsiding. "I don't care how beautiful the house is. It's haunted, and always will be. Three people have died here, and you"—he paused—"you lost your hand." The two men fell silent awhile. "Bad luck is what this place is," Cole continued a few moments later. "Like a fucking monument to greed, and *we* built it. Three rubes, fallin' all over each other to pick up Gretchen's spare change."

"You heard what I said, though?" Bart asked. "Didn't you, Cole? We can't tell anybody what happened. *No one.* Ever."

"Yeah," Cole said, "I heard you, buddy. Just keep it stowed away. I get it."

"I'm fucking serious, Cole," Bart said, pointing a finger in Cole's direction.

"Don't worry, buddy," Cole said, his voice now almost eerily calm. "Nobody'll ever know what you did."

Bart stood and waded out of the hot springs, drying himself with one of the ratty towels they'd kept in the trailer. "I imagined a much different dip in these springs when we were finished," Bart said. "I thought there'd be champagne, caviar, maybe some glitzy lights...."

"I'm tired, Bart," Cole said, reaching for another towel inside the bag.

"We should move the trailer, too," Bart said. "At least park it across the bridge, in that turnaround. I don't think it's something Gretchen ought to see as she pulls in here for the first time in weeks."

Cole nodded. "Good idea."

They dressed quickly and then double-teamed the trailer, picking up the detritus of the past four months of their life. Hanging over all the stale sweat of dirty socks was the slight smell of meth, a light odor that someone else may have taken for vinegar or ammonia but which to the two men was unmistakably and inextricably linked to this place and time in their lives. Cole walked down the hill and drove his truck back up the driveway; then he hitched the trailer up and swung it around, before driving it back and away from the house. Looking in his rearview mirror, it was as if the house were watching him with wide golden eyes under a heavy rectangular brow.

Once the trailer was relocated, they left the windows open to air it out, and Bart lit a few scented candles, the lights of which seemed cheerful and true to the holiday.

Bart lumbered back uphill. The hot springs had actually relaxed him some, leaving his body as limber as he'd felt since before the start of this project, as loose, really, as he'd felt in years. Cole was nowhere to be found outside, but inside the garage his shoes and socks were neatly arranged near the bottom of the stairs leading to the first floor. Bart set his new cowboy boots right next to them and plodded up the stairs.

He found Cole stroking a nondescript wall, his fingertips touching the finished surface as if he were reading Braille.

"I punched a hole in this wall," Cole said weakly, "right here."

"You sure?" Bart asked, walking over to stand beside his friend. "Looks fine to me."

"I'm sure," Cole said. "Right here."

Then he pointed down the hall, to the doorway of one of the bedrooms.

"And there, too. Teddy must've patched 'em up right away."

"Did a helluva job, then," Bart said, raising his eyebrows. "Why'd you do that?"

"I was out of my mind," Cole answered. "Maybe I still am."

"Hey," Bart said, "come on, now. Don't say that. We just have to get through tonight. She'll be here in less than twelve hours, Cole. We get the house cleaned up, make sure things are spic-and-span, then we can crash in the trailer for a few hours. Get some shut-eye."

Cole nodded his weary head, and they went to work, sweeping and mopping floors, vacuuming, spraying Windex on all the glass and the surfaces of the gleaming new appliances. They wore thin white cotton gloves, careful not to leave their prints on anything; not the doorknobs or mirrors, not the countertops or the stainless steel of the refrigerator. They wanted the house to appear as it should—totally fresh and unlived in. But for Cole in particular, this cleaning reminded him of the days after they—*he still couldn't quite believe it*—murdered Bill and José. Those days of frantically cleaning blood off the floor, ceiling, and walls of the garage. Of disposing of clothing and anything that might yield some forensic evidence of that horrible evening.

Just before dawn, after they'd both walked through the house three different times, inspecting for the slightest flaws anywhere, they walked down the driveway to the trailer and, like two boys at the end of a long sleepover, fell asleep in the narrow bed, their backs to each other, the mountains growing brighter in the east.

39

"Merry Christmas," her driver said, as he passed her a stiff paper cup of hot coffee sealed up tight. "We've got a bit of a drive ahead of us."

The SUV left Jackson, driving quiet roads southeast of town. In the backseat, Abby studied plans of the house on her phone. Looking at the topographic map of the site, she could hardly believe the sharp elevation changes that defined the valley and the mountain rising straight up from it. Without even laying eyes on the land, Abby felt a queasiness in her gut. This was a landscape that ought to be preserved, not gated off and developed. She'd gone to college for conservation biology, but there she was, flying on private planes, acting as some rich lady's assistant in a land deal.

She checked her emails and texts. Still no word from Gretchen.

The SUV slowed and made a left turn onto a gravel road before coming to a stop.

"You need to make any calls or send any messages?" the driver said, leaning back to address her. "This'll probably be your last best chance. I doubt we'll get much of a signal from here on."

Abby stared at Gretchen's contact information before typing a quick text:

> JUST ARRIVING TO YOUR PROPERTY. DRIVING TO HOUSE NOW. HOPE YOU FEEL BETTER TODAY? MERRY CHRISTMAS.

She gave the driver a nod, and they resumed the journey, proceeding slowly along an icy gravel road that could only be described as treacherous. The drifts the snowplows had piled up stood taller than the SUV itself, the sides of the driveway marked with tall wooden poles, bright orange flags adorning the tops of the markers.

"Holy shit," the driver muttered softly, as he stared ahead to where the river boiled and frothed. "This is *your* house we're driving to?" He glanced at the young woman in his rearview mirror.

"No, no," she said, meeting his eyes. "My employer's."

"She must be a very private person."

She's dying, Abby thought, before replying quietly, "Yes, she'll never be . . ."

"She'll never be able to keep this road open all winter," he continued. "We're lucky the snows have been so light. Another month, heck, another few days, everything'll be buried."

At five and ten miles an hour, it took forever to reach the turnaround at the end of the road, just before the river and bridge leading up to the house. And then there they were, finally. Abby pressed her face close to the window, the cliff-faces rising up majestically over the house, steam rising from the hot springs, and the sunlight warming that whole valley as if to plate it all in gold foil.

"My lord," Abby said. "Have you ever seen anything so beautiful?"

The driver parked the SUV near a camping trailer and three pickup trucks, all emblazoned with a triangle logo, and they sat for a moment, idling and staring out the windows.

"No," he replied. "I haven't. Never seen anything like this."

"I know this isn't probably part of your job description," Abby said, "but I wonder if you might escort me up there? Inside, I mean? I really don't know what to expect."

Which was the truth. If the house wasn't complete, or hadn't been completed to Gretchen's specifications, what would she tell the men who awaited her inside the house? After all their work, after crafting such a beautiful structure, how could she possibly withhold their rewards? And on Christmas morning, no less? She, of all people. And how would they respond to her, this young proxy, when all along they'd expected Gretchen? When they had so clearly toiled, and all for that one woman's benefit.

"Are you kidding me?" the driver said, grinning. "I can't come this close and *not* see the inside."

They left the warm confines of the vehicle and walked slowly across the bridge. The driveway was salted, which made the going easier. As the elevation steepened, their strides up toward the hot springs grew more labored, and finally they approached the steaming pool, where the driver removed his gloves and touched the water's surface.

"This place is like Shangri-La," he said, staring up at the cliff-faces all aglow in the morning light.

Together, they walked to the garage, where Abby pushed open a door to reveal a perfectly clean concrete floor. There was room there for three vehicles.

Three vehicles, she thought. *For one woman who may never drive again.*

She followed the sound of voices and the smell of freshly brewed coffee up a beautiful hickory staircase and onto the expansive next floor, where three men, perhaps a decade older than her, hunched around a commanding granite kitchen island, all of them sipping coffee out of paper cups. At the first sight of her, they stood right up, straightening their backs and smoothing the fronts of their

button-down shirts. The most youthful-looking of the three pulled at
the lapels of what looked to be a brand-new black blazer. The biggest
of the men seemed to be missing all the fingers of his left hand, his
right hand cradling that stump. The last man looked utterly haggard,
so bedraggled and thin he might have crawled out of a culvert, though
his hair was combed, and something in his eyes shone like pride, or
perhaps just relief. Then, as the driver also came up those stairs behind her and stood on that first floor, his eyes wide and his mouth
open as he reached the main floor, Abby noticed something cross all
three men's faces, and their eyes squinted with confusion and anger.

"Who are *you*?" the haggard one asked. "Where's Gretchen? What
the fuck's going on here?" His face was red, and veins were popping
on his neck and forehead.

The young one intercepted him as he moved toward Abby, barking
like a rabid dog. "Where's Gretchen, huh? Where is she? We did *our*
job! We DID OUR JOB! Where is *she*?"

"Now hold on," the driver said loudly, his voice booming in that
wide-open space as he stepped between Abby and the men. "Let's all
just calm down, all right? This young woman is here on behalf of her,
uh, employer. Isn't that right, miss?"

"Yes," Abby said. "I'm, uh, I am Gretchen's assistant."

"Where *IS* she?" the bedraggled one bellowed.

"Calm him down," the driver said to the other two men, "or I'm
going to escort this young woman back to her hotel and whatever
meeting you fellas here were expecting just ain't gonna happen."

"He's right, Cole," said the young one in the blazer. "Let's all take
a deep breath."

"Better have our money. She better have our fucking money. All
we been through."

"I've got your money," Abby managed. "But first, maybe you ought
to introduce yourselves, and then I can tell you who *I* am and, um, why
Gretchen isn't here."

"Of course. I'm Teddy Smythe, miss."

"Bart Christianson."

"Cole McCourt."

"Would you like a cup of coffee, miss?" Teddy asked. "I just got this French press for this morning's housewarming, and, uh, well, anyway, coffee tastes a little strong to *me*, but it's nice and hot."

"No thank you, Mr. Smythe," Abby said, managing a small smile.

"So, where's Gretchen?" Cole said again, though a little less menacingly this time.

They all stood around the kitchen island, each of them with their arms crossed across their chest.

"I'm afraid she's very ill," Abby explained. "Well, I think I can level with you, because you'll find out soon enough anyway. . . . She's dying."

Bart shook his head. "You have to be fucking kidding with us," he said.

"I am not," Abby said. "It's stage IV cancer. She and I were set to board a plane together yesterday to fly out here, and just before we left . . . well, she collapsed. I haven't even heard from her yet today."

"I *knew* this place was fucked from the get-go," Bart said, covering his face with that remaining hand. "All that, and for a woman who might never *see* the place."

"I wouldn't bet against her," Abby said with some force. "As you know, Gretchen is incredibly tough and driven, and she's got the best doctors in the world. I truly believe the one thing keeping her alive all these months is the idea of living out her final days in this house. Look, I know you gentlemen are angry at her, and perhaps you have a right to be. But please, trust me, *no one* has ever wanted to stand here, in this beautiful house on this morning, more than Gretchen. And know this: You three have fulfilled her dream. That must mean something."

"Pretty expensive coffin," Cole said, hanging his head just above the island's surface.

"Jesus," Bart said, "take it easy, Cole. She doesn't deserve that."

"Oh, *fuck* off, Bart," Cole replied. "You really think she cared about us? About our well-being? She even send any flowers to your hospital room? Did you get a card? Did she even text you? Let's be fucking real, for once."

"Still, I don't wish anything bad on her," Bart said. "She didn't do this to me." He held up his left arm. "She didn't *make* us take this project. Didn't hold a gun to our heads."

"No," Cole replied, "but she burned us down, used us up. And you know it."

An uncomfortable pause settled over the kitchen.

"Well." Abby sighed. "I say we get down to business, because I'm sure you gentlemen want to get paid. I'm here to do several things. To inspect the house, and assuming everything is right, reward you your bonuses, and then to sign the final draw. After which, I can, uh, take the keys and basically send you on your way."

"Send us on our way, huh?" Cole sneered. "You know Bart here lost all the fingers on his hand working on this house? You have any idea what we've been through, lady?" He dearly wished that he had brought the Mason jar of Bart's fingers with him, so that he might have handed it to this woman. *That* would make a fitting housewarming present, now, wouldn't it?

"I'm sorry," Abby admitted, meeting his eyes. "I'm just—I'm just the messenger."

"Maybe I can guide you around the house," Teddy interjected. "I think you'll find everything's in order."

Teddy began where they stood, in the kitchen. He motioned toward the one-of-a-kind cabinets, the specially imported granite, the commercial-grade windows, and the top-of-the-line appliances. He suggested Abby open the cutlery drawer and showed her the high-end hardware of the adjustable shelves in several of the cabinets.

"None of us have ever seen a project of this quality," he said. "From the cement work to the bathroom tiling, everything's top-quality, all the way through, and exquisitely finished." He took a shameful amount of pride in the use of that word, *exquisitely*.

From room to room they moved, Abby's defenses slowly melting as she was overcome by the thoughtfully decorated Christmas tree in front of those wide windows, or the way in which the men had perfectly arranged all the furniture for which she'd supervised delivery. It was all well and truly clear: These three men had done everything in their power to create a special moment for Gretchen when she arrived here, and now she felt a deep sympathy for them. They were like little boys on Christmas morning who somehow had been promised a glimpse of Santa Claus, only to be confronted by his loud absence, or perhaps some dull, shopping-mall impostor.

As they passed the fieldstone fireplace, Abby asked, "And what about Bill? We haven't heard from him in a month or more. I know Gretchen was in contact with local authorities, but she's been so absorbed in her own work and with her health in decline . . ."

The tour had by then wound back toward the kitchen, where Bart promptly insinuated himself.

"Yeah, after he completed the fireplace, that was the last we heard from him," Bart said. "And we tried, too. He's owed a pretty healthy chunk of change, for one thing. Both him and his assistant, José."

"Do you think something could have happened to them?" Abby asked. "I mean, the way Gretchen described Bill, he just seemed so . . . I don't know—dependable. And strong. She is very, very concerned about him."

"You know what they say," Bart put in, with a wry tone that felt off to Abby. "It's the quiet ones you gotta keep an eye on."

"What are you suggesting?" she asked. "That Bill wasn't who he appeared to be?"

"Hey, these are the building trades," Bart said. "We see all kinds, miss. Look, we've got no idea what happened to Bill, or José, for that matter. But we've seen it all. Nothing would surprise us."

"Well, what *do* you think could have happened to them?" she asked. "Did you check with the police?"

"I really don't know," Bart said. "Maybe they went to visit José's family down in old Mexico. Or maybe they took a much-needed vacation together to Greece. Maybe they drove off one of these scary mountain roads and somebody'll find 'em come spring. Who knows? But after they finished their work for Gretchen, that was the end of *our* obligation to 'em. We're just waiting for a bill, so we can officially settle up."

"So, you never called the police?"

"And tell them what? We haven't seen an invoice yet?" Bart scoffed.

"The sheriff *has* been here," Cole said, almost calmly. He gestured toward Bart. "Came not long after the accident. It isn't fair to say we haven't been in touch with the authorities. We've seen him a few times, actually, all the way back to when that fella came to get his forgotten tool."

Abby bit her lower lip and surveyed the men.

"Well, what do you think, miss?" Teddy asked, desperately trying to redirect the conversation, eager to get things back on track. "Would you say the house is in order?"

She took a deep breath, then smiled.

"Gentlemen," she began, "congratulations. I'm happy to communicate to Gretchen that the house is one hundred percent complete and *beautifully* built. I really can't think of a single objection she might have."

There was a long moment of silence when the men simply stared at one another, and then at this messenger, Abby, a total stranger to them, and this chauffeur, another stranger, before Teddy cheered wildly, jumping up and down, hugging Cole, who merely stood there, as if a pillar of salt, suffering Teddy's affection, even as Bart, off to the side, began sliding down one of the walls until he sat on the gleaming wood floor, his head between his knees.

"So today, I will make out two checks to True Triangle," Abby said, leaning onto the island and flourishing the checkbook and one of Gretchen's Montblanc pens. "The first is your bonus for finishing the house on time. That check is in the amount of five hundred and twenty-five thousand dollars, to be split between the three of you. The second check is another bonus that my employer wanted very much to reward you with because of the hardships you've endured, including the loss of your hand, Mr. Christianson. That check is for three hundred thousand dollars, again, to be divided by the three of you.

"I'll be in town for the next several days," she continued. "If you finish your final draw, we can bring all this to a close before I leave. In fact, that's what Gretchen would prefer. She says you three deserve as much."

Then she handed the checks to Teddy, whom she reckoned seemed the most responsible of the group. He held the two slips of paper in his hand as if they were sacred scrolls, just staring at them.

"Now," Abby said, "if you'll excuse me, gentlemen, I'd like to take some pictures to send to Gretchen."

She shook their hands and drifted off to snap photographs of the Christmas tree, before suddenly remembering something and returning to the kitchen area.

"Oh," Abby said, "one other thing—I forgot the keys."

Teddy reached into his pocket and placed two gold keys into the palm of her hand.

"Thank you," she said. "You've done great work. You should all be truly very proud. And here is my telephone number, if you need me." And with that, she handed him a small slip of paper before turning her back to them and continuing to take photos.

The men stayed put, unsure what to do with themselves, though not exactly wanting to leave the house.

"Come on," Teddy said. "Let's get a drink."

"It's Christmas," Bart replied. "Shouldn't you be home with the kids?"

"Oh, there's time for that," Teddy said, "but first we ought to celebrate, don't you think?"

"I agree," said Cole, who above all did not want to be left alone right then.

They converged on the Chinatown Restaurant, one of the few businesses open on Christmas Day. Past the lobby's red gumball machines and faux golden dragons and lions, the men were seated in a dining room with plastic bamboo plants and wall-mounted televisions. In their hometown, back in Utah, the three men had often visited a Chinese restaurant called the Pagoda, a near magical place with a shallow wishing well, where three orange koi swam their endless circuits, where the brilliantly red dining room was a dark mystery, the walls papered in rich textured patterns, the background music trickling just above the dining room's soundtrack of competing voices, clattering silverware, and the distant frying sounds of the woks at work. But this place was just a rectangle in the center of a woebegone strip mall.

"Christ, this is depressing," Bart said.

"Well, let's have a drink," Teddy suggested, perusing the menu. "Maybe a mai tai?"

Cole sat stoically, passing his finger over the flame of the candle at the center of their table.

Their server arrived, and Teddy ordered their drinks and several entrées; then the men just sat there, quietly, avoiding eye contact and unsure where they stood.

"Cole," Bart said finally, "I told Teddy this already, but after we deposit those checks and split up the bonuses, I think I need to bow out. If you guys get the paperwork started, I'll sign whatever you need. But I think you understand. Might be for the best if I disappear for a while. Truth is, I ain't any use to you now anyways. Like tits on a bull."

Cole cleared his voice, then went about smoothing the red linen of their tablecloth. "Yeah," he began, "might not be a bad idea to deal *me* out, too. I, uh . . . I'm gonna need to get back to the straight and narrow before I . . ." His voice drifted off, the other two giving him whatever time he needed. "But I'll tell you something."

Just then their drinks arrived, and each man took up his goblet of mai tai.

"We built a helluva beautiful house out there," Cole finished. "Here's to us: Long live the True Triangle."

They touched glasses with as much festiveness as they could summon then sat quietly, unsure how to proceed with the rest of their lives, but certain of their crimes and newfound wealth.

40

A bby sat alone in the conference room, staring out the window. The space was so quiet she could hear the ice cubes in the glass before her crack and resettle. A bookish-looking young man entered the room with a file folder tucked under his arm. They shook hands, and he unbuttoned his suit jacket before sitting down and briefly cleaning the lenses of his glasses.

"Ms. Saunders, my name is Aarav Reddy, and I am the attorney tasked with executing Gretchen Connors's will and estate. I know we've spoken over the telephone and communicated through email, but I just wanted to say how sorry I am for your loss. Now, um, you may not have known it, but Gretchen was pretty methodical when it came to her estate documents, and she was incredibly grateful to you for your help, especially in her final days."

Abby nodded her head. "She was the best boss I ever had," she said, looking out the window.

"Well, Ms. Saunders, I'm happy to report that Ms. Connors named you as a beneficiary in her will. She left you two hundred and fifty thousand dollars, in fact, and her Range Rover, which is housed at the Jackson Hole Airport, near the house you visited."

Abby continued staring vacantly out the window.

"Do you understand what I just said?" Reddy asked after a moment. "Miss? Or is it, ma'am? I'm not sure—"

"Her whole life meant so little in the end, didn't it?" Abby said suddenly.

"What?"

"She went from her penthouse to work and back, every day for thirty years. Took about two weeks' worth of vacation every year. The bare minimum, probably just so she wouldn't attract attention to the fact that she rarely stopped thinking about work. She didn't even live long enough to see that house of hers. Just accumulated a bunch of money, and . . . for *what*?"

Reddy remained silent.

"Did she have any relatives?"

Reddy cleared his throat. "I'm, uh, not normally at liberty to share that kind of information, Ms. Saunders, but seeing as you were not only Gretchen's assistant but also her friend, I can tell you that she had one cousin and also a great-aunt, who each stand to inherit a significant portion of her estate. The rest is to be split between several charities. And you, of course."

He reached into the folder for a small manila envelope, which he slid across the table to Abby.

"Those are the keys to the Range Rover," he explained. "And this," he said, passing her an envelope, "is her gift to you."

Abby held the keys in her hand. "I'd rather she was still alive," Abby said. "That's what I want. I mean, she wasn't the warmest woman I ever met, but . . . God, what a *waste*."

A quiet descended over the conference room.

"And what are your plans, then, um, if you don't mind me asking?" Reddy asked. "Will you be headed back out there?"

"I think so," Abby said. "Yeah. Probably in a week or so. I sort of liked it out there. Liked the mountains."

Reddy sat quietly, lightly drumming his fingers on the table, his work there all but done.

"You work a lot?" she asked him.

"Me? I've got a ten-month-old baby girl," he answered, "a hundred grand in law school debt, forty more for undergraduate. What can I say?" He shrugged his shoulders. "I'm on the treadmill."

She stood from the table, the keys and envelope tightly clasped in her fists.

You're running, all right, she thought. *And you ain't going anywhere fast.*

She rented a single-wide several miles outside Jackson and off the highway, but close enough to a nearby creek so that the traffic noises were somewhat muted. Initially, she knew not a soul and felt very awkward driving Gretchen's Range Rover around town, the odometer reading less than five thousand miles. Three days after she'd taken receipt of the vehicle, an eighteen-wheeler kicked up a stone that left part of the windshield a matrix of cracks. The next morning, walking out to the Range Rover, she was suddenly overcome with the desire to kick the vehicle as hard as she possibly could and did so, leaving a decent-size dent in the back-right quarter-panel. For good measure, she ran a key across the passenger-side door. The following day she regretted both the dent and the scratch because she realized what she *should* have done.

"Shit," she sighed.

She drove the Range Rover to a used-car dealership and asked the owner, an old man with a white mustache and sweat-stained cowboy hat, how much he could give her in trade for the vehicle.

"This vehicle stolen?" he asked. *Vee-hickel*, he pronounced it.

"Nope," she replied. "I got the title, free and clear."

"Somehow, you don't seem like the Range Rover type to me," he said, peering at her worn blue jeans, flannel shirt, leather belt, wind-blown hair, and sunburnt face.

"I sort of inherited it," she said.

"Well," he sighed, "it's a beaut. Won't take me long to unload it."

Circling the Range Rover, he made a whistling sound that conveyed as much admiration as incredulity. "Got a dent over there," he said, pointing. "And a helluva scratch over here. Plus, the windshield needs replacin'."

"You can fix all that in a matter of hours," she said. "This vehicle's barely been driven. It still smells new. So, let's not dick around here. Try to lowball me and I'll walk."

"All right, all right, lady," he said, brushing at his mustache. "Geez, I ain't trying to cheat ya. Just stating the facts. Now, what're ya in the market for?"

She drove off in a brown 1988 Chevy Custom DeLuxe pickup truck plus a sizable five-figure check in her pocket. The shocks were mushy, but the tape deck worked, and inside the glove compartment she found one lonely cassette tape. She popped it in, cranked the volume, and was pleased to hear the opening chords of "Folsom Prison Blues." Glancing in the rearview as she was pulling out of the lot, she saw the old man remove his ten-gallon hat, scratch his head, then turn his back to her and do a little jump in the air, clicking the heels of his cowboy boots.

She smiled and felt like she was righting something askew in the universe. Like straightening a painting hanging crookedly off a gallery wall.

41

Bart pushed the skiff out of the white-sand shallows, into turquoise waters, his shoulder against the stern. When the boat
was in three feet of water and with waves lapping against the
bow, he flopped in, then worked his way back toward the twenty-five-
horse outboard motor. He lighted a cigarette, inhaling a delicious nim-
bus of smoke. With his good hand, he yanked on the motor's starter
cord, an oily blue cloud of exhaust rising into the midmorning air as
he scooted away from shore toward the smaller island just southeast,
where he'd found work as a maintenance man at a resort hotel. It
wasn't as sexy as his visions of tending bar, but the hours were better
and his interactions with guests gratifyingly minimal.

He tied the skiff to a pier, shook hands with one of the fishing
guides, and walked into the nearby kitchen for an egg sandwich and a
cup of coffee, kissing all the female cooks on their cheeks as he made
his way to the manager's office for that day's work orders.

"A leaky sink in unit nine, a loose doorknob in two, and I'd like you to give seven a fresh coat of paint," his manager said brusquely, never meeting Bart's eyes. "Nobody checking in there for a week, so you've got time."

"I'll get right on it," Bart said, and he meant it. On Bocas del Toro, time moved differently; underneath an unrelenting sun, minutes and hours congealed, and expectations took on the value of dreams: If things happened, great; if not, no worries, man. Still, Bart kept up the old work ethic, nonetheless. He loved being an employee, frankly— loved clocking out at the end of the day, loved learning Spanish from the other workers. He couldn't understand why he hadn't moved down here ten years earlier. The management appreciated the fact that his English was perfect, not to mention the steady pace of his work. Viewing Bart as basically indefatigable, they'd taken to calling him El Caballo. He delighted in this. Nobody'd ever given him a nickname before.

Just after five, he punched out, made his way out to the skiff, started the engine, and pointed the craft back across the bay toward the beach and the little town where he and Margo lived in a small concrete cabana, little more than a bedroom, kitchen, small living room, and porch. A humble barbecue grill outside and two cheap plastic deck chairs. That was it. And it was just fine. He'd bought her a surfboard for her birthday that leaned against the wall outside their front door, and in the early mornings or just before dusk he'd sit on the beach and watch her ride the board as the rollers combed toward shore.

Eight hundred yards from the beach, the engine abruptly quit. Bart lifted the little gasoline tank and discovered it empty. The sun was sinking quickly. He found the oars stowed under the benches and set their pins in either gunwale before realizing that a one-handed man did not a natural oarsman make. He sat on the center bench, feeling the sun burn his forehead. He lighted another cigarette.

He had not meant to kill Bill, he realized months earlier. He had meant to kill himself. Or some part of himself. The whole thing still gnawed at him, of course filled his guts with loathing. Many a night he stared at the ceiling of their cabana, puzzling out his best path forward, some balance between morality and happiness. The right thing to do would be to leave this life, haul himself back to Jackson, and confess. But hadn't he suffered and sacrificed enough? Was this new life too much to ask? He'd never harm another soul, as long as he lived, he could promise that. And, too, he was angry at Cole and Teddy, at Gretchen. Angry for being used. Her hundreds of thousands—hell, millions—meant nothing, after all. All that money was just chump change to her. Chump change off a fortune she couldn't even take with her.

For she was right all along. Time. Time was the thing he couldn't get back. And his hand, of course. He'd given everything to her, and that house. From what he'd heard, she had died shortly after the new year. Just that young woman, Abby, by her side in some big-city hospital. And now, the house sat empty. He imagined once the teenagers in Jackson Hole heard about it, heard about this abandoned temple at the end of a road up to heaven, with a hot springs steaming the huge glass windows, why, it wouldn't take long before there would be graffiti on the garage doors and broken beer bottles littering the driveway. How long, he wondered, until the first stone was thrown at all those inviting walls of glass? How long before someone broke in and ruined the place?

Or maybe some other plutocratic type would snatch it up from the estate, take care of it, even as they hoarded all that natural beauty to themselves.

Come to think of it, maybe he preferred those barbarian teenagers.

He exhaled smoke.

A few days prior, he'd been absent-mindedly painting one of the hotel guest rooms when he was interrupted by his boss, who stood in the doorway, looking at him dourly. Behind the boss stood a local constable and two lieutenants.

"Come on," the boss said. "Quickly."

He nodded his head, then carefully wrapped the wet paintbrush in a plastic bag and hammered the metal lid tightly back onto the paint can. He'd thought all along how easy it had been; escaping down here flush with money, setting up this new life, and far, far behind him, two dead bodies and all those crystal meth days. . . . Of course, it couldn't end this way.

Bart stood, and with the police leading the way, he followed them to the largest private cabana on the property. His boss walked behind him, saying nothing. Bart assumed he was being escorted to his own interrogation, his own extradition—perhaps his own execution. Imagined that old Wyoming sheriff sitting in the cabana, a glass of iced tea sweating beside his hairy knuckles while the old man ran an already soaked handkerchief across his glossy forehead.

The local police parted and made a path for Bart, standing on either side of the door.

"Open it," his boss said, nodding.

Bart fumbled for the master key, his hand trembling, found the proper key. He used the stub of his left hand to steady that right arm, and in a moment, glanced at one of the Panamanian cops, who was staring at the stump with something like disgust etched on his face.

The lock turned, and the door eased open. The cops slid around him and into the cabana.

"You go," his boss ordered, pointing into the cabana.

Bart shuffled in, his shoulders slumped in defeat.

But then his boss moved past him, into the cabana's master bedroom, where, through a set of French doors, Bart could see the cops standing, encircling a bed.

Despite the open windows and the scent of the ocean and tropical flowers, Bart could smell the meth in the bedroom. And as he stood just inside the room, he pieced together what happened to the guest lying dead, half covered by bedsheets. On the bedside table was a small mound of cocaine, framed by bottles of rum. Near the dead man's hand, on the bedsheet, was a pipe, its black bowl leaving a dark stain on the white sheets.

"*Déjanos*," the constable said.

Bart drifted out of the room and back toward the guest room he had been painting. Inside that room, he locked the door, slid down to the floor, covered his face with his hand, and closed his eyes, a strange mélange of relief, regret, and horror sweeping over him.

The skiff drifted slowly back to shore. On the beach he spotted what looked to be someone waving at him with two arms, like a person signaling for a rescue. He waved back, suspecting it was Margo. He rarely carried his cell phone anymore and did not have it then, as perhaps he ought to have. The figure on the beach entered the water and appeared to be swimming in a straight line toward him.

He allowed himself to enjoy the last heat of the day. The flat of the ocean. The moisture in the air. The dry burn of the cigarette. He felt healthy again and allowed himself to close his eyes and feel the ocean moving gently beneath the skiff.

"You okay?" Margo called out.

He smiled, startled out of his reverie. She was twenty-five yards off, swimming strongly.

"Yeah," he said. "Ran out of gas."

"What about the oars?" she called, spitting out salt water.

He pulled her aboard, her skin glistening like a dolphin's, then held up his left arm, as if it were the first time she might have seen his stump. "Ever seen a one-handed man row a boat?" he asked.

"Poor baby," she said. "Get in the stern. I'll row you back."

He watched her strong arms move in that particular rhythm. Looked at her long, beautiful feet in the dirty bilge water, her stomach muscles clenching with each pull.

"You sure you're okay?" she asked. "You look sad."

He smiled bravely. "Couldn't be happier," he replied.

When they were perhaps a hundred yards from shore, he unbuttoned his shirt, his pants, and removed his socks and boots, right down to his underwear.

"What are you doing?" she asked, frowning. "Bart?"

He bent down and kissed her firmly, their tongues weaving over each other. Her mouth tasted like cold gin and lime; her skin smelled of the salt water and sunscreen.

"Race you back home!" he yelled, diving out of the skiff.

He moved below the surface for several kicks, before rising up into the sunset-painted waters and then turning onto his back, floating, to stare up at the blue, blue sky. The truth of it was, he didn't have any interest in ever racing anyone, or anything, not ever again.

He backstroked slowly back to shore, and when his feet touched sand, he stood and there she was, looking at him with a blend of curiosity and affection. Together, they pulled the skiff up onto the sand and then made their way back to the cabana.

42

You know what "mortgage" means in Latin, don't you? Teddy's grandfather used to say. *"Death-pledge." Think about that.*

Nevertheless, the following spring, Teddy and Britney bought Penny Abrams's house in town, paying more than fifty percent down in cash. With what money remained, Teddy hired on a framing crew he trusted to rip off the roof, construct a second floor, and finish the basement, complete with new egress windows to brighten its subterranean position. Two months later, the house was unrecognizable. At twenty-two hundred square feet, it was no monstrosity, but each of the girls now had her own room, and for the first time since they were married, Teddy and Britney had a backyard where, on summer nights, they sat together in the darkness, holding hands and listening to the tourist bustle several blocks away.

"I can't believe you did it," Britney said on one of those evenings, not long after they were finally moved in. "I mean, I've always believed in you. Always knew you were a hard worker, but . . ."

"But what?" Teddy asked.

"I just feel like—you know, like our dreams are actually coming true."

Three months after the house was finished, Teddy's phone rang at a jobsite. It was Britney.

"You better get home quick," she said. "Some folks are here to see you."

Teddy didn't need any introductions to know who the sad-faced trio of visitors sitting in his living room were, ignoring the cups of coffee Britney had offered them. It was José's family, come up from Mexico to search for their son, their brother. His parents were short people, well-dressed, with suspicious eyes. They didn't speak any English. That duty was left to his younger sister, a woman who might have been twenty years old, Marisol.

"How can you not know where my brother is?" she asked. "He worked for you. Don't you care about your workers?"

The question stabbed Teddy right in his heart. She was right, of course. Bill and José had been their employees, and True Triangle had been responsible for them, responsible for them beyond just scratching checks or barking out orders.

"Well, see . . . ," Teddy stumbled, "now, I don't know a lot about most of our contractors. Like, for example, after that job, I never seen any of those window installers ever again. Or the tile guy." Teddy saw an opportunity to plant a seed of doubt. "Did you check with ICE, or the INS? Maybe the federales picked him up on something. These days they're doing that kind of thing. Swooping down on a jobsite and just picking up everyone." Teddy wasn't actually sure this was true, but it sounded true enough.

"Mr. Symthe," Marisol began, "José wasn't working at a meat-packing plant outside of Omaha. He wasn't picking strawberries in

Salinas. He is a skilled stonemason. A married father of four, I might add. His wife is beside herself."

Teddy scratched at his head; did not meet Marisol's eyes, though he could feel the woman staring a searing-hot hole right through him.

"Look, I am happy to give you José's wages. I want to."

Just then he was relieved to stand and walk briskly into the kitchen, where he had kept two checks—already written out and dated several months earlier—stored in a cupboard for just such a moment as this. He stood for a time in the kitchen, the envelopes in his hands, trying to imagine that reality he had long ago fabricated: Bill and José walking down the driveway toward their trucks and waving back at Teddy, Bart, and Cole like lifelong friends. He tried to picture them altogether in Mexico, drinking beers and barbecuing together.

When he returned to the living room, he handed José's mother the checks and sat down heavily.

"I'm sorry there isn't more that I can do," he said. "José was my friend. Bill, too. Most talented stonemasons I ever met. And maybe if you leave me your contact information, why, if I ever run into him, or hear word, I'll let you know immediately." He passed Marisol a pen and piece of paper.

These things she held in her hand disgustedly, as if all she wanted to do was throw them back into Teddy's face.

"*No me gusta este hombre*," her father said in a low voice. "*El sabe algo.*"

"*He criado niños*," her mother added. "*Su cara está mintiendo.*"

"We're so sorry," Britney said, tears freely wetting her cheeks. "How horrible for you all. And his family. I think we ought to pray, don't you, Teddy?"

Marisol stared at her father until finally he nodded and reached for the hands of Britney and her mother. Toward the end of the prayer, and only for an instant, Teddy opened his eyes, and he saw that Marisol and her father were staring directly at him; he quickly bowed his head again, and this time, he prayed fervently to God that these people would never hound him again. He wasn't sure that he could keep up with this charade if they did.

He kept the company name. None of his new clientele knew that he'd once had two partners, and if they'd ever heard of Cole Mc-Court, they certainly didn't connect the murderer to Teddy, this soft-spoken, reliable Mormon, often seen about town, shuttling his daughters from one event to the next. The in-towners, of course *they* knew; knew about the ill-fated multimillion-dollar house up by those hot springs. And they knew that no fewer than three men had died there. But the blessing of a tourist town, perhaps, is that memories are short. The influx of California marijuana money and social media millionaires didn't especially care what Teddy had or had not done. All they cared about was that he was capable of building them a beautiful house and responsible enough to return their phone calls. Which, of course, he was; and like a loyal golden retriever, Teddy delighted at pleasing his new masters.

He did update the logo. Now, instead of a single triangle, there were three triangles, interlocked, the tallest triangle in the middle. Though he'd never tell anyone as much, that triangle was him—the last man standing, the tallest mountain in a proud old range, now mostly eroded away.

And sitting in his backyard on some night, long after Britney and the girls had fallen asleep, poking at the embers of a dying fire, he even imagined himself somewhere in the future, a state legislator, well-liked by his peers on both sides of the aisle, even as they talked about him behind his back: his lack of education, his limited travels, the fact that he wouldn't share a drink of Scotch with them. But he could see himself, in a well-tailored suit, cowboy boots, bolo tie, and Stetson, looking every inch the successful entrepreneur and family man, a leader in his ward, and the rare sort of politician who overlooked no one, perhaps because earlier in his life, everyone had overlooked him.

43

The sheriff walked out onto the sun-drenched patio of the treatment center, followed by a counselor who all but tugged at his arm to waylay him. A patient in a hammock practically spilled himself onto the ground when he saw the lawman and quickly speed-walked out to one of the many therapeutic paths leading into the desert. Conversation stilled in and around the rectangular-shaped pool. All eyes were on Cole, where he sat on a lounge chair reading Edward Abbey's *Desert Solitaire*. He let out a little sigh of relief and stood to shake the sheriff's hand.

"You weren't an easy man to find," the sheriff said. "Your buddy Teddy was pretty tight-lipped about your whereabouts. And your other amigo, Bart, up and disappeared like a fart in the wind. Turns out, it was your ex-wife who tipped us off. Guess she forwarded some mail on to you."

Cole nodded his head, smiling grimly. *Poetic justice*, he thought. "How can I help you, Sheriff?"

"Well, I'll cut to the chase. Two men disappear off your jobsite—two of your own contractors—and you have no idea where they went. And the thing is, your company would've owed those two men a lot of money. So, in my line of work, that sort of gives you a motive. 'Specially if they were gonna rat you out for all them drugs you boys were doing."

Cole's smile faded, and his lips pursed tightly.

"See," the sheriff said, "the way I figure it, you boys did something to them two stonemasons. Now, I can't yet *prove* that, but here's the thing: Your old dealer was just found dead in his house. Gunshot, back of the head. Probably pissed off the wrong gang, is my theory. Older fella like that, working alone; he was vulnerable to competition.

"I got any number of people who put you and him together on multiple occasions. Got a waitress, a few building contractors, a gas station attendant. Even some checks written out to him. Gotta say, I wouldn't a pegged you as an addict, Cole. You wouldn't probably remember this, but a few years back, when you and your partners were just starting off, you did a fine job for my brother-in-law. Built a little stand-alone coffee shop in a parking lot by the grocery store."

Cole smiled, remembering that project fondly. How little they'd even known about what they were doing back then.

"Hell, a year ago, I'da thought you were angling for great things. Maybe run for president of the Chamber of Commerce or Board of County Commissioners. But I heard you fell off. Got the junk in your system. Guess that's why you're down here."

He spat into the desert gravel.

"Unless," he said, staring at Cole, "you're just hiding out, on the lam."

Cole remained quiet.

"See, it took us a while to figure out Jerry owned himself an old ranch outside of town. Suppose it was originally his parents' or somethin'. Lonely place. I took a walk around the perimeter. Thought I might find a grave or two. Never did come across anything like that. Them two men disappeared without a trace."

The sheriff removed his hat and scratched at his head.

"Christ, it's hot down here. Anyway, turns out, though, we did find something. Lo and behold, we come across a goddamned good-ole-fashion *clue*. In a locked-up barn of all places. Now what do you think we found, Cole?"

The two men stared at each other for a few seconds.

Cole took a deep breath. "A pickup truck."

The sheriff, who must have been prepared for a battle of wits, took a step back then, sizing this fellow he was talking to anew.

Cole shook his head. "Now, I'm going to say two things, Sheriff, before I ask for my attorney," Cole said, "and I hope like hell you're listening to me."

"I'm listening."

"First, it was me that killed both those men. I was crazy on crystal meth and paranoid as all get-out. I was going days without sleep, hallucinating, the whole thing. Whatever you may think, it wasn't about money. There was plenty of money to be had. We would have paid those men. Would have happily paid them. But I was a lunatic then. A fuckin' zombie. And, well, I'm sincerely very sorry about what I done. I truly am."

He took a deep breath and continued.

"Two, my partners didn't know nothin' about any of it. I hid it from them. All of it. They weren't even at the house with me when I killed both them men or later, when I hid the bodies. Jerry was the one who helped me. So you want to pin it on someone other than me, you can pin it on him, that sumbitch who got me hooked on meth in the first place.

"And now I'd like to speak to my attorney," Cole said, "if you please."

He held up his arms for the handcuffs, an expensive watch encircling that right wrist, glinting brightly in the desert sun.

44

Gretchen Connors's closest existing heirs were a forty-something insurance agent named Blake Connors, a younger cousin on her father's side, and her mother's sister, Rosalind. They bounced up the gravel road to the house, Aarav Reddy driving.

"How's business?" Reddy asked Blake amiably enough.

"Oh, steady," Blake replied, his eyes scanning the mountainsides to the right of the vehicle. He'd never intended to become an insurance agent but somehow slipped into that life after college, when he realized with a start that he had no entrepreneurial dreams, no skills, and no interest in further schooling. So he returned to his hometown, where his good looks, height, and smile combined with a generational understanding of the town's dynamics to make him a natural-born salesperson of home, auto, and life insurance policies.

The trouble was, he and Lindsay were still ninety-six grand deep in student loans between them, there was the new three-hundred-thousand-dollar mortgage on their house, two car payments, a new boat, and, of course, their annual spring vacation to Corpus Christi. It all added up. Or didn't. Between their two jobs there was never anything extra to save—*never*—and the thing that kept him up at nights was the notion that, as their small town aged, so did his clients. One day soon enough, he worried, that well would run dry.

"I don't know why she left any of this property to me," Rosalind groused as Reddy eyeballed her in the rearview mirror. "I'm eighty-six years old in a week. I can't be bumping up and down these roads." She ran a pale, blue-veined hand over her wrist, consulting her watch. "I *do* hope we'll be back to town before my television program comes on."

"Not much for the mountains, I take it, Rosalind?" Blake said, turning in his seat to peer at the old woman.

No, indeed. She had no intention of ever living in this ridiculous house Gretchen had left her part of, and was already desperate to return to her condo on Hutchinson Island, Florida, where the vistas to her east were as wide as the Atlantic Ocean, while to the west, that comfortably predictable stretch of strip malls, chain restaurants, car dealerships, and golf courses running all the way to Lake Okeechobee and the Everglades. Everything you could possibly want. And not a driveway or sidewalk to shovel *ever*. Whereas this wild place filled her with an unnameable dread, from the roaring of the river and the clouds scraping the mountaintops, to this godforsaken gravel road, pitted and rutted, it seemed, about every ten feet, which had the effect of making her feel as if they were driving to the end of the earth.

"I do want to see the house, though," she sighed. "See what all the hullabaloo is about."

"Yeah, just speaking for myself, it's awful hard to imagine paying the taxes," Blake said, shaking his head with exaggerated disbelief. "Especially given how rarely anyone'd even get out to use the place."

"There is a condition in Gretchen's will, I should mention," Reddy said, "whereby all taxes will be paid by the estate for a period of ten years. It certainly was not her intention to bankrupt anyone with the gift of this house."

"Buddy, I've got three kids," Blake continued. "So, unless we were to just, you know, pick up and relocate . . . I mean, what kind of life would they have back up in here? We'd be like . . . homesteaders or something. The Swiss Family Robinson. Can you imagine all the driving you'd have to do? Into town for every soccer game or church function?" He glanced at his phone. "I mean—look at this, *no signal*. No signal. I don't even see any telephone lines. It's like the Stone Age out here."

"With all due respect," the attorney said, "I suspect one reason Gretchen left the house in part to you, Mr. Connors, is because you *do* have a family. Gretchen loved this land because it was where she spent summers as a kid. I imagine she thought that maybe you and your family might enjoy this land, too, and now, this house, set *on* it. Even if only as a place to occasionally vacation."

Rosalind stared at this phony insurance man from the backseat, in which she jostled and shook like the palm trees outside her condo back home. She found herself agreeing with the sap, even as she recognized in him the same self-loathing, snake-oil salesman streak she'd encountered hundreds of times in her life—from her own insurance man, to start with, to the Realtor she'd worked with down in Florida. That kind of job never ended; that was the thing. Every interaction was a future mark, or prospect, a lead that might open a new door to other leads, like wandering through an infinite mansion, where most of the doors were locked, but behind a very few were rooms of undeniable gain. It had to do something to a person, this kind of endless opportunism, had to rot them from the core on outwards.

She thought with fondness of her own living quarters back home: the small galley kitchen, the one small bedroom, the living room with a little deck overlooking the ocean, and that single tiny bathroom. Not much, maybe, but it was all *hers*, and she knew her neighbors; knew the deli workers at her local grocery store, who cut and weighed her shaved turkey; and trusted the men who changed the oil on her aged Cadillac. She walked six miles a day on the same stretch of beach, monitoring the delicate nests of the sea turtles and chatting with the same deeply tanned fishermen and beachcombers she saw every day, old men who greeted her kindly behind impenetrable sunglasses, who chatted about the weather around the Marlboros they smoked. And this was all she wanted for however many days she had left on this earth. It was more than enough for her.

Whereas, this place? Who would she even talk to out here? And what if something were to happen to her? The thought of lying help-less on some wet marble bathroom floor, her hip in splinters, her screams booming and echoing in vain around some grandiose house no one needed ... it was something out of a nightmare. A person might as well just stay quiet under those circumstances and wait for death to come. At least back at her condo the walls were thin enough that her neighbors would eventually come running, and the nearest hospital was all of three miles away. She could practically crawl to it.

"I think," Reddy said evenly, "you may want to reserve any judg-ments until you actually see the house. Please—out of respect for Gretchen."

At the bridge, they finally crossed onto new pavement and a relief settled over them all. The house ahead of them was indeed breathtak-ing in that morning light, the steam steadily rising up, framing that end of the house and the cliffs. . . .

The attorney helped Rosalind out of the vehicle as courteously as he knew how, and then rather meaningfully begged their pardon to retrieve a house key secreted away some hundred yards from the house. In truth, a copy of the house key dangled off his own keyring, but he wanted to give the heirs time to stand where they were, in that devastating silence, taking in the colors and smells and rarefied light of that place. After five minutes of pretending to look through the grasses and scree, he trotted back to the house, a key held triumphantly in one hand.

"Got it," he called.

Blake dipped his long, thin, pale fingers into the hot springs as the attorney approached. "I've heard some cultures believe hot springs are entrances to hell," he said. "I don't know about that, but I did hear a rumor three men died here while it was under construction. Any truth to that?"

"Well," Reddy began, "one of those deaths you're referring to did happen here, that's true. It was a terrible accident."

"And the other two?" Blake asked.

"Those gentlemen worked on this house," the attorney said, removing his glasses to breathe condensation on the lenses. "But I couldn't say for sure exactly where they disappeared to. All of that is still being sorted out by the police. But it really doesn't concern us here."

"Sounds like lawyer-speak to me," Rosalind said.

"Well, would you like to have a look at the house?" the attorney offered. "I know you're both busy people."

The attorney unlocked the front door, adjacent to the garage, and guided the old woman into an entryway-mudroom, a long, narrow rectangle of a room with a native stone floor, built-in cubbies for shoes, and a window offering a view up into the mountains. From the mudroom, they followed a hallway at the back of the foundation and garage and up the stairs to the main floor.

"I don't like all this climbing," she complained. "And the altitude. Yeesh. I feel a little dizzy."

"I wonder how much she even had into this place," Blake said. "Five mil? Ten? Fifteen?"

Reddy ignored him, and when they stood on the main floor and turned toward that bank of windows looking back toward the river and mountains, the attorney was pleased with their reactions. They stood where they were, mouths agape, like two pilgrims visiting a faraway cathedral.

"It *is* beautiful," Rosalind whispered. "Like living in a painting. Or looking *out* of a painting."

Blake began roaming the floor plan.

"Feels a little cold in here to me," he complained. "You know? I think I'd feel like I was encased in a crystal or somethin'. Can't really imagine my kids in this space. I'd be afraid they'd ruin it, for one thing. I mean, everything in here's painted white and all brand-new. Kids need comfort."

But it was not just a matter of taste or practicality; in his head, he imagined unlocking the value of the place, paying off all their debts and becoming instantly and unexpectedly *free*. Were they to set a good price on this rich woman's folly, they could move to the biggest house back home. Or even to a city with more upside, more opportunities, more glitz. No destination was unthinkable. Their lives would be entirely different and, he could not help thinking, better.

Room to room they wandered, running their hands over the new satin-painted walls and granite counters, and standing before the windows to stare out at the mountains or down at the hot springs. After a half hour, Rosalind returned to Reddy's side.

"Okay, then," she said. "I believe I'm ready to go."

"Me, too," Blake said. "It's a beautiful house. No doubt about that."

Aarav Reddy had known Gretchen since graduating from law school. Though they worked at separate firms and in separate areas of practice, Gretchen often sent him referrals because, as he remembered her often writing in emails, "*Aarav is not only diligent and talented, he represents his clients with dignity, compassion, and a true understanding of their final intentions. . . .*" He thought about her then and realized he knew very little about her, save for the fact that she was the most responsive attorney he had ever dealt with, returning emails efficiently in completely transparent and readable messages. And when it was needed, she often called him, if for only a matter of minutes, to iron out some detail or to confirm that her clients had managed to get in contact with him. In their final meeting together, he had asked her about the wisdom of leaving something as personal as a house like this to these two heirs, but she'd insisted.

"This land is sacred to me, Aarav," she had said, "and to my family, and I just *know* that once they see the house and the springs, they'll want to preserve it, too. I'm sure of it."

"What about your aunt?" Reddy pressed. "Isn't she a little old to make this kind of move? To such a remote house? Are you sure you won't reconsider?"

"If Rosalind isn't interested, then Blake will be, I know it. He's got a young family, and I know this place will resonate with him. The hot springs, the hiking, the skiing. Can you imagine, Aarav? Having exclusive access to something like this? It's the very definition of priceless."

Gretchen's health was clearly failing during that final face-to-face meeting. She seemed to have been whittled away, her arms and legs painfully thin, her once red hair streaked with so much more gray, her skin taking on a pale, yellowish cast. Still, she was as animated as ever when she talked about the house.

Aarav locked the door and turned, somewhat defeatedly, to leave. He stood now, holding a gleaming, polished wood box in his hands.

"There is one final thing," Aarav said, "Gretchen asked to have her ashes spread here. Would either of the two of you care to . . ." Aarav's voice trailed off.

Neither Blake nor Rosalind stopped forward, so it was Aarav who quickly gauged the direction of the light wind before opening the box's lid and shaking Gretchen's ashes out and into the hot springs.

Then they stood quietly for several moments, watching as the ashes drifted down into the pool. Blake and Rosalind were polite but it was clear that both parties wanted to sell the house, and that was that.

By and by they slowly walked down the driveway to Aarav's vehicle, making the trip back to Jackson without so much as a single word.

45

A month later, Loney Wilkins sat at his kitchen table eating oatmeal with blueberries as he absent-mindedly pored over the *Jackson Hole News & Guide*.

"Mornin', hon," his wife said, pecking him on the top of his head.

"Mornin'," he said.

"Where you off to today?"

He checked his watch, wiped his mustache, and stretched his arms over his head. "I don't know yet, but I'm glad you asked."

"You are?" she said, smiling.

Loney and Eula had been married almost forty years, and there were few occasions left where he might surprise her, but this perhaps was one; he saw something in her eyes like delight.

"Care to take a ride with me today?" he asked, pushing back from the table.

She kissed him lightly on the lips and then rose to pour herself a cup of coffee.

"Well, I had planned on some grocery shopping, and maybe to swing by church, but . . ."

"Oh, all that can wait," he said, waving off her excuses. "Come on now, it's a beautiful day."

"All right," she agreed. "I'll pack us a picnic."

The work was part-time but kept him busy, and the real estate company didn't trouble him much. Report to the office each Monday, Wednesday, and Friday morning. Collect a list of addresses in need of FOR SALE signs, and another list indicating where to pick up signs from properties successfully sold. Thirty hours a week, no benefits. But the company covered his oil changes and mileage, they never quibbled about his hours, and the pay wasn't half bad. Fifty-nine years old, Loney knew his options were limited. Ranching hadn't been for him, and he wasn't much for the new tourism in town; couldn't imagine working at a ski resort or helping a bunch of flatlanders up into the saddle of some nag. No, this work suited him fine. Left him to drive around in his truck with his books-on-tape, his Garcia y Vega cigars, and a handy gazetteer for finding those out-of-the-way places.

At the office he picked up the day's work—three signs to plant and two to pick up. Four of the addresses were in town or nearby, the last address was some forty minutes away, he was told. He recognized the highway, of course, but not the address. That was part of the fun of this job; discovering new country and with a particular kind of access that softened landowners and homeowners alike. Often, if he simply laid on the politeness and courtesy, they'd allow him to explore at least a little of their ranch, and on a few occasions he trailered a horse and made a day of it, just as he had back as a teenager with his beloved uncle Samuel.

Eula finished chatting with a woman she knew, and Loney held the door for her as they walked out into the early-summer morning.

He was glad for her company. It was true he liked the solitude of the job, liked listening to his books and the radio and the podcasts she helpfully loaded onto his phone, but he was grateful that day for her steady monologue of observations and the fact that she held each sign for him as he tamped gravel and dirt around its base. That was actually quite helpful.

After they finished his assignments in town, he drove them out into the mountains, southeast of town, the terrain growing wilder and wilder still.

"You mind punching that address into my phone?" Loney asked.

"Sure thing," she said, her bare feet suntanning on the dashboard.

He took the phone back from her and peered down at the route.

"Sonuvabitch," he said very quietly.

"Everything okay?" she asked.

"Oh sure—everything's fine," he said. "We're just . . . We're headed to a place I used to know, back when I was a kid, working for my uncle."

"You used to talk about that country all the time when we first started up," she said. "Back when you were a real cowboy." She swatted his shoulder playfully.

"Long time ago," he said.

"Doesn't seem so long ago to *me*," she said. "Lord, we were young, though."

There was no reason for it, he supposed, but his anxiety grew the closer they pushed toward the address, and as he turned off onto that gravel road and parked the truck, he remembered everything, could all but see Gretchen's family as they unloaded their things from the station wagon and stood there in the sunlight, gawking at the river and mountains, and how he fell in love with her, at first sight, how he lost the ability to breathe, think, or speak. How she reduced him to nothing.

He unloaded the last sign and carried it to a spot beside the road where he began digging a hole. Eula left the truck to help him hold the sign in place, and when it was secure, he dusted off his hands and exhaled deeply.

"Well," he said, "I suppose we ought to head on back."

"But we haven't even eaten our picnic," she protested, "and I'd love to see this house. If it's the one I think it is, s'posed to be pretty special."

"All right," he said, nodding. "Of course. Yeah, let's check it out."

And so, they drove on, up and up and up. It was different, of course, from what he remembered, the road taking a fair amount of the wildness out of the equation. Still, it was gorgeous.

"So beautiful," she murmured. "Loney, you know who owns this property?" She reached for his paperwork and the property's listing.

He hadn't thought of Gretchen in a long, long time, and could not have said for sure whether it was even still her family that owned the property. He hadn't seen her in almost forty years, and especially in those early decades of estrangement or separation, there had been no Internet, no Facebook or Instagram or Twitter. When a person was gone from your life, they were gone. And even now, with the advent of personal computers and social media, Loney wasn't the type to post a photograph of himself for all to see. He preferred the world the way it was.

"No idea," he said, not exactly outright lying but not volunteering any information either.

"Loney," she said, "they're listing this place, it says, for fifty million dollars. Can that be *right*?"

But his mind was elsewhere, where he stood at a fence line in an alpine pasture some forty years earlier, he and his uncle stringing and tightening new barbed wire around a sun-bleached and lichen-decorated cedar post.

Stay away from that girl, Samuel told him. *Unless you intend to marry her. And young and dumb as you are, you shouldn't be marrying anyone anyhow.*

We're just friends, Loney said quietly.

I ain't stupid, Samuel went on. *I seen you two. I know what's going on. But, Loney, that girl could be president someday. You have to let her go.*

She don't belong here. She needs to go her way, go to college, and all the way beyond that.

Loney winced and ran a hand over his jawline, remembering how he'd laughed at his uncle, at that notion of Gretchen being president, that bright, curious, independent girl being president someday. And how his uncle had quit their fencing to stand up and stare right into him, right into that headstrong seventeen-year-old he was then.

I tell you what, his uncle said. *I believe in that girl. I never met her equal. And I don't expect I ever will either.*

What his uncle wanted to say, Loney understood, even then, was, *I love her.*

"Oh," his wife said quietly, and then, reaching for his hand, "there it is. . . . Would you look at that?"

At the turnaround, they passed over a bridge and proceeded slowly up toward the house.

He parked near those familiar hot springs, feeling an acute sense of cognitive dissonance. This house, the paved driveway, the bridge . . . none of it jibed with his memories of the place, so raw. Gone were the small gravel squares where he and Samuel erected the family's tents each year to start with. And gone, too, was the wooden cabin that later replaced those platforms. Gone, the horse paths grooved along the creek and river . . .

"I could die a happy woman up here." Eula laughed. "You know, if we had a spare fifty million dollars. We could skinny-dip right here in our own private springs and have some horses, maybe truck in some black dirt for a little garden."

He turned slowly around, examining the majestic valley that cupped this house.

"This place is a like a private kingdom," she said with a laugh. "Totally apart from the world."

She pointed down to the river. "It even has a moat," she said.

"No drawbridge," he countered.

"Yeah, but it does have a bridge, though," she said, kissing his cheek and patting his biceps. "Now, where's a good place to eat?" she asked. "Maybe down by the river?"

"All right," he said. "Yeah, that sounds good."

They spent the afternoon there, lingering in the generous pine-scented shadows, walking up and down the creek, reclining on an outspread blanket, their eyes closed, the dappled sunlight warming their skin.

"Are you sure you're okay?" she asked him later in the afternoon. "You've been awfully quiet since we got here."

"Yeah," he lied for the second time that day, despite the fact he truly never was dishonest to his wife. "I just got a little headache is all."

"We can go," she offered. "Maybe you can bring me back to get the sign when it sells."

"Hold on," he said. "I have to check on something."

He hiked back up to the house and, standing near the springs, looked south, out across the valley to the meadow just above the tree line on that far ridge. He could not be sure, but he thought he saw some pale glitter far over there, though he supposed his eyes were not what they once were.

"You do know something about this place, don't you?" Eula asked, then turned to follow his gaze. "What is that light out there? Is someone signaling us?"

"Naw," Loney began, "prolly just a piece of mica or quartz, reflecting the sun."

"It looks like a mirror, though," she continued, "not some random rock, but like someone's trying to get our attention."

He kicked at the gravel, sighed. "It's a grave," he said quietly.

"A grave?" she repeated.

"Long story. Can I tell you on the way home?"

"Well, now you've really piqued my interest, cowboy."

"Next time, we'll bring some horses. It'd take us all afternoon just to get over there," he said, remembering the last time he'd visited those cairns. "Come to think of it, that'd be a real decent thing to do. We could even bring some flowers." He meant to go on, to say something to the effect that he might be the last person on earth to know what those cairns meant, but his voice failed him, for somehow, he knew Gretchen was gone, that that was the only possible explanation for why this land, and the house, would be for sale. A coolness swept through his body, and he grimaced, then bit his lower lip, before turning his back to Eula and covering his mouth with a forearm.

They drove back down the valley, the river always on their left, and made their way back on home. Where the gravel road met the highway, Loney Wilkins glanced in the rearview mirror, but there was nothing much to see except the cloud of dust rising into the blue, blue late-afternoon sky. He turned right and eased onto the road as his wife reached for his hand.

TRUE TRIANGLE CONSTRUCTION

Building Heaven on Earth

*

Established—2016

ACKNOWLEDGMENTS

The author would like to thank the following individuals, organizations, and businesses for their support, wisdom, and enthusiasm during the writing and editing of this novel: Beargrass Writing Retreat, Marcus Burke, Alex and Cynthia Butler, Bette Butler, Eleanor Butler, Henry Butler, Regina Butler, Angus Cargill, Patrizia Chendi, Guia Cortassa, Giulio D'Antona, Chris Dombrowski, the Eau Claire *Leader-Telegram*, Julian Emerson, Peter Geye, Nicholas Gulig, Jim and Lynn Gullicksrud, Crystal Halvorson and Bill Hogseth, the Hempel family, Tracy Hruska, the Jackson office of the Bridger-Teton National Forest, Gary Johnson, Sally Kim, John Larison, the L.E. Phillips Public Library, Raphaëlle Liebaert, Massie McQuilkin, Rob McQuilkin, Chris and Sara Meeks, Nik Novak, Ben Percy, SHIFT Cyclery & Coffee Bar, Luis Solano, Charmaine and Josh Swan, Mike Tiboris, Chiara Tiveron, *Volume One*, Hilary and Mike Walters, and Jade Wong-Baxter.

The author would also like to thank all the booksellers, journalists, and librarians worldwide who continue to support his career.